NIGHT TRAIN TO LISBON

PASCAL MERCIER

Translated from the German by

Barbara Harshav

Atlantic Books
London

Originally published in 2004 in Germany by Carl Hanser Verlag.

This edition originally published in the United States of America by Grove Atlantic Ltd.

This updated paperback edition published in Great Britain in 2009
by Atlantic Books, an imprint of Grove Atlantic Ltd.

Copyright © Carl Hanser Verlag Muenchen Wien 2004

The moral right of Pascal Mercier to be identified
as the author of this work has been asserted by him in accordance with
the Copyright, Designs and Patents Act of 1988.

Translation © Barbara Harshav 2008

The moral right of Barbara Harshav to be identified
as the translator of this work has been asserted by her in accordance with
the Copyright, Designs and Patents Act of 1988.

The epigraphs are taken from:
Coplas de don Jorge Manrique by Jorge Manrique,
translated by Henry Longfellow (Boston: Allen & Ticknor, 1833)
The Complete Essays of Montaigne by Michel de Montaigne,
translated by Donald M. Frame (Stanford: Stanford University Press, 1948)
The Selected Prose of Fernando Pessoa by Fernando Pessoa,
translated by Richard Zenith (New York: Grove Press, 2002)

15

A CIP catalogue record for this book is available from the British Library.

ISBN: 978 1 84354 713 6

Typeset in Adobe Garamond by Ellipsis Books Limited, Glasgow

Printed in the UK by CPI Group (UK) Ltd, Croydon, CR0 4YY

Atlantic Books
An imprint of Grove Atlantic Ltd
Ormond House
26–27 Boswell Street
London WC1N 3JZ

www.atlantic-books.co.uk

Nuestras vidas son los ríos
que van a dar en la mar,
qu'es el morir

Our lives are rivers, gliding free
to that unfathomed, boundless sea,
the silent grave!

Jorge Manrique

*Nous sommes tous de lopins et d'une contexture si informe
et diverse, que chaque piece, chaque momant, faict son jeu.
Et se trouve autant de difference de nous à nous mesmes,
que de nous à autruy.*

We are all patchwork, and so shapeless and diverse in
composition that each bit, each moment, plays its own
game. And there is as much difference between us and
ourselves as between us and others.

Michel de Montaigne, Essays, Second Book, 1

*Cada um de nós é vários, é muitos, é uma prolixidade
de si mesmos. Por isso aquele que despreza o ambiente não é o
mesmo que dele se alegra ou padece. Na vasta colónia do nosso
ser há gente de muitas espécies, pensando
e sentindo diferentemente.*

Each of us is several, is many, is a profusion of selves. So
that the self who disdains his surroundings is not the same
as the self who suffers or takes joy in them. In the vast
colony of our being there are many species of people who
think and feel in different ways.

Fernando Pessoa, O Livro do Desassossego

NIGHT TRAIN
TO LISBON

PART I
THE DEPARTURE

1

The day that ended with everything different in the life of Raimund Gregorius began like countless other days. At quarter to eight, he came from Bundesterrasse and stepped on to the Kirchenfeldbrücke leading from the heart of the city to the Gymnasium. He did that every day of the school term, always at quarter to eight. Once when the bridge was blocked, he made a mistake in the Greek class. That had never happened before nor did it ever happen again. For days, the whole school talked of nothing but this mistake. The longer the debate lasted, the more it was thought that he had been misheard. At last, this conviction won out even among the students who had been there. It was simply inconceivable that Mundus, as everyone called him, could make a mistake in Greek, Latin or Hebrew.

Gregorius looked ahead at the pointed towers of the Historical Museum of the city of Bern, up to the Gurten and down to the Aare with its glacier-green water. A gusty wind drove low-lying clouds over him, turned his umbrella inside out and whipped the rain in his face. It was then that he noticed the woman standing in the middle of the bridge. She had leaned her elbows on the railing and was reading – in the pouring rain – what looked like a letter. She must have been holding the sheet with both hands. As Gregorius came closer, she suddenly crumpled the paper, kneaded it into a ball and threw the ball into space with a violent movement. Instinctively, Gregorius had walked faster and was now only a few steps away from her. He saw the rage in her pale, rain-wet face. It wasn't a rage that could be expressed in words and then blow over. It was a grim rage turned inward that must have been smouldering in her for a long time. Now the woman leaned on the railing with outstretched arms, and slipped her heels out of her shoes. *Now she jumps.* Gregorius abandoned the umbrella to a gust of wind that drove it over the railing, threw his briefcase full of school notebooks to the ground and uttered a string of curses that weren't part of his usual vocabulary. The briefcase opened and the notebooks slid on to the wet pavement. The woman turned around. For a few moments, she watched unmoving as the notebooks darkened with the water. Then she pulled a felt-tipped pen from her coat pocket, took two steps, leaned down to Gregorius and wrote a line of numbers on his forehead.

'Forgive me,' she said in French, breathless and with a foreign accent. 'But I mustn't forget this phone number and I don't have any paper with me.'

Now she looked at her hands as if she were seeing them for the first time.

'Naturally, I could have . . .' And now, looking back and forth between Gregorius's forehead and her hand, she wrote the numbers on the back of the hand. 'I . . . I didn't want to keep it, I wanted to forget everything, but when I saw the letter fall . . . I had to hold on to it.'

The rain on his thick glasses muddied Gregorius's sight and he groped awkwardly for the wet notebooks. The tip of the felt pen seemed to slide over his forehead again. But then he realized it was the fingers of the woman, who was trying to wipe away the numbers with a handkerchief.

'It is out of line, I know . . .' And now she started helping Gregorius gather up the notebooks. He touched her hand and brushed against her knee, and when the two of them reached for the last notebook, they bumped heads.

'Thank you very much,' he said when they stood facing each other. He pointed to her head. 'Does it hurt?'

Absently, looking down, she shook her head. The rain beat down on her hair and ran over her face.

'Can I walk a few steps with you?'

'Ah . . . yes, of course,' Gregorius stammered.

Silently they walked together to the end of the bridge and on towards the school. His sense of time told Gregorius that it was after eight and the first class had already begun. How far was 'a few steps'? The woman had adjusted to his pace and plodded along beside him as if she might follow him all day. She had pulled the wide collar of her coat so high that, from the side, Gregorius could only see her forehead.

'I have to go in here, into the Gymnasium,' he said, stopping. 'I'm a teacher.'

'Can I come along?' she asked softly.

Gregorius hesitated and ran his sleeve over his wet glasses. 'Well . . . it's dry there,' he said at last.

She went up the stairs, Gregorius held the door open for her, and then they stood in the hall, which seemed especially empty and quiet now that classes had started. Her coat was dripping.

'Wait here,' said Gregorius and went to the cloakroom to get a towel.

At the mirror, he dried his glasses and wiped his face. The numbers could still be seen on his forehead. He held a corner of the towel under the warm water and was about to start rubbing them out when he suddenly stopped. *That was the moment that decided everything*, he thought when he recalled the event hours later. That is, he realized that he really didn't *want* to wipe away the trace of his encounter with the enigmatic woman.

He imagined appearing before the class with a phone number on his face, he, Mundus, the most reliable and predictable person in this building and probably in the whole history of the school, having worked here for more than thirty years, impeccable in his profession, a pillar of the institution, a little dull perhaps, but respected and even feared in the university for his astounding knowledge of ancient languages. He was affectionately teased by his students who put him to the test every year by calling him in the middle of the night and asking about some remote passage in an ancient text, only to receive information that was both dry and exhaustive, including a critical commentary with other possible meanings, all of it presented without a trace of anger at the disturbance. Mundus, a man with an impossibly old-fashioned, even archaic first name that you simply *had to* shorten, and *couldn't* shorten any other way. It was a name that perfectly suited the character of this man, for what he carried around in him as a philologist was in fact no less than a whole world, or rather several whole worlds, since along with those Latin and Greek passages, his head also held the Hebrew that had amazed several Old Testament scholars. *If you want to see a true scholar,* the Rector would say when he introduced him to a new class, *here he is.*

And this scholar, Gregorius thought now, this dry man who seemed to some to consist only of dead words, and who was spitefully called The Papyrus by some colleagues who envied him his popularity – this scholar would shortly enter the classroom with a telephone number written on his forehead by a desperate woman apparently torn between rage and love, a woman in a red leather coat with a soft, southern voice that sounded like an endless hesitant drawl that drew you in merely by hearing it.

When Gregorius had brought her the towel, the woman had used it to rub her long black hair, which she had then combed back so that it spread over her coat collar like a fan. The janitor entered the hall and, when he saw Gregorius, cast an amazed look at the clock over the exit and then at his watch. Gregorius nodded to him, as he always did. A student hurried past, looked back in surprise and went on his way.

'I teach up there,' Gregorius said to the woman and pointed up through a window to another part of the building. Seconds passed. He felt his heart beat. 'Do you want to come along?'

Later, Gregorius couldn't believe he had really said that; but he must have done, for he recalled the screech of his rubber soles on the linoleum and the clack of the woman's boots as they walked together to the classroom.

'What's your mother tongue?' he had asked her.

'*Português*,' she had answered.

The *o* she pronounced surprisingly as a *u*; the rising, strangely constrained lightness of the *é* and the soft *sh* at the end came together in a melody that sounded much longer than it really was, and that he could have listened to all day long.

'Wait,' he said, took his notebook out of his jacket pocket and ripped out a page: 'For the number.'

His hand was on the doorknob when he asked her to say *Português* once more. She repeated it, and for the first time he saw her smile.

The chatter broke off abruptly when they entered the classroom. Instead, an amazed silence filled the room. Later, Gregorius remembered the moment precisely: he had enjoyed this surprised silence, the look of incredulity on the faces of his students as they gazed at the bedraggled couple in the doorway. He had also enjoyed his delight at being able to feel in a way he would never have believed possible.

'Perhaps there?' said Gregorius to the woman and pointed to an empty seat at the back of the room. Then he advanced, greeted the class as usual, and sat down behind the desk. He had no idea how he could explain the woman's presence and so he simply had them translate the text they were working on. The translations were halting, and he caught some bewildered looks among the students for he – he, Mundus, who recognized every mistake, even in his sleep – was now overlooking dozens of errors.

He tried not to look at the woman. Yet, every time he did so, he was struck by the damp strands of hair that framed her face, the white clenched hands, the absent, lost look as she gazed out of the window. Once she took out the pen and wrote the phone number on the page from his notebook. Then she leaned back in her seat and hardly seemed to know where she was.

It was an impossible situation and Gregorius glanced at the clock: ten more minutes until break. Then the woman got up and walked softly to the door. When she reached it, she turned round to him and put a finger to her lips. He nodded and she repeated the gesture with a smile. Then the door closed behind her with a soft click.

From this moment on, Gregorius no longer heard anything the students said. It was as if he was completely alone and enclosed in a numbing silence. He found himself standing at the window and watching the woman in the red coat until she had disappeared from view. He felt the effort not to run after her reverberate through him. He kept seeing the finger on her lips that could mean so many things: *I don't want to disturb you*, and *It's our secret*, but also, *Let me go now, this can't go on.*

When the bell rang for the break, he was still standing at the window. Behind him, the students left more quietly than usual. Later he went out too, left the building through the back door and went across the street to the public library where nobody would look for him.

For the second part of the double class, he was on time as always. By then he had rubbed the numbers off his forehead, after writing them down in his notebook, and the narrow fringe of grey hair had dried. Only the damp patches on his jacket and trousers revealed that something unusual had happened. Now he took the stack of soaked notebooks out of his briefcase.

'A mishap,' he said tersely to the reassembled class. 'I stumbled and they slipped out, in the rain. Nevertheless, the corrections should still be legible; otherwise, you will have to interpret them as best you can.'

An audible sigh of relief went through the room. Now and then, he still caught a curious look or heard the occasional whisper. Otherwise, everything was as before. He wrote the most frequent errors on the board, then he left the students to work on their own.

Could what happened to him in the next quarter of an hour be called a decision? Later, Gregorius was to keep asking himself this question and he could never be sure of the answer. But if it wasn't decision – what was it?

It began when he suddenly looked at the students bending over their notebooks as if he were seeing them for the first time.

Lucien von Graffenried, who had secretly moved a piece in the annual chess tournament in the school auditorium where Gregorius had played simultaneous matches against a dozen students. Gregorius had noticed it immediately, and after the moves on the other boards, he looked at him calmly. 'That's beneath you,' he said as Lucien's face flamed red. And then made sure that the game ended in a draw.

Sarah Winter, who had stood outside the door of his flat at two in the morning because she didn't know what to do about her unwanted pregnancy. He had made her tea and listened, nothing more. 'I'm so glad I followed your advice,' she said a week later. 'It would have been much too early to have a baby.'

Beatrice Lüscher with the regular, precise handwriting who had grown old frighteningly fast under the burden of her

always perfect achievements. René Zingg, always at the lowest
end of the scale.

And naturally, Natalie Rubin. A girl who was grudging with
her favours, a bit like a courtly maiden of the past, reserved,
idolized and feared for her sharp tongue. Last week, after the
bell rang for the break, she had stood up, stretched like someone
at ease in her own body, and taken a colourful sweet out of
her shirt pocket. On the way to the door, she had unwrapped
it and, as she passed Gregorius, had put it to her mouth. It
had just touched her lips when she broke off the movement,
turned to him, held the sweet out and asked: 'Want it?' Amused
at his astonishment, she had laughed her strange light laugh
and made sure her hand touched his.

Gregorius went through each one. At first he seemed to be
only drawing up an interim balance sheet of his feelings for
them. Then, as he reached the middle of the rows of benches,
he found himself thinking: *How much life they still have before
them; how open their future still is; how much can still happen
to them; how much they can still experience!*

Português. He heard the melody and saw the woman's face
as, with closed eyes, it had emerged from the towel, white as
alabaster. One last time, he slid his eyes over the heads of the
students. Then he stood up slowly, went to the door, took the
still damp coat off the hook and, without saying a word,
walked out of the room.

His briefcase, together with the textbooks that had
accompanied him for a lifetime, remained behind on the desk.
At the top of the stairs, he paused as he remembered how he
had taken them to be rebound every couple of years, always
to the same shop, where they had laughed at the worn, dog-
eared, pages that felt almost like blotting paper. As long as the
briefcase lay on the desk, the students would assume that he
was coming back. But that wasn't why he had left the books
behind or why he now resisted the temptation to go back for

them. If he left now, he also had to take his leave of those books. He felt that very strongly, even if at this moment, on the way out, he had no idea what it really signified.

In the entrance hall, his look fell on the little puddle that had formed when the woman in the dripping coat had waited for him to come out of the cloakroom. It was the trace of a visitor from another, faraway world, and Gregorius regarded it with a devotion usually reserved for archaeological finds. Only when he heard the janitor's shuffling step did he tear himself away and hurry out of the building.

Without turning round, he walked to the corner, where he could look back at the Gymnasium unseen. With a sudden force he wouldn't have expected of himself, he felt how much he loved this building and everything it stood for and how much he would miss it. He checked the numbers again: forty-two years ago, as a fifteen-year-old student, Gregorius had entered it for the first time, wavering between anticipation and apprehension. Four years later, he had left the school with his diploma in hand, only to come back again four years later as a substitute for the Greek teacher who had been in an accident, the teacher who had once opened the ancient world to him. The student substitute turned into a permanent substitute, who was thirty-three by the time he finally took his university exams.

He had done that only because Florence, his wife, had urged him to. He had never thought of a doctorate; if anyone asked him about it, he had only laughed. Such things didn't matter. What did matter was something quite simple: to know the ancient texts down to the last detail, to recognize every grammatical and stylistic detail and to know the history of every one of those expressions. In other words: to be *good*. That wasn't modesty – his demands on himself were utterly immodest. Nor was it eccentricity or a warped kind of vanity. It had been, he sometimes thought later, a silent rage aimed at a pompous world, an unbending defiance against the world of show-offs who had made his father suffer all his life because he had been only a museum attendant. Others, who knew much less than he – ridiculously less, to tell the truth – had gained degrees and lucrative positions: they seemed to belong to another, unbearably superficial world with standards he despised. In the Gymnasium, no one would ever have come up with the idea of dismissing him and replacing him with somebody with a degree. The Rector, himself a philologist of ancient languages, knew how good Gregorius was – much better than he himself – and he knew that the students would have risen in revolt if their teacher had been replaced. When he finally did take the examination, it seemed absurdly simple to Gregorius, and he handed in his paper in half the time. He had always held it against Florence a bit that she had made him abandon his defiance.

Gregorius turned around and walked slowly towards Kirchenfeldbrücke. When the bridge came into view, he had the amazing feeling, both upsetting and liberating, that, at the age of fifty-seven, he was about to take his life into his own hands for the first time.

2

At the spot where the woman had read the letter in the pouring rain, he stood still and looked down. It was only now that he realized how deep the drop was. Had she really wanted to jump? Or had that only been an unreasonable fear on his part, going back to Florence's brother who had also jumped off a bridge? Except that Portuguese was her mother tongue, he didn't know the slightest thing about the woman. Not even her name. Naturally, it was absurd to expect to see the scrunched-up letter from up here. Nevertheless he stared down, his eyes aching with the effort. Was that dark dot his umbrella? He felt in his jacket to make sure that the notebook with the number written on his forehead by the nameless Portuguese woman was still there. Then he walked to the end of the bridge, uncertain where to go next. He was in the course of running away from his previous life. Could somebody who intended to do that simply go home?

His eye fell on Hotel Bellevue, the oldest, most distinguished hotel in the city. Thousands of times he had passed by without ever going in. Now he realized that, in some vague way, it had been important to him to know that it was there; he would have been upset to learn that the building had been torn down or had stopped being a hotel, even though it had never entered his mind that he, Mundus, had any reason to go there. Timorously, he now approached the entrance. A Bentley stopped, the chauffeur got out and went inside. When Gregorius followed him, he had the feeling of doing something absolutely revolutionary, indeed forbidden.

The lobby with the coloured glass dome was empty and the carpet absorbed all sound. Gregorius was glad the rain had stopped and his coat was nearly dry. Treading lightly in his heavy, clumsy shoes he went on into the dining room. Only two of the tables were occupied. Light notes of a Mozart divertimento created the impression that one was far away from everything loud, ugly and oppressive. Gregorius took off his coat and sat down at a table near the window. No, he said to the waiter in the light beige jacket, he wasn't a guest at the hotel. He felt under scrutiny: the rough turtleneck sweater under the worn-out jacket with the leather patches on the elbows; the baggy corduroy trousers; the sparse fringe of hair around the powerful bald head; the grey beard with the white specks that always made him look a bit unkempt. When the waiter had gone off with his order, Gregorius nervously checked whether he had enough money on him. Then he leaned his elbows on the starched tablecloth and looked over towards the bridge.

It was absurd to hope that the woman would appear there once again. She must have gone back over the bridge and then vanished into an alleyway in the Old City. He pictured her sitting at the back of the classroom absently gazing out of the window. He saw her wringing her white hands. And again he saw her alabaster face surface from the towel, exhausted and vulnerable. *Português*. Hesitantly, he took out the notebook and looked at the phone number. The waiter brought his breakfast with coffee in a silver pot. Gregorius let the coffee grow cold. Once he stood up and went to the telephone. Halfway there, he turned round and went back to the table. Then he paid for the untouched breakfast and left the hotel.

It was years since he had been in the Spanish bookshop on Hirschengraben. Once, every now and then, he had bought a book for Florence that she had needed for her dissertation on San Juan de la Cruz. On the bus, he had sometimes leafed through it, but at home he had never touched her books. Spanish – that was her territory. It was like Latin and yet completely different from Latin, and that bothered him. It went against the grain with him that words in which Latin was so evident came out of contemporary mouths – on the streets, in supermarkets, in cafés; that they were used to order Coke, to haggle and to curse. He found the idea hard to bear and brushed it quickly aside whenever it came to him. Naturally, the Romans had also haggled and cursed. But that was different. He loved the Latin sentences because they bore the calm of everything past. Because they didn't make you say something. Because they were speech beyond talk. And because they were beautiful in their immutability. Dead languages – people who talked about them like that had no idea, really no idea, and Gregorius could be harsh and unbending in his contempt for them. When Florence spoke Spanish on the phone, he had to close the door. That offended her and he couldn't explain why.

The bookshop smelt wonderfully of old leather and dust. The owner, an ageing man with a legendary knowledge of Romance languages, was busy in the back room. The front room was empty except for a young woman, a student apparently. She sat at a table in a corner reading a slim book with a yellowed binding. Gregorius would have preferred to be alone. The sense that he was standing here only because the melody of a Portuguese word wouldn't leave his mind, and maybe also because he hadn't known where else to go, that feeling would have been easier to bear without witnesses. Now and then, as he walked along the rows of books, he occasionally tilted his glasses to read a title on a high shelf: but as soon as he had read it, it had been forgotten. As so often, he was alone with his thoughts, and his mind was closed to the outside world.

When the door opened, he turned round quickly. He saw, to his disappointment, that it was the postman and realized that, contrary to his intention and against all reason, he was still waiting for the Portuguese woman. Now the student closed the book and got up. But instead of putting it on the table with the others, she stood still, let her eyes slide again over the yellowed binding, stroked it with her hand; only a few seconds later did she put the book down on the table, as softly and carefully as if it might crumble to dust with a nudge. Then, for a moment, she stood at the table and it looked as if she might reconsider and buy the book. But she went out, her hands deep in her coat pockets and her head down. Gregorius picked up the book and read: AMADEU INÁCIO DE ALMEIDA PRADO, UM OURIVES DAS PALAVRAS, LISBOA 1975.

The bookseller came in, glanced at the book and pronounced the title aloud. Gregorius heard only a flow of sibilants; the half-swallowed, hardly audible vowels seemed to be only a pretext to keep repeating the hissing *sh* at the end.

'Do you speak Portuguese?'

Gregorius shook his head.

'*A Goldsmith of Words.* Isn't that a lovely title?'

'Quiet and elegant. Like dull silver. Would you say it again in Portuguese?'

The bookseller repeated the words. Aside from the words themselves, you could hear how he enjoyed their velvety sound. Gregorius opened the book and leafed through it until he reached the first page of text. He handed it to the man, who looked at him with surprise and pleasure and started reading aloud. As he listened, Gregorius closed his eyes. After a few sentences, the man paused.

'Shall I translate?'

Gregorius nodded. And then he heard sentences that stunned him, for they sounded as if they had been written for him alone, and not only for him, but for him on this morning that had changed everything.

Of the thousand experiences we have, we find language for one at most and even this one merely by chance and without the care which it deserves. Among all these unexpressed experiences are those that are hidden and which have given our life. Its shape, its colour and its melody. If we then, as archaeologists of the soul, turn to examine these treasures, we will discover how confusing they are. The object of our examination refuses to stand still, the words glance off the experience we are left with a lot of contradictions. For a long time, I thought this was a defect, something that had to be overcome. Now I think differently: that it is the recognition of the confusion that is the key to understanding these intimate yet enigmatic experiences. That sounds strange, even bizarre, I know. But ever since I have seen the issue in this light, I have the feeling of being really awake and alive for the first time.

'That's the introduction,' said the bookseller and started leafing through it. 'And now he seems to begin, passage after passage, to dig for all the buried experiences. To be the archaeologist of himself. Some passages are several pages long and others are quite short. Here, for example, is a fragment that consists of only one sentence.' He translated:

Given that we can live only a small part of what there is in us – what happens to the rest?

'I'd like to have the book,' said Gregorius.

The bookseller closed it and ran his hand over the binding as affectionately as the student had.

'I found it last year in the junk box of a second-hand bookshop in Lisbon. And now I remember: I bought it because I liked the introduction. Somehow I lost sight of it.' He looked at Gregorius, who felt awkwardly for his briefcase. 'I give it to you as a gift.'

'That's . . .' Gregorius began hoarsely and cleared his throat.

'It cost pretty much nothing,' said the bookseller and handed him the book. 'Now I remember you: San Juan de la Cruz. Right?'

'That was my wife,' said Gregorius.

'Then you're the classical philologist of Kirchenfeld, she talked about you. And later I heard somebody else talk about you. It sounded as if you were a walking encyclopaedia.' He laughed. 'Definitely a popular encyclopaedia.'

Gregorius put the book in his coat pocket and held out his hand. 'Thank you very much.'

The bookseller accompanied him to the door. 'I hope I haven't . . .'

'Not at all,' said Gregorius and touched his arm.

On Bubenbergplatz, he stood and looked around him. Here he had spent his whole life, here he knew his way around, here he was at home. For someone as nearsighted as he was, that was important. For someone like him, the city he lived in was like a shell, a cosy cave, a safe haven. Everything else meant danger. Only someone who had such thick glasses could understand that. Florence hadn't understood it. And, maybe for the same reason, she hadn't understood that he didn't like flying. He didn't like getting on an aeroplane and arriving a few hours later in a completely different world, with no time to take in individual images along the way. It bothered him. *It's not right,* he had said to Florence. *What do you mean – not right?* she had asked, irritated. He couldn't explain it and so she had often flown by herself or with others, usually to South America.

Gregorius stood at the display window of Bubenberg Cinema. The late show was a black-and-white film of a novel by Georges Simenon: *L'homme qui regardait passer les trains.* He liked the title and looked for a long time at the stills. In the late seventies, when everybody bought colour televisions, he had tried in vain for days to get another black-and-white set. Finally he had brought one home from the dump. Even after he got married, he had stubbornly held on to it, keeping it in his study; when he was by himself, he ignored the colour set in the living room and turned on the old rattle-trap that flickered, the images rolling occasionally. *Mundus, you're impossible,* Florence had said one day when she found him before the ugly, misshapen box. When she had started addressing him as the others did, and even at home he was treated like a factotum of the city of Bern – that had been the beginning of the end. When the colour television had vanished from the flat with his divorced wife, he had breathed a sigh of relief. Only years later, when the black-and-white picture was unwatchable, did he buy a new colour set.

The stills in the display window were big and crystal clear. One showed the pale alabaster face of Jeanne Moreau, stroking damp strands of hair off her forehead. Gregorius tore himself away and went into a nearby café to examine more closely the book by the Portuguese aristocrat who had tried to express himself and his mute experiences in words.

Only now, as he leafed slowly one by one through the pages, with a bibliophile's careful attention, did he discover a portrait of the author, an old photo, yellowed at the time the book was printed, where the once black surfaces had faded to dark brown, the bright face on a background of coarse-grained shadowy darkness. Gregorius polished his glasses, put them back on and, within a few minutes, was completely engrossed in the author's face.

The man might have been in his early thirties and he radiated an intelligence, a self-confidence, and a boldness that literally dazzled Gregorius. The bright face with the high forehead was thatched with luxuriant dark hair that seemed to shine dully and was combed back like a helmet, with some strands falling next to the ears in soft waves. A narrow Roman nose gave the face great clarity, emphasized by strong eyebrows, as if painted with a broad brush and breaking off at the edges, thus concentrating attention on the centre of the forehead. The full curved lips that wouldn't have been surprising in the face of a woman, were framed by a thin moustache and a trimmed beard, and the black shadows it cast on the slim neck gave Gregorius the impression of a certain coarseness and toughness. Yet, what determined everything were the dark eyes. They were underscored by shadows, not shadows of weariness, exhaustion or illness, but shadows of seriousness and melancholy. In his dark look, gentleness was mixed with an air of intrepidity and inflexibility. The man was a dreamer and a poet, thought Gregorius, but at the same time, someone who could resolutely direct a weapon or a scalpel. You would be advised to get out of his way when his eyes flamed, eyes that could keep an army of powerful giants at bay, eyes that were no stranger to black looks. As for his clothing, only the white shirt collar with the knot of a tie could be seen, and a jacket Gregorius imagined as a frock coat.

It was almost one o'clock when Gregorius surfaced from his absorption with the portrait. Once again, the coffee had grown cold in front of him. He wished he could hear the voice of the Portuguese man and see how he moved. Nineteen seventy-five: if he was then in his early thirties, as it seemed, he was now slightly over sixty. *Português.* Gregorius recalled the voice of the nameless Portuguese woman and transposed it to a lower pitch in his mind, but without turning it into the voice of the bookseller. It was to be a voice of melancholy clarity, corresponding precisely with the visage of Amadeu de Prado, the author. He tried to make the sentences in the book resonate with this voice. But it didn't work; he didn't know how the individual words were pronounced.

Outside, his chess-playing student Lucien von Graffenried passed by the café. Gregorius was surprised and relieved to find that he didn't flinch. He watched the boy go by and thought of the books he had left on the desk. He had to wait until classes resumed at two o'clock. Only then could he go back to the bookshop to buy a Portuguese language textbook.

3

As soon as Gregorius put on the first record at home and listened to the first Portuguese sentences, the phone rang. The school. The ringing wouldn't stop. He stood next to the phone and tried out sentences he could say. *Ever since this morning I've been feeling that I'd like to make something different out of my life. That I don't want to be your Mundus any more. I have no idea what the new one will be. But I can't put it off any longer. That is, my time is running out and there may not be much more of it left.* Gregorius spoke the sentences aloud. They were right, he knew that; he had said few sentences in his life that were so precisely right as these. But they sounded empty and bombastic when they were spoken aloud, and it was impossible to say them into the phone.

The ringing had stopped. But it would start again. They were worried and wouldn't rest until they had found him; something could have happened to him. Sooner or later, the doorbell would ring. Now, in February, it always got dark early. He wouldn't be able to turn on a light. In the centre of the city, the centre of his life, he was attempting to flee and had to hide in the flat where he had lived for fifteen years. It was bizarre, absurd, and sounded like some potboiler. Yet it was *serious*, more serious than most things he had ever experienced and done. But it was impossible to explain it to those who were searching for him. Gregorius imagined opening the door and inviting them in. Impossible. Utterly impossible.

Three times in a row, he listened to the first record of the course, and slowly got an idea of the difference between the written and the spoken language, and of all that was swallowed in spoken Portuguese. His unerring memory for word formation kicked in.

The phone kept ringing at ever shorter intervals. He had taken over an antiquated phone from the previous tenant with a permanent connection he couldn't pull out. The landlord had insisted that everything remain as it was. Now he found a blanket to muffle the ringing.

The voices guiding the language course wanted him to repeat words and short sentences. Lips and tongue felt heavy and clumsy when he tried it. The ancient languages seemed made for his Bernese mouth, and the thought that you had to hurry didn't appear in this timeless universe. The Portuguese, on the other hand, always seemed to be in a hurry, like the French, which made him feel inferior. Florence had loved it, this carefree elegance, and when he saw how easily it came to her, he had fallen silent.

But now everything was different. Gregorius *wanted* to imitate the impetuous pace of the man and the woman's dancing lightness like a piccolo, and repeated the same sentences again and again to narrow the distance between his stolid enunciation and the twinkling voice on the record. After a while, he understood that he was experiencing a great liberation; the liberation from his self-imposed limitation, from a slowness and heaviness expressed in his name and the slow, measured steps of his father walking ponderously from one room of the museum to another; liberation from an image of himself, even when he wasn't reading, as someone bending myopically over dusty books; an image he hadn't drawn systematically, but that had grown slowly and imperceptibly; the image of Mundus created not only by himself but also by many others who had found it convenient to be able to view him as this silent museum-like figure. It seemed to Gregorius that he was stepping out of this image as if from a dusty oil painting on the wall of a forgotten wing in the museum. He walked back and forth in the dim illumination of the lightless flat, ordered coffee in Portuguese, asked for a street in Lisbon, enquired about someone's profession and name, answered questions about his own profession, and conducted a brief conversation about the weather.

And all at once, he started talking with the Portuguese woman he had met on the bridge that morning. He asked her why she was furious with the letter-writer. *Você quis saltar? Did you want to jump?* Excitedly, he held the new dictionary and grammar book before his eyes and looked up expressions and verb forms he lacked. *Português.* How different the word sounded now! Before, it had possessed the magic of a jewel from a distant, inaccessible land and now it was like one of a thousand gems in a palace whose door he had just pushed open.

The doorbell rang. Gregorius tiptoed to the record player and turned it off. They were young voices, student voices, conferring outside. Twice more, the shrill ring cut through the dim silence where Gregorius waited, stock-still. Then he heard the footsteps receding on the stairs.

The kitchen was the only room that faced the back and had a Venetian blind. Gregorius pulled it down and turned on the light. He took out the book by the Portuguese aristocrat and the language books he had also bought, sat down at the table and started translating the first text after the introduction. It was like Latin but quite different from Latin, and now it didn't bother him in the slightest. It was a difficult text, and it took a long time. Methodically and with the stamina of a marathon runner, Gregorius selected the words and combed through the tables of verbs until he had deciphered the complex verb forms. After a few sentences, he was gripped by a feverish excitement and he got some paper to write down the translation. It was almost nine o'clock when he was finally satisfied:

PROFUNDEZAS INCERTAS. UNCERTAIN DEPTHS. *Is there a mystery underlying human actions? Or are human actions just what they seem?*

It is extraordinary, but the answer changes in me with the light that falls on the city and the Tagus. If it is the enchanting light of a shimmering August day that produces clear, sharp-edged shadows, the thought of a hidden human depth seems bizarre and like a curious, even slightly touching fantasy, like a mirage that arises when I look too long at the waves flashing in that light. On the other hand, if city and river are clouded over on a dreary January day by a dome of shadowless light and boring grey, I am certain that all human action is an extremely imperfect, utterly helpless expression of a hidden life of unimagined depths that presses to the surface without ever being able to reach it.

And to this upsetting unreliability of my judgement is added another experience that plunges my life continually in to distressing uncertainty: that, in this matter, the really most important one for us human beings, I waver even when it concerns myself. For when I sit outside my favourite café, basking in the sun, and overhear the tinkling laughter of the passing Senhoras, my whole inner world seems filled to the depths, and is revealed to me more fully because of these pleasant feelings. Yet, if a disenchanting, sobering layer of clouds pushes in before the sun, with one fell swoop, I am sure there are hidden depths and abysses in me, where unimagined things could break out and sweep me away. Then I quickly pay and hastily seek diversion in the hope that the sun might soon break out again and restore the reassuring superficiality.

Gregorious turned to the picture of Amadeu de Prado and leaned the book against the table lamp. Sentence after sentence, he read the translated text gazing into the bold, melancholy eyes. Only once before had he done something like that: when he had read Marcus Aurelius's *Meditations* as a student. A plaster bust of the emperor had stood on the table, and when he worked on the text, he seemed to be doing it under the aegis of his silent presence. But between then and now there was a difference, which Gregorius felt ever more clearly as the night progressed, without being able to put it into words. He knew only one thing as two o'clock approached: with the sharpness of his perception, the Portuguese aristocrat had awoken in him an alertness and precision of feeling even more keenly than the wise emperor, whose meditations he had devoured as if they were aimed directly at him. In the meantime, Gregorius had translated another note:

PALAVRAS NUM SILÊNCIO DE OURO. WORDS IN GOLDEN SILENCE. *When I read a newspaper, listen to the radio or overhear what people are saying in the café, I often feel an aversion, even disgust at the same words written and spoken over and over – at the same expressions, phrases, and metaphors repeated. And the worst is, when I listen to myself I have to admit that I too endlessly repeat the same things. They're so horribly frayed and threadbare, these words, worn out by constant overuse. Do they still have any meaning? Naturally, words have a function; people act on them, they laugh and cry, they go left or right, the waiter brings the coffee or tea. But that's not what I want to ask. The question is: are they still an expression of* thoughts? *Or only effective sounds that drive people in one direction or the other?*

Sometimes I go to the beach and stand facing the wind, which I wish were icy, colder than we know it in these parts. I wish it would blow all the hackneyed words, all the inspid habits of language out of me so that I could come back with a cleansed mind, cleansed of the banalities of the same talk. But the next time I have to say anything everything is as before. The cleansing I long for doesn't come automatically. I have to do something, and I have to do it with words. But what? It's not that I'd like to switch from my own language into another. No, it has nothing to do with that. And I also tell myself: You can't invent a new language. But do I really want to?

Maybe it's like this: I'd like to rearrange Portuguese words. The sentences that would emerge from this new order must not be odd or eccentric, not exalted, affected or artificial. They must be archetypal sentences in Portuguese so that you have the feeling that they originated directly and from the transparent, sparkling nature of this language. The words must be as unblemished as polished marble, and they must be pure as the notes in a Back partita, which turn everything that is not themselves into a perfect silence. Sometimes, when I am feeling more tolerant about the linguistic morass, I think, it could be the easy silence of a living room or the relaxed silence between lovers. But when I am totally possessed by rage over the clichéd use of words, then it must be nothing less than the clear, cool silence of outer space, where I make my solitary way as the only person who speaks Portuguese. The waiter, the barber, the conductor – they would be startled if they heard the new use of words and amazed by the beauty and clarity of the sentences. They would be – I imagine – compelling sentences, incorruptible and firm like the words of a god. At the same time, they would be without exaggeration and without pomposity, precise and so succinct that you couldn't take away one single word, one single comma. Thus they would be like a poem, plaited by a goldsmith of words.

Hunger made Gregorius's stomach ache and he forced himself to eat something. Later he sat with a cup of tea in the dark living room. What now? Twice more the doorbell had rung, and the last time he had heard the stifled buzz of the phone was shortly before midnight. Tomorrow they would file a missing person's report and then the police would appear at the door some time. He could still go back. At a quarter to eight he could walk across the Kirchenfeldbrücke, enter the Gymnasium and explain his enigmatic absence with some story that would make him look ridiculous, but that was all, and it suited him. They would never learn anything of the enormous distance he had covered internally in less than twenty-four hours.

But that was it: he *had* covered it. And he didn't want to let himself be forced by others to undo this silent journey. He took out a map of Europe and considered how you got to Lisbon by train. Train information, he learned on the phone, didn't open until six o'clock. He started packing.

It was almost four when he sat in the chair, ready to leave. Outside, it had started snowing. Suddenly all his courage deserted him. It was a crackpot idea. A nameless, confused Portuguese woman. Yellowed notes of a Portuguese aristocrat. A language course for beginners. The idea of time running out. You don't run away to Lisbon in the middle of winter because of that.

At five, Gregorius called Constantine Doxiades, his eye specialist. They had often called each other in the middle of the night to share their common suffering from insomnia. Sleepless people were bound by a wordless solidarity. Sometimes he played a blind game of speed chess with the Greek, and afterwards Gregorius could sleep a little before it was time to go to school.

'Doesn't make much sense, does it?' said Gregorius at the end of his faltering story. Doxiades was silent. Gregorius was familiar with that. Now he would shut his eyes and pinch the bridge of his nose with thumb and index finger.

'Yes, indeed, it does make sense,' said the Greek now. 'Indeed.'

'Will you help me if, on the way, I feel I can't go on?'

'Just call. Day or night. Don't forget the spare glasses.'

There it was again, the laconic certainty in his voice. A medical certainty, but also a certainty that went far beyond anything professional; the certainty of a man who took time to formulate his thoughts so they were later expressed in valid judgements. For twenty years, Gregorius had been going to this doctor, the only one who could remove his fear of going blind. Sometimes, he compared him with his father, who, after his wife's premature death, seemed – no matter where he was or what he did – to dwell constantly in the dusty safety of a museum. Gregorius had learned young that it was very fragile, this safety. He had liked his father and there had been moments when the feeling was even stronger and deeper than simple liking. But he had suffered from the fact that his father was not someone you could rely on, could not hold on to, unlike the Greek, whose solid judgement you could trust. Later, he had sometimes felt guilty about this. The safety and self-confidence his father didn't have weren't something a person could control or be accused of lacking. You had to be lucky with yourself to be a self-confident person. And his father hadn't had much luck, either with himself or with others.

Gregorius sat down at the kitchen table and drafted letters to the Rector. They were either too abrupt or too apologetic. At six, he called train information. From Geneva, the journey took twenty-six hours; it would take him through Paris and Irún in the Basque region, where he would connect with with the night train to Lisbon, arriving at eleven in the morning. Gregorius booked a one-way ticket. The train to Geneva left at eight-thirty.

Finally he got the letter right.

Honoured Rector, Dear Colleague Kägi,
   You will have learned by now that I left class yesterday without an explanation and didn't come back, and you will also know that I have remained incommunicado. I am well, nothing has happened to me. But, in the course of the day yesterday, I had an experience that has changed a great deal. It is too personal and still much too obscure for me to put it on paper yet. I must simply

ask you to accept my abrupt and unexplained act. You know me well enough, I think, to know that it is not the result of imprudence, irresponsibility or indifference. I am setting off on a distant journey and if and when I will return is an open question. I don't expect you to keep the position open for me. Most of my life has been closely intertwined with this Gymnasium, and I am sure I will miss it. But now, something is driving me away from it and it could well be that this action is final. You and I are both admirers of Marcus Aurelius, and you will remember this passage in his Meditations: 'Do wrong to thyself, do wrong to thyself, my soul; but later thou wilt no longer have the opportunity of respecting and honouring thyself. For every man has but one life. But yours is nearly finished, though in it you had no regard for yourself but placed thy felicity in the souls of others . . . But those who do not observe the impulses of their own minds must of necessity be unhappy.'

Thank you for the trust you have always shown me and for the good co-operation. You will find – I'm sure – the right words to explain my decision to the students, words that will let them know how much I liked working with them. Before I left yesterday, I looked at them and thought: How much time they still have before them!

In the hope of your understanding and with best wishes for you and your work, I remain yours,

Raimund Gregorius

P.S. I left my books on the desk. Would you pick them up and make sure nothing happens to them?

Gregorius mailed the letter at the railway station and boarded the train. He found a seat at the window and his hands shook as he polished his glasses and made sure he had his passport, ticket and address book. When the train left for Geneva, it was snowing big, slow flakes.

4

For as long as possible, Gregorius's eyes clung to the last houses of the city. When they had finally and irrevocably disappeared from view, he took out his notebook and started writing down the names of the students he had taught over the years. He started with the previous year and worked backwards into the past. For every name he sought a face, a characteristic gesture and a telling episode. He had no trouble with the last three years, but then he kept having the feeling that somebody was missing. In the mid-nineties, the classes consisted of only a few faces and names, and then the chronological sequence blurred. What remained were only a few boys and girls who stood out.

He shut the notebook. From time to time, in the city, he had run into a student he had taught many years earlier. They weren't boys and girls now, but men and women with spouses, professions and children. He was taken aback when he saw the changes in their faces: sometimes a premature bitterness, a harried look, a symptom of serious illness. But what usually startled him was the simple fact that the altered faces indicated the incessant passing of time and the merciless decline of all living things. Then he looked at his hands with their first age spots, and sometimes he took out photos of himself as a student and tried to visualize what it had been like to live through this long stretch to the present, day after day, year after year. On such days, he was jumpier than usual and then would appear unannounced at Doxiades's office so that he could once again dispel his fear of going blind. Encounters with former students who had lived many years abroad, on other continents, in other climates, with other languages, threw him off balance the most. *And you? Still in Kirchenfeld?* they asked, and their movements showed their impatience to move on. At night, after such an encounter, first he would defend himself against these questions and later against the feeling of having to defend himself.

And now, with all this going through his head, he sat in the train, after more than twenty-four hours without sleep, and travelled towards a future as uncertain as any he had ever had to contemplate.

The stop in Lausanne was a temptation. Across the same platform was the train to Bern. Gregorius caught it and looked at the clock. If he took a taxi to Kirchenfeld, he could still make the fourth period. The letter – he would have to catch the postman tomorrow or ask Kägi to give him back the envelope unopened. Unpleasant but not impossible. Now his look fell on the notebook on the compartment table. Without opening it, he saw the list of student names. And all of a sudden, he understood: what had started as the temptation to hold on to something familiar after the last houses of Bern slipped away, had become more like a farewell as the hours passed. To be able to part from something, he thought as the train started moving, you had to confront it in a way that created internal distance. You had to turn the unspoken, diffuse self-understanding it had wrapped around you into a clarity that showed what it meant to you. And that meant it had to congeal into something with distinct contours. Something as distinct as the list of the many students who had meant more to his life than anything else. Gregorius felt as if the train, now rolling out of the railway station, was leaving a piece of him behind, as if he was marooned on an ice floe that had come loose in a mild earthquake, in an open cold sea.

As the train picked up speed, he fell asleep and woke up only when he felt it draw to a halt at Geneva. On the way to the French high-speed train, he was as excited as if he had set out for a trip on the Trans-Siberian Railway. As soon as he had taken his seat, the carriage filled up with a group of French tourists. Hysterical chatter filled the car, and when someone in an open coat bent over him to put a suitcase on the storage shelf, Gregorius's glasses were knocked off. Then he did something he had never done before: he took his things and moved into first class.

The few opportunities he had had to travel first class had been twenty years ago. It had been Florence who had urged it; he had followed her and sat down on the expensive cushion feeling like a fraud. *Do you find me boring?* he had asked her after one of those trips. *What? But Mundus, you can't ask me such a thing!* she had said and ran her hand through her hair as she always did when she was at a loss. Now, when the train started moving, as Gregorius stroked the elegant upholstery with both hands, his act seemed like a belated, childish revenge he didn't really understand. He was glad nobody was sitting near by who could have witnessed the foolish feeling.

He was shocked at the extra amount he had to pay the conductor, and when the man had gone, he counted his money twice. He whispered the pin number of his credit card to himself and wrote it in the notebook. Shortly after, he tore out the page and threw it away. In Geneva, it had stopped snowing and now he saw the sun again for the first time in weeks. It warmed his face behind the windowpane and he calmed down. He had always had much too much money in his savings account, he knew that. *What's going on with your money?* said the bank clerk when she saw how much had accumulated because he withdrew so little. *You must* do *something with your money!* She invested it for him and so, over the years, he had become a prosperous man who seemed oblivious to his prosperity.

Gregorius thought of the two Latin books he had left on the desk this time yesterday. The name *Anneli Weiss* was on the flyleaf, written in ink in a childish hand. In his youth there wasn't money for new books, so he had scoured the city until he found used copies in second-hand bookshops. When he produced his find, his father's Adam's apple had moved fiercely; it always did when something weighed on his mind. At first, Gregorius was bothered by the strange name in the book. But then he had imagined the previous owner as a girl with white knee socks and windblown hair, and soon he wouldn't have exchanged the used book for a new one at any price. Nevertheless, he had later enjoyed being able to buy old texts in beautiful, expensive editions with the money he started earning as a substitute teacher. That was now more than thirty years ago, and still seemed a little unreal to him. Only recently, he had stood at his bookshelves and marvelled that he had been able to afford such a library.

Slowly, these memory images were distorted into dream images in which the slim book where his mother wrote down what she earned from cleaning kept popping up like a tormenting will-o'-the-wisp. He was glad when he was awakened by the noise of a smashing glass further up the carriage.

An hour to Paris. Gregorius sat down in the dining car and looked out on to a bright, early spring day. And there, all of a sudden, he realized that he was in fact making this trip – that it wasn't only a possibility, something he had thought up during a sleepless night, but something that really and truly was taking place. And the more space he gave this feeling, the more it seemed to him that the relation of possibility and reality was beginning to change. Kägi, his school and all the students listed in his notebook really had existed, but only as possibilities that had been accidentally realized. But what he was experiencing in this moment – the sliding motion and muted thunder of the train, the slight clink of the glasses on the next table, the odour of rancid oil coming from the kitchen, the smoke of the cigarette the cook now and then puffed – possessed a reality that had nothing to do with mere possibility, but was filled with the density and overwhelming inevitability that marked something utterly real.

Gregorius sat before the empty plate and the steaming cup of coffee and had the feeling of never having been so awake in his whole life. And it seemed to him that it wasn't a matter of degree, as when you slowly shook off sleep until you were fully alert. It was different. It was a different, new *kind* of wakefulness, a state of being in the world that he had never known before. When the Gare de Lyon came in sight, he went back to his seat and afterwards, when he set foot on the platform, it seemed to him as if, for the first time, he was fully aware of getting off a train.

5

The force of memory hit him unprepared. He hadn't forgotten that this had been their first railway station, their first arrival together in a foreign city. Naturally he hadn't forgotten that. But he hadn't figured that, when he stood here, it would be as if no time at all had elapsed. The green iron girders and the red pipes. The arches. The translucent roof.

'Let's go to Paris!' Florence had suddenly said at the first breakfast in his kitchen, arms wound around a drawn-up leg.

'You mean . . .'

'Yes, now. Right now!'

She had been his student, a pretty, usually dishevelled girl who turned all heads with her provocative moodiness. From one term to the next, she had become first-rate in Latin and Greek, and the first time he entered the optional Hebrew class that year, she was sitting in the front row. But Gregorius would never have even dreamed it could have anything to do with him.

The matriculation exam came and another year went by before they met in the university cafeteria and sat there until they were thrown out.

'What a blind worm you are!' she said when she took off his glasses. 'You didn't notice anything! *Everybody* knew! *Everybody!*'

It was correct, thought Gregorius, in the taxi taking him to Gare Montparnasse, that he was a person who didn't notice such things – one who was so inconspicuous even to himself that he couldn't have believed that someone could have strong feelings for him – *him*! But with Florence he was right in the end.

'You never really meant *me*.' Those were the only accusing words he had said to her during their five-year marriage. They had burned like fire and everything seemed to turn to ashes.

She had looked at the floor. In spite of everything, he had hoped for denial. It hadn't come.

La Coupole. Gregorius hadn't expected to drive along Boulevard Montparnasse and see the restaurant where their separation had been sealed without a word. He asked the driver to stop and looked silently for a while at the red awning with the yellow letters and the three stars left and right. It had been an honour for Florence, a doctoral student, to be invited to this conference on Romance literature. On the phone, she had sounded ecstatic, almost hysterical, he thought, so he had hesitated to meet her for the weekend as arranged. But then he had gone and had met with her new friends in this famous restaurant, whose reputation for the most exquisite food and the most expensive wines had proved to him as soon as he entered that he didn't belong here.

'One more moment,' he said to the driver and crossed the street.

Nothing had changed, and he immediately saw the table where he, very unsuitably dressed, had faced those literary hotshots boldly. They had been talking about Horace and Sappho, he remembered, as he now stood in the way of the hurrying and irritated waiters. Nobody could keep up with him as he quoted verse after verse, crushing to dust the witty *aperçus* of the well-dressed gentlemen of the Sorbonne with his Bernese accent, one after the other, until the table grew silent.

On the way home, Florence had sat alone in the dining car while the aftershock of his rage slowly ebbed and gave way to a sadness that he had needed to stand up to her like that; for that's what it was naturally about.

Lost in those distant events, Gregorius had forgotten the time and now the taxi driver had to drive at breakneck speed to get him to Gare Montparnasse on time. When he finally sat breathless in his seat and the train for Irún started moving, a sense that had assaulted him in Geneva returned: that it was the train and not he who decided that this very real trip carrying him further out of his former life, hour after hour, station after station, would continue. For three hours, until the train reached Bordeaux, there would be no more stops, no possibility of turning back.

He looked at the clock. At school, the first day without him was coming to an end. At this time, the six students of Hebrew would be waiting for him. At six, after the double class, he had sometimes gone with them to a café, and then he had talked to them of the historical growth and contingency of the biblical texts. Ruth Gautschi and David Lehmann, who wanted to study theology and worked the hardest, kept finding a reason not to go along. A month ago he had questioned them about it. They had the feeling that he was taking something away from them, they had answered evasively. Naturally, these texts could also be examined philologically. After all, they were the Holy Scriptures.

Gregorius recommended to the Rector that a theology student should be hired to teach Hebrew, one of his former students. With her copper-coloured hair, she had sat in the same place as Florence once had. But his hope that that might not be accidental had been in vain.

For a few moments his head was perfectly empty, then Gregorius again pictured the face of the Portuguese woman emerging white, almost transparent, from behind the towel. Once again, he stood at the mirror in the school cloakroom and felt that he didn't want to wipe away the phone number the enigmatic woman had written on his forehead. Once again, he stood up at his desk, took the damp coat off the hook and walked out of the classroom.

Português. Gregorius started, opened his eyes, and looked out at the flat French landscape, where the sun was now low on the horizon. The word that had been like a melody lost in a dreamy expanse, had suddenly lost its force. He tried to retrieve the magical sound of the voice, but what he managed to grasp was only a rapidly fading echo, and the vain attempt only strengthened the feeling that the precious word, the basis of this whole crazy trip, had slipped away. And it didn't help that he still knew precisely how the speaker on the language record had pronounced the word.

He went to the bathroom and held his face under the chlorinated water for a long time. Back in his seat, he took the book by the Portuguese aristocrat out of his bag and started translating the next passage. At first, it was mainly an escape, a desperate attempt, despite the fear, to keep on believing in this trip. But after the first sentence, the text fascinated him again as much as it had in his kitchen the previous night.

NOBREZA SILENCIOSA. SILENT NOBILITY. *It is a mistake to believe that the decisive moments of a life when its direction changes for ever must be marked by sentimental loud and shrill dramatics, manifested by violent inner surges. This is a sentimental fairy tale invented by drunken journalists, flashbulb happy film-makers and readers of the tabloids. In truth, the dramatic moments of a life-determining experience are often unbelievably low-key. It has so little in common with the bang, the flash, or the volcanic eruption that, at the moment it happens, the experience is often not even noticed. When it unfolds its revolutionary effect, and ensures that a life is revealed in a brand-new light, with a brand-new melody, it does that silently and in this wonderful silence resides its special nobility.*

From time to time, Gregorius glanced up from the text and looked out to the west. In the remaining brightness of the twilight sky, it seemed the sea could now be imagined. He put the dictionary away and shut his eyes.

If I could see the sea just once, his mother had said six months before her death, as if she felt that the end was near; *but we simply can't afford that.*

What bank will give me a loan, Gregorius heard the father say, *and for such a thing?*

Gregorius had been angry with him for his placid resignation. And then, he, who was still a student in Kirchenfeld, had done something that surprised him so much he never shook off the feeling that maybe it hadn't really happened.

It was late March, early spring. People hung their coats over their arms, and mild air streamed into the annexe through the open window. The annexe had been put up a few years earlier because the Gymnasium had outgrown the main building, and it had become a tradition to put the seniors there. Moving to the annexe seemed the first step towards graduation. Feelings of liberation and fear balanced each other. *One more year and then it was finally over . . . One more year and then you had to . . .* These alternating feeling were expressed in the way the students strolled to the annexe, nonchalant and scared at the same time. Even now, forty years later in the train to Irún, Gregorius could feel how it had been to be in his body back then.

The afternoon began with Greek. It was the Rector who taught them, Kägi's predecessor. He had the most beautiful Greek handwriting you could imagine; he drew the letters ceremonially, and the loops especially – as in Omega or Theta, or when he pulled the Eta down – were the purest calligraphy. He loved Greek. *But he loved it in the wrong way,* thought Gregorius at the back of the classroom. His way of loving it was a conceited way. It wasn't by celebrating the words. If it had been that – Gregorius would have liked it. But when this man wrote out the most difficult verb froms, he celebrated not the *words*, but rather *himself* as one who knew them. The words thus became ornaments to him, he adorned himself with them, they turned into something like the polka-dotted bow tie he wore year in, year out. They flowed from his writing hand with the signet ring as if they too were a kind of signet ring, a conceited jewel and just as superfluous. And so, the Greek words really stopped being *Greek* words. It was as if the gold dust from the signet ring corroded their Greek essence that was revealed only to those who loved it for its own sake. Poetry for the Rector was like an exquisite piece of furniture, a fine wine or an elegant evening gown. Gregorius had the feeling that the Rector robbed him of the verses of Aeschylus and Sophocles with this smugness. He seemed to know nothing of Greek theatre. Or rather, he knew everything about it, was often in Greece, guided educational tours there and came back with a suntan. But he didn't *understand* anything about it – even if Gregorius couldn't have said what he meant by that.

He had gazed out of the open window of the annexe and thought of his mother's words, words which had exacerbated his rage at the Rector's conceit, even though he couldn't have explained the connection. He felt the blood pulse in his throat. A look at the board assured him that it would take the Rector a while to finish the sentence he had started before he turned round to explain it to the students. As the others went on writing with bent backs, he pushed his chair back without a sound. He left the open notebook on his desk. With the tense slowness of someone preparing a surprise attack, he took two steps to the open window, sat down on the sill, swung his legs over and was outside.

The last thing he saw inside the classroom was the amazed and amused face of Eva, the girl with red hair, freckles, and the squint that had always rested on him mockingly, to his despair, on the boy wearing the thick glasses with the cheap and ugly frames. She turned to her benchmate and whispered something in her ear. 'Unbelievable!' She said it all the time. And so she was called *Unbelievable*. 'Unbelievable!' she had said when she heard about her nickname.

Gregorius had walked quickly to Bärenplatz. It was a market, and you made your way slowly from one stall to another. When the crowd forced him to stop at a stand, his eye fell on the open cashbox, a simple metal case with one compartment for coins and another for notes, which formed a thick pile. The market woman was now bending over, fiddling with something on the stand, her broad behind jutting out in the coarse cloth of a checked dress. Gregorius had slowly pushed his way towards the cashbox, his look circling over the people near by. With two steps, he was behind the counter, had grabbed the bundle of notes and plunged into the crowd. When he went up the street to the railway station, panting, and forcing himself to walk calmly, he expected somebody to call him from behind or take hold of him. But nothing had happened.

They lived on Länggasse, in a grey apartment house with dirty plasterwork, and when Gregorius mounted the staircase, which smelt of cabbage from morning to night, he saw himself surprising his sick mother with the announcement that she would soon be seeing the sea. Only when he reached the apartment door did he realize that the whole thing was impossible, absolutely ludicrous. How was he to explain to her, and later to his father, how he had suddenly come by so much money? He, who had no experience of lying?

On the way back to Bärenplatz, he bought an envelope and stuck the bundle of notes inside. The woman in the checked dress had a tear-stained face when he returned to her stand. He chose some fruit and when she was busy with the scales at the other end of the stall, he pushed the envelope under the vegetables. Shortly before the end of break, he was back at school, had climbed into the annexe through the open window and sat down in his seat.

'Unbelievable!' said Eva when she saw him and she began to regard him with more respect than before. But that was less important than he had thought. More important was that the discovery about himself made in the past hour didn't inspire any horror in him, but only a great amazement that reverberated for weeks.

When the train left Bordeaux station for Biarritz it was getting dark and Gregorius saw himself reflected in the window. What would have become of him if the person who had taken the money out of the cashbox back then had determined his life instead of the one who began to love the ancient silent words so much that he granted them sovereignty over everything else? What did that breakout have in common with this one now? Anything?

Gregorius reached for Prado's book and searched for the laconic note the man in the Spanish bookshop on Hirschengraben had translated for him:

Given that we can live only a small part of what there is in us — what happens to the rest?

In Biarritz, a man and woman got on, stood by the seat in front of Gregorius and discussed their seat reservation. *Vinte e oito.* It took him a while to identify the repeated sounds as Portuguese words and to confirm his assumption: twenty-eight. He concentrated on what they were saying and now and then in the next half-hour he managed to make out a few words. Tomorrow morning, he would arrive in a city where most of what the people said would be incomprehensible to him. He thought of Bubenplatz, Bärenplatz, Bundesterrasse, the Kirchenfeldbrücke. Meanwhile, it had become pitch-dark outside. Gregorius felt for his money, his credit cards, and his spare pair of glasses. He was feeling anxious.

At the French border town of Hendaye the carriage emptied. When the Portuguese couple noticed that, they panicked and grabbed their suitcases from the shelf. '*Isto ainda não é Irún,*' said Gregorius: This isn't yet Irún. It was a sentence from the language course record; only the name of the town was different. The Portuguese people hesitated because of his awkward pronunciation and the slowness with which he strung the words together. But they looked out and now they saw the railway station sign. '*Muito obrigada*,' said the woman. '*De nada*,' replied Gregorius. The Portuguese couple sat down, the train went on.

Gregorius was never to forget this scene. They were his first Portuguese words in the real world and they worked. That words could cause something in the world, make someone move or stop, laugh or cry: even as a child he had found it extraordinary and it had never stopped impressing him. How did words do that? Wasn't it like magic? But at this moment, the mystery seemed greater than usual, for these were words he hadn't even known yesterday morning. A few minutes later, when he set foot on the platform of Irún, all fear had vanished, and he walked confidently towards the Lisbon train.

6

It was ten o'clock when the train that would cross the Iberian Peninsula the next morning started moving; the dreary railway station lamps slid past one after another into the dark. The compartment next to Gregorius had remained empty. Two compartments down, towards the dining car, a tall slim man with greying hair was leaning against his door. 'Boa noite,' he said when their eyes met. 'Boa noite,' said Gregorius.

When he heard the awkward pronunciation, a smile flitted over the stranger's face. It was a chiselled face with clear, definite features, and there was something distinguished and reserved about it. The man's dark clothing was conspicuously elegant and made Gregorius think of the lobby of an opera house. Only the loosened tie didn't fit. Now the man folded his arms over his shirt, leaned his head against the door and shut his eyes. With his eyes shut, the face looked very white and radiated fatigue, a fatigue that must have come from other things than the late hour. When the train had reached its full speed a few minutes later, the man opened his eyes, nodded to Gregorius, and disappeared into his compartment.

Gregorius would have given anything to be able to fall asleep, but even the monotonous beat of the wheels didn't help. He sat up in the bed and pressed his forehead against the window. Desolate little railway stations slid past, milky, diffuse light bulbs, illegible place-names, parked baggage carts, a head with a cap in a railway halt, a stray dog, a rucksack half-concealing a blond mop of hair. The certainty granted by the first

Portuguese words began to crumble. *Just call. Day or night.* He heard Doxiades's voice and thought of their first meeting twenty years earlier, when the Greek still had a strong accent.

'Blind? No. You've just had a bad time with your eyes. We check the retina regularly. Besides, there are lasers now. No reason to panic.' On the way to the door, he had stood still and looked at him intensely. 'Any other concerns?'

Gregorius had shaken his head mutely. Only a few months later did he tell Doxiades that he had seen the divorce from Florence coming. The Greek had nodded, it seemed not to surprise him. *Sometimes we're afraid of something because we're afraid of something else,* he had said.

Shortly before midnight, Gregorius went into the dining car. It was empty except for the man with greying hair who was playing chess with the waiter. In fact, the car was closed, the waiter indicated, but then he got Gregorius a mineral water and beckoned him to join them. Gregorius quickly saw that the man, who had put on a pair of gold-framed glasses, had fallen into the waiter's cunning trap. With his hand on the chess piece, the man looked at him before he made his move. Gregorius shook his head and the man withdrew his hand. The waiter, a man with calloused hands whose coarse features didn't seem to suggest a brain for chess, looked up surprised. Now the man with the gold-framed glasses turned the board towards Gregorius and gestured to him to play in his place. It was a long, tough struggle and it was two o'clock when the waiter gave up.

Afterwards, when they stood at his compartment door, the man asked Gregorius where he was from and they spoke in French. He took this train every two weeks, the man said, and only once had he been able to beat this waiter, while he usually beat others. He introduced himself: José António da Silveira. He was, he said, a businessman and sold porcelain in Biarritz; and he took the train because he was afraid of flying.

'Who knows the real reasons for his fear?' he said after a pause and now the exhaustion Gregorius had noted earlier appeared again on his face.

Then, when he explained how he had taken over his father's little business and had built it into a big firm, he talked about himself as if about somebody else, who had made thoroughly understandable but altogether wrong decisions. And it sounded the same when he talked of his divorce and the two children he hardly saw any more. Disappointment and sadness were in his voice, and what impressed Gregorius was his lack of self-pity.

'The problem is,' said Silveira, as the train stopped at Valladolid station, 'that we have no grasp of our life as a whole. Neither forward nor backward. If something goes well, we just attribute it to good luck.' An invisible hammer tested the brakes. 'And how do you come to be on this train?'

They sat on the bed in Silveira's compartment as Gregorius told his story. He left out the Portuguese woman on the Kirchenfeldbrücke. That was something he could tell Doxiades, not a stranger. He was glad Silveira didn't ask to see Prado's book. He didn't want anybody else to read it and pass comment on it.

There was silence when he had finished. Silveira's mind was busy, Gregorius saw from the way he turned his signet ring and the brief, shy glances he cast at him.

'And you just got up and left the school? Just like that?'

Gregorius nodded. Suddenly he regretted talking about it; something precious had been endangered. Now he wanted to get some sleep, he said. Silveira took out a little notebook. Would he repeat to him the words of Marcus Aurelius about the impulses of one's soul? When Gregorius left his compartment, Silveira sat bent over his notebook copying down the words.

Gregorius dreamed of red cedars. The words *cedros vermelhos*

kept flickering through his restless sleep. It was the name of
the publisher of Prado's book. He hadn't paid any special
attention to it previously. It was only Silveira's question of how
he could get in touch with the author that reminded him he
would first have to find this publishing house. Maybe Amadeu
de Prado had published the book privately, Gregorius thought
as he fell asleep; then the red cedars would have had a meaning
known only to him. In his dream, Gregorius wandered with
the mysterious name on his lips and the phone book under
his arm, through the twisted, steeply rising streets of Lisbon,
lost in a faceless city, knowing only that it was set on hills.

When he awoke at six o'clock and saw the name Salamanca
before his compartment window, out of the blue, a sluicegate
of memory opened that had remained closed for four decades.
The first thing it released was the name of another city: *Isfahan*.
Suddenly it was there, the name of the Persian city where he
had wanted to go after he finished school. The name bearing
so much mysterious strangeness touched Gregorius at this
moment, like the code of another possible life he hadn't dared
live. And as the train left Salamanca station, once again he
lived through the feelings of thirty years earlier when another
life had both opened and closed.

It had started when, after a year of study, the Hebrew
teacher had them read the Book of Job. For Gregorius, it had
been intoxicating when he started understanding the sentences
and a path opened for him leading into the Orient. In Karl
May, the Orient sounded very German, not only because of
the language. Now, in the Book of Job, which he had read
from cover to cover, it sounded like the Orient. Eliphaz of
Telman, Bildad of Shuach, Zofar of Na'ama: even the names
of Job's three friends, in their bewitching foreignness, seemed
to come from beyond all oceans. What a wonderful, dreamlike
world that was!

Afterwards, for a while, he had wanted to become an

Orientalist. Someone who knew his way around in *Morgenland*, the East, he loved the German word, it led out of Länggasse into a bright light. Shortly before graduation, he had applied for the position of tutor to the children of a Swiss industrialist in Isfahan. Reluctantly – worried about him, but also fearing the vacuum he would leave behind – his father had given him the thirteen francs thirty for a Persian grammar, and he had written the unfamiliar Oriental characters on the small blackboard in his room.

But then a dream had begun haunting him, one he seemed to dream all night long. It had been a very simple dream and part of the torment was this simplicity, which seemed to increase the more frequently the image returned. For in fact the dream had consisted of only a single image: hot Oriental sand, desert sand, white and scorching, had blown on to his glasses from the smouldering breath of Persia and had settled like a white-hot crust, robbing him of all sight, melting the lenses of his glasses.

After two or three weeks, when the dream kept popping up and haunting him far into the day, he had taken back the Persian grammar and returned the money to his father. He was allowed to keep the three francs thirty and it had been as if he now possessed Persian money.

What would have become of him if he had overcome the fear of the scorching dust of the Orient and had gone to Isfahan? Gregorius thought of how cold-bloodedly he had reached into the cashbox of the market woman. Would that have enabled him to cope with everything that would have assailed him in Isfahan? *The Papyrus.* Why did that decades-old joke that hadn't bothered him hurt so much all of a sudden?

Silveira's place was empty when Gregorius entered the dining car in the morning, and the Portuguese couple with whom he had exchanged his first Portuguese words in the early evening were already on their second cup of coffee.

He had spent an hour lying awake in bed, thinking about the postman who would enter the lobby of the Gymnasium at nine and give the mail to the janitor. Today, his letter would be there. Kägi wouldn't be able to believe his eyes. Mundus was running away from his life. Anybody else, but not him. The news would make the rounds, upstairs and down, and the students on the steps at the entrance would talk of nothing else.

Gregorius had gone through his colleagues in his mind, imagining what they would think, feel and say. As he did so, he had made a discovery that jolted him: he wasn't sure of a single one of them. At first, things had looked different: Burri, for instance, an army major and enthusiastic churchgoer, found it incomprehensible, perverse, and reprehensible, because of the effect his disappearance would have on the students; Anita Mühletaler, who had just gone through a divorce, tilted her head pensively, she could imagine such a thing, even if not for herself; Kalbermatten, the skirt-chaser and secret anarchist from Saas-Fee, might say in the staffroom: 'Why not?'; while Virginie Ledoyen, the French teacher, whose prissy appearance contrasted glaringly with her sparkling name, would react to the news with an executioner's look. All that seemed quite predictable at first. But then it occurred to Gregorius that he had seen the devout paterfamilias, Burri, a few months ago with a blonde in a short dress who seemed to be more than an acquaintance; how petty Anita Mühletaler could be when students raised hell; how cowardly Kalbermatten was about resisting Kägi; and how easily students who knew how to flatter her could wind Virginie Ledoyen around their little finger and make her drop her strict agenda.

Could something be inferred from that? Something about their attitude to him and his surprising action? Could concealed understanding or even secret envy be assumed? Gregorius had sat up in bed and was looking out at the landscape steeped in the silvery shimmering green of the olive groves. His familiarity with his colleagues all these years turned out to be curdled ignorance that had become deceptive habit. And was it indeed important – really *important* – to know what they thought of him? Was it only because of his thick head that he didn't know that or was he becoming aware of a strangeness that had always existed between him and them, but had been hidden behind social rituals?

Compared with the face that had become open in the dim light of the compartment last night – open to the feelings that thrust out from inside, and open to the look from outside that sought to fathom them – this morning, Silveira's features were closed. At first glance, it looked as if he regretted exposing himself to a total stranger in the intimacy of the compartment smelling of blankets and disinfectant, and Gregorius sat down hesitantly at his table. But he soon understood: it wasn't retreat and rejection that was expressed in the firm, controlled features, but rather a pensive sobriety suggesting that the encounter with Gregorius had perplexed Silveira, had provoked surprising feelings he was now trying to figure out.

He pointed to the phone next to his cup. 'I've reserved a room for you in the hotel where I put up my business partner. Here's the address.'

He handed Gregorius a business card with the information written on the back. He had to look through some papers before they arrived, he said, and prepared to stand up. But then he leaned back again and the way he looked at Gregorius proved that something had occurred to him. Had he never regretted devoting his life to ancient languages? he asked. That surely meant a very quiet, withdrawn life.

Do you find me boring? It occurred to Gregorius how the question he had asked Florence back then had preoccupied him on the trip yesterday and something of that must have shown on his face. Silveira said hastily, please don't mis-understand, he was only trying to imagine how it would be to live a life that was so completely different from his own.

It had been the life he had wanted, said Gregorius, and even as the words took shape in him, he became aware of defiance in his tone. Only two days ago, when he had stepped on to the Kirchenfeldbrücke and seen the Portuguese woman reading the letter, he wouldn't have had any reason for this defiance. He would have said exactly the same thing, but his words would have contained no trace of obstinacy.

And why are you sitting here, then? Gregorius was afraid of the question and for a moment, the elegant Portuguese man seemed like an inquisitor.

How long does it take to learn Greek? Silveira asked next. Gregorius breathed a sigh of relief and plunged into an answer that was much too long. Could he write down a few words for him in Hebrew, here on the napkin? asked Silveira.

And God said, Let there be light; and there was light, wrote Gregorius and translated it for him.

Silveira's phone rang. He had to go, he said, when he finished his conversation, and thrust the napkin into his jacket pocket. 'What was the word for light?' he asked, standing up, and he repeated it to himself on his way to the door.

The broad river outside must already have been the Tejo. Gregorius started: that meant they would soon be arriving. He returned to his compartment, which had been converted back into a regular compartment with a cushioned bench, and sat down at the window. He didn't want the journey to end. What was he to do in Lisbon? He had a hotel. He would give the porter a tip, close the door, rest. And then?

Hesitantly, he picked up Prado's book and leafed through it.

SAUDADE PARADOXAL. PARADOXICAL YEARNING. *For 1,922 days I attended the Liceu where my father sent me, the strictest school*

*in the whole country, they said. 'You don't need to become a
scholar,' he said, and tried a smile that, as usual, failed. By the
third day. I realized that I had to count the days so as not to be
crushed by them.*

As Gregorius was looking up the verb *crush* in the dictionary,
the train pulled into the city's Santa Apolónia railway station.

The few sentences had captivated him. They were the first
that revealed something about the external life of the Portuguese
man. A student at a strict school, who counted the days, and
the son of a father whose smile usually failed. Was that the
origin of the restrained rage conveyed in the other sentences?
Gregorius couldn't have said why, but he wanted to know more
about this rage. He had glimpsed the first brushstrokes in a
portrait of somebody who lived here in this city. Somebody
he wanted to know. Lisbon seemed to grow towards him in
these sentences. As if it had just stopped being a thoroughly
strange city.

He took his suitcase and stepped out on to the platform.
Silveira had waited for him. He took him to the taxi and gave
the driver the address of the hotel. 'You have my card,' he said
to Gregorius and waved a brief goodbye.

7

When Gregorius woke up, it was late afternoon and twilight was sinking over the cloud-draped city. Soon after he arrived, he had climbed under the bedspread in his clothes and had slipped into a leaden sleep, despite the feeling that he really couldn't allow himself any sleep, for there were a thousand things to do, things he couldn't name but no less urgent for that. On the contrary, the fact that they were nameless made it all the more imperative to tackle them at once to prevent something bad from happening, something that also couldn't be named. Now, as he washed his face in the bathroom, he felt with relief the fear of missing something, and feeling guilty about it, fall away along with his numbness.

During the next hour, he sat at the window and tried in vain to bring order to his thoughts. Now and then, his eye was drawn to the unpacked suitcase in the corner. When night fell, he went down to reception and had them enquire at the airport if there was still a flight to Zurich or Geneva. There were none, and when he went up in the elevator, he was amazed at how relieved he felt. Then he sat on the bed in the dark and tried to interpret the surprising relief. He dialled Doxiades's number and let the phone ring ten times before he hung up. He opened the book by Amadeu de Prado and read on from where he had stopped at the railway station.

Six times a day I heard the jingle of bells announcing the beginning of class and sounding as if monks were being called to their prayers.

Thus it was 11,532 times that I clenched my teeth and went back into the gloomy building from the schoolyard instead of following my imagination, which sent me through the school-gate and out to the port, to a ship's rail, where I would then lick the salt from my lips.

Now, thirty years later, I keep coming back to this place. There isn't the slightest practical reason for it. So why? I sit on the mossy, crumbling steps at the entrance and have no idea why my heart is in my mouth. Why am I full of envy when I see the students with brown legs and light hair going in and out as if they were at home here? What is it? Why do I envy them? Recently, when the window was open on a hot day, I listened to the various teachers and heard the stuttering answers of anxious students to questions that had made me tremble too. Sitting inside there once more – no, that was certainly not what I wanted. In the cool dark of the long corridor, I met the janitor, a man with a protruding, birdlike head, advancing towards me with a suspicious look. 'What are you searching for here?' he asked, when I passed him. He had an asthmatic falsetto voice that sounded as if it came from the hereafter. 'I went to school here,' I said and was filled with contempt for myself when I heard how hoarse my voice sounded. For a few seconds, an eerie silence reigned in the corridor. Then the man behind me shuffled off. I felt I had been caught red-handed. But why?

On the last day of finals, we had all stood behind our benches, the school caps on our heads, as if we were lined up for morning roll call. With measured tread, Senhor Cortês went from one boy to another, announced the results with his usual strict expression and with the same look, he handed us our diplomas. Joyless and pale, my assiduous benchmate took his and held it in his folded hands like a Bible. Giggling, the boy at the bottom of the class, the girls' suntanned favourite, let his diploma fall to the floor like a piece of litter. Then we went out into the midday heat of a July day. What could, what should, be done with all the time that lay

*before us, open and unshaped, feather-light in its freedom and
lead-heavy in its uncertainty?*

*Neither before nor since have I experienced anything that
revealed so cogently and impressively as the following scene how
different people are. The boy at the bottom of the class was the
first to take off his cap; he spun around and threw it over the
fence of the schoolyard into the pond next door where it was slowly
soaked and finally disappeared under the waterlilies. Three or four
other boys followed his example and one cap remained hanging
on the fence. My benchmate then straightened his cap, anxious
and indignant, you couldn't tell which feeling predominated in
him. What would he do tomorrow morning when there was no
more reason to put on the cap? But what was most impressive was
what I observed in the shadowy corner of the schoolyard. Half
hidden behind a dusty bush, a boy was trying to stow his cap in
his schoolbag. He didn't simply want to stuff it in, that was plain
from the hesitant movements. He tried to place it carefully this
way and that; finally he made room for it by taking out a few
books which he now wedged awkwardly under his arm. When he
turned and looked around, you could read in his eyes the hope
that nobody had observed him in his shameful act, along with a
last trace of the childish thought, wiped out by experience, that
you could become invisible by averting your eyes.*

*I can still feel today how I twisted my own sweaty cap back
and forth. I sat on the warm moss of the entrance steps and thought
of my father's imperious wish that I might become a doctor – one
who might release people like him from pain. I loved him for his
trust and cursed him for the crushing burden he imposed on me
with his touching wish. Meanwhile, some students from the girls'
school had come over. 'Are you glad it's over?' asked Maria João
and sat down next to me. She examined me. 'Or are you sad
about it, after all?'*

*Now I finally seem to know what keeps compelling me to return
to the school: I'd like to go back to those minutes in the schoolyard*

when the past had dropped from us and the future hadn't yet begun. Time came to a halt and held its breath, as it never did again. Was it Maria João's suntanned knees and the fragrance of soap in her light dress that I'd like to go back to? Or is it the wish – the dreamlike, nostalgic wish – to stand once again at that point in my life and be able to take a completely different direction to the one that has made me who I am now?

There's something strange about this wish, because the one who wishes it isn't the one who, still untouched by the future, stands at the crossroads. Instead, it is the one marked by the future-become-past who wants to go back to the past, to revoke the irrevocable. Would he want to revoke it if he hadn't suffered it? To sit once more on the warm moss holding his cap – it's the absurd wish to go back in time and take oneself – the one marked by events – on this journey. And is it conceivable that the boy back then would have defied the father's wish and not gone to medical school – as I sometimes wish today? Could he have done it and be me? At that time no perspective of experience could have made me want to take another fork at the crossroads. So what good would it do me to turn back time and, extinguishing one experience after another, to turn myself into the boy who was addicted to the fresh fragrance of Maria João's dress and the sight of her tanned knees? The boy with the cap – he would have had to be quite different from me to take another direction, as I wish for myself today. But then, if he had, he wouldn't have become a man who would later wish to return to the previous crossroads. Can I wish myself to be him? I wouldn't want to be him. But this would only be because I am not him, only as the fulfilment of wishes that aren't his. If, in fact, I were him – I couldn't wish for what would satisfy me as him, as my own wishes might, because I wouldn't have them at all if they had already been fulfilled.

Yet I am certain I will soon wake up again with the wish to return to the school and give in to a yearning whose object can't

exist because you can't even think it. Can there be anything more
absurd than this: to be moved by a wish that has no conceivable
object?

It was nearly midnight before Gregorius was finally sure he
understood the difficult text. So Prado was a doctor and had
become one because his father, whose smile usually failed, had
had this imperious wish, a wish that had originated not in
dictatorial arbitrariness or paternal vanity, but had developed
out of the helplessness of chronic pain. Gregorius opened the
phone book. There were fourteen listings under the name of
Prado, but there was no *Amadeu* among them, no *Inácio* and
no *Almeida*. Why had he assumed that Prado lived in Lisbon?
Now he looked in the business directory for the publisher
Cedros Vermelhos: nothing. Would he have to search through
the whole country? Did that make sense? Even the slightest
sense?

Gregorius set out to walk in the night-time city. He had
been doing that since his mid-twenties when he lost the capacity
to fall asleep easily. Countless times, he had walked through
the empty streets of Bern after midnight, had stopped from
time to time and listened like a blind man to the few footsteps
coming or going. He loved to stand at the dark display windows
of the bookshops and feel that, because others were sleeping,
all these books belonged only to him. With slow steps, he now
turned the corner out of the side street of the hotel into the
broad Avenida da Liberdade and went towards the Baixa, the
lower part of town where the streets were arranged like a
chessboard. It was cold, and a fine fog formed a milky halo
around the old-fashioned street lamps with their gold light.
He found a coffee shop where he had a sandwich and coffee.

Prado kept returning to sit on the steps of his school and
imagine how it would have been to live a completely different
life. Gregorius thought of the question Silveira had put to him

and to which he had answered defiantly that he had lived the life he wanted. He felt that the image of the doubting doctor on the mossy steps and the question of the doubting businessman in the train had shifted something in him, something that would never have happened in the familiar streets of Bern.

Now the only other man in the café paid and left. With sudden inexplicable haste, Gregorius also paid and followed the man. He was an old man who dragged one leg and stood still every now and then to rest. Gregorius followed him at a distance into Bairro Alto, the upper part of the city, until he disappeared behind the door of a narrow, shabby house. Now the light went on in the first floor, the curtain was pushed aside, and the man stood at the open window, a cigarette between his lips. From the protective dark of a doorway, Gregorius looked past him into the lighted flat. A sofa with cushions of worn-out needlepoint. Two unmatched armchairs. A glass cabinet with crockery and small, colourful porcelain figures. A crucifix on the wall. Not a single book. How was it to be this man?

After the man had closed the window and pulled the curtains closed, Gregorius emerged from the doorway. He had lost his orientation and took the next street down. Never had he followed anybody like this with the thought of how it would be to live another life instead of his own. It was a brand-new kind of curiosity that had taken hold of him and it suited the new alertness he had experienced on the train journey and when he had arrived at the Gare de Lyon in Paris, yesterday or whenever it was.

Now and then he paused and looked around him. The ancient texts, his ancient texts, they were also full of characters who lived a life, and to read and understand the texts had always also meant reading and understanding this life. So why was everything so new now when it concerned both the

Portuguese aristocrat and the limping man? On the damp cobblestones of the steep streets, he put one uncertain foot before the other and breathed a sigh of relief when he recognized the Avenida da Liberdade.

The blow caught him unprepared, for he hadn't heard the rollerblader coming. He was a giant who hit Gregorius on the temple with his elbow as he overtook him and ripped off his glasses. Dazed and suddenly sightless, Gregorius stumbled a few steps and to his horror felt himself stepping on the glasses and crushing them underfoot. A wave of panic washed over him. *Don't forget the spare glasses,* he heard Doxiades say on the phone. Minutes passed until his breathing grew calm. Then he knelt down on the street and felt for the glass splinters and the fragments of the frame. What he could feel he brushed together and knotted into his handkerchief. Slowly he groped his way back to the hotel.

The night porter jumped up, in fright when Gregorius entered the lobby with blood dripping from his temple. In the elevator, he pressed the porter's handkerchief to the wound and then ran along the corridor, opened his door with trembling fingers and tumbled on to the suitcase. He felt tears of relief when his hand touched the cool metal case of the spare pair of glasses. He put them on, washed off the blood, and stuck the Band-Aid the porter had given him on the scratch on his temple. It was two-thirty. At the airport nobody answered the phone. At four he fell asleep.

8

If Lisbon hadn't been steeped in that bewitching light the next morning, Gregorius thought later, things might have taken a completely different turn. Maybe he would have gone to the airport and taken the next flight home. But the light dispelled any temptation to turn back. Its glow made the past very distant, almost unreal, under its luminosity, the only possibility was to move forward into the future whatever it might bring. Bern and its snowflakes were far away and it was hard for Gregorius to believe that only three days had passed since he had met the enigmatic Portuguese woman on the Kirchenfeldbrücke.

After breakfast, he dialled José António da Silveria's number and reached his secretary. Could she recommend an ophthalmologist who spoke German, French or English, he asked. Half an hour later, she called back, gave him greetings from Silveria and the name of a doctor his sister went to, a woman who had worked for a long time at the university clinics in Coimbra and Munich.

Her office was in the Alfama quarter, the oldest part of the city, behind the citadel. Gregorius walked slowly through the luminious day and avoided anybody who could have bumped into him. Sometimes he stood still and rubbed his eyes behind the thick lenses. So this was Lisbon, the city he had come to because, while looking at his students, he had suddenly seen his life from the other end, and because a book by a Portuguese doctor had fallen into his hands and its words sounded as if they were aimed at him.

The rooms he entered an hour later didn't look like a doctor's office at all. The dark wood panelling, the original paintings, and the thick carpet gave the impression that you were in the home of a noble family, where everything had its solid form and life proceeded without a sound. It didn't surprise Gregorius that nobody was in the waiting room. No one who lived in such rooms needed to accept patients. Senhora Eça would come in a few minutes, said the woman at the reception desk. Nothing about her indicated a medical assistant. The only thing that hinted at commercial matters was a bright monitor full of names and numbers. Gregorius thought of Doxiades's slightly shabby office and the cocky medical assistant. Suddenly he had the feeling of committing treason and when one of the high doors opened and the doctor appeared, he was glad to be relieved of the uncomfortable thought.

Doutora Mariana Conceição Eça was woman with big dark eyes he felt he could trust. In fluent German, with a mistake only here and there, she greeted Gregorius as a friend of Silveira, and already knew why he was here. Why should he feel any need to apologize for his panic about the broken glasses? she asked. Naturally, somebody as nearsighted as he was had to feel he had a spare pair of glasses.

All at once, Gregorius calmed down, sank deep into the chair at her desk and wished he never had to stand up again. The woman seemed to have unlimited time for him. Gregorius had never had this feeling with any doctor, not even Doxiades; it was unreal, almost as in a dream. He had expected her to measure the spare glasses, make the usual eye tests, and then send him to the optician with a prescription. Instead, she made him tell her the history of his nearsightedness, stage by stage, concern after concern. When he finally handed her the glasses, she gave him a searching look.

'You're a man who doesn't sleep well,' she said.

The examination lasted more than an hour. The instruments looked different from those of Doxiades, and Senhora Eça studied the background of his eyes with the detail of somebody becoming familiar with a brand-new landscape. But what impressed Gregorius the most was that she repeated the test for visual acuity three times. In between were pauses when she made him walk around and started a conversation about his profession.

'How well one sees depends on so many things,' she said smiling when she noted his amazement.

At last, there was a diopter number that was clearly different from the usual one and the value for the two eyes was further apart than usual. Senhora Eça saw his confusion.

'Let's just try it out,' she said and touched his arm.

Gregorius wavered between resistance and trust. Trust won. The doctor gave him the business card of an optician and then she called the shop. Her Portuguese voice brought back the magic he had felt when the enigmatic woman on the Kirchenfeldbrücke had pronounced the word *português*. Suddenly being in this city made sense, a sense that couldn't be explained; on the contrary, it was part of this sense that it musn't be violated by trying to capture it in words.

'Two days,' said the doctor after she hung up. 'With the best will in the world, says César, the glasses can't be ready any sooner.'

Now, Gregorius took the little volume by Amadeu de Prado out of his jacket pocket, showed her the strange name of the publisher and told of the futile search in the phone book. Yes, she said, distracted, it sounds like a private publisher.

'And the red cedars – it wouldn't surprise me if they were a metaphor for something.'

Gregorius had thought the same: a metaphor or a code for something secret – bloody or beautiful – hidden under the colourful, wilted foliage of a life story.

The doctor went into another room and came back with an address book. She opened it and ran her finger along a page.

'Here. Júlio Simões,' she said, 'a friend of my late husband, a second-hand book dealer who always seemed to us to know more about books than anyone else alive, it was really weird.'

She wrote down the address and explained to Gregorius where it was.

'Give him my best. And call in with the new glasses. I'd like to know if I've done it right.'

When Gregorius turned around on the staircase, she was still standing in the doorway, with one hand on the lintel. If Silveira had called her, she might also know that he had run away. He would gladly have told her about it and as he went down the stairs, his steps were hesitant, as if he was reluctant to leave.

The sky was coated with a fine white veil that softened the gleam of the sunlight. The optician's shop was near the ferry across the Tagus. César Santarém's surly face lit up when Gregorius told him who had sent him. He looked at the prescription, weighed the glasses Gregorius gave him in his hand and then said in broken French that they could be made of lighter material and put in a lighter frame.

That was the second time in a short period that someone had cast doubt on the judgement of Constantine Doxiades, and it seemed to Gregorius that his former life was being taken out of his hands, a life spent, as long as he could remember, with heavy glasses on his nose. Uncertainly, he tried on frame after frame and finally let himself be tempted by Santarém's assistant, who knew only Portuguese and talked like a waterfall, to choose a narrow reddish frame that seemed much too stylish and chic for his broad, square face. On the way to the Bairro Alto, where Júlio Simões's second-hand bookshop was, he kept telling himself that the new glasses could be spare glasses and didn't need to be worn, and when he finally stood before the bookshop, he had recovered his internal balance.

Senhor Simões was a wiry man with a sharp nose and dark eyes emanating a mercurial intelligence. Mariana Eça had called and told him the issue. Half the city of Lisbon, thought Gregorius, seemed to be concerned with calling on his behalf and directing him on; he couldn't remember ever experiencing such a thing before.

Cedros Vermelhos – there was no such publisher, said Simões, in the thirty years that he had been in the book business, of that he was sure. *Um Ourives das Palavras* – no, he had never heard of that title either. He leafed through the book, read a sentence here and there, and it seemed to Gregorius that he was waiting for his memory to bring something to light. Finally, he looked once more at the year of publication. Nineteen seventy-five – he had still been in college in Porto and wouldn't have heard of a book that appeared as a private publication, especially not if it had been printed in Lisbon.

'If there is anybody who would know,' he said and filled his pipe, 'it's old Coutinho, who had the shop here before me. He's close to ninety and is nuts, but his memory for books is phenomenal, a genuine miracle. I can't call him because he can barely hear, but I'll write you a few lines to give him.'

Simões went to his desk in the corner, wrote something on a notepad, and put it in an envelope.

'You have to be patient with him,' he said when he gave Gregorius the envelope. 'He's had a lot of bad luck in his life and is a bitter old man. But he can also be very nice when you take the right tone with him. The problem is that you never know in advance what the right tone is.'

Gregorius stayed in the second-hand bookshop a long time. Getting to know a city through the books in it – he had always done that. His first trip abroad as a student had been to London.

On the way back to Calais, he had realized that, except for the Youth Hostel, the British Museum and the many bookshops around it, he had seen practically nothing of the city. *But the same books could also be anywhere else!* said the others and shook their heads at all the things he had missed. *Yes, but in fact they weren't anywhere else*, he had replied.

And now he stood before the ceiling-high shelves filled with Portuguese books that he couldn't read and reflected on how quickly he had established contact with the city. When he had left the hotel that morning, he had thought he had to find Amadeu de Prado as fast as possible to give a meaning to his stay here. But then there had been Mariana Eça's dark eyes, reddish hair and black velvet jacket and now there were all these books with names of previous owners that reminded him of Anneli Weiss's handwriting in his Latin book.

O Grande Terramoto. Except that it took place in 1755 and had devastated Lisbon, he knew nothing about the great earthquake that had shaken faith in God for so many people. He took the book off the shelf. The next book, standing crooked, was titled *A Morte Negra* and about the plague of the fourteenth and fifteenth centuries. With both books under his arm, Gregorius went to the literature section on the other side of the room. Luis Vaz de Camões; Francisco de Sá de Miranda; Fernão Mendes Pinto; Camilo Castelo Branco. An entire universe he had never heard of, not even from Florence. José Maria Eça de Queirós, *O Crime do Padre Amaro.* Hesitantly, as if it was something forbidden, he took the volume off the shelf and added it to the two others. And then, all of a sudden, he stood before it: Fernando Pessoa, *O Livro do Desassossego.* It really was unbelievable, but he had gone to Lisbon without thinking that he was going to the city of the assistant book-keeper Bernardo Soares, who worked on Rua dos Douradores and whose thoughts Pessoa had written down – thoughts that

were lonelier than all thoughts in the world, before or after
him.

Was it so unbelievable? *The fields are greener in description
than in their greenness.* This sentence by Pessoa had led to the
shrillest episode between him and Florence in all their years
together.

She had been sitting in the living room with colleagues,
to the accompaniment of laughter and clinking glasses.
Gregorius had gone in there reluctantly because he needed a
book. As he entered, somebody was reading a sentence aloud.
Isn't that a brilliant sentence? one of Florence's colleagues had
called out, shaking his artist's mane and putting his hand on
Florence's bare arm. *Only very few will understand this sentence,*
Gregorius had said. All at once, the room filled with an
embarrassed silence. *And you're one of these chosen ones?* Florence
asked in a cutting tone. With exaggerated slowness, Gregorius
had taken the book off the shelf and had left the room without
a word. It was some minutes before he heard voices and
laughter again.

Afterwards, when he had seen *The Book of Disquiet* somewhere, he had quickly passed it by. They had never spoken of
the episode again. It was part of everything that hadn't been
worked through when they split up.

Now, Gregorius took the book off the shelf.

'Do you know what this unbelievable book seems like to
me?' asked Senhor Simões, tapping the price into the cash
register. 'It's as if Marcel Proust had written the essays of
Michel de Montaigne.'

Gregorius was exhausted when, with his heavy bags, he
approached the memorial to Camões on Rua Garrett. But he
didn't want to go back to the hotel. He had come to this city
and he wanted to experience more of this feeling of belonging
so that he could be sure he wouldn't call the airport again
tonight to book a return flight. He drank a coffee and then

boarded the tram that would take him to the Cemitério dos Prazeres, near the home of Vítor Coutinho, the crazy old man who might know something about Amadeu de Prado.

9

In the hundred-year-old Lisbon tram, Gregorius travelled back to the Bern of his childhood. The car that took him, bumping, shaking and ringing through Bairro Alto, looked just like the one he had ridden through the streets of Bern for hours when he was still too young to have to pay the fare. The same lacquered wooden slat benches, the same bell-pulls next to the strap handles hanging down from the ceiling, the same metal lever the driver operated to brake and accelerate and whose workings Gregorius understood as little today as he had back then. At some time, when he was already wearing a sixth-form cap, the old trams were replaced with new once. The other students scrambled to ride in the new trams because they were quieter and smoother, and not a few were late to class because they had waited for one of them. Gregorius hadn't trusted himself to say it, but it bothered him that the world changed. He mustered all his courage, went to the tram depot and asked a workman what had happened to the old cars. They would be sold to Yugoslavia, said the man. He must have seen the boy's unhappiness, for he went into the office and came back with a model of the old car. Gregorius guarded it as a precious, irreplaceable find from a prehistoric time. He pictured it as the Lisbon tram rattled and screeched to a stop in the final loop.

It had never crossed Gregorius's mind that the old Portuguese aristocrat might be dead. Only now did the thought come to him as he stood at the cemetery gates. Slowly and apprehensively, he wandered through the lanes of the necropolis lined with simple little mausoleums.

It might have been half an hour later when he came upon a tall sepulchre of white weather-spotted marble. Two tablets with ornate corners and edges had been hewn in the stone. AQUI JAZ ALEXANDRE HORÁCIO DE ALMEIDA PRADO QUE NASCEU EM 28 DE MAIO DE 1890 E FALECEU EM 9 DE JUNHO DE 1954, was written on the top tablet, and AQUI JAZ MARIA PIEDADE REIS DE PRADO QUE NASCEU EM 12 DE JANEIRO DE 1899 E FALECEU EM 24 DE OUTUBRO DE 1960. On the bottom tablet, which was clearly lighter and less mossy, Gregorius read: AQUI JAZ FÁTIMA AMÉLIA CLEMÊNCIA GALHARDO DE PRADO QUE NASCEU EM 1 DE JANEIRO DE 1926 E FALECEU EM 3 DE FEVEREIRO DE 1961, and under that, with less patina on the letters, AQUI JAZ AMADEU INÁCIO DE ALMEIDA PRADO QUE NASCEU EM 20 DE DEZEMBRO DE 1920 E FALECEU EM 20 DE JUNHO DE 1973.

Gregorius stared at the last date. The book in his pocket had appeared in 1975. If this Amadeu de Prado was the doctor who had attended the strict Liceu of Senhor Cortês and had later, while sitting on its mossy steps, asked himself how it would have been to become somebody else – then he wouldn't have published his writings himself. Somebody else had done it, probably a private publisher. A friend, a brother, a sister. If this person was still alive after twenty-nine years, that was who he had to find.

But the name on the tomb could also be a coincidence. Gregorius wanted it to be, he wanted it with all his might. He knew how disappointed he would be and how dejected he would become if he couldn't meet the melancholy man who had wanted to re-order the Portuguese language because it was so hackneyed in its old form.

Nevertheless, he took out his notebook and wrote down all the names along with the dates of births and deaths. This

Amadeu de Prado had been fifty-three when he died. He had lost his father at the age of thirty-four. Had that been the father whose smile had mostly failed? The mother had died when he was forty. Fátima Galhardo – that could have been Amadeu's wife, a woman who had been only thirty-five and had died when he was forty-one.

Once more Gregorius let his eyes slide over the tomb and only now did he notice an inscription on the pedestal, half covered with wild ivy: QUANDO A DITADURA É UM FACTO A REVOLUÇÃO É UM DEVER. *When dictatorship is a fact, revolution is a duty.* Had the death of this Prado been a political death? The Revolution of the Carnations in Portugal, the end of the dictatorship, had taken place in the spring of 1974. So this Prado hadn't lived through it. The inscription sounded as if he had died as a resistance fighter. Gregorius took out the book and looked at the picture. It could be him, he thought, it would suit the face and the restrained rage behind everything he wrote. A poet and a language mystic who had taken up arms and fought against Salazar.

At the cemetery gate, he tried to ask the man in uniform how you could find out who a grave belonged to. But his few Portuguese words weren't adequate. He took out the notepaper on which Júlio Simões had written the address of his predecessor, and set out.

The house Vítor Coutinho lived in looked as if it could tumble down at any moment. Set back from the street, it was hidden behind other houses and its lower floor was overgrown with ivy. There was no bell and Gregorius stood helpless in the courtyard for a while. Just as he was about to leave a voice barked from one of the upper windows:

'*O que é que quer?*' What do you want?

The head at the window was framed with white locks that merged seamlessly into a white beard, and on the nose was a pair of glasses with broad, dark frames.

'*Pergunta sobre livro*,' Gregorius called out as loud as he could and held up Prado's notes.

'*O quê?* the man asked and Gregorius repeated his words.

The head disappeared and the door buzzed. Gregorius entered a corridor with overflowing bookshelves up to the ceiling and a worn-out Oriental rug on the red stone floor. It smelt of stale food, dust and pipe tobacco. On the creaky steps, the white-haired man appeared, a pipe between dark teeth. A coarse checked shirt of washed-out indefinable colour drooped over his baggy corduroy trousers; on his feet were open sandals.

'*Quem é?* he asked with the exaggerated loudness of the hard of hearing. The light brown, amberish-coloured eyes under the gigantic eyebrows had the look of someone whose rest had been disturbed.

Gregorius handed him the envelope with the message from Simões. He was Swiss, he explained in Portuguese, and added in French: a philologist of ancient languages and searching for the author of this book. When Coutinho didn't react, he started on a loud repetition.

He wasn't deaf. The old man interrupted him in French, and now a cunning grin appeared on the lined, weatherbeaten face. Deafness – that was useful shield against all the twaddle you were subjected to.

His French had an eccentric accent, but the words came, albeit slowly, in a confident order. He scanned Simões's lines, then pointed to a room at the end of the corridor, to which he led the way. On the kitchen table, next to a half-eaten tin of sardines and a half-full glass of red wine, lay an open book. Gregorius went to the chair at the other end of the table and sat down. Then the old man came to him and did something surprising: He took off Gregorius's glasses and put them on himself. He blinked, looked here and there, while swinging his own glasses in his hand.

'So, we've got that in common,' he said at last and returned the glasses to Gregorius.

The solidarity of those who go through the world with thick glasses. All of a sudden, all the annoyance and defensiveness had disappeared from Coutinho's face, and he reached for Prado's book.

Without a word, he looked at the portrait of the doctor for a few minutes. He stood up now and then, absent as a sleepwalker, and once poured Gregorius a glass of wine. A cat slipped in and sidled around his legs. He didn't notice it, took off his glasses, and grasped the bridge of his nose with thumb and index finger, a gesture that reminded Gregorius of Doxiades. In the next room, a grandfather clock was ticking. Now he emptied his pipe, took another from the shelf and filled it. More minutes passed until he began to speak, softly and in the timbre of distant memory.

'It would be wrong if I said I knew him. You can't even speak of an encounter. But I did see him, twice, in the doorway of his treatment room, in a white coat, his brows raised, waiting for the next patient. I was there with my sister, whom he was treating. Jaundice. High blood pressure. She swore by him. Was, I think, a little bit in love with him. No wonder, a fine figure of a man, with a personality that hypnotized people. He was the son of the famous Judge Prado, who took his own life, many said, because he could no longer bear the pains of his hunched back. Others conjectured that he couldn't forgive himself for staying in office under the dictatorship.

'Amadeu de Prado was a much loved, even esteemed doctor. Until he saved the life of Rui Luís Mendes, a member of the secret police, the one called The Butcher. That was in the mid-sixties, shortly after I turned fifty. After that, people avoided him. That broke his heart. From then on, he worked for the Resistance, but nobody knew it; as if he wanted to atone for rescuing Mendes. It came out only after his death. He died, as I remember, quite surprisingly of a cerebral haemorrhage, one year before the revolution. Lived at the end with Adriana, his sister, who idolized him.

'She must have been the one who had the book printed, I even have an idea who published it, but the firm closed down a long time ago. A few years later, the book popped up in my second-hand bookshop. I put it in some corner, didn't read it, had an aversion to it, don't really know why. Maybe because I didn't like Adriana, even though I hardly knew her. She worked as his assistant and both times I was there her overbearing way with patients got on my nerves. Probably unfair of me, but that's how I've always felt.'

Coutinho leafed through the book. 'Good sentences, it seems. And a good title. I didn't know he was a writer. Where did you get it? And why have you come looking for him?'

The story Gregorius told him sounded different from the one he had told José Antonio da Silveira on the night train. Mainly because he also mentioned the enigmatic Portuguese woman on the Kirchenfeldbrücke and the phone number written on his forehead.

'Do you still have the number?' asked the old man, who liked the story so much that he opened another bottle of wine.

For a moment, Gregorius was tempted to take out the notebook. But he felt this was going too far; after the episode with the glasses, he wouldn't put it past the old man to call the number. Simões had said he was nuts. That couldn't mean that Coutinho was confused; there was no question of that. What he seemed to have lost in his solitary life with the cat was any sense of distance and proximity.

No, said Gregorius now; he no longer had the number. Too bad, said the old man. He didn't believe a word of it, and suddenly they sat across from each other like total strangers.

There was no Adriana de Almeida Prado in the phone book, said Gregorius after an embarrassed pause.

That didn't mean anything, growled Coutinho. If she was still alive, Adriana had to be close to eighty, and old people sometimes got unlisted numbers; he had done that recently. And if she had died, her name would also have been on the tombstone. The address where the doctor had lived and worked, no, he no longer knew that after forty years. Somewhere in Bairro Alto. It wouldn't be too hard for him to find the house, for it was a house with a lot of blue tiles on the façade and there weren't many blue houses in Lisbon. *O consultório azul*, the blue practice, it was called.

When Gregorius left the old man an hour later, they had drawn close again. Gruff distance and surprising complicity alternated irregularly in Coutinho's behaviour, without any obvious reason for the abrupt changes. Stunned, Gregorius followed him through the house that was more like a library. The old man was uncommonly well-read and possessed a huge number of first editions.

He was well-versed in Portuguese names, too. The Prados, Gregorius learned, were a very old family that went back to João Nunes do Prado, a grandson of Afonso III, king of Portugal. Eça? Went back to Pedro I and Inês de Castro and was one of the most distinguished names in all of Portugal.

'My name is indeed even older and also linked with the royal house,' said Coutinho, and his pride was evident despite the irony.

The old man envied Gregorius his knowledge of ancient languages and on the way to the door, he suddenly pulled a Greek–Portuguese edition of the New Testament off the shelf.

'No idea why I give this to you,' he said, 'but that's how it is.'

As Gregorius went through the courtyard, he knew he would never forget that sentence. Or the old man's hand on his back softly pushing him out.

The tram rattled through the early dusk. He would never

find the blue house at night, thought Gregorius. The day had lasted an eternity, and now, exhausted, he leaned his head against the misted panes of the tram. Was it possible that he had been in this city only two days? And that only four days, not even a hundred hours, had passed since he had left his Latin books on the desk? At Rossio, the most famous square in Lisbon, he got out and trudged to the hotel with the heavy bag from Simões's second-hand bookshop, made even heavier by Coutinho's gift.

10

Why had Kägi talked to him in a language that sounded like Portuguese, but wasn't? And why had he complained about Marcus Aurelius without saying a single word about him?

Gregorius sat on the edge of the bed and rubbed the sleep from his eyes. In his dream the janitor had been there, in the corridor of the Gymnasium, hosing down the place where he had stood with the Portuguese woman when she dried her hair. Before or after, you couldn't tell, Gregorius had gone with her into Kägi's office to introduce her to him. He must not have opened a door to it; suddenly they had simply been standing before his gigantic desk, a little like petitioners who had forgotten their petition; but then the Rector suddenly wasn't there any more, the desk and even the wall behind it had disappeared, and they had had a clear view of the Alps.

Now Gregorius noted that the door to the minibar was ajar. At some time during the night, he had woken up from hunger and had eaten the peanuts and the chocolate. Before that, the overflowing postbox of his Bern flat had tormented him, all the bills and junk mail, and all of a sudden, his library was in flames before it became Coutinho's library, where there were nothing but charred Bibles, an endless row of them.

At breakfast, Gregorius took second helpings of everything and then sat there to the annoyance of the waiter, who was preparing the dining room for lunch. He had no idea how to proceed. Just now he had listened to a German couple making their tourist plans for the day. Lisbon didn't interest him for sightseeing, as a tourist setting. Lisbon was the city where he had run away from his life. The only thing he could imagine doing was taking the ferry across the Tagus to see the city from a different perspective. But he really didn't want to do that either. What did he want?

In his room, he assembled the books he had collected: the two about the earthquake and the Black Death, the novel by Eça de Queirós, *The Book of Disquiet*, the New Testament, the language books. Then he packed his bag tentatively and put it by the door.

No, that wasn't it either. Not only because of the glasses he had to pick up the next day. To land in Zurich now and get off the train in Bern just wasn't possible; it wasn't possible any more.

What else? Was this what came from thoughts of time running out and death: that all of a sudden you no longer knew what you wanted? That you didn't know your own mind? That you lost the obvious familiarity with your own wishes? And in this way became strange and a problem to yourself?

Why didn't he set off in search of the blue house where Adriana de Prado might still be living, thirty-one years after her brother's death? Why was he hesitating? Why was there suddenly a barrier?

Gregorius did what he had always done when he was unsure: he opened a book. His mother, a country girl from the flatlands around Bern, had seldom picked up a book, at most a sentimental novel by Ludwig Ganghofer and then it took her weeks to read. His father had discovered reading as an antidote to boredom in the empty halls of the museum, and after he had acquired the taste, he read everything that came to hand. *Now you're escaping into books, too,* said his mother when her son also discovered reading. It had hurt Gregorius that she saw it like that and that she didn't understand when he spoke of the magic and luminosity of good writing.

There were the people who read and there were the others. Whether you were a reader or a non-reader – it was soon apparent. There was no greater distinction between people. People were amazed when he asserted this and many shook their heads at such crankiness. But that's how it was. Gregorius knew it. He *knew* it.

He sent the chambermaid away and in the next few hours he sank into an attempt to understand a note by Amadeu de Prado, whose title had leapt to his eye as he leafed through the book.

O INTERIOR DO EXTERIOR DO INTERIOR. THE INSIDE OF THE OUTSIDE OF THE INSIDE. *Some time ago – it was a dazzling morning in June, the morning brightness flooded unmoving through the streets – I was standing in the Rua Garrett at a shop window where the blinding light made me look at my reflection instead of at the merchandise. It was annoying to stand in my own way – particularly since the whole thing was like an allegory of the way I usually stood by me – and I was about to make my way inside through the shadowy funnels of my hands, when behind my reflection – it reminded me of a threatening storm shadow that changed the world – the figure of a tall man emerged. He stood still, took a packet of cigarettes out of his shirt pocket, and stuck one between his lips. As he inhaled the first drag, his look strayed and finally fixed on me. We humans: what do we know of one another? I thought, and acted – to keep from meeting his reflected look – as if I could easily see the display in the window. The stranger saw a gaunt man with greying hair, a narrow, stern face and dark eyes behind round lenses in gold frames. I cast a searching glance at my reflection. As always, I stood with my square shoulders straighter than straight, my head higher than my size really allowed, and leaning back a trace and it was undoubtedly correct what they said, even those who liked me: I looked like an arrogant misanthrope who looked down on everything human, a* misanthrope with a mocking comment ready for everything and everyone. That was the impression the smoking man must have had.

How wrong he was! For sometimes I think: I exaggerate standing and walking that way in protest against my father's irrevocably crooked body, his torment, to be bowed down by Bechterev's disease, to have to aim your eyes at the ground like a tortured slave who didn't trust himself to meet his master with a raised head and a direct look. It is perhaps as if, by stretching myself, I could straighten my proud father's back or, with a backward, magical law of effect make sure his life would be less bowed and enslaved to pain than it really was – as if through my attempt in the present, I could strip the tormented past of its reality and replace it with a better, freer one.

And that wasn't the only delusion my appearance must have produced in the stranger behind me. After an endless night which had brought neither sleep nor consolation, far be it from me to look down on another. The day before, I had informed a patient in the presence of his wife that he didn't have long to live. You have to, I had persuaded myself before I called the two of them into the consulting room, they have to plan for themselves and the five children – and anyway: part of human dignity consists of the strength to look your fate, even a hard one, in the eye. It had been early evening; through the open balcony door a light warm wind brought the sounds and smells of a dying summer day, and if this soft wave of brightness could have been enjoyed in freedom and oblivion, it could have been a moment of happiness. If only a sharp, ruthless wind had whipped the rain against the windowpane! I had thought, as the man and woman across from me sat on the very edge of their chairs, hesitant yet full of scared impatience, eager to hear the verdict that would release them from the fear of an impending death, so they could go downstairs and mix with the strolling passers-by, a sea of time before them.

I took off my glasses and pinched the bridge of my nose between *thumb and forefinger before I spoke. The two must have recognized the gesture as a harbinger of an awful truth, for when I looked up they had grasped each other's hands, which looked as if they hadn't done so for decades. That choked me so that the anxious wait seemed even longer. I spoke down to these hands, so hard was it to confront the nameless horror in their eyes. The hands clenched each other, the blood leached from them, and it was this image of a bloodless, white knot of fingers that robbed me of sleep and that I tried to drive away when I went out for the walk that had led me to the reflecting shop window. (And I had tried to drive away something else in the lighted streets: the memory of my rage at my clumsy words announcing the bitter message that had later been turned against Adriana only because she, who takes care of me better than a mother, had forgotten to buy my favourite bread. If only the white-gold light of the morning would extinguish this injustice that wasn't untypical for me!)*

The man with the cigarette, now leaning on a lamp post, let his look wander back and forth between me and what was happening in the street. What he saw of me could have revealed nothing about my self-doubting fragility that didn't accord much with my proud, even arrogant posture. I put myself into his look, reproduced it in me, and from that perspective absorbed my reflection. The way I looked and appeared – I thought – I had never been that way for a single minute in my life. Not at school, not at university, not in my practice. Is it the same with others: that they don't recognize themselves from the outside? That the reflection seems like a stage set full of crass distortion? That, with fear, they note a gap between the perception others have of them and the way they experience themselves? That the familiarity of inside and the familiarity of outside can be so far apart that they can hardly be considered familiarity with the same thing?

The distance from others, where this awareness moves us, becomes even greater when we realize that our outside form doesn't appear to others as to our own eyes. Human beings are not viewed like houses, trees and stars. They are seen with the expectation of being able to encounter *them in a specific way and thus making them a part of our own Imagination trims them to suit our own wishes and hopes, but also to confirm our own fears and prejudices. We don't even get safely and impartially to the outside contours of another person. On the way, the eye is diverted and blurred by all the wishes and fantasies that make us the special, unmistakable human beings we are. Even the outside world of an inside world is still a piece of our inside world, not to mention the thoughts we have about the inside world of strangers and that are so uncertain and unstable that they say more about ourselves than about others. How does the man with the cigarette view an exaggeratedly upright man with a gaunt face, full lips and gold-framed glasses on the sharp, straight nose that seems to me to be too long and too dominant? How does this figure fit into the framework of the pleasure and displeasure and into the remaining architecture of his soul? What does his look exaggerate and stress in my appearance, and what does it leave out as if it didn't even exist? It will inevitably be a caricature that the smoking stranger forms of my reflection, and his notion of my notional world will pile up caricature on caricature. And so we are doubly strangers, for between us there is not only the deceptive outside world, but also the delusion that exists of it in every inside world.*

Is it an evil, this strangeness and distance? Would a painter have to portray us with outstretched arms, desperate in the vain attempt to reach the other? Or should a picture show us in a pose expressing relief that there is this double barrier that is also a protective wall? Should we be grateful for the protection that guards us from the strangeness of one another? And for the freedom it makes possible? How would it be if we confronted each other unprotected by the double refraction represented by the interpreted body? If, because nothing stood between us, we tumbled into each other?

As he read Prado's self-description, Gregorius kept looking at the portrait at the front of the book. In his mind, he turned the doctor's helmet of combed hair grey and put gold-framed glasses with round lenses on him. Haughtiness, even misanthropy, others had seen in him. Yet, as Coutinho said, he had been a beloved, even esteemed doctor. Until he had saved the life of a member of the secret police. After that, he was despised by the same people who had loved him. It had broken his heart and he had tried to make up for it by working for the Resistance.

How could a doctor need to atone for something every doctor did – had to do – the opposite of a transgression? Something, thought Gregorius, couldn't be right in Coutinho's account. Things must have been more complicated, more involved. Gregorius leafed through the book. *Nós homens, que sabemos uns dos outros? We humans: what do we know of one another?* For a while, Gregorius kept leafing through it. Maybe there was a note about this dramatic and regrettable turn in Prado's life?

When he found nothing, he left the hotel at twilight and made his way to Rua Garrett, where Prado had seen his reflection in the display window and where Júlio Simões's second-hand bookshop was.

There was no sunlight today to make the display window into a mirror. But after a while, Gregorius found a brightly lit clothing store with an enormous mirror where he could look at himself through the windowpane. He tried to do what Prado had done: to put himself into a stranger's look, to reproduce it in himself and absorb his reflection from this look. To encounter himself as a stranger might see him.

That was how his students and colleagues had seen him. That was what their Mundus looked like. Florence had also seen him like that, first as an infatuated student in the front row, later as a wife, to whom he had become an increasingly ponderous and boring husband, who used his learning more often to destroy the magic, the high spirits and the chic of her world of literary celebrities.

They all had the same image before them and yet, as Prado said, each had seen something different in the others because every piece of a human being's outside world seen was also a piece of an inside world. The Portuguese man had been sure that in not one single minute of his life had he been as he appeared to others; he hadn't recognized himself in his outside – familiar as it was – and was deeply frightened at this strangeness.

Now a boy hurrying past bumped into Gregorius, who recoiled. Fear at being shoved coincided with the upsetting thought that he had no certainty equal to the doctor's. Where had Prado acquired his certainty that he was completely different from the way others saw him? He talked about it as of a bright light inside that had always illuminated him, a light that had meant both great familiarity with himself and great strangeness in the view of others. Gregorius shut his eyes and imagined himself back in the dining car on the trip to Paris. The new kind of wakefulness he had experienced there, when he realized that his trip was actually taking place – was it somehow connected with the amazing awareness the Portuguese man had possessed about himself, an awareness whose price had been loneliness? Or were these two completely different things?

People said to Gregorius that he went through the world in a posture, as if he were always bent over a book and constantly reading it. Now he stood up straight and tried to imagine how it was to straighten the pain-crooked back of your own father by standing with an exaggeratedly straight back and an especially high head. In the sixth form, he had had a teacher who suffered from Bechterev's disease. Such people shoved their heads into their necks to keep from having to look at the ground all the time. They looked the way Prado had described the janitor he met on his visit to the school: like a bird. Horrible jokes about the crooked figure made the rounds and the teacher took revenge with a malicious, punishing strictness. What must it have been like to have a father who had to spend his life in this humiliating posture, hour after hour, day after day, at the judge's bench and at the dinner table with his children?

Alexandre Horácio de Almeida Prado had been a judge, a famous judge, as Coutinho had said. A judge who had administered the law under Salazar – a man who had broken every law. A judge who perhaps couldn't forgive himself and therefore sought death. *When dictatorship is a fact, revolution is a duty*, was inscribed on the pedestal of the Prados' tomb. Was it there because of the son who had joined the Resistance? Or because of the father who had recognized the truth of the sentence too late?

On the way down to the big square, Gregorius realized that knowing these things was now more urgent than the ancient texts that had once dominated his life. Why? The judge had been dead for half a century, the revolution was thirty years ago, and the son's death was also part of that distant past. So why? What did all that have to do with him? How could it have happened that a single Portuguese word and a phone number written on his forehead had torn him out of his orderly life and involved him, far from Bern, in the life of Portuguese people who were no longer alive?

In the bookshop on Rossio, a photo biography of António de Oliveira Salazar, the man who had played a crucial, perhaps fatal role in Prado's life, leapt to his eyes. The dust jacket showed a man, dressed all in black, with an overbearing but not insensitive face and with a hard, even fanatical look that did however reveal intelligence. Gregorius leafed through it. Salazar, he thought, was a man who had sought power but not one who had seized it with blind brutality and dull violence, nor one who had enjoyed it like an excess of rich food at an orgiastic banquet. To gain power and hold it for so long, he had sacrificed everything in his life that had stood in the way of the absolute discipline that governed it. The price had been high, you could tell that from the stern features and the effort of the rare smile. And the repressed needs and impulses of this barren life amid the sumptuousness of government – distorted beyond recognition by the rhetoric of state – had found an outlet in merciless execution orders.

Gregorius lay awake in the dark and thought of the great distance there had always been between him and world affairs. Not that he hadn't been interested in political events abroad. In April 1974, when the dictatorship of Portugal came to an end, some of his generation had gone there and he had offended them by saying that he didn't care for political tourism. Nor was he uninformed, but it always felt as if he were reading Thucydides when he read the newspaper or watched the news. Or was there a connection with the impeccable character of Switzerland? Or was it because of his fascination with words, communicating horrid, bloody and unjust things? And maybe with his nearsightedness?

When his father, who hadn't gone further than non-commissioned officer, spoke of the time when his company had been stationed on the Rhine, Gregorius always had the feeling of something unreal, whose significance was mainly that it could be remembered as exciting and possibly something that stood out from the banality of the rest of his life. Once, his father had blurted out: *We were scared, scared to death, for it could easily have been different and then maybe you wouldn't even exist.* He hadn't shouted, his father never did that; nevertheless, they had been furious words that Gregorius heard with shame and had never forgotten.

Was that why he now wanted to know what it had been

like to be Amadeu de Prado? To move closer to his world through this understanding?

He turned on the light and reread the following sentences:

NADA. NOTHING. *Aneurysm. Every moment can be the last. Without the slightest premonition, in total ignorance, I will walk through an invisible wall, behind which is nothing, not even darkness. My next step can be the step through this wall. Isn't it illogical to be afraid of it, knowing that I shall no longer experience this sudden extinction?*

Gregorius called Doxiades and asked him what an aneurysm was. 'I know the word means a dilation. But of what?' It was the expansion of an arterial blood vessel through innate or acquired changes in the wall, said the Greek. Yes, in the brain, too, quite often. People didn't usually notice anything and it could be fine for a long time – decades. Then the vessel would suddenly burst and that was the end. Why did he want to know that in the middle of the night? Was anything wrong? And where was he anyway?

Gregorius felt he had made a mistake in calling the Greek. The words that would have suited their long intimacy eluded him. Stiff and hesitant, he said something about the old tram, about an odd second-hand bookseller, and the cemetery where the dead Portuguese man lay. It made no sense and he knew it. There was a pause.

'Gregorius?' Doxiades asked at last.

'Yes?'

'How do you say chess in Portuguese?'

Gregorius could have hugged him for the question.

'*Xadrez,*' he said and the dryness in his mouth had disappeared.

'Everything all right with the eyes?'

Now the tongue stuck to the palate again. 'Yes.' And after another pause, Gregorius asked:

'Do you have the impression that people see you as you are?'

The Greek burst out laughing. 'Of course *not*!'

Gregorius was flabbergasted that somebody, Doxiades of all people, could laugh about that when Amadeu de Prado was deeply horrified. He picked up Prado's book, as if to hold on to himself.

'Is everything really all right?' the Greek asked into the new silence.

Yes, said Gregorius, everything's fine.

They ended the conversation in the usual way.

Gregorius lay in the dark, distraught, and tried to figure out what had come between him and Doxiades. He was, after all, the man whose words had given him the courage to make this trip, despite the snow that had started falling in Bern. He had put himself through university by working as a taxi driver in Thessaloniki. *A pretty rough bunch, the taxi drivers*, he had once said. Now and then, a coarse word would escape him. As when he cursed or dragged fiercely on a cigarette. The dark stubble and the thick black hair on his arms looked wild and uncontrollable at such moments.

So he considered it natural that others failed to see him as he was. Was it possible that this didn't matter at all to some people? And was that a lack of sensibility? Or a desirable internal independence? It was growing light when Gregorius finally fell asleep.

11

It can't be, it's impossible. Gregorius took off the new, feather-light glasses, rubbed his eyes and put them back on. It *was* possible: he could see better than ever. That was especially true for the top half of the glasses, through which he looked out at the world. Things literally seemed to jump at him, as if they were crowding up to attract his look. And since he no longer felt the previous weight on his nose, which had made the old glasses a protective bulwark, they seemed importunate, even threatening, in their new clarity. The new impressions also made him a little dizzy, and he took the glasses off. A smile flitted over César Santarém's gruff face.

'And now you don't know if the old or the new ones are better?' he said.

Gregorius nodded and stood before the mirror. The narrow, reddish frames and the new lenses that no longer looked like martial barriers before his eyes made him into somebody else. Somebody whose appearance was important. Somebody who wanted to look elegant, chic. OK, that was an exaggeration; but still, Santarém's assistant, who had talked him into buying the frames, gestured her appreciation in the background. Santarém saw it. '*Tem razão,*' he said, She's right. Gregorius felt rage rising in him. He put on the old glasses, had the new ones packed up, and quickly paid.

Mariana Eça's office in the Alfama quarter was half an hour's walk from the optician's. It took Gregorius four hours. It began with him sitting down whenever he found a bench, sitting down and changing his glasses. With the new glasses the world was bigger and for the first time, space really had three dimensions where things could extend unhindered. The Tagus was no longer a vague brownish surface, but a river, and the Castelo de São Jorge projected into the sky in three directions, like a real citadel. But the world was a strain like that. Indeed it was also lighter with the light frames on the nose; the heavy steps he was used to taking no longer suited the new lightness in his face. But the world was closer and more oppressive; it demanded more of you, but its demands weren't clear. When they became too much for him, these obscure demands, he retreated behind the old lenses that kept everything at a distance and allowed him to doubt whether there really was an outside world beyond words and texts, a doubt that was dear to him and without which he really couldn't imagine life at all. But he could no longer forget the new view either and in a little park, he took out Prado's notes and tried out the new glasses.

O verdadeiro encenador da nossa vida é o acaso – um encenador cheio de crueldade, misericórdia e encanto cativante. Gregorius couldn't believe his eyes: he hadn't understood any of Prado's sentences so easily: *The real director of our life is accident – a director full of cruelty, compassion and bewitching charm.* He shut his eyes and gave in to the sweet illusion that the new glasses would make all the Portuguese man's other sentences accessible to him in this way – as if they were a fabulous magical instrument that made the meaning of the words visible through their external contours. He grasped the glasses and adjusted them. He was beginning to like them.

I'd like to know if I've done it right – the words of the woman with the big eyes and the black velvet jacket; words that had surprised him because they had sounded like those of an ambitious schoolgirl with little self-confidence and didn't suit the certainty she radiated. Gregorius watched a girl on rollerblades. If the rollerblader had held his elbow at a different angle that first evening – missing his temple – he wouldn't now be on the way to see this woman – or torn between an imperceptibly veiled and a dazzlingly clear field of vision that lent the world this unreal reality.

In a bar, he drank a coffee. It was lunchtime; the bar was full of well-dressed men from an office building next door. Gregorius looked at his new face in the mirror, then the whole figure, as the doctor would see it later. The baggy corduroy trousers, the rough turtleneck and the old anorak contrasted with the many tailored jackets, the matching shirts and ties around him. Nor did they suit the new glasses, not at all. It angered Gregorius that the contrast bothered him; from one sip of coffee to another, he became increasingly annoyed about it. He thought of the way the waiter in the Hotel Bellevue had scrutinized him on the morning of his flight, and how it hadn't mattered to him; on the contrary, with his shabby look, he had felt he was standing up to the hollow elegance of the surroundings. Where had this certainty gone? He put on the old glasses, paid, and left.

Had the grand houses next to and across from Mariana Eça's office really been there on his first visit? Gregorius put on the new glasses and looked around. Doctors, lawyers, a wine company, an African embassy. He was sweating under the thick jumper, and at the same time he felt on his face the cold wind that had swept the sky clear. Behind which window was the consulting room?

How well one sees depends on so many things, she had said. It was a quarter to two. Could he just go up there without an appointment? He walked on a few streets and stopped outside a men's clothing shop. *You really might buy something new for a change.* To the student Florence, the girl in the front row, his indifference to his outward appearance had been attractive. This attitude had soon got on her nerves as his wife. *After all, you don't live alone. And Greek isn't enough for that.* In the nineteen years he had lived alone again, he had been in a clothes shop only two or three times. He was glad that nobody had scolded him for it. Were nineteen years' defiance enough? Hesitantly, he entered the shop.

The two saleswomen took all conceivable pains with him, the only customer, and finally they summoned the manager. Gregorius kept looking at himself in the mirror: first in suits that made him into a banker, an opera-goer, a bon vivant, a professor, an accountant; then in jackets, from the double-breasted blazer to the sports jacket suitable for a ride in the castle grounds; finally in leather. He didn't understand a single one of the enthusiastic Portuguese sentences bombarding him and kept shaking his head. Finally, he left the shop in a grey corduroy suit. He looked at himself uncertainly in a display window a few buildings away. Did the fine scarlet polo neck he had also let himself be pressured into, match the red of the new spectacle frames?

Quite suddenly, Gregorius lost his nerve. With fast, furious steps, he walked to the public toilet on the other side of the street and put his old things back on. When he passed an alleyway with a mountain of junk at the entrance, he put down the bag with the new clothes. Then he walked slowly in the direction of the doctor's apartment.

As soon as he entered the building, he heard the door open upstairs and then he saw her coming down in a flowing coat. Now he wished he had kept the new clothes.

'Oh, it's you,' she said and asked how the new glasses were.

As he was telling her, she came close to him, grasped the new glasses and tested whether they were sitting right. He smelled her perfume, a strand of her hair stroked his face, and for a fleeting moment, her movement merged with that of Florence the first time she had taken off his glasses. When he spoke of the unreal reality things had assumed all of a sudden, she smiled and then looked at her watch.

'I have to catch the ferry to pay a visit.' Something in his face must have made her wonder, for she paused as she was leaving. 'Have you ever been on the Tagus? Would you like to come along?'

Later, Gregorius no longer remembered the drive down to the ferry. Only that, with a single liquid motion, she had pulled into a parking place that seemed much too small. Then they were sitting on the upper deck of the ferry and Mariana Eça was telling him about the uncle she wanted to visit, her father's brother.

João Eça lived in a nursing home up in Cacilhas, barely spoke a word and replayed famous chess games all day long. He had been an accountant in a big firm, a modest, unprepossessing, inconspicuous man. It had never occurred to anybody that he was working for the Resistance. The disguise was perfect. He was forty-seven when Salazar's thugs caught up with him. As a communist, he was sentenced to life in prison for high treason. Two years later, Mariana, his favourite niece, went to collect him from the prison.

'That was in the summer of 1974, a few weeks after the revolution. I was twenty-one and was studying in Coimbra,' she said now, her face averted.

Gregorius heard her swallow, and now her voice became raw, in an effort not to break.

'I never got over how much he had changed. He was only forty-nine, but torture had made him into a sick old man. He had had a full, deep voice; now he spoke in a hoarse soft voice, and his hands that had played Schubert, mainly Schubert, were disfigured and constantly shaking.' She took a breath and sat up very straight. 'Only the incredibly direct, fearless look in his grey eyes – it was still there. It took years before he could tell me about his time in prison: they had held a white-hot iron before his eyes to make him talk. They kept coming closer, and he had expected to sink into a wave of darkness at any minute. But his eyes didn't flinch from the iron and when they had finished with him he could still see his torturers' faces.

This unbelievable courage gave them pause. "Since then, nothing can scare me any more," he said, "literally nothing." And I am sure he didn't reveal anything.'

The ferry had docked.

'Over there,' she said, and now her voice recovered its usual firmness; 'that's the home.'

She pointed to a ferry that described a big arc, so the city could be seen from another perspective. Then she stood still for a moment, her hesitation revealing the awareness of an intimacy between them, which had happened surprisingly fast and couldn't be allowed to continue, and perhaps also her doubts as to whether it had been right to expose so much of João and herself. When she finally went off towards the care home, Gregorius looked after her for a long time and imagined her standing at the prison gates at the age of twenty-one.

He went back to Lisbon and then made the whole trip over the Tagus again. João Eça had been in the Resistance, Amadeu de Prado had worked for the Resistance. *Resistência*: the doctor had naturally used the Portuguese word – as if, for this matter, this sacred matter, there could be no other. In her mouth, the word, softly urgent, had an intoxicating sonority, it was a word with a mythical gleam and a mystical aura. An accountant and a doctor, five years apart. Both had risked everything, both had worked under perfect cover, both had been masters of silence. Had they known each other?

When he was back on land, Gregorius bought a city map with an enlarged inset of Bairro Alto. Sitting in a café he worked out the route he would follow in search of the blue house where Adriana de Prado, old and without a telephone, might still be living. By the time he left the café, darkness was falling. He caught a tram to the Alfama quarter. After a while, he found the alleyway with the pile of rubbish. The bag with his new clothes in was still there. He picked it up, hailed a cab and was driven to the hotel.

12

Early the next morning, Gregorius awoke to a day that was grey and foggy. Quite contrary to habit, last night he had fallen asleep quickly and plunged into a flood of dream images of ships, clothes, and prisons. Even though it was incomprehensible, the whole thing had not been unpleasant and was far from a nightmare. The confused, rhapsodic changing scenes were set off by an inaudible voice that possessed an overwhelming presence and belonged to a woman whose name he had sought with feverish haste, as if his life depended on it. Just as he woke up, the word for which he had been searching came to him: Conceição – the beautiful, fairy-tale part of the doctor's full name on the brass plate at the entrance to her office: Mariana Conceição Eça. When he spoke the name softly to himself, another dream scene surfaced, in which a woman of quickly changing identity took off his glasses before pressing them firmly on his nose, so firmly that he still felt the pressure.

It had been one in the morning and getting back to sleep was inconceivable. So he had leafed through Prado's book and been drawn to a note with the title CARAS FUGAZES NA NOITE. FLEETING FACES IN THE NIGHT.

Encounters between people, it often seems to me, are like trains passing at breakneck speed in the night. We cast fleeting looks at the passengers sitting behind dull glass in dim light, who disappear from our field of vision almost before we perceive them. Was it really a man and a woman who flashed past like phantoms, who came out of nothing into the empty dark, without meaning or purpose? Did they know each other? Did they talk? Laugh? Cry? People will say: That's how it is when strangers pass one another in rain and wind and there might be something in the comparison. But we sit opposite people for longer, we eat and work together, lie next to each other, live under the same roof. Where is the haste? Yet everything that gives the illusion of permanence, familiarity, and intimate knowledge: isn't it a deception invented to reassure, with which we try to conceal and ward off the flickering, disturbing haste because it would be impossible to live with it all the time? Isn't every exchange of looks between people like the ghostly brief meeting of eyes between travellers passing one another, intoxicated by the inhuman speed and the shock of air pressure that makes everything shudder and clatter? Don't our looks bounce off others, as in the hasty encounter of the night, and leave us with nothing but conjectures, slivers of thoughts and imagined qualities? Isn't it true that it's not people who meet, but rather the shadows cast by their imaginations?

How would it have been, Gregorius thought, to be the sister of somebody whose loneliness spoke from such depths? Of somebody who, in his reflections, had revealed such a merciless consistency but whose words did not sound despairing or even agitated? How would it have been to assist him in his work, give injections and help bandage his patient. What his writings about distance and strangeness between people had meant for the atmosphere in the blue house? Had he kept his thoughts to himself or had the house been the place, the only place, where he had given them free rein? Were they apparent in the way he went from room to room, picked up a book and decided what music he wanted to listen to? What sounds best expressed lonely thoughts? Were they sounds that heightened his loneliness or were they melodies and rhythms that were like balm to the ear?

With these questions in his mind, Gregorius had slipped back into a light sleep towards morning. He had found himself standing before a narrow blue door, torn between the wish to ring the bell and the certainty that he had no idea what he would say to the woman who opened the door. On waking, he went down to breakfast in the new clothes and wearing the new glasses. The waitress gave a start when she noticed his changed appearance, and then a smile flashed over her face. And now, on this grey, foggy Sunday morning, he was on his way to find the blue house old Coutinho had talked about.

He had explored only a few streets in the upper part of the city when he saw the man he had followed home on his first evening in Lisbon, smoking at a window. In daylight the house looked even narrower and shabbier than it had then. The interior of the room was in shadow, but Gregorius caught a glimpse of the tapestry of the sofa, the glass cabinet with the colourful porcelain figures and the crucifix. He stopped and tried to catch the man's eye.

'*Uma casa azul?*' he asked.

The man held his hand to his ear and Gregorius repeated the question. It provoked a surge of words he didn't understand accompanied by gestures with the cigarette. As the man spoke, a very old, bent woman came to his side.

'*O consultório azul?*' Gregorius asked now.

'*Sim!*' shouted the old woman in a creaky voice and then once again: '*Sim!*'

She gesticulated excitedly with her stick-thin arms and shrivelled hands and after a while, Gregorius realized that she was waving him inside. Hesitantly, he entered the house that smelt of mould and rancid oil. He felt as if he had to push through a thick wall of nauseating smells to reach the door where the man was waiting, a fresh cigarette between his lips.

Limping, he led Gregorius into the living room, mumbled some question and gestured a vague invitation to sit on the tapestry-covered sofa.

In the next half-hour, Gregorius struggled to find some meaning in the mostly incomprehensible words and ambiguous gestures of the two old people who were trying to explain what it had been like forty years ago, when Amadeu de Prado had been the local doctor. There was respect in their voices, a respect you feel for someone far above you. But another feeling also filled the room, which Gregorius recognized only gradually as shyness originating in a long-ago accusation that it was difficult to expunge from the memory. *After that, people avoided him. That broke his heart,* he heard Coutinho say, after telling him how Prado had saved the life of Rui Luís Mendes, the Butcher of Lisbon.

Now the man pulled up a trouser leg and showed Gregorius a scar. '*Ele fez isto.*' He did it, he said, and ran his nicotine-stained fingertips over it. The woman rubbed her temples with her shrivelled fingers and then made the gesture of flying away: Prado had made her headaches disappear. And then she too showed him a small scar on a finger where a wart had probably been removed.

Later, when Gregorius asked himself what had been the decisive factor that had finally made him ring the bell at the blue door, he always recalled these two old people whose bodies bore traces of the doctor who was respected, then ostracized and finally won their respect again. It had been as if his hands had come back to life.

When they had given him directions to Prado's former office, Gregorius got up to leave. Head to head, they watched him from the window and it seemed to him that there was envy in their look, a paradoxical envy that he could do something they no longer could: meet Amadeu de Prado by making his way into the doctor's past.

Was it possible that the best way to be sure of yourself was to know and understand someone else? Even someone whose life had been completely different and based on a different logic from your own? How did curiosity about another life coexist with the awareness that your own time was running out?

Gregorious stood at the counter of a small bar and drank a coffee. It was the second time he had had stood here. An hour ago, he had climbed up to Rua Luz Soriano and stood a few steps away away from Prado's old office, a three-storey house that he had recognized not only because of the blue ceramic tiles, but because all the windows were covered with high arches painted dark blue. The paint was old and crumbling and there were damp patches where black moss grew rampant. The blue paint was also peeling off the cast-iron bars on the bottom of the windows. Only the blue front door had an impeccable coat of paint as if someone wanted to say: This is what matters.

His heart pounding, Gregorius had looked at the door with the brass knocker. *As if my whole future were behind this door*, he had thought. Then he had gone to a bar a few doors away and struggled with the threatening feeling that he was losing his grip. He had looked at his watch: it had been six days ago since he had taken the damp coat off the hook in the classroom and run away from the security of his life without a single backward glance. He had reached into the pocket of this coat and groped for the key to his flat in Bern. And suddenly, as withan attack of ravenous hunger, he was assailed by the desire to read a Greek or Hebrew text; to see the beautiful Oriental letters that hadn't lost any of their fabulous elegance for him even after forty years; to make sure that, during the past six confusing days, he hadn't lost any of his ability to understand everything they expressed.

In the hotel was the New Testament, in Greek and

Portuguese, that Coutinho had given him; but the hotel was some distance away; it was the urge to read it here and now, not far from the blue house, that threatened to consume him, even before the door had opened. He had quickly paid for his coffee and set off in search of a bookshop where he could find such texts. But it was Sunday and the only one he found was closed; it was a religious bookshop with Greek and Hebrew titles in the window. He had leaned his forehead on the fog-damp windowpane and again felt overcome by the temptation to go to the airport and take the next plane to Zurich. It was a relief to see that he could experience the impulse as a surging and ebbing fever and patiently wait for it to pass. Finally he had slowly retraced his steps to the bar near the blue house.

Now he took Prado's book out of the pocket of his new jacket and looked at the bold, intrepid face of the Portuguese man. A doctor who had practised his profession with rock-hard consistency. A resistance fighter who put himself in mortal danger to expiate a guilt that didn't exist. A goldsmith of words whose deepest passion had been to put into words the silent experiences of human life.

Suddenly Gregorius was struck by the fear that someone quite different might now live in the blue house. The doorbell had no nameplate. He quickly left some coins for his coffee on the counter and rushed to the house. Before the blue door, he took two deep breaths and very slowly let the air escape from his lungs. Then he rang the bell.

A rattling chime that sounded as if it came from a medieval fortress reverberated excessively loudly through the house. Nothing happened. No light, no steps. Once again, Gregorius forced himself to be calm, then he rang again. Nothing. He turned round and leaned against the door, exhausted. He thought of his flat in Bern. He was glad that his time there was over. Slowly, he shoved Prado's book into his coat pocket, touching the cool metal of the house key as he did so. Then he broke away from the door and was about to leave.

At that moment, he heard steps inside. Someone was coming down the stairs. Through a window, a lamp could be seen. The steps approached the door.

'*Quem é?*' called a sharp female voice.

Gregorius didn't know what he should say. He waited in silence. Seconds passed. Then a key was turned in the lock and the door opened.

PART II
THE ENCOUNTER

13

In her strict, nun-like beauty the tall woman in black who stood before him could have come from a Greek tragedy. The pale gaunt face was framed by a crocheted kerchief she held together under her chin with a hand, a slim, bony hand with protruding dark veins that revealed her old age more clearly than the features of her face. From deep-set eyes shining like black diamonds, she examined Gregorius with a bitter look that spoke of deprivation, self-control and self-denial. These eyes could flame, thought Gregorius, if someone opposed the unbending will of this woman, who held herself straight as a candle and bore her head a little higher than her size really allowed. An icy glow came from her and Gregorius had no idea how he was to face up to her. He couldn't even remember how to say 'Good morning' in Portuguese any more.

'*Bonjour*,' he said hoarsely as the woman silently observed him, and then he pulled Prado's book out of his coat pocket, opened it at the portrait and showed it to her.

'I know that this man, a doctor, lived and worked here,' he went on in French. 'I . . . I wanted to see where he lived and to talk with somebody who knew him. They're such impressive sentences that he wrote. Wise sentences. Wonderful sentences. I'd like to know what the man was like who could write such sentences. What it was like to live with him.'

The change in the woman's stern white face, glowing faintly against the black of the kerchief, was hardly discernible. Only someone with the special wakefulness Gregorius possessed at that moment could have seen that the taut features relaxed a little – a tiny bit – and the look lost a trace of its chilly sharpness. But she remained silent and time began to stretch.

'*Pardonnez-moi, je ne voulais pas . . .*' Gregorius now began. He took two steps away from the door and fumbled in his coat pocket, which suddenly seemed too small to accommodate the book. He turned to go.

'*Attendez!*' said the woman. The voice now sounded less irritated and a shade warmer than just now, behind the door. And in French, the same accent resonated as in the voice of the nameless Portuguese woman on the Kirchenfeldbrücke. It sounded like an order you didn't dare refuse, and Gregorius thought of Coutinho's comment about the overbearing way that Adriana had treated the patients. He turned back to her, the bulky book still in his hand.

'*Entrez,*' said the woman, moving back from the door and pointing upstairs. She locked the door with a big key that seemed to come from another century, and then followed him upstairs. When she released the hand with the white knuckles from the banister and went past him into the parlour, he heard her gasping and he was aware of an astringent fragrance that could have come from either a medicine or a perfume.

Never had Gregorius seen such a room, not even in the movies. It seemed to stretch over the entire house. The immaculately shining parquet floor consisted of rosettes in a variety of different kinds and tints of wood and extended as far as the eye could see. One's gaze was then drawn to the trees beyond, that now, at the end of February, presented a tangle of black boughs rising into the blue grey sky. In one corner was a round table with a French-style sofa and three chairs, the seats of olive green velvet, the curved backs and legs of reddish wood – in another corner a shiny black grandfather clock, whose gold pendulum was still, the hands stopped at six twenty-three. And in the corner by the window was a grand piano, covered with a heavy throw of black brocade, laced with shining gold and silver threads.

Yet, what impressed Gregorius more than anything else were the endless shelves of books built into the ochre-coloured walls. Small Art Nouveau lamps ran along the wall above them, and the coffered ceiling combined the ochre tone of the walls, mixed with dark red geometric patterns. *Like a monastery library*, thought Gregorius, *like the library of someone who had received a classical education and came from an affluent home.* He didn't dare walk along the walls of books but his eye quickly found the Greek classics in the dark blue, gold-inscribed Oxford volumes; further back he caught sight of Cicero, Horace, the writings of the Church Fathers, the *Obras Completas* of San Ignacio. He hadn't been in this house even ten minutes and was already wishing he would never have to leave it again. It simply *must* be Amadeu de Prado's library. *Was* it?

The woman's voice brought him back to the present. 'Amadeu loved the room, the books. "I have so little time, Adriana," he often said, "much too little time to read. Maybe I should have become a priest." But he wanted the practice to be open at all times, from morning to night. "Anyone who has pain or fear can't wait," he used to say when I saw his exhaustion and tried to restrain him. Reading and writing he did at night when he couldn't sleep. Or maybe he couldn't sleep because he had the feeling that he must read, write, and meditate, I don't know. It was a curse, his sleeplessness, and I'm sure, without this suffering and without his restlessness, his eternal, breathless search for words, his brain would have held out much longer. Maybe he'd still be alive. He would have been eighty-four years old this year, on December 20.'

Without asking him a single question and without introducing herself to him, she had spoken of her brother, his suffering, his devotion, his passion and his death. All the things

– her words and her changing expressions left no doubt – that
had been most important in her life. And she had spoken of
them so abruptly, as if she had a right to expect that Gregorius,
in a lightning-fast, unearthly metamorphosis outside all time,
had turned into a denizen of her mind and an omniscient
witness of her memories. He was someone who carried the
book with the mysterious sign of the *Cedros vermelhos*, the red
cedars, and that was enough to give him entry to the sacred
region of her thoughts. How many years had she been waiting
for someone like him to appear, someone she could talk to
about her dead brother? Nineteen seventy-three had been the
year of death on the tombstone. So, Adriana had lived in this
house by herself for thirty-one years, thirty-one years alone
with the memories and the emptiness left behind by her brother.

So far she had held the kerchief together under her chin,
as if to hide something. Now, she took her hand away; the
crocheted kerchief parted to reveal a black velvet ribbon
encircling her neck. Gregorius was never to forget this view
of the dividing cloth, exposing the broad ribbon over the white
lines of the neck; it crystallized into a firm, precisely detailed
image and later, when he knew what the ribbon hid, it became
an icon of his memory, along with Adriana's gesture of checking
whether the ribbon was still in place. This was an action that
seemed to happen to her rather than be performed by her, and
yet it was a gesture into which she sank completely and that
seemed to say more about her than anything she did deliberately
and consciously.

The kerchief had slipped far back and now Gregorius saw
her greying hair, with a few strands that still recalled the previous
black. Adriana gripped the sliding kerchief, raised it and pulled
it forward, embarrassed, paused a moment, and then ripped
it off her head defiantly. Their eyes met for a moment and
hers seemed to say: *Yes, I've grown old.* She bent her head, a
curl slid over her eyes, her torso collapsed and then, slowly

and as if lost, she ran the hands with the dark purple veins over the kerchief in her lap.

Gregorius pointed to Prado's book, which he had put on the table. 'Is that all Amadeu wrote?'

The few words worked a miracle. Adriana straightened up, threw her head back, ran both hands through her hair, and then looked at him. It was the first time a smile appeared on her features; mischievous and conspiratorial, it made her look twenty years younger.

'*Venha, Senhor.*' Come. All traces of her overbearing manner had vanished from her voice; the words didn't sound like an order, not even like a demand. It was more like an announcement that she would show him something, let him in on something hidden and mysterious, and it suited the promised intimacy and complicity that she had apparently forgotten he didn't speak Portuguese.

She led Gregorius along a corridor and up to the second floor and from there up to the attic, gasping as she took one stair after another. At one of the two doors, she halted. It could have been merely to catch her breath but later, when Gregorius sorted out the images of his memory, he was sure it had also been a moment of hesitation, of doubt as to whether she really should show the stranger this holy of holies. At last she turned the knob, as softly as if she were visiting a sickroom, and the care with which she opened the door – only a crack at first and then pushing it open slowly – gave the impression that, as she climbed the stairs, she had gone back more than thirty years in time and was entering the room expecting to meet Amadeu in it, writing and meditating, maybe even sleeping.

Gregorius was dimly conscious of the thought that he was dealing with a woman who was straying on to a narrow ridge that separated her present, visible life from another whose invisibility and chronological distance was much more real to her, and that it would take only a feeble shove, perhaps only a gust of wind, to make her plunge and vanish irrevocably into the past of life with her brother.

In fact, in the big room they now entered, time had stood still. It was furnished with ascetic sparseness. At one end, facing the wall, was a desk and a chair. At the other end, a bed with a small rug beside it, like a prayer rug. In the centre was a reading chair with a standard lamp and next to it mountains of messy piles of books on the bare floorboards. Nothing else. The room was a sanctuary, a chapel to the memory of Amadeu Inácio de Almeida Prado, doctor, resistance fighter and goldsmith of words. The cool, eloquent silence of a cathedral prevailed here, the impassive rustle of a room filled with frozen time.

Gregorius stood still in the doorway; this wasn't a room a stranger could simply walk around in. And even if Adriana now moved among the few objects, it was different from normal movement. Not that she walked on tiptoe or that her gait was at all artificial. But her slow steps had something ethereal, thought Gregorius, something dematerialized and almost timeless and spaceless about them. That also applied to the movements she made as she went to the pieces of furniture and stroked them softly, barely touching them.

She did that first with the desk chair, a match for the chairs in the parlour with its round seat and curved back. It stood at an angle from the desk, as if someone had risen hastily and pushed it back. Gregorius instinctively waited for Adriana to straighten it and only when she had affectionately stroked all its corners without changing anything did he understand: the crooked position of the chair was where Amadeu had left it thirty years and two months earlier, and not to be changed at any cost. That would have been as if someone were trying with Promethean arrogance to rescue the past from its inalterability or to overturn the laws of nature.

What was true of the chair was also true of the objects on the desk, which was slightly tilted to make it easier to read and write. On it, in a precarious position, was an enormous book open in the middle; in front of it, a pile of pages, the top one, as far as Gregorius could make out with an effort, with only a few words written on it. Adriana softly stroked the wood with the back of her hand and then touched the bluish porcelain cup on the red copper tray, along with a sugar bowl full of sweets and an overflowing ashtray. Were these things also old? Thirty-year-old coffee grounds? Cigarette butts more than a quarter of a century old? The ink in the open fountain pen must have crumbled to fine dust or dried to a black lump by now. Would the light bulb in the richly decorated table lamp with the emerald green shade still burn?

There was something else that amazed Gregorius, but it took him a while to grasp it: there was no dust on anything. He shut his eyes and now Adriana was only a spirit with visible outlines sliding through the room. Had this spirit regularly wiped off the dust, on eleven thousand days? And grown grey doing it?

When he opened his eyes again, Adriana was standing before a towering pile of books that looked as if it could topple over at any minute. She was looking down at a thick, oversized book on the cover of which was a picture of the human brain.

'*O cérebro sempre o cérebro,*' she said softly and accusingly. The brain, always the brain. '*Porquê não disseste nada?*' Why do you say nothing?

Now there was anger in her voice, resigned anger, eroded by time and the silence with which her dead brother had responded for decades. He had told her nothing of the aneurysm, thought Gregorius, nothing of his fear and the awareness that his life could come to an end at any time. Only from the notes had she learned of it. And through all the grief, she had been furious that he had denied her the intimacy of this knowledge.

Now she glanced up and looked at Gregorius as if she had forgotten him. Only slowly did her mind return to the present.

'Oh yes, come here,' she said in French and, with firmer steps than before, she went back to the desk, where she pulled open two drawers. In them were thick piles of papers, pressed between cardboard covers and tied several times with red ribbons.

'He started that shortly after Fátima's death. "It's a struggle against the internal paralysis," he said, and a few weeks later: "Why on earth didn't I start it before! You're not really awake when you don't write. And you have no idea who you are. Not to mention who you *aren't*." Nobody was allowed to read it, not even me. He removed the key and always carried it around with him. He was . . . he could be very distrusting.'

She shut the drawers. 'I'd like to be alone now,' she said abruptly, with a trace of hostility, and as they went down the stairs, she didn't say another word. When she had opened the front door, she stood there silent, angular and stiff. She wasn't a woman to whom you offered your hand.

'*Au revoir et merci*,' said Gregorius and turned hesitantly to leave.

'What's your name?'

The question came louder than necessary; it sounded a little like a hoarse bark that reminded him of Coutinho. She repeated the name: *Gregoriusch*.

'Where do you live?'

He told her the name of the hotel. Without a word of farewell, she shut the door and turned the key.

14

On the Tagus, the clouds were reflected. They chased the sun-glittering surfaces, slid over them, swallowed the light and let it pierce through the shadows. Gregorius took off his glasses and covered his face with his hands. The feverish change between dazzling brightness and threatening shadow pressing with unusual sharpness through the new glasses was a torment for unprotected eyes. Just now, at the hotel, after he had woken up from a light and uneasy afternoon nap, he had tried on the old glasses again. But now their dense heaviness felt disturbing, as if he had to push his face through the world with a tedious burden.

Uncertain and even a little strange to himself, he had sat on the edge of the bed for a long time and tried to decipher and sort out the confusing experiences of the morning. In his most recent dream, haunted by a mute Adriana with a marble pallor, the colour black had prevailed, a black with the disconcerting quality of adhering to objects – all objects – no matter what their colour or how bright they were. The velvet ribbon around Adriana's neck seemed to be choking her, for she was constantly tugging at it. Then she grasped her head with both hands and she wasn't trying to protect the skull so much as the brain. Towers of books, one after another, collapsed and for a moment of tense expectation, blended with apprehension and the guilty conscience of the voyeur, Gregorius had sat at Prado's desk. On it lay a sea of fossils and in the middle a half-written page, whose lines paled to illegibility when he strained to read it.

While he was busy remembering these dream images, it sometimes seemed to Gregorius that the visit to the blue house really hadn't taken place – as if the whole thing had been only an especially vivid dream, where the difference between waking and dreaming was faked. Then he grabbed his head too and when he had recovered the sense of the reality of his visit and pictured the figure of Adriana clearly, stripped of all dreamlike elements, he mentally rehearsed the hour he had spent with her thought for thought, movement for movement, word for word. Sometimes he felt a chill when he thought of her stern, bitter look, with its irreconcilability towards distant events. An eerie feeling had crept over him when he saw her floating through Prado's room, completely lost in the past, and close to madness. Then he wanted to put the crocheted cloth gently back around her head to grant her tormented spirit a break.

The way to Amadeu de Prado led through this hard yet fragile woman, or rather, it led through the dark corridor of her memory. Did he want to take that on? Was he up to it? He, who was called 'The Papyrus' by his spiteful colleagues because he had lived more in ancient texts than in the modern world?

It was crucial to find other people who had known Prado; not only seen him, like Coutinho, and known him as a doctor, like the limping man and the old woman of yesterday, but had really known him, as a friend, perhaps as a comrade in the Resistance. It would be hard, he thought, to learn anything from Adriana about it; she considered the dead brother her exclusive property, that much had become clear when, looking down at the medical book, she had spoken directly to him. She would deny, or use all means to keep away, anybody who attempted to question the only real picture of him – which was hers and hers alone.

Gregorius had looked up Mariana Eça's number and called her after hesitating a long time. Would she have any objection if he visited João, her uncle, in the home? He now knew that Prado had also been in the Resistance and perhaps João had known him. There was a silence and Gregorius was about to apologize for the suggestion when Mariana said pensively, 'Of course I have nothing against it; on the contrary, a new face might be good for him. I'm only wondering whether he would accept it. He can be very brusque, and yesterday he was even more taciturn than usual. In any case, you must have a reason for your visit.'

She was silent.

'I think I know something that might help. I wanted to take him a new recording of Schubert's sonatas yesterday. He wants to hear only Maria João Pires. I don't know whether it's the sound or the woman or a bizarre form of patriotism. But he will like this recording. I forgot to take it with me. You can call at my house and take it to him. My messenger, as it were. That should make your visit easier.'

He had drunk tea in Mariana's house, a red-gold steamy Assam, and told her about Adriana. He wanted her to say something about it, but she merely listened to his account in silence. But when he mentioned the used coffee cup and the full ashtray that had apparently been there for three decades, she narrowed her eyes like somebody who suddenly thinks he's picked up an important clue.

'Be careful,' she said to him as they parted. 'With Adriana, I mean. And let me know how it goes with João.'

And now, with Schubert's sonatas in his bag, he took the ferry to Cacilhas to visit a man who had gone through the hell of torture without losing his composure. Once again. Gregorius covered his face with his hands. If somebody had prophesied a week ago, when he had sat in his Bern flat correcting Latin notebooks, that seven days later, in a new suit and with new glasses, he would be sitting on a boat in Lisbon, hoping to learn something from a tortured victim of the Salazar regime about a Portuguese doctor and poet who had been dead for more than thirty years – he would have considered him crazy. Was he still Mundus, the myopic bookworm, who had taken fright because a few snowflakes had fallen in Bern?

The boat docked and Gregorius slowly climbed up to the retirement home. How would they understand each other? Did João Eça speak anything but Portuguese? It was Sunday afternoon people who were paying visits to the home, and you could recognize them by the bunches of flowers they carried. At the home, the old people sat wrapped in blankets on the narrow balconies because the sun kept disappearing behind clouds. Gregorius got João's room number at the gate. Before he knocked, he inhaled and exhaled slowly a few times; it was the second time that day that he had stood at a door with a pounding heart, not knowing what was in store for him.

His knock wasn't answered, not even the second time. He had already turned to go when he heard the door open with a slight squeak. He had expected to see a man in shabby clothing, who often didn't get properly dressed, but sat in his bathrobe at the chess board. The man who appeared in the doorway, noiseless as a ghost, was quite different. He wore a dark blue cardigan sweater over a brilliant white shirt with a red tie, trousers with an impeccable crease and shiny black shoes. He kept his hands hidden in his sweater pockets and the bald head with the few cropped hairs over the protruding ears was turned slightly to the side, like someone who doesn't want to deal with anything. João Eça was old and he may have been ill, as his niece had said, but the look in his grey squinting eyes seemed to pierce whatever they saw. A broken man he was not. It would be better, thought Gregorius instinctively, not to have him as an enemy.

'*Senhor Eça?*' said Gregorius. '*Venho da parte de Mariana, a sua sobrinha. Trago este disco. Sonatas de Schubert.*' Those were words he had looked up on the boat and had then repeated to himself several times.

Eça stood still in the doorway and looked at him. Gregorius had never had to endure such scrutiny and after a while, he looked away. Now Eça pulled the door wide open and beckoned him in. Gregorius entered a meticulously tidy, room furnished only with what was most necessary. For a fleeting moment, he thought of the luxurious rooms in which the ophthalmologist lived, and asked himself why she hadn't found her uncle a better place to live. The thought vanished with Eça's first words:

'Who are you?' he asked in English. The words came lightly, and yet they had authority, the authority of a man who had seen everything and was nobody's fool.

Holding the record, Gregorius told him something about himself in English and explained how he had met Mariana.

'Why are you here? Not because of the record, surely.'

Gregorius put the record on the table and took a breath. Then he pulled Prado's book out of his pocket and showed him the portrait.

'Your niece thought you might have known him.'

After a brief glance at the picture, Eça closed his eyes. He swayed a little, then, with eyes still shut, he went to the sofa and sat down.

'Amadeu,' he said into the silence and then again: 'Amadeu. *O sacerdote ateu.* The godless priest.'

Gregorius waited. One wrong word, one wrong gesture, and Eça wouldn't say another word. He went to the chessboard and looked at the game in progress. He had to risk it.

'Hastings 1922. Alekhine beats Bogolyubov,' he said.

Eça opened his eyes and looked at him in amazement.

'Tartakover was once asked whom he considered the greatest chess player. He said: "If chess is a battle – Lasker; if it's a science – Capablanca; if it's an art – Alekhine."'

'Yes,' said Gregorius. 'The sacrifice of both rooks reveals the imagination of an artist.'

'Sounds like envy.'

'It is. It simply wouldn't occur to me.'

On Eça's weatherbeaten, peasant features, the trace of a smile appeared.

'If it makes you feel better, not to me either.'

Their eyes met, then each looked straight ahead. Either Eça was preparing to continue the conversation, thought Gregorius, or the meeting was at an end.

'Up there in the alcove is some tea,' said Eça. 'I'd also like a cup.'

At first, Gregorius was taken aback to be asked to do what the host usually did. But then he saw Eça's hands balled into fists in his sweater pockets and he understood that he didn't want Gregorius to see his disfigured, shaking hands, the remaining proof of his torture. And so he made tea for both of them. Gregorius waited. From the next room came the laughter of visitors. Then all was quiet again.

The silent way Eça finally took his hand out of his pocket to take the cup was like his silent appearance at the door. He kept his eyes shut as if he thought the disfigured hand would thus be invisible to others too. The hand was covered with traces of cigarette burns, two fingernails were missing, and it shook as if with palsy. Now Eça glanced searchingly at Gregorius: was he up to the sight? Gregorius's horror flowed over him like an attack of weakness; he held it in check, and brought his cup calmly to his mouth.

'You can only fill mine halfway.'

Eça said it softly, in a strained voice, and Gregorius was never to forget those words. He felt a burning in his eyes that indicated tears and then he did something that was to shape the relationship between him and this flayed man for ever: he took Eça's cup and drank half of the hot tea himself.

Tongue and throat burned. It didn't matter. Calmly, he put the half-full cup back and turned the handle to Eça's thumb. Now the man looked at him at length, and this look too was etched deep in his memory. It was a look that blended incredulity and gratitude, a gratitude that was only tentative, for Eça had long ago given up expecting anything from others that called for this. Shaking, he lifted the cup to his lips, waited for a favourable moment and then drank in hasty sips. There was a rhythmic clinking when he put the cup back on the saucer.

Now he took a packet of cigarettes from his sweater pocket, put one between his lips and brought the trembling flame to the tobacco. He smoked in deep, calm drags and the shaking diminished. He held the hand with the cigarette so that the missing fingernails weren't visible. The other hand had once more disappeared in the sweater pocket. He looked out of the window as he began to speak.

'I met him the first time in the autumn of 1952, in England, on the train from London to Brighton. I was taking a language course for my firm; they sent me to learn foreign correspondence. It was the Sunday after the first week and I was going to Brighton because I missed the sea. I grew up by the sea, in the north, in Esposende. The compartment door opened and in came this man with shining hair that sat on his head like a helmet, with these unbelievable eyes, bold, soft and melancholy. He was making a long trip with Fátima, his new wife. Money never mattered to him, not then and not later. I learned that he was a doctor who was fascinated mainly by the brain. A diehard materialist, who had originally wanted to be a priest. A man who had an unusual attitude towards a lot of things, not absurd, but paradoxical.

'I was twenty-seven, he was five years older. He was vastly superior to me in everything. In any case, that's how I felt on that journey. He was the son of an aristocratic Lisbon family, I the son of farmers from the north. We spent the day together, strolled on the beach, ate together. At some point, we started talking about the dictatorship. *Devemos resistir.* We must resist, I said. I still remember the words. I remember them because they seemed crass spoken to a man who had the chiselled face of a poet and sometimes used words I had never heard of.

'He lowered his eyes, looked out of the window, nodded. I had touched on a subject he was uncomfortable with. It was the wrong subject for a man on his honeymoon. I spoke of other things but he was no longer really involved and left the conversation to Fátima and me. "You're right," he said when we parted, "of course you're right." And clearly he was talking of the Resistance.

'When I thought of him on the way back to London, it seemed to me that he, or a part of him, wanted to go back to Portugal with me instead of continuing his trip. He had asked me for my address and it had been more than a courtesy towards a travelling acquaintance. In fact, they soon broke off the trip and returned to Lisbon. But that had nothing to do with me. Adriana, his older sister, had had an abortion and almost died from it. He wanted to check on her as he didn't trust the doctor. A doctor who distrusted doctors. That's how he was. That was Amadeu.'

Gregorius pictured Adriana's bitter, unreconciled look. He was beginning to understand. And what about the younger sister? But that had to wait.

'Thirteen years passed until I saw him again,' Eça went on. 'It was in the winter of 1965, the year the secret police murdered Delgado. He had learned my new address from the company and one evening, he stood at my door, pale and unshaved. The hair that had once gleamed like black gold had become dull, and his look spoke of his pain. He told me how he had saved the life of Rui Luís Mendes, a high-ranking officer in the secret police, called the Butcher of Lisbon, and how his previous patients were now avoiding him. He felt ostracized.

'"I want to work for the Resistance," he said.

'"To make up for it?"

'He looked down, embarrassed.

'"You haven't done anything wrong," I said. "You're a doctor."

'"I want to do something," he said. "You understand: *do*. Tell me what I can do. You know your way around."

'"How do you know that?"

'"I know it," he said. "I've known it since Brighton."

'It was dangerous. For us much more than for him. Because for a resistance fighter, he didn't have – how should I put it – the right make-up, the right character. You have to have patience, be able to wait, you have to have a head like mine, a peasant's skull, not the soul of a sensitive dreamer. Otherwise you risk too much, slip up, endanger everything. Cold-bloodedness, he did have that, almost too much of it, he tended to be daring. But he lacked the persistence, the stubbornness, the ability to do nothing, even when the opportunity seems to favour action. He sensed that I thought that, he sensed the thoughts of others even before they had begun to think them. It was hard for him; it was, I think, the first time in his life that anyone had ever said to him: You can't do that, you lack the ability for that. But he knew I was right, he was anything but blind about himself, and he accepted that the tasks would be small and nondescript at first.

'I kept reminding him that, above all, he must resist the temptation to let his patients know he was working for us. He wanted it to atone for a supposed breach of loyalty towards Mendes's victims. And this plan really only had meaning for him if the people who blamed him for it learned of it. If he could manage to reverse their contemptuous judgement. This wish was paramount in him, I knew that, and it was his and our greatest enemy. He flared up whenever I talked of it, acted as if I underestimated his intelligence, I, nothing but an accountant, and five years younger than he. But he knew that, on this point, I was right. "I hate it when somebody knows as much about me as you do," he said once. And grinned.

'He had overcome his yearning, his ludicrous yearning for forgiveness for something that hadn't been wrong, and made no mistakes, or none that had any consequences.

'Mendes secretly protected him, his lifesaver. In Amadeu's office, messages were passed, envelopes with money changed hands. There was never a search, as there usually was. Amadeu was furious about that, that's how he was, the godless priest. He wanted to be taken seriously. Being spared wounded his pride, which was rather like the pride of a martyr.

'For a while, that conjured up a new danger: the danger that he might want to provoke Mendes with daredevil acts so that he would withdraw his protection. I spoke to him about it. Our friendship hung on a silk thread. This time he didn't admit that I was right. But he became more controlled, more cautious.

'Shortly after, he brilliantly carried out two delicate operations that only someone like him could have undertaken, someone who knew the railway network inside out. Amadeu did, he was crazy about trains, rails and points, knew every type of locomotive and above all he knew every railway station in Portugal, even the smallest. He knew whether it had a signal box or not, for that was one of his obsessions: that you could determine the direction of the train by twisting a lever. This simple mechanical operation fascinated him and ultimately it was his knowledge of these things, his crazy railway patriotism that saved the lives of our people. The comrades who weren't happy that I accepted him, because they thought his refined manner could be dangerous for us, changed their minds.

'Mendes must have been eternally grateful to him. In prison, I wasn't allowed any visits, not even Mariana, and certainly not comrades who were suspected of belonging to the Resistance. With one exception: Amadeu. He was permitted to come twice a month and he could choose the day and even the hour. It violated all the rules.

'And he came. He always came and stayed longer than agreed; the guards were afraid of his furious look when they mentioned the time. He brought me medicines, some to help the pain and some to help me sleep. They let him bring them in but took them away from me afterwards. I never told him that, he would have tried to tear down the walls. Tears flowed down his cheeks when he saw what they had done to me. Tears that were naturally tears of sympathy, but even more tears of impotent rage. It wouldn't have taken much for him to become violent towards the guards; his damp face was red with rage.'

Gregorius looked at Eça and imagined his grey, piercing eyes watching the white-hot iron that threatened to blind him approaching in a hissing glow. He felt the unbelievable strength of this man who could be defeated only by death.

'Amadeu brought me the Bible, the New Testament. Portuguese and Greek. That and the Greek grammar he threw in were the only books they let through in the two years.

'"You don't believe a word of it," I said to him when they came to take me back to the cell.

'He smiled. "It's a beautiful text," he said. "An amazingly beautiful language. And pay attention to the metaphors."

'I was amazed. I had never really read the Bible, knew only quotations, like everybody does. I was amazed at the strange blend of the relevant and the bizarre. Sometimes we talked about it. *A religion whose centre is a scene of execution, I find disgusting*, he once said. *Just imagine if there had been a gallows, a guillotine or a garrotte. Just imagine how our religious symbolism would look then.* I had never seen it in those terms. I was even a little frightened because the sentences had a special significance between those walls.

'That's how he was, the godless priest: he thought things

through to the end. He *always* thought them through to the end, no matter how black the consequences were. Sometimes he could be brutal, sometimes self-lacerating. Maybe that was why, except for me and Jorge, he had no friends; you had to be able to put up with certain things. He was unhappy that Mélodie had broken off contact with him, he loved his little sister. I saw her only once; she looked light and cheerful, a girl who didn't seem to touch the ground, I could imagine that she wouldn't be able to handle her brother's melancholy side; he could be like a boiling volcano before an eruption.'

João Eça shut his eyes. Exhaustion was written on his face. It had been a trip back in time and he may not have talked so much in years. Gregorius would like to have asked much more about the little sister with the wonderful name, about Jorge and Fátima, and also whether Eça had started learning Greek then. He had listened breathlessly, forgetting his burning throat. Now it burned again and his tongue was thick. In the middle of his story, Eça had offered him a cigarette. He had the feeling he couldn't refuse it, it would have been as if he had ripped the invisible thread spun between them. He couldn't drink the tea from Eça's cup and then refuse his tobacco, who knows why, and so he put the first cigarette of his life between his lips. He watched the trembling flame in Eça's hand anxiously and then puffed timorously and sparingly so as, not to cough. He cursed his irrationality and at the same time he felt with amazement that he wouldn't want to have missed the sensation of the hot smoke poisoning his burnt mouth.

A shrill signal startled Gregorius.

'Dinner,' said Eça.

Gregorius looked at his watch: five thirty. Eça saw his amazement and grinned scornfully.

'Much too early. Like in the slammer. It's not for the convenience of the inmates, it's for the sake of the staff.'

Might he visit him again? asked Gregorius. Eça looked over

at the chess table. Then he nodded mutely. It was as if an armour of wordlessness had closed in around him. When he noticed that Gregorius wanted to give him his hand, he vigorously buried both hands in the sweater pockets and looked at the floor.

On the crossing back to Lisbon Gregorius noticed little. He walked through the Rua Augusta, through the chessboard of the Baixa, to Rossio, deep in thought. The longest day of his life seemed to be coming to an end. Later, in bed in the hotel room, he remembered how he had leaned his forehead against the fog-damp window of the religious bookshop that morning and waited for the urgent desire to go to the airport to subside. Then he had met Adriana, drunk Mariana Eça's red-gold tea, and with her uncle had smoked his first cigarette with a burnt mouth. Had all that really happened in one single day? He looked at the picture of Amadeu de Prado. Everything new he had learned about him today changed his features. He began to live, the godless priest.

15

'*Voilà. Ça va aller?* It's not exactly comfortable, but . . .' said Agostinha, the trainee at *Diario de Noticias,* Portugal's traditional newspaper, somewhat embarrassed.

Yes, said Gregorius, that would do, and sat down in the gloomy alcove with the microfilm reader. Agostinha, who had been introduced to him by an impatient editor as a student of history and French, seemed only too glad to help him. He had the impression that, upstairs, where the phone was constantly ringing and the computer screens were flickering, she was tolerated more than needed.

'What are you looking for?' she asked now. 'I mean, it's none of my business . . .'

'For the death of a judge,' said Gregorius. 'For the suicide of a famous judge in 1954, on June 9. He may have killed himself because he had Bechterev's disease and could no longer bear the pain, but maybe also from a sense of guilt because, during the dictatorship, he kept on administering the law and did not refuse to comply with the unjust regime. He was sixty-four when took his life. So, he didn't have long to go before retirement. Something must have happened that made it impossible for him to wait. Something to do with his illness or something at court. That's what I'd like to find out.'

'And . . . and why do you want to find this out? *Pardon* . . .' Gregorius took out Prado's book and let her read:

PORQUÊ, PAI? WHY, FATHER? *'Don't take yourself so seriously,' you used to say when somebody complained. You sat in your chair, where nobody could sit, the cane between your thin legs, the gouty deformed hands on the silver knob, the head – as always – stretched down and forward. (My God, if only I could see you once standing tall, head up, befitting your pride!* Only one single time! *But the thousandfold view of the twisted back, it extinguished every other memory, and not only that, it also paralysed the imagination.) The many pains you had to endure in your life lent authority to your repeated admonition. No one dared contradict. Not only externally; internally, too, contradiction was forbidden. We children did parody your words, far away from you there was scorn and laughter, and even Mamã, when she scolded us about it, sometimes gave herself away with the trace of a smile we greedily pounced on. But the liberation was only make-believe, like the helpless blasphemy of the pious.*

Your words held. They held until that morning when I went off to school apprehensively, with wind-whipped rain in my face. Why wasn't my apprehension about the gloomy schoolrooms and the joyless cramming to be taken seriously? Why shouldn't I take it seriously that Maria João treated me like air, when I could think of hardly anything else? Why were your pains and the judiciousness they had bestowed on you the measure of all things? 'Considered from the standpoint of eternity,' you sometimes added, 'that does lose significance.' Full of rage and jealousy of Maria João's new friend, I left school, trudged home and sat down across from you after dinner. 'I want to go to another school,' I said in a voice that sounded more solid than it felt internally. 'This one is unbearable.' 'You take yourself too seriously,' you said and rubbed the silver knob of the cane. 'What, if not myself, should I take seriously?' I asked. 'And the standpoint of eternity – there is none.'

The room filled with a silence that threatened to explode. Such a thing had never happened. It was unheard of and coming from your favourite child made it even worse. Everyone expected an outburst with your voice cracking, as usual. Nothing happened. You put both hands on the knob of the cane. An expression appeared on Mamã's face that I had never seen. It made it clear – I later thought – why she had married you. You got up without a word, only a slight groan of pain was to be heard. You didn't appear at supper. Ever since this family had existed, that had never happened. When I sat down to dinner the next day, you looked at me calmly and a little sadly. 'What other school are you thinking of?' you asked. During recess, Maria João had asked me if I wanted an orange. 'It's over,' I said.

How can you tell whether to take a feeling seriously or treat it as a carefree mood? Why, Papá, didn't you talk to me before you did it? So that I would at least know why you did it?

'I understand,' said Agostinha, and then went on searching among the microfiches for a record of the death of Judge Prado.

'Nineteen fifty-four, that was the strictest year of censorship,' she said. 'I know about that, I wrote my senior essay on press censorship. What the *Diaro* prints doesn't have to be true. Especially if it was a political suicide.'

The first thing they found was the obituary that appeared on June 11. The wording was extremely terse, reflecting the Portuguese attitude to suicide at the time, *Faleceu*, Gregorius knew the word from the cemetery. *Amor, recordação*, terse ritual jargon. Underneath, the names of the closest relatives: Maria Piedade Reis de Prado; Amadeu; Adriana; Rita. The address. The name of the church where the mass would be held. That was all. Rita, thought Gregorius – was that the Mélodie João Eça had spoken of?

Now they looked for an article. In the first week after June 9, there was nothing. 'No, no, go on,' said Agostinha when Gregorius wanted to give up. The article appeared on June 20, far back in the local section:

'Yesterday, the Minister of Justice announced that Alexandre Horácio de Almeida Prado, who served as an outstanding judge on the Supreme Court for many years, died last week as the result of a long illness.'

Next to it was a picture of the judge, a surprisingly large one considering the brevity of the article. A severe face with a pince-nez on a chain, a goatee and a moustache, a high forehead, as high as his son's, a greying but still full head of hair, white stand-up collar with folded corners, black tiepin, a very white hand supporting his chin; everything else was lost in the dark background. A cleverly taken photo, no trace of the torment of the subject's crooked back, or of the gout in his hands, the figure emerging silent and ghostly from the darkness, white and imperious, tolerating neither objection nor contradiction. A judge who couldn't have been anything but a judge. A man of iron rigidity and stony consistency, even towards himself, A man who would judge himself if he were lacking. A father whose smile usually failed. A man who had had something in common with António de Oliveira Salazar: not his cruelty, not his fanaticism, not his ambition and his desire for power, but the rigidity, even mercilessness towards himself. Was that why he had served him for so long, the man in black with the strained face under the derby hat? And ultimately, could he not forgive himself for promoting the cruelty, a cruelty that could be seen in the shaking hands of João Eça, hands that had once played Schubert?

Died as the result of a long illness. Gregorius felt himself growing hot with rage.

'That's nothing,' said Agostinha, 'that's nothing compared with some of the distortions I've seen. The silent lying.'

On the way out, Gregorius asked her about the street mentioned in the obituary. He was glad that she was apparently needed now in the editorial office.

'That you make the history of this family so much . . . so

much your own ... is ...' she said after they had shaken hands.

'Strange, you think? Yes, it is strange. Very strange. For me, too.'

16

It wasn't a palace, but a house for wealthy people who could spread out as much as they liked, one room more or less didn't matter; there would be two or even three bathrooms. Here the hunched judge had lived, he had walked through this house on a cane with a silver knob, struggling grimly against the continual pain, accompanied by the conviction that you shouldn't take yourself so seriously. Did he have his study in the square tower, whose arched windows were separated from one another with small pillars? There were so many balconies set at different angles, with finely carved wrought-iron bars, that Gregorius imagined each of the five family members must have had one if not two to himself. He thought of the narrow, badly soundproofed rooms in which his own family had lived, the museum guard and the cleaning woman with their nearsighted son, who sat in his room at a simple wooden table and chanted complicated Greek verb forms against the drone of the neighbours' radio. The tiny balcony, too narrow for a parasol, had been white-hot in the summer and he had hardly ever ventured on to it, repelled by the kitchen odours that wafted around it. The judge's house, on the other hand, was like a paradise of vastness, shadow and silence. Everywhere, high, spreading conifers with knotty trunks and interwoven branches that came together in small, shadowy roofs that sometimes looked like pagodas.

Cedars. Gregorius started. *Cedars. Cedros vermelhos.* Were they really cedars? *The* cedars soaked in red for Adriana? *The* trees whose imaginary colour took on such meaning that they came to mind when she sought a name for the invented publisher? Gregorius stopped some passers-by and asked if they were cedars. Their amazement at the question of a bizarre foreigner was evident from the shrugs and raised eyebrows. Yes, said a young woman at last, they were cedars, especially big and beautiful ones. Now he imagined himself living in the house looking out at the lush dark greenery around it. What could have happened? What could have changed the green into red? Blood?

Behind the tower window appeared a female figure in bright clothes, her hair up; light, almost hovering, she walked here and there, busy without haste. Now she took a burning cigarette from somewhere, and smoke rose to the high ceiling. She evaded a sunbeam that fell into the room through the cedars and apparently blinded her, then she suddenly vanished. *A girl who didn't seem to touch the ground,* João Eça had called Mélodie, whose real name must have been Rita. *His little sister.* Could there have been such a big difference in age that today she could still move as nimbly and smoothly as the woman in the tower?

Gregorius walked on and entered a coffee shop in the next street. Along with the coffee, he bought a packet of cigarettes, the same brand he had smoked at Eça's yesterday. As he puffed he pictured the students in Kirchenfeld standing in front of the bakery a few streets away, smoking and drinking coffee out of paper cups. When had Kägi introduced the ban on smoking in the staffroom? Now he tried to inhale but a scorching cough took his breath away. He put the new glasses on the counter, coughed and rubbed the tears from his eyes. The woman behind the counter, a chain-smoking matron, grinned. '*É melhor não começar,*' Better not start, she said, and Gregorius was proud that he understood her, even if the understanding came with hesitation. He didn't know what to do with the cigarette and finally put it out in the glass of water next to the coffee cup. The woman cleared away the glass with a lenient shake of her head. He was a bloody beginner, what could you do?

Slowly he returned to the gate of the cedar house, once again uncertain whether to ring the doorbell. Just then the front door opened and the woman from the tower room came out with an impatient German shepherd dog on a leash. Now she was wearing blue jeans and running shoes; only the light blouse seemed the same. She walked the few steps to the gate on tiptoe, pulled by the dog. *A girl who didn't seem to touch the ground.* Despite all the grey in the ash-blonde hair, she still looked like a girl even now.

'*Bom dia,*' she said, raising her eyebrows inquiringly and looked at him with clear eyes.

'I . . .' Gregorius began uncertainly in French, feeling the unpleasant aftertaste of the cigarette, 'a long time ago, a judge lived here, a famous judge, and I'd like . . .'

'That was my father,' said the woman and blew a loose strand of hair off her face. She had a light voice that suited the watery grey of her eyes and she spoke French without an accent. *Rita* was good as a name, but *Mélodie* was simply perfect. 'Why are you interested in him?' she asked.

'Because he was the father of this man,' and now Gregorius showed her Prado's book.

The dog tugged at the leash.

'Pan, sit,' said Mélodie. 'Pan.'

The dog sat down. She shoved the loop of the leash in the crook of her arm and opened the book. '*Cedros ver . . .*' she read, and from one syllable to the next, her voice grew softer until, finally, it died out completely. She leafed through the book and looked at her brother's portrait. Her light face, covered with tiny freckles, had become darker and swallowing seemed difficult for her. She looked at the picture, intently, like a statute beyond space and time, and once she ran the tip of her tongue over her dry lips. Now she leafed through some more pages, read two sentences, went back to the picture, then to the title page.

'Nineteen seventy-five,' she said. 'He had already been dead two years. I didn't know anything about the book. Where did you get it?'

As Gregorius told her, she ran her hand softly over the grey binding and the movement reminded him of the student in the Spanish bookshop in Bern. She didn't seem to be listening any more and he broke off.

'Adriana,' she said now. 'Adriana. And not a single word. *É próprio dela*,' That's typical of her. At first, there was only amazement in the words; then he detected bitterness and the melodious name no longer suited her. She gazed into the distance, past the citadel, over the valley of the Baixa, to the hill of Bairro Alto. As if she wanted to strike the sister up there in the blue house with her angry look.

They stood mutely facing each other. Pan panted. Gregorius felt like an interloper, a voyeur.

'Come, let's have some coffee,' she said, and it sounded as if she leapt light-footed over her resentment. 'I want to look at the book. Pan, you're out of luck,' and with these words, she dragged the dog back into the house.

It was a house that breathed life, a house with toys on the steps, that smelled of coffee, cigarette smoke and perfume, with Portuguese newspapers and French magazines lying around, with open CD cases and a cat licking the butter on the breakfast table. Mélodie shooed the cat away and poured them coffee. The blood that had just now flooded her face had subsided and only a few red spots hinted at her recent excitement. She reached for her glasses and began to read pieces of what her brother had written. Now and then, she bit her lips. Once, without taking her eyes off the book, she took off her jacket and blindly fished a cigarette out of the packet in its pocket. Gregorius noticed that she was breathing heavily.

'That part about Maria João and changing schools – that must have been before I was born. We were sixteen years apart in age. But Papá – he was like it says here, just like that. He was forty-six when I was born. I was an accident, conceived in the Amazon, on one of the few trips Mamá could tempt him to go on. I can't even imagine Papá on the Amazon. When I was fourteen, we celebrated his sixtieth birthday; it seems to me that I only knew him as an old man, a stooped, strict old man.'

Mélodie paused, lit another cigarette, and looked straight ahead. Gregorius hoped she would talk about the judge's death. But her thoughts were moving in another direction for now her face lit up.

'Maria João. So he knew her even as a kid. I didn't know that. An orange. Apparently he loved her even then. Never stopped. The great, untouched love of his life. It wouldn't surprise me if he never even kissed her. But nobody, no woman, measured up to her. She got married, had children. None of it mattered. When he had problems, real cares, he went to her. In a certain sense, she, only she, knew who he was. He knew how to create intimacy with shared secrets, he was a master at that art, a virtuoso. And we knew: if there was anybody who knew all his secrets, it was Maria João. Fátima suffered from it, and Adriana hated her.'

Was she still alive? asked Gregorius. Recently she had lived outside in the Campo de Ourique, near the cemetery, said Mélodie, but it had been many years since she had encountered her there at his grave, a friendly yet cool meeting.

'She, a peasant girl, always kept her distance from us, the nobles. That Amadeu was also one of us – she acted as if she didn't know that. Or as if it was something accidental, external, that had nothing to do with him.'

What was her last name? Mélodie didn't know. 'She was simply Maria João to us.'

They went out of the tower room and into the main part of the house, where there was a loom.

'I've done a thousand things,' she said, laughing at Gregorius's curious look. 'I was always the flighty one, the unpredictable one, so Papá didn't know what to do with me.'

For a moment, the light voice darkened like a fleeting cloud blotting out the sun, then the moment passed and she pointed to the photographs on the wall showing her in a variety of surroundings.

'As a waitress in a bar; playing hooky, as a garage attendant; and here, you have to look at this: my orchestra.'

It was a street orchestra with eight girls, all playing violins and all wearing Mao caps, the peaks turned to the side.

'Do you recognize me? I've turned my peak to the left, all the others to the right. That means I was the leader. We made money, pretty good money. We played at weddings and parties; we were a hot item.'

Abruptly she turned away, went to the window and looked out.

'Papá didn't like it, my drifting. Shortly before his death – I was on the road with the *moças de balão*, the balloon girls, as we were called – I suddenly saw Papá's official car at the kerb. In the driving seat was Felipe, the chauffeur who picked him up every morning at ten to six and took him to the courthouse; he was always the first one there. Papá sat in the back as always and now he looked at us. Tears shot into my eyes and I made one mistake after another in playing. The car door opened and Papá clambered out, laboriously, his face twisted with pain. He stopped the traffic with his cane – even now he radiated the authority of a judge – and came over to us. For a while he stood among the spectators at the back, then he made his way to the open violin cases in which we collected the money. Without looking at me, he tossed in a handful of coins. The tears ran down my face and they had to finish the rest of the piece without me. As the car drove off, Papá waved with his gouty hand and I waved back, but then I sat down on the steps of a house and cried my eyes out. I don't know if it was more out of joy that he had come or out of sadness that he had not come before.

Gregorius let his gaze wander over the photos. Mélodie had been a girl who sat on everyone's lap and made everyone laugh and when she wept, it was over as quickly as a short downpour on a sunny day. She played truant from school, but got away with it because she charmed the teachers with her bewitching impudence. She went on to tell me how she had learned French overnight, as it were, and called herself after a French actress named Élodie. The others turned it into Mélodie, a word invented for her because her presence was as beautiful and fleeting as a melody. Everybody fell in love but nobody could hold on to her.

'I loved Amadeu, or let's say I would have liked to love him, but it was hard, the way you love a monument. And he *was* a monument, even when I was little. Everybody looked up to him, even Papá, but most of all Adriana, who took him away from me with her jealousy. He was nice to me, the way you're nice to your kid sister. But I would have liked to be taken seriously by him, not just patted like a doll. Not until I was twenty-five and about to get married did I get a letter from him, a letter from England.'

She opened a desk and took out a fat envelope. The yellowed stationery was covered to the margins with calligraphic letters in dark black ink. Mélodie cast her eye down it and then began to translate what Amadeu had written to her from Oxford, a few months after his wife's death.

Dear Mélodie,
    It was a mistake to make this trip. I thought it would help me if once again I saw the things Fátima and I had seen together.

But it hurts me and I'm coming back earlier than planned. I miss you and so I'm sending you what I wrote last night. Perhaps in this way, I can come closer to you with my thoughts.

OXFORD: JUST TALKING. *Why does the nocturnal silence among the cloistered buildings seem so lifeless to me, so queasy and desolate, so completely vapid and without charm? So completely different from the Rua Augusta, which flashes with life even at three or four in the morning when no human souls are out and about? How can it be, where the bright unearthly shining stone encloses buildings with sacred names, cells of scholarship, exquisite libraries, rooms of dusty velvet silence, where perfectly shaped sentences are spoken, weighed pensively, refuted, and defended? How can that be?*

'Come on,' *said the red-haired Irishman to me as I stood before the poster announcing a lecture titled* 'Lying to Liars', 'let's listen to this; might be fun.' *I thought of Father Bartolomeu, who had defended Augustine: to repay lies with lies would be the same as repaying robbery with robbery, sacrilege with sacrilege, adultery with adultery. And that in view of what happened then in Spain and in Germany! We had quarrelled as so often and he didn't lose his gentleness. He never lost it, this gentleness, not one single time, and when I sat down in the lecture hall next to the Irishman, all of a sudden I missed him terribly and felt homesick.*

It was unbelievable. The lecturer, a pointy nosed, pointy prissy spinster, sketched in a creaky voice a casuistic of lying that couldn't have been more nitpicking or farther from reality. A woman who must never have lived in the web of lies of a dictatorship where lying well can be a question of life or death. Can God create a stone He couldn't lift? If not, then He isn't almighty; if yes, then He isn't either, for now there is a stone He cannot lift. That was the kind of scholasticism that poured forth into the room from a woman made of parchment, with an artificial bird's-nest of grey hair on her head.

But that wasn't what was really unbelievable. What was really incomprehensible was the discussion, as it was called. Cast into and enclosed in the grey lead frame of polite empty British phrases, the people spoke perfectly past one another. Constantly they said *they understood each other, answered each other. But it wasn't so. No one, not a single one of the discussants, showed the slightest indication of a change of mind in view of the reasons presented. And suddenly, with a fear I felt even in my body, I realized: that's how it* always *is. Saying something to another: how can we expect it to affect anything? The current of thoughts, images and feelings that flows through us on every side, has such force, this torrential current, that it would be a miracle if it didn't simply sweep away and consign to oblivion all words anyone else says to us, if they didn't by accident, sheer accident, suit our own words. Is it different with me? I thought. Did I really* listen *to anybody else? Let him into me with his words so that my internal current would be diverted?*

'How did you like it?' asked the Irishman as we walked along Broad Street. I didn't say everything, I said only that I had found it eerie how everybody had been talking only to themselves. 'Well,' he said, 'well.' And after a while: 'It's just talking, you know; just talking. People like to talk. Basically, that's it. Talking.' 'No meeting of minds?' I asked. 'What?' he shouted and howled with laughter. 'What!' And then he shot the ball he had been carrying the whole time on to the pavement. I would like to have been the Irishman, an Irishman who dared to appear in All Souls College for the evening lecture with a bright red football. What wouldn't I have given to be Irishman!

I think I know now why the nocturnal silence in this illustrious place is such a bad silence. The words, all of them destined to oblivion, have died out. That wouldn't matter, they die out in the Baixa too. But there, no one pretends that it's more than talk, people talk and enjoy talking, as they enjoy licking ice cream, so the tongue can take a break from words. While here, everyone always acts as if it were different. As if it were enormously

important, *what they said. But they, too, have to sleep in their
self-importance, and then a silence remains that smells rotten
because cadavers of pomposity are lying around everywhere and
stinking without words.*

'He hated them, the pompous asses, *os presunçosos*, whom
he also called *os enchouriçados*, the windbags,' said Mélodie
and put the letter back in the envelope. 'He hated them
everywhere: in politics, medicine, journalism. And he was
merciless in his condemnation. I liked his condemnation because
it was incorruptible, relentless, even against himself. I didn't
like it when it became murderous, destructive. Then I got out
of the way of my monumental brother.'

Next to Mélodie's head, a photo hung on the wall that
showed them dancing together, she and Amadeu. His movement
wasn't really stiff, thought Gregorius; and yet you could see
that he was a stranger to it. Later, when he thought about it,
he came up with the right word: dancing was somehow
inappropriate for Amadeu.

'The Irishman with the red ball in the sacred college,' said
Mélodie into the silence. 'It moved me very much at that time,
this passage in the letter. It seemed to me that it expressed a
longing he never spoke of otherwise: to be able to be a boy
who played with a ball just once. He learned to read at the
age of four and from then on he read everything he could; he
was bored to death at the Liceu where he skipped a grade
twice. At twenty, he really knew everything and sometimes
asked himself what else there was to learn. And yet he never
knew how to play ball.'

The dog barked and then some children, who must have
been her grandchildren, burst in. Mélodie gave Gregorius her
hand. She knew he had wanted to learn much more, about
cedros vermelhos for instance, and about the death of the judge.
Her look proved that she was aware of it. It also proved that

she wouldn't be willing to say any more today, even if the children hadn't arrived.

Gregorius sat down on a bench at the Castelo and thought about the letter Amadeu had sent from Oxford to his little sister. He had to find Father Bartolomeu, the gentle teacher. Prado had had an ear for the various kinds of silence, an ear granted only to insomniacs. And he had said of the evening's lecturer that she was made of parchment. Only now was Gregorius aware that he winced at that comment and, for the first time, had recoiled internally from the godless priest with the murderous judgement. *Mundus, the Papyrus. Parchment and papyrus.*

Gregorius went down the hill towards the hotel. In a shop he bought a chess set. For the rest of the day, until late at night, he tried to win against Alekhine by not accepting the sacrifice of the two rooks, unlike Bogolyubov. He missed Doxiades and put on his old pair of glasses.

17

They aren't texts, *Gregorius. What people say aren't* texts. *They simply talk.* It had been a long time since Doxiades had said that to him. What people said was often so unconnected and contradictory, he had complained to him, that it passed straight from their minds. The Greek found it touching. If, like him, you had been a taxi driver in Greece, and in Thessaloniki to boot, then you knew – and knew it as certainly as few other things – that you couldn't tie people down to what they said. Often, they talked only for the sake of talking. And not only in the taxi. To be able to take them at their word was something only a philologist could do, particularly a philologist of ancient languages, dealing all day with immutable words.

If you couldn't take people at their word, what else should be done with their words? Gregorius had asked. Doxiades had laughed: 'Use them as a chance to talk yourself! So that it keeps going on, talking.' And now the Irishman in Prado's letter to his little sister had said something that sounded quite similar and he hadn't said it about fares in Greek taxis, but about professors at All Souls' College in Oxford. He had said it to a man who was so disgusted by worn-out words that he wanted to be able to re-order the Portuguese language.

Outside it was pouring with rain, and had been for two days now. It was as if a magic curtain shielded Gregorius from the outside world. He wasn't in Bern and he was in Bern; he was in Lisbon and he wasn't in Lisbon. He played chess all day long and forgot positions and moves, something that had never happened to him before. Sometimes he caught himself holding a piece in his hand and not knowing where it came from. Downstairs, at meals, the waiter had to keep asking him what he wanted, and once he ordered dessert before soup.

On the second day, he had called his neighbour in Bern and asked her to empty the postbox; the key was under the doormat. Should she forward the mail? Yes, he said, and then he called back and said no. Leafing through the notebook, he came upon the phone number the Portuguese woman had written on his forehead. *Português*. He picked up the phone and dialled. When it rang, he hung up.

The Koiné, the Greek of the New Testament, bored him, it was too simple; but looking at the other, the Portuguese section in Coutinho's edition, had a certain appeal. He called various bookshops and asked for Aeschylus and Horace, or even Herodotus and Tacitus. They barely understood him and when he was finally successful, he couldn't pick up the books because it was raining so hard.

In the business directory, he looked for language schools where he could learn Portuguese. He called Mariana Eça and wanted to tell her about his visit to João, but she was in a hurry and not paying attention. Silveira was in Biarritz. Time stood still and his world stood still because his will faltered as it had never done before.

Sometimes he stood gazing vacantly out of the hotel window, reviewing in his mind what the others – Coutinho, Adriana, João Eça, Mélodie – had said about Prado. It was a bit as if the outlines of a landscape emerged out of the fog, still veiled, but recognizable, as in a Chinese pen-and-ink drawing. Only once in these days did he leaf through Prado's notes and then he got stuck on this passage:

AS SOMBRAS DA ALMA. THE SHADOWS OF THE SOUL. *The stories others tell about you and the stories you tell about yourself: which come closer to the truth? Is it so clear that they are your own? Is one an authority on oneself? But that really isn't the question that concerns me. The real question is: in such stories, is there really a difference between true and false? In stories about the outside, surely. But when we set out to understand someone on the inside? Is that a trip that ever comes to an end? Is the soul a place of facts? Or are the alleged facts only the deceptive shadows of our stories?*

On Thursday morning, under a clear blue sky, Gregorius went to the newspaper offices and asked Agostinha, the trainee, to find out if there had been a Liceu in the thirties where you could learn ancient languages and where some of the teachers were priests. She searched eagerly and when she found it, she showed him the place on the city map. She also found the office of the appropriate church, called and enquired about a Father Bartolomeu, who had taught in the Liceu, it must have been about 1935. That could only have been Father Bartolomeu Lourenço de Gusmão, she was told. He was way over ninety by now and seldom received visitors; what was it about? Amadeu Inácio de Almeida Prado? They would ask the priest and call back. The call came a few minutes later. The priest was willing to talk to someone who was interested in Prado after all this time. He looked forward to the visit in the late afternoon.

Gregorius went in search of the former Liceu, where the student Prado had quarrelled with Father Bartolomeu about Augustine's intransigent ban on lying without the priest ever losing his gentleness. It was to the east of the city and was surrounded by high, old trees. The building with its pale yellow walls could almost have been taken for a former grand hotel of the nineteenth century, were it not for the absence of balconies and the narrow bell tower. The building was thoroughly dilapidated. The plaster was peeling, the windowpanes were blind or smashed, tiles were missing from the roof, the gutters were rusted and one corner was broken off.

Gregorius sat down on the entrance steps, which had been mossy even on Prado's nostalgic visits. That must have been in the late sixties. Here he had sat and asked himself how it would have been if, thirty years before, at this fork in the road, he had taken the other turning. If he had resisted his father's touching but imperious wish and not gone to medical school.

Gregorius took out his notes and leafed through them . . .

the dreamlike, bombastic wish to stand once again at that point in my life and be able to take a completely different direction than the one that has made me who I am now . . . To sit once more on the warm moss and hold the cap – it's the absurd wish to go back behind myself in time and take myself – the one marked by events – along on this journey.

Over there was the decomposing fence around the schoolyard where the boy at the bottom of the class had flung his cap in the pond with the waterlilies after finals, more than sixty-seven years ago. The pond had long since dried up; only a hollow, carpeted with ivy, remained.

The building behind the trees must have been the girls' school, from where Maria João had appeared, the girl with tanned knees and the fragrance of soap in her light dress, the girl who had become the great untouched love in Amadeu's life, the woman who, in Mélodie's estimation, was the only one who knew who he had really been; a woman of such significance that Adriana had hated her, even though he may not have given her a single kiss.

Gregorius closed his eyes. He imagined himself back in Kirchenfield, at the corner of the building from where he had looked back, unseen, at the Gymnasium after he had run away in the middle of class. Once more he had the feeling that had hit him with unexpected force ten days before and had showed him how much he loved this building and all that it stood for, and how much he would miss it. It was the same feeling and yet it was different because it was no longer one and the same. It hurt him to feel that it was no longer what it had once been. He stood up, let his eyes roam over the peeling, fading yellow of the façade, and now all of a sudden it didn't hurt any more. The pain gave way to a hovering feeling of curiosity and he pushed open the door, which was now ajar and whose rusty hinges screeched as in a horror movie.

An odour of damp and mould struck him as he entered. After a few steps, he almost slipped, for the uneven stone floor was covered with a film of damp dust and rotten moss. Slowly, his hand on the banister, he went up the worn stairs. The panels of the swing door that opened to the upper floor were stuck together with so many spiders' webs that there was a dull sound of ripping when he pushed them open. He started, as frightened bats fluttered through the hall. Then there was a silence he had never before experienced: in it, you could hear the years.

The door to the Rector's office was easy to recognize; it was trimmed with fine wood-carvings. This door was also stuck and gave way only after several shoves. He entered a room where there seemed to be only one thing: an enormous black desk on curved and carved legs. Everything else – the empty dusty bookshelves, the bare tea table on the bare rotting floorboards, the Spartan chair – appeared insignificant beside it. Gregorius wiped off the seat of the chair and sat down behind the desk. The Rector at that time was named Senhor Cortês, the man with the measured pace and the strict expression.

Gregorius had stirred up dust; the fine particles danced in a cone of sunlight that had entered the room. The deep silence made him feel like an interloper and for a long moment he forgot to breathe. Then curiosity triumphed and he pulled open the drawers of the desk, one after another. A piece of rope, a mouldy shaving from a sharpened pencil, a crinkled stamp from 1969, cellar smells. And then, in the bottom drawer, a Hebrew Bible, thick and heavy, bound in grey linen, faded, worn, with blisters of dampness on the cover; *Biblia Hebraica* in gold letters that had taken on black shadows.

Gregorius hesitated. The Liceu, as Agostinha had found out, had not been a religious school. The Marquês de Pombal had driven the Jesuits out of Portugal in the mid-eighteenth century, and something similar had happened again in the early twentieth century. In the late 1940s, orders like the Maristas had founded a few Colégios, but that had been after Prado finished school. Until then, there had only been public Liceus, which occasionally employed priests as teachers of ancient languages. So why this Bible? And why in a drawer of the Rector's desk? A simple mistake, a meaningless accident? An invisible silent protest against those who had closed the schools? A subversive forgetting, directed against the dictatorship and unnoticed by its stooges?

Gregorius read. Carefully he turned the crinkly pages of thick paper that felt dank and mouldy. The cone of sunlight shifted. He buttoned up his coat, pulled up the collar and shoved his hands in the sleeves. After a while, he stuck one of the cigarettes he had bought on Monday between his lips. Now and then he had to cough. Outside, beyond the half-open door, something swished by that must have been a rat.

He read in the Book of Job and he read with a pounding heart. Eliphaz of Teman, Bildad of Shuah and Zofar of Na'ama. *Isfahan*. What would the name of the family have been where he would have taught? In the Francke bookshop in those days, there had been a book of photographs of Isfahan, of the mosques, the squares, the mountains all around veiled by sandstorms. He couldn't afford to buy it and had therefore gone to Francke every day to leaf through it. After his dream of white-hot sand that would blind him had forced him to withdraw his job application, he hadn't gone back to Francke for months. When he finally did go back, the book was no longer there.

The Hebrew letters had blurred before Gregorius's eyes. He rubbed his wet face, cleaned the glasses and read on. Something of Isfahan, the city of blinding, had remained in his life: from the start he had read the Bible as poetry, linguistic music played faintly from the dark blue and gold of the mosques. *I have the feeling that you don't take the text seriously,* Ruth Gautschi had said and David Lehmann had nodded. Had that really been only last month?

Can there be anything more serious than poetic seriousness? he had asked the two of them. Ruth had looked down. She liked him. Not like Florence back then, in the front row; she would never have wanted to take off his glasses. But she liked him and now she was torn between this affection and the disappointment, perhaps even the horror, that he desecrated God's word by reading it as a long poem and hearing it as a series of oriental sonatas.

The sun had disappeared from Senhor Cortês's room and Gregorius was freezing. He had been living in the past for hours, and had failed to notice the desolation of the room. Now he stood up and walked stiffly out to the corridor and up the stairs to the classrooms.

The rooms were full of dust and silence. If they were distinct from each other, it was in the degree of dilapidation. In one there was an enormous damp patch on the ceiling; in another, the washbasin hung crookedly because a rusted screw had broken; in a third a shattered glass lampshade lay on the floor, the bare bulb still hanging from the ceiling. Gregorius worked the light switch: nothing, neither here nor in the other rooms. A deflated football lay in a corner, the jagged remains of the smashed windowpanes flashed in the afternoon sun. *And yet he never knew how to play ball,* Mélodie had said about her brother who had skipped two grades in this building because at the age of four he had already begun reading through the library.

The classrooms were off long corridors like a barracks. Gregorius inspected them one after another. Once he tripped over a dead rat, then stood still, trembling, and wiped his hands, which had nothing to do with it, on his coat. From one of the classrooms you could look over at the girls' school, but half the building was concealed by the trunk of a gigantic pine tree. Amadeu de Prado would have chosen a seat near the bank of windows. So he could see Maria João at her desk no matter where she was sitting. Gregorius sat down in the seat with the best view and strained to see. Yes, he could have seen her in her bright dress that smelt of soap. They had exchanged looks and when she took an exam, Amadeu had wished he could guide her hand. Had he used opera glasses? In the aristocratic house of a Supreme Court judge, there must have been some. Alexandre Horácio wouldn't have used them if he ever sat in a box at the opera. But perhaps his wife, Maria Piedade Reis de Prado, had in the six years she had lived after his death? Had his death been a liberation for her? Or had it made time stand still and frozen her feelings, as with Adriana?

Back on the ground floor, Gregorius opened a pair of lofty doors and found himself in the school dining hall. In one wall there was a hatch and behind it the former kitchen, where only rusty pipes still remained, sticking out of the tiled walls. The long dining table had been left. Was there an auditorium?

He found it on the other side of the building. Tightly fixed benches, a stained-glass window missing two panes, in front a raised lectern with a small lamp. A separate bench, probably for the school staff. The silence of a church hung over the auditorium, a silence that wouldn't be ended with arbitrary words. A silence that made sculptures of words, monuments of praise, warning or scathing judgements.

Gregorius went back to the Rector's office. Undecided, he held the Hebrew Bible in his hand. He already had it under his arm and was on his way to the exit when he turned back. He lined the damp drawer where it had lain with his sweater and put the book inside. Then he made his way to Belém, at the other side of the city, where Father Bartolomeu Lourenço de Gusmão lived in a church home.

18

'Augustine and the lies – that was only one of a thousand things we fought about,' said Father Bartolomeu. 'We fought a lot without ever getting into a fight. For, you see, he was a hothead, a rebel, and a boy with a quicksilver intelligence. He was a gifted speaker, who swept through the Liceu like a whirlwind for six years, and became a legend.'

The priest was holding Prado's book and now ran the back of his hand over the portrait. It could have been a smoothing action or it could have been a caress. Gregorius pictured Adriana, stroking Amadeus's desk with the back of her hand.

'He's older here,' said the priest. 'But it's him. That's how he was, exactly.'

He rested the book on the blanket that covered his legs.

'Back then, as his teacher, I was in my mid-twenties and it was an unbelievable challenge for me to have to stand up to him. He split the faculty into those who damned him to hell and those who loved him. Yes, that's the right word: some of us were in love with him – with his boldness, his overflowing generosity and tough determination, his brazen contempt for the world, his fearlessness, and his fanatical enthusiasm. He was full of audacity, an adventurer you could easily imagine exploring the seas, singing, preaching, and firmly resolved to protect the inhabitants of distant continents against every degrading infringement of occupation, with the sword if need be. He was willing to challenge everyone, even the devil, even God. No, it wasn't megalomania, as his opponents said, it was only flourishing life and a volcanic outburst of awakening forces, a shower of sparks of flashing inspiration. No doubt he was full of arrogance, this boy. But it was so boisterous, so great, this arrogance, that you overcame your resistance and viewed him in amazement like a natural wonder with its own laws. Those who loved him saw him as a rough diamond, an unpolished gem. Those who rejected him were offended by his lack of respect, which could wound. They saw him as an aristocratic prig, favoured by fate, showered not only with money but also with talent, beauty and charm, as well as the irresistible melancholy that made women love him. It seemed unfair that he was so much better endowed than others. This made him a magnet for envy and resentment. Yet even those who felt resentment were secretly full of admiration. He was a boy who could touch heaven.'

Memory had carried the priest far from the room they were in, a room that was spacious and filled with books. Although it, too, was in a nursing home, as evidenced by the medical instruments and the bell over the bed, it bore no comparison with João Eça's miserable room up in Cacilhas. Gregorius had liked Father Bartolomeu from the start, the lanky, gaunt man with the snow-white hair and deep-set clever eyes. He had to be well over ninety, if he had taught Prado, but there was nothing senile about him, no sign that he had lost any of the alertness that had countered Amadeu's impetuous challenges seventy years before. He had slim hands with long, finely shaped fingers, as if they had been created to turn the pages of precious old books. With these fingers, he now leafed through Prado's book. But he didn't read it; moving the paper was like a ritual to bring back the distant past.

'All the things he had read when he crossed the threshold of the Liceu at the age of ten in his small, tailor-made frock coat! Many of us caught ourselves secretly calculating whether we could keep up with him. And then, after class, he sat in the library soaking up all the thick books, page after page, line after line. He had an incredible memory and as incredibly concentrated, rapt look on his face when reading. Even the loudest noise would not disturb him. "When Amadeu finishes reading a book," said another teacher, "it has no more letters. He devours not only the meaning, but also the printers' ink."

'That's how it was: the books seemed to disappear inside him, leaving empty husks on the shelf afterwards. The landscape of his mind behind the impudent high forehead expanded with breathtaking speed; from one week to the next, new ideas took shape in it, remarkable associations and inspirations that always amazed us. Sometimes he hid in the library and went on reading all night with a torch. The first time, his mother was in a sheer panic when he didn't come home. But more and more she got used to the fact that her boy tended to violate all the rules and she took a certain pride in it.

'Many a teacher was afraid when Amadeu's concentrated look fell on him. Not that it was a rejecting, provoking or belligerent look. But it gave the teacher only one chance to get it right. If you made a mistake or showed uncertainty, he didn't look contemptuous, or even disappointed. No, he simply averted his eyes, didn't want to make you feel bad, was polite and friendly as he left. But it was precisely this tangible desire not to wound that was destructive. I myself experienced it and other teachers confirmed it: even when they were preparing their lessons, they pictured this testing look. For some, it was the look of the examiner, taking them back to the classroom; others likened it to an athlete facing a strong opponent. I didn't know anybody who hadn't experienced it: that Amadeu Inácio de Almeida Prado, the precocious, alert son of the famous judge, was in the study with you when you were preparing something difficult, something that could trip you up, even as a teacher.

'Nevertheless, despite being so demanding he wasn't a

monolithic whole. There were chinks in his armour, and sometimes you felt you didn't know your way around him at all. When he became aware of the consequences of his arrogant excesses, he was flabbergasted and tried everything to make up for it. And there was also the other Amadeu, the good, helpful comrade. He could sit with a fellow pupil all night to help him prepare for an exam, revealing a modesty and an angelic patience that shamed everybody who had maligned him.

'The attacks of melancholy belonged to yet another Amadeu. When they descended it was almost as if a completely different soul had temporarily settled in him. He became extremely nervous, the slightest noise made him flinch, like a whiplash. And woe to anyone who offered a consoling or encouraging comment at such moments: then he leapt on you in fury.

'He could do so much, this richly blessed boy. There was only one thing he couldn't do: celebrate, play, let himself go. His immense alertness and his passionate need to maintain control got in his way. No alcohol. And no cigarettes, that only came later. But enormous amounts of tea; he loved the red-gold glow of a heavy Assam and brought a silver pot from home for it, which he ultimately gave to the cook.'

But what about this girl? Maria João, Gregorius interjected.

'Yes. And Amadeu loved her. People would smile at his chaste admiration of her to hide their envy; it was envy of a feeling that occurs really only in fairy tales. He loved her and adored her. Yes, that was it: he *adored* her – even if that's not usually said of children. But so many things were different about Amadeu. And she wasn't an especially pretty girl, no princess, far from it. Nor was she a good student, as far as I know. Nobody really understood it, at least not the other girls in the school, who would have given anything to attract the eyes of the noble prince. Maybe it was simply that she wasn't dazzled by him, not overwhelmed like all the others. Maybe that was what he needed: somebody to be on an equal footing with him, with words, looks and movements that liberated him from himself with their naturalness and ordinariness.

'When Maria João came over and sat down next to him on the steps, he seemed to become completely calm, freed of the burden of his alertness and quickness, the weight of his incessant presence of mind, the torment of having constantly to outdo and surpass himself. Sitting next to her, he could listen to the ringing of the bells that called pupils to class, and looking at him, you had the impression he'd like to have stayed there for ever. Then Maria put her hand on his shoulder and pulled him back from the paradise of a precious effortlessness. It was always she who touched him; never did I see his hand rest on hers. When she was about to go back to her school, she'd tie hers shiny black hair into a ponytail with a rubber band. Every time she did it he looked at her as if he were under a spell; he must have loved it very much, this movement. One day, it was no longer a rubber band, but a silver hairclasp, and you could see from his face that it was a gift from him.'

Like Mélodie, the priest couldn't remember the girl's married name either.

'Now that you ask me, it seems to me that we didn't *want* to know the name; as if it would have been *disturbing* to know it,' he said. 'A little bit the way you don't ask about the family names of saints. Or Diana or Electra.'

A nurse in a nun's habit came in.

'Not now,' said the priest when she reached for the blood-pressure cuff.

He said it with gentle authority, and suddenly Gregorius understood why this man had been so good for young Prado: he possessed precisely the kind of authority he had needed to test his limits, and maybe also to liberate himself from the strict, austere authority of his father.

'But we would like a cup of tea,' said the priest and charmed the nurse with his smile. 'An Assam, and make it strong so the red-gold glows properly.'

The priest shut his eyes and was silent. He didn't want to let go of the distant time when Amadeu de Prado had given Maria João a silver hairclasp. Actually, thought Gregorius, he wanted to continue talking about his favourite student, with whom he had debated Augustine and a thousand other things. With the boy who could have touched the sky. The boy whose shoulder he would like to have put his hand on, like Maria João.

'Maria and Jorge,' the priest went on with his eyes shut, 'they were like his patron saints. Jorge O'Kelly. In him, the future pharmacist, Amadeu found a friend, and it wouldn't surprise me if he had been his only real friend, aside from Maria. In many respects, O'Kelly was his complete opposite and sometimes I thought: he needs him to be *whole*. With his peasant skull, the tousled hair and his heavy, awkward manner, he could seem limited, and on parents' days, I saw some of the grander parents look at him askance when he passed them. He was so inelegant in his crumpled shirt, shapeless jacket and the same black tie he always wore askew in protest against the regulations.

'Once, in the school corridor, Amadeu and Jorge came towards us, me and my colleague, who said afterwards: "If I had to explain in a dictionary the definition of elegance and its polar opposite, I would simply depict these two boys. Any further commentary would be superfluous."

'Jorge was someone with whom Amadeu could rest and take a break from his fast pace. When he was with him, after a while, he also slowed down; Jorge's ponderousness rubbed off on him. Also in chess. At first it made him mad when Jorge brooded eternally over a move; in his world-view, his quicksilver metaphysics, it wasn't right that somebody who needed so long to gather his thoughts could ultimately win.

But then he began to inhale Jorge's calm, the calm of someone who always seemed to know who he was and where he belonged. It sounds crazy but I think it got to the point that Amadeu *needed* the regular defeats against Jorge. He was unhappy the few times he won; it must have been as if the rock face he could usually hold on to had given way.

'Jorge knew exactly when his Irish ancestors had come to Portugal, he was proud of his Irish blood and knew English well, even if his mouth wasn't really made for the English words. And in fact, you wouldn't have been surprised to meet him in an Irish farmyard or a country pub, and if you imagined that, he suddenly looked like the young Samuel Beckett.

'Even then, he was a diehard atheist, I don't know how we knew that, but we did. Despite that, he would often quote the family motto: *Turris fortis mihi Deus.* He read the Russian, Andalusian, and Catalan anarchists and played with the idea of crossing the border and fighting against Franco. That he later went into the Resistance: anything else would have surprised me. All his life he was a romantic without illusions, if there is such a thing. And this romantic had two dreams: to become a pharmacist and to play a Steinway. The first dream he realized; even today he stands in a white coat behind the counter of the shop on the Rua dos Sapateiros. Everybody laughed at the second dream, Jorge most of all. For his coarse hands with the broad fingertips and the grooved nails were better suited to the school double bass, which he tried for a while, until, in an attack of despair at his lack of talent, he sawed so violently on the strings that the bow broke.'

The priest drank his tea and Gregorius noticed, disappointed, that the drinking became a slurping. Suddenly, he was an old man whose lips no longer obeyed him completely. His mood had also changed; grief and wistfulness crept into his voice as he spoke of the vacuum Prado had left behind when he finished school.

'Naturally, we all knew that, in the autumn, when the heat subsided and a golden shadow lay on the light, we'd no longer meet him in the corridors. But nobody talked about it. In parting, he shook hands with all of us, forgot no one, thanked us with such warm, refined words – I still remember them – that for a moment I thought: like a president.'

The priest hesitated and then he said: 'They shouldn't have been so well-formed, those words. They should have been more halting, clumsy, groping. Something more like unhewn stone. A little less like polished marble.'

And Prado should have said a goodbye to him, Father Bartolomeu, that was different from the others, thought Gregorius. With more personal words, perhaps with an embrace. He had hurt the priest by treating him like one of the others. It still rankled, seventy years later.

'In the first few days of the new school year, I walked through the numbed school by his absence. I had to keep saying to myself: you must no longer expect to see his helmet of hair approaching, you must no longer hope that his proud figure will come round the corner and you can watch him explaining something to somebody and moving his hands in that inimitably eloquent way. And I'm sure it was the same with others, even though we didn't talk about it. Only once did I hear someone say: "Everything's been so different ever since." There was no question but that he was talking about the absence of Amadeu. That his soft baritone voice was no longer heard around the school. It wasn't only that you didn't see him any more, didn't meet him any more. *You saw his absence* and encountered it as something tangible. His not being there was like the sharply outlined emptiness of a photo with a figure cut out, in which the missing figure is now more important, more dominant, than all the others. That's exactly how we missed Amadeu: through his precise absence.

'It was years before I met him again. He was studying up

in Coimbra and now and then I heard something about him through a friend who assisted one of the professors of medicine with lectures and courses on dissection. Even there, Amadeu had quickly become a legend. Not as brilliant though experienced professors, with prizes for excellence, leading authorities in their field, felt tested by him. Not because he knew more than they did, not yet. But he was insatiable in his need for explanations, and there must have been dramatic scenes in the lecture halls when he proved with his merciless Cartesian perspicacity that something propounded as an explanation really wasn't.

'Once he mocked a particularly vain professor by comparing his explanation with that of a doctor ridiculed by Molière for identifying the soporific potency of a remedy with its *virtus dormitivia*. He could be merciless when he encountered vanity. Merciless. The knife opened in his pocket. *It's an unrecognized form of stupidity,* he would say, *you have to forget the cosmic meaninglessness of all our acts to be able to be vain and that's a glaring form of stupidity.*

'When he was in this mood, you would not want to cross him. They soon discovered that in Coimbra. And they discovered something else: that he had a sixth sense for the planned reprisals of others. Jorge also possessed such a sense, and Amadeu managed to cultivate it independently. When he imagined that someone wanted to show him up, he sought the most remote chess move you could make and prepared himself meticulously for it. It must have been the same with the faculty in Coimbra. In the lecture hall, when he was summoned to the board and asked about arcane matters, he refused the chalk offered by the avenging professor with a malicious smile, and took his own chalk out of his pocket. "Aha," he must have said contemptuously on such occasions, and then he filled the board with anatomical sketches and physiological or biochemical formulas. "*Must* I know that?" he asked when he had once miscalculated. The other's grin couldn't be seen, but it could be heard. You just couldn't get to him.'

For the last half-hour, they had been sitting in the dark. Now the priest turned on the light.

'I buried him. Adriana, his sister, wanted it. He had collapsed on Rua Augusta, which he loved especially, at six in the morning, when his incurable insomnia had driven him into the city. A woman who came out of her house with a dog called an ambulance. But he was already dead. The blood from a burst aneurysm in the brain had extinguished the radiant light of his consciousness for ever.

'I hesitated. I didn't know what he would have thought of Adriana's request. *Burial is a matter for others, the dead have nothing to do with it*, he had once said. It had been one of his chilly sentences that made many people fear him. Was it still true?

'Adriana, who certainly could be a dragon, a dragon who protected Amadeu, was helpless as a child in the face of the things death demands of us. And so I decided to comply with her request. I would have to find words that would do justice to his silent spirit. After decades when he had no longer looked over my shoulder when I prepared words, now he was there again. His life force was extinguished, but it seemed to me that the white, irrevocably silent countenance demanded even more from me than the face that had challenged me so often when it was vividly alive.

'My words at the grave not only had to honour the dead man. I knew that O'Kelly would be there. In his presence, I couldn't possibly speak words dealing with God and what Jorge would call *His empty promises*. The way out was for me to talk about my experiences with Amadeu and of the inextinguishable traces he had left behind in all those who knew him, even his enemies.

'The crowd at the cemetery was unbelievable. All the people

he had treated, including people he had never charged for his services. I allowed myself one single religious word: *Amen.* I pronounced it because Amadeu had loved the word and because Jorge knew that. The sacred word died away in the silence of the graves. Nobody moved. It started raining. The people wept, fell into each other's arms. Nobody turned to go. The heavens opened and the people were soaked to the skin. But they still stood by the grave. Simply stood there. I thought: they want to stop time, they want to keep it from flowing away so that it doesn't drive their beloved doctor away from them, as every second does with everything that has happened before it. At last, after they must have stood there for half an hour, there was movement that started the oldest ones who could no longer remain on their feet. It took another hour for the cemetery to empty.

'When I finally decided to go too, something remarkable happened, something I later dreamed of sometimes, something with the unreality of a scene in a Buñuel film. Two people, a man and a young woman of restrained beauty, came towards each other from either end of the path to the grave. The man was O'Kelly, the woman I didn't know. I couldn't know it, but I felt it: the two knew each other. It seemed like an intimate knowing and as if this intimacy was linked with a catastrophe, a tragedy that also involved Amadeu. Each had to cover an equal distance to the grave and they seemed to adapt the speed of their steps precisely to one another, so they arrived at the same time. Their eyes did not meet once on the way, but were directed at the ground. That they avoided looking at each other created a greater closeness between them than any exchange of looks could have done. Nor did they look at each other when they stood side by side at the grave and seemed to breathe in harmony. The dead man seemed to belong to them alone and I felt I had to leave. To this day, I don't know what kind of secret bound the two people or what it had to do with Amadeu.'

A bell rang, it must have been the signal for supper. A trace of irritation hovered over the priest's face. He flung the blanket off his legs, went to the door and locked it. Back in his chair, he reached for the light switch and turned off the lamp. A cart dragging crockery rolled through the corridor. Father Bartolomeu waited until it was silent again before he went on.

'Or perhaps I do know something, or imagine it. That is, a good year before his death, Amadeu suddenly arrived at my door in the middle of the night. All his self-confidence was gone. His features were agitated and so were his breath and his movements. I made tea and he smiled fleetingly when I brought out the biscuits he had been crazy about as a student. Then the tormented expression reappeared on his face.

'Clearly I couldn't press him, couldn't even ask anything. I remained silent and waited. He was struggling with himself as only he could: as if victory and defeat in this struggle would decide life and death. And perhaps it was really so. I had heard rumours that he was working for the Resistance. As he gazed straight ahead, breathing with an effort, I considered what growing old had done to him: the first age spots on the slim hands, the weary skin under the sleepless eyes, the grey strands in the hair. And suddenly, I saw with horror that he looked neglected. Not like a tramp. The neglect was less apparent than that: the untended beard, little hairs growing out of his ears and nose, carelessly cut fingernails, a yellowish sheen on the white tie, unpolished shoes. As if he hadn't been home for days. And there was an irregular twitch of the eyelids that looked like the consequence of a lifelong strain.

'"One life for many lives. You can't calculate like that. Can you?" Amadeu spoke in a strained voice, and behind the words were both outrage and the fear of doing something wrong, something unforgivable.

'"You know what I think about that," I said. "I haven't changed my mind since then."

"'And if it were *really* many?'"

"'Do *you* have to do it?'"

"'On the contrary, I have to *prevent* it.'"

"'He knows too much?'"

"'She. She's become a danger. She wouldn't hold out. She would talk. The others think so.'"

"'Jorge too?' It was a shot in the dark and it hit home.

"'I don't want to talk about that.'"

'Silent minutes passed. The tea grew cold. It was tearing him up. Did he love her? Or was it simply because she was a human being?

"'What's her name? *Names are the invisible shadows with which others clothe us and we them.* Do you remember?'"

'Those were his own words in one of the many remarks he had amazed us all with.

'For a brief moment, the memory freed him and he smiled.

"'Estefânia Espinhosa. A name like a poem, isn't it?'"

"'How will you do it?'"

"'Over the border. Into the mountains. Don't ask me where.'"

'He disappeared through a garden gate and that was the last time I saw him alive.

'After what happened in the cemetery, I kept thinking about this nocturnal conversation. Was the woman Estefânia Espinhosa? Had she come from Spain, where she had heard the news of Amadeu's death? And when she walked towards O'Kelly, was she walking towards the man who had wanted to sacrifice her? Did they stand, not moving and not looking at each other, at the grave of the man who had sacrificed a lifelong friendship to save the woman with the poetic name?'

Father Bartolomeu turned on the light. Gregorius stood up.

'Wait,' said the priest. 'Now that I have told you all these things, you should also read this.' And from a bookcase, he took an ancient folder, held together by faded ribbons. 'You're a classical philologist, you can read this. It's a copy of Amadeu's speech at the graduation ceremony. He made it especially for me. Latin. Magnificent. Unbelievable. You saw the lectern in the auditorium, you say. He delivered it right there.

'We were prepared for something special, but nothing like this. From the first sentence, a breathless silence prevailed. And it became more silent and more breathless, this silence. The sentences from the pen of a seventeen-year-old iconoclast, who spoke as if he had already lived a whole life, were like whiplashes. I began to ask myself what would happen when the last word had been spoken. I was afraid. Afraid for this thin-skinned adventurer who knew what he was doing and yet didn't know, whose vulnerability was every bit equal to his verbal force. But also afraid for those of us who might not be up to it. The teachers sat there very stiff, very straight. Some had shut their eyes and seemed to be busy erecting a protective wall internally against this barrage of blasphemous accusations, a bulwark against a blasphemy that wouldn't have been thought possible in this room. Would they still talk to him? Would they resist the temptation to defend themselves with a condescension that turned him back into a child?

'The last sentence, you'll see, contains a threat, touching and frightening, for you imagined a volcano behind it spitting fire, and if it didn't, it might be destroyed by its own fervour. Amadeu didn't utter it loudly or with clenched fists, this sentence, but softly, almost gently, and to this day I don't know if it was a deliberate ploy to increase its effectiveness, after the firm tone in which he had delivered the bold, ruthless sentences, or if he had suddenly lost his nerve and, with the gentleness in his voice, wanted to ask for forgiveness in advance.

'The last word was spoken. Nobody moved. Amadeu straightened the sheets of paper, slowly, his eyes aimed at the lectern. Now there was nothing more for him to do, absolutely nothing. But you can't leave the lectern after such a speech without the audience taking sides in some sense. It would be a defeat of the worst sort: as if you hadn't said anything at all.

'I felt like standing up and applauding. If only because of the brilliance of this daredevil speech. But then I thought: you can't applaud blasphemy, polished as it may be. No one can, least of all a priest, a man of God. And so I remained sitting. The seconds passed. The silence couldn't have lasted much longer, otherwise it would be a catastrophe, for him as well as for us. Amadeu raised his head and stretched his back. His glance went to the stained-glass window and stayed there. It wasn't intentional, no dramatic trick, I'm sure of that. It was completely instinctive and illustrated, as you will see, his speech. It showed that he *was* his speech.

'Maybe that was enough to break the ice. But then something happened that seemed to everyone in the hall like a joking proof of God's existence: a dog started barking outside. At first, it was a short, dry bark that scolded us for our petty, humourless silence; then it turned into a long-drawn-out wail, as if echoing the misery of the whole occasion.

'Jorge O'Kelly burst out laughing, and after a second of fear, others followed him. I think that Amadeu was taken aback for a moment; humour was the last thing he had counted on. But it was Jorge who had started, so it had to be all right. The smile that appeared on Amadeu's face was a little forced, but it lasted, and as other dogs now joined in the wailing, he left the lectern.

'Only now did Senhor Cortês, the Rector, wake up from his paralysis. He stood up, went to Amadeu and shook his hand. Does a handshake show if a person is glad to know that it will be the last? Senhor Cortês said a few words to Amadeu, which were drowned out by the dogs' wailing. Amadeu answered, and as he spoke, he recovered his self-confidence; you could see that in his movements as he shoved the scandalous manuscript into the pocket of his frock coat as if stowing something precious in a safe place. Finally, he bent his head, looked the Rector straight in the eye, and turned to the door where Jorge was waiting for him. O'Kelly put his arm around his shoulders and pushed him out.

'Later, I saw the two of them in the park. Jorge was talking and gesticulating, Amadeu was listening. The pair of them reminded me of a trainer going over a fight with his protégé. Then Maria João came up. Jorge touched his friend on the shoulders with both hands and pushed him, laughing, towards the girl.

'The teachers hardly mentioned the speech afterwards. I wouldn't say that it was hushed up. Rather it was that we didn't find the words or the tone to exchange views about it. And maybe many were also glad about the unbearable heat that day. It meant we didn't have to say: "Impossible!" or "There may be some truth in it." Instead we could say: "What a scorcher!"'

19

How could it be, thought Gregorius, that he was riding in the hundred-year-old tram through the Lisbon evening with the feeling that he was departing, thirty-eight years too late, for Isfahan? He had got out on the way back from Father Bartolomeu and collected the dramas of Aeschylus and the poems of Horace from the bookshop. Then, as he walked to the hotel, something had bothered him and his steps became slower and more hesitant. For some minutes, he was assailed by the repulsive smell of rancid chicken fat from a street vendor near by. Despite this it had seemed enormously important to stand still *now* and find out what was troubling him. Had he ever before tried so intensely to understand himself?

Outside he was wide awake, but not yet inside. It sounded like something quite obvious when Father Bartolomeu had said that about Prado. As if every grown-up knew about inside and outside alertness. *Português.* Gregorius had pictured the Portuguese woman on the Kirchenfeldbrücke leaning on the ledge with outstretched arms, her heels sliding out of her shoes. *Estefânia Espinhosa. A name like a poem,* Prado had said. *Over the border. Into the mountains. Don't ask me where.* And then, suddenly, without understanding how it happened, Gregorius knew what he had felt in himself without realizing: it: he didn't want to read Prado's speech in the hotel room, but in the abandoned Liceu, where he had delivered it. There, where the Hebrew Bible lay in the drawer on his sweater. There, with rats and bats.

Why did he feel so strongly that it would have far-reaching consequences if, instead of going on to the hotel, he retraced his steps to the Liceu? Shortly before it closed, he had slipped into a hardware shop and bought the the most powerful torch they had. And now he sat again in one of the old trams and rattled to the underground that would take him out to the Liceu.

When he had decided to return there, Gregorius had in his mind's eye the cone of sunlight that had strayed into Senhor Cortês's office at noon. In the darkness of early evening the school building lay silent like a sunken ship at the bottom of the sea.

He sat down on a bench and thought of the student who had broken into the Bern Gymnasium at night a long time ago, and from the Rector's office had made phone calls all over the world costing thousands of francs, out of revenge. Hans Gmür was his name and he answered to it with defiance. Gregorius had paid the bill and persuaded Kägi not to press charges. He had met with Gmür in town and tried to find out what he wanted to avenge. It didn't work. 'Just revenge,' the boy simply kept saying. He looked exhausted behind his apple cake and seemed consumed by a resentment as old as himself. When they parted, Gregorius had watched him as he walked away. Somehow, he admired Gmür a little, he later told Florence, or at least envied him.

'Just imagine: he sits in the dark at Kägi's desk and calls Sydney, Belém, Santiago, even Peking. Always the embassies where they speak German. He has nothing to say, absolutely nothing. He simply wants to hear the open line buzz and feel the sinfully expensive seconds pass. Rather splendid, isn't it?'

'And you of all people say that? A man who would like to pay his bills even before they arrive? And not owe anybody anything?'

'Exactly,' he had said. 'Exactly.'

Florence had adjusted her ultra-stylish glasses, as she always did when he said such things.

Now Gregorius switched on the torch and followed the beam of light to the entrance of the Liceu. In the dark, the creaking of the door sounded much louder than it had in the daytime, and it also made him sound much more like an intruder. The noise of startled bats flooded through the building. Gregorius waited until it had subsided before he went through the swing door to the ground floor. He swept the light like a broom over the stone floor of the corridor, to avoid stepping on a dead rat. It was chilly here at this time of day and he went first to the Rector's office to get his sweater.

He looked at the Hebrew Bible. It had belonged to Father Bartolomeu. In 1970, when the Liceu was closed as a hotbed of communists, the priest and Senhor Cortês's successor had stood in the Rector's empty office, furious and impotent. 'We needed to do something, something symbolic,' the priest had said. And so he had left his Bible in the desk drawer. The Rector had looked at him and grinned. 'Perfect. The Lord will get them,' he had said.

Gregorius sat down in the auditorium on the bench reserved for the school staff, where Senhor Cortês had listened to Prado's speech with a stony expression. He took Father Bartolomeu's folder out of the bookshop bag, removed the bands and unfolded the sheets which Amadeu had straightened on the lectern after the speech, enveloped in embarrassed, horrified silence. It was written in the same black ink he had seen on the letter Prado had sent to Mélodie from Oxford. Gregorius aimed the beam of the torch at the shimmering yellowish paper and began to read.

REVERENCE AND LOATHING FOR THE WORD OF GOD
I would not like to live in a world without cathedrals. I need their beauty and grandeur. I need them against the vulgarity of

*the world. I want to look up at the illuminated church windows
and let myself be blinded by the unearthly colours. I need their
lustre: I need it against the dirty colours of the uniforms. I want
to let myself be wrapped in the austere coolness of the churches. I
need their imperious silence. I need it against the witless bellowing
of the barracks yard and the witty chatter of the yes-men. I want
to hear the rustling of the organ, this deluge of ethereal tones. I
need it against the shrill farce of marches. I love praying people.
I need the sight of them. I need it against the malicious poison
of the superficial and the thoughtless. I want to read the powerful
words of the Bible. I need the unreal force of their poetry. I need
it against the dilapidation of the language and the dictatorship
of slogans. A world without these things would be a world I would
not like to live in.*

*But there is also another world I don't want to live in: the
world where the body and independent thought are disparaged,
and the best things we can experience are denounced as sins. The
world that demands love of tyrants, slavemasters, and cutthroats,
whether their brutal boot steps reverberate through the streets with
a deafening echo or they slink with feline silence like cowardly
shadows through the streets and pierce their victims in the heart
with flashing steel. What is most absurd is that people are exhorted
from the pulpit to forgive such creatures and even to love them.
Even if someone really could do it: it would mean an unparalleled
dishonesty and merciless self-denial whose cost would be total
deformity. This commandment, this crazy, perverse commandment
to love your enemy is apt to break people, to rob them of all
courage and self-confidence and to make them supple in the hands
of the tyrants so they won't find the strength to stand up to them,
with weapons, if necessary.*

*I revere the word of God for I love its poetic force. I loathe the
word of God for I hate its cruelty. The love is a difficult love for
it must incessantly separate the luminosity of the words and the
violent verbal subjugation by a complacent God. The hatred is a*

difficult hatred for how can you allow yourself to hate words that are part of the melody of life in this part of the world? Words that taught us early on what reverence is? Words that were like a beacon to us when we began to feel that the visible life can't be all of life? Words without which we wouldn't be what we are?

But let us not forget: These are the same words that call on Abraham to slaughter his own son like an animal. What do we do with our rage when we read that? What should we think of such a God? A God who blames Job for arguing with Him, he who knows and understands nothing? Who, after all, was it who created him like that? And why is it less unjust if God hurls someone into misery for no reason than if a common mortal does? In fact, isn't Job's complaint perfectly justified?

The poetry of the divine words is so overwhelming that it silences everything and every protest becomes wretched yapping. That's why you can't just put *away the Bible, but must* throw *it away when you have enough of its unreasonable demands and of the slavery it inflicts on us. It is a joyless God far from life speaking out of it, a God who wants to constrict the enormous compass of a human life – the big circle that can be drawn when it is left free – to the single, shrunken point of obedience. Grief ridden and sin laden, parched with subjugation and the indignity of confession, with the cross of ashes on our forehead, we are to go to the grave in the thousandfold refuted hope of a better life at His Side. But how could it be better on the side of One who just robbed us of all joy and freedom?*

And yet they are bewitchingly beautiful, the words that come from Him and go to Him. How I loved them as an altar boy! How drunk they made me in the glow of the altar candles! How clear, how evident it seemed that these words were the measure of all things! How incomprehensible it seemed to me that other words were also important to people, every one of them could mean only damnable dissipation and the loss of the essential! Even today I stand still when I hear a Gregorian chant and for an idle moment

I am sad that the old drunkenness has been wiped out irrevocably by rebellion. A rebellion that shot up in me like a flame the first time I heard these two words: sacrificium intellectus.

How are we to be happy without curiosity, without questions, doubt and arguments? Without joy in thinking? The two words, like a sword-stroke cutting off our head, they mean nothing less than a demand to live our feelings and acts against our thinking, they are the summons to a complete split, the order to sacrifice what is the core of our happiness: the internal unity and coherence of our life. The slave in the galley is chained, but he can think what he wants. But what He, our God, demands of us is that we force our slavery into our depths with our own hands and do it willingly and joyfully. Can there be a greater mockery?

In His omnipresence, the Lord observes us day and night, every hour, every minute, every second, He keeps a ledger of our acts and thoughts, He never lets us alone, never spares us a moment completely to ourselves. What is man without secrets? Without thoughts and wishes that only he, he alone, knows? The torturers, of the Inquisition and of today, they know: cut off his retreat, never turn off the light, never leave him alone, deprive him of sleep and silence: he will talk. That torture steals our soul means it demolishes the solitude with ourselves that we need like air to breathe. Did the Lord our God not consider that He was stealing our soul with His unbridled curiosity and revolting voyeurism, a soul that should be immortal?

Who could in all seriousness want to be immortal? Who would like to live for all eternity? How boring and stale it must be to know that what happens today, this month, this year, doesn't matter: endless more days, months, years will come. Endless, literally. If that was how it was, would anything count? *We would no longer need to calculate time, nothing could be missed, we wouldn't have to rush. It would be the same if we did something today or tomorrow, all the same. A million omissions would become nothing before eternity, and it would make no sense to regret something for there would always be time to make up for it. Nor could we live for the day, for this happiness lives on the awareness of passing time; the idler is an adventurer in the face of death, a crusader against the dictate of haste. When there is always and everywhere time for all and everything: How should there still be room for the joy of wasting time?*

A feeling is no longer the same when it comes the second time. It dies through the awareness of its return. We become tired and weary of our feelings when they come too often and last too long. In the immortal soul, a gigantic weariness and a flagrant despair must grow in view of the certainty that it will never end, never. Feelings want to develop and we through them. They are what they are because they retreat from what they used to be and because they flow towards a future where they will diverge. If this stream flowed into infinity, thousands of feelings must emerge in us that we, used to a time, cannot even imagine. So that we really don't know what is promised us when we hear of the eternal life. How would it be to be us in eternity, devoid of the consolation of being some day released from the need to be us? We don't know, and it is a blessing that we never will. For one thing we do know: it would be hell, this paradise of immortality.

It is death that gives the moment its beauty and its horror. Only through death is time a living time. Why does the Lord, *the omniscient God, not know that? Why does He threaten us with an endlessness that must mean unbearable desolation?*

I would not like to live in a world without cathedrals. I need the lustre of their windows, their cool stillness, their imperious silence. I need the deluge of the organ and the sacred devotion of praying people. I need the holiness of words, the grandeur of great poetry. All that I need. But just as much I need the freedom and hostility against everything cruel. For the one is nothing without the other. And no one may force me to choose.

Gregorius read the text three times with increasing

amazement. It displayed a rhetorical ability and stylistic elegance equal to Cicero; a force of thought and an honesty of feelings reminiscent of Augustine. Comparable virtuosity on an instrument played by a seventeen-year-old, he thought, would have had people talking of a child prodigy.

As for the closing sentence, Father Bartolomeu was right: it was moving, the threat. Who did it refer to? He would always choose hostility to the cruel, this boy. If necessary, he would sacrifice cathedrals to it. The godless priest would build his own cathedrals, if only those of golden words, to defy the vulgarity of the world. His hostility to cruelty would become even more bitter.

Perhaps the threat was not so empty? When he stood at the lectern, had Amadeu unknowingly anticipated what he would do thirty-five years later: refuse to comply with the plans of the Resistance movement, and Jorge's plans, and save Estefânia Espinhosa?

Gregorius wished he could hear his voice and feel the molten lava on which his words flowed. He took out Prado's book and shone the torch on the portrait. An altar boy he had been, a child whose first passion had been for the altar candles and the sacred words that had seemed sacrosanct in their bright glow. But then words from other books had displaced them, words that had run riot in him until he had become someone who placed all strange words on the gold scales and crafted his own.

Gregorius buttoned his coat, shoved his cold hands in the opposite sleeves and lay down on the bench. He was exhausted. Exhausted from the effort of listening and the fever of understanding. But also exhausted from the inner alertness that this fever generated. For the first time he missed the bed in his Bern flat where, reading, he would wait for the moment when he could finally fall asleep. He thought of the Kirchenfeldbrücke before the Portuguese woman had stood on the bridge and transformed it. He thought of his Latin books on the desk in the classroom. Ten days ago now. Who had introduced the *ablativus absolutus* in his place? Explained the structure of *The Iliad*? In the Hebrew class, they had recently discussed Luther's choice of words when he decided to let God be a *jealous* God. He had explained to the students the enormous distance between the German and the Hebrew text, a breathtaking distance. Who would now continue this discussion?

Gregorius was freezing. The last underground train had left long ago. There was no telephone or taxi and it would take hours to walk back to the hotel. Beyond the door of the auditorium, the soft sweeping rustle of the bats was heard. Now and then, a rat squeaked. Beyond that, the silence of the tomb.

He was thirsty and was glad to find a sweet in his coat pocket. When he shoved it in his mouth, he pictured Natalie Rubin's hand offering him the brightly coloured sweet. For a split second, it had looked as if she wanted to put it in his mouth herself. Or had he only imagined that?

She stretched and laughed when he asked her how he was to find Maria João, when nobody seemed to know her last name. They had been standing for days beside a cooked chicken stall at the cemetery of Prazères, he and Natalie, for it had been there that Mélodie had last seen Maria. It became winter and it started snowing. The train for Geneva started to draw out of Bern railway station. Why had he boarded? asked the stern conductor, and in first class to boot. Frantically Gregorius searched all his pockets for the tickets. When he awoke and sat up with stiff limbs, it was growing light outside.

20

In the first underground train, he was the only passenger for a while and the train seemed to be just another episode in the silent, imaginary world of the Liceu where he had spent the night. Then Portuguese people started to board the train, working people, who had nothing to do with Amadeu de Prado. Gregorius was grateful for their sober, surly faces akin to the faces of people who got on the bus on the Länggasse early in the morning. Could he live here? Live and work, whatever that might be?

The hotel porter observed him anxiously. Was he all right? Had something happened to him? Then he handed him a thick envelope with a red wax seal. It had been delivered yesterday afternoon by an old woman who had waited for him until late that night.

Adriana, thought Gregorius. Of all the people he had met here, only she would seal a letter like that. But the porter's description didn't fit her. And she wouldn't have come herself, not a woman like her. It must have been the housekeeper, the maid whose task would be to remove all the dust from Amadeu's room in the attic so that nothing indicated the passage of time. Everything was fine, Gregorius assured the porter once again and went upstairs.

Queria vê-lo! I would like to see you. *Adriana Soledade de Almeida Prado.* That was all the letter said. Written on expensive stationery, in the same black ink that Amadeu had used, in a hand that looked both awkward and affected. It was as if the writer had laboured over every word. Had she forgotten that he knew no Portuguese and that they had spoken French with each other?

For a moment, Gregorius was scared by the laconic words that sounded like an order summoning him to the blue house. But then he saw the pale face and black eyes with the bitter look, he saw the woman walking on the rim of the abyss through the room of the brother who could not be allowed to die, and the words no longer sounded imperious, but rather like a cry for help from the hoarse throat with the mysterious black velvet ribbon.

He examined the black lion, apparently the heraldic symbol of the Prados, embossed on top of the stationery, right in the middle. The lion suited their father's sternness and the dreariness of his death, it suited Adriana's black shape, and it also suited the merciless audacity in Amadeu's nature. But it didn't suit Mélodie, the light-footed, flighty girl who was the result of unusual carelessness on the bank of the Amazon. Or their mother, Maria Piedade Reis. Why didn't anybody ever talk about her?

Gregorius took a shower and slept until noon. He was pleased that he had managed to look after his own needs first and let Adriana wait. Could he have done that in Bern?

Later, on the way to the blue house, he called at Júlio Simões's second-hand bookshop and asked him where he could buy a Persian grammar. And what was the best language school if he should decide to learn Portuguese.

Simões laughed. 'All at the same time, Portuguese and Persian?'

Gregorius's irritation lasted only a moment. The man couldn't know that, at this point in his life, there was no difference between Portuguese and Persian; that in a certain sense, they were one and the same language. Simões also enquired about his search for Prado and whether Coutinho had been able to help him. An hour later, just before four o'clock, Gregorius rang the bell of the blue house.

The woman who opened the door might have been in her mid-fifties.

'*Sou Clotilde, a criada,*' she said. I'm the maid.

She ran one hand, marked by a life of housework, through her grey hair and checked whether the bun was in place.

'*A Senhora está no salão,*' she said and led the way.

Like the first time, Gregorius was overwhelmed by the size and elegance of the parlour. His eye fell on the grandfather clock. It still showed six twenty-three. Adriana was sitting at the table in the corner. The acrid smell of medicine or perfume hung in the air again.

'You're late,' she said.

The letter had prepared Gregorius for such stern words. As he sat down at the table, he felt astonished at how well he coped with this old woman's acerbic style. How easy it was for him to see her whole manner as an expression of pain and loneliness.

'I'm here now,' he said.

'Yes,' she said. And then, after a while, once more: 'Yes.'

Without a sound and unnoticed by Gregorius, the maid had come to the table.

'*Clotilde,*' said Adriana, '*liga o aparelho.*' Turn on the machine.

Only now did Gregorius notice the box. It was an ancient tape recorder, a monster with tape spools as big as plates. Clotilde pulled the tape through the slit in the tape head and fastened it in the empty spool. Then she pushed a button and the spools began to turn. She left the room.

For a while, only crackling and swooshing were heard. Then a woman's voice said:

'*Porquê não dizem nada?*' Why do you say nothing?

Gregorius didn't understand any more, for what now came out of the machine was to his ears a chaotic jumble of voices, covered by swooshing and loud sounds that must have been caused by clumsy handling of the microphone.

'Amadeu,' said Adriana as a single male voice was heard. Her usual hoarseness had intensified as she uttered the name. She ran her hand over her throat and tightened the black velvet ribbon as if she wanted to press it tighter to her skin.

Gregorius put his ear to the loudspeaker. The voice was different from what he had imagined. Father Bartolomeu had talked of a soft baritone voice. The pitch was right, but the timbre was harsh, you felt that this man could speak with cutting sharpness. Did it also have something to do with the fact that the only words Gregorius understood were '*não quero*', I don't want to?

'Fátima,' said Adriana, when a new voice emerged from the jumble. The contemptuous way she uttered the name said everything. Fátima had been in the way. Not only in this conversation. In every conversation. She hadn't been worthy of Amadeu. She had illegitimately laid claim to him. It would have been better if she had never entered his life.

Fátima had a soft, dark voice and you observed that it wasn't easy for her to prevail. In the softness, was there also the demand to be listened to with special attention and tolerance? Or was it merely the swooshing that produced this impression? Nobody interrupted her, and ultimately the others let her have her say.

'Everyone is always so considerate of her, so damn considerate,' said Adriana, as Fátima was still speaking. 'As if her lisp were a dreadful fate that excused everything, all religious sentimentalism, simply everything.'

Gregorius hadn't heard the lisp, it had drowned in the accompanying static.

The next voice belonged to Mélodie. She talked at a fast pace, seemed to blow deliberately into the microphone and then burst out laughing. Adriana turned away in disgust and looked out of the window. When she heard her own voice, she quickly reached for the switch and turned it off.

For a few minutes, Adriana looked at the machine that had brought the past into the present. It was the same look as on Sunday, when she had looked down at Amadeu's books and had spoken to the dead brother. She must have heard the recording hundreds, perhaps thousands of times. She knew every word, every rustle, every crack and swoosh. It was as if now, too, she was sitting with the others, over in the family home where Mélodie now lived. So why should she speak except in the present tense or in a past tense that was as if it were only yesterday?

'We couldn't believe our eyes when Mamã brought the thing home. She's impossible with machines, just impossible. Afraid of them. Always thinks she'll break them. And then she brings home a tape recorder of all things, one of the first ones you could buy.

'"No, no," Amadeu said when we talked about it later. "It's not because she wants to immortalize our voices. It's something quite different. It's to make us pay attention to her again."

'He's right. Now that Papá is dead and we have the office here, her life must seem empty to her. Rita hangs around and seldom visits her. Fátima does go to see her every week, but that doesn't help Mamã much.

'"She'd prefer to see you," she says to Amadeu when she comes back.

'Amadeu doesn't want to visit her any more. He doesn't say it, but I know. He's a coward when it comes to Mamã. The only cowardice in him. He who usually faces up to unpleasant things, all of them.'

Adriana gripped her throat. For a moment, it seemed as if she'd start talking about the secret hidden behind the velvet ribbon, and Gregorius held his breath. But the moment passed and now Adriana's look returned to the present.

Could he listen again to what Amadeu says on the tape? asked Gregorius.

'*Não me admira nada*,' That doesn't surprise me. Adriana began to quote and then repeated every one of Amadeu's words from memory. It was more than a quotation. It was an impersonation which not even a good actor could have bettered. It was perfect. Adriana *was* Amadeu.

Gregorius understood *não quero* and could make out something new: *ouvir a minha voz de fora*. Hearing my voice from outside.

As she came to the end, Adriana began to translate. That the whole thing was possible, no, that didn't surprise him, said Prado. He knew the technical principle from medicine. *But I don't like what it does with words.* He didn't want to hear his voice from outside, he didn't want to inflict that on himself, he disliked himself enough already. And he hated the permanence of the spoken word: you usually spoke in the liberating awareness that most of it would be forgotten. He found it frightening to have to think that everything would be preserved, every thoughtless word, every tasteless remark. It reminded him of the indiscretion of God.

'He only mutters that,' said Adriana. 'Mamã doesn't like such things and it confuses Fátima.'

The machine, it destroyed the freedom of forgetting, Prado said. *But I'm not scolding you, Mamã, it's also a lot of fun. You mustn't take everything your clever son says so seriously.*

'Why the hell do you always try to appease her?' Adriana flew off the handle. 'When she tortured you so much in her gentle way! Why can't you simply stand up for what you think? Like you always do! *Always!*'

Could he listen to the tape once more, for the voice? asked Gregorius. The request touched her. As she rewound the tape, she had the face of a little girl, surprised and happy that the grown-up found it as important as she did.

Listening to Prado's words, Gregorius put the book with the portrait on the table and stared at it until the voice seemed to come from the subject's lips. Then he looked at Adriana and was scared. She must have been looking at him constantly and he saw that her face had opened; all the severity and bitterness was gone and what remained was an expression welcoming him into the world of her love and admiration for Amadeu. '*Be careful. With Adriana, I mean,*' he heard Mariana Eça say.

'Come,' said Adriana. 'I'd like to show you where we work.'

Her step was firmer and faster than before when she led the way down to the ground floor. She was going to her brother in the office, she was needed, no time to lose; *someone who has pain or fear can't wait*, Amadeu used to say. Unerringly, she put the key in the lock, opened the door and turned on all the lights.

Thirty-one years ago, Prado had treated his last patients here. A fresh paper cloth was spread on the examining table. On the instrument cabinet were the sort of syringes no longer in use today. In the middle of the desk sat an index card file of patients, one of the cards inserted at an angle. Next to it the stethoscope. In the wastepaper basket a wad of bloody cottonwool. Hanging from the door, two white coats. Not a particle of dust.

Adriana took one of the white coats off the hook and put it on. 'He always hangs his on the left, he's left-handed,' she said as she did up the buttons.

Gregorius began to fear the moment when she got stuck in the past, where she moved like a sleepwalker. But it wasn't yet time for that. With a relaxed face, that began to glow with a zeal for work, she opened the medicine cabinet and checked the stocks.

'We're almost out of morphine,' she murmured. 'I'll have to call Jorge.'

She closed the cabinet, stroked the paper cover on the examining table, straightened the scales with her toes, checked whether the washbasin was clean, and then stood at the desk with the card file. Without touching the crooked card or even looking at it, she began talking about the patient.

'Why did she go to this bungler, this back-street abortionist? Well, she doesn't know how awful it was for me. But everybody knows that Amadeu takes good care of you in such cases. That he doesn't give a damn about the law when a woman's in trouble. Etelvina and another child, that's quite impossible. Next week, says Amadeu, we have to decide whether she needs follow-up treatment in the hospital.'

His older sister had an abortion and had almost died from it, Gregorius heard João Eça say. It was eerie to him. Here, downstairs, Adriana sank even deeper into the past than upstairs in Amadeu's room. Upstairs was a past which she could attend only from outside. With the book, she had erected a belated memorial to it. When her brother had sat there smoking and drinking coffee at the desk, the old-fashioned fountain pen in his hand, she couldn't reach him, and Gregorius was sure she had burned with jealousy at the solitude of his thoughts. Here, in the office, it had been different. She had heard everything he said, had discussed the patients with him and had assisted him in his work. Here he was all hers. For many years, this had been the centre of her life, the place of her most living present. Her face, which, despite the traces of age was young and beautiful at this moment, expressed her wish to be able to remain for ever in that present, not to have to leave the eternity of those happy years.

The moment of awakening wasn't far off. Adriana's fingers groped uncertainly to make sure the white coat was buttoned up. The gleam of the eyes began to die out, the slack skin of the old face drooped, the bliss of time past departed the room.

Gregorius didn't want her to wake up and return to the

cold solitude of her life, where Clotilde had to put on the tape for her. Not now; it would be too cruel. And so he risked it.

'Rui Luís Mendes. Did Amadeu treat him here?'

It was as if he had taken a syringe from the tray and injected her with a drug that raced through the dark veins. A wave of trembling went through her, the bony body shook feverishly and her breathing was heavy. For a moment Gregorius was alarmed and cursed his stupidity. But then the convulsions died down, Adriana's body grew still, the flickering look subsided, and now she went over to the treatment table. Gregorius waited for the question of how he knew about Mendes. But Adriana was a long way back in the past.

She put her flat hand on the paper covering the treatment table. 'It was here. Right here. I can see him lying there as if it were only minutes ago.'

And then she began to talk. The museum-like rooms came alive with the force and passion of her words; the heat and the disaster of that distant day when Amadeu Inácio de Almeida Prado, lover of cathedrals and merciless enemy of all cruelty, had done something, the consequences of which would never leave him, something he couldn't cope with and couldn't put behind him, even with the ferocious clarity of his intellect. Something that lay like a sticky shadow over the last years of his smouldering life.

It had happened on a hot, damp August day in 1965, shortly after Prado's forty-fifth birthday. In February, Humberto Delgado, the former candidate of the centre-left opposition in the presidential election of 1958, was murdered when he tried to return from Algerian exile across the Spanish border. The Spanish and Portuguese police were blamed for the murder, but everybody was convinced that it had been the work of the secret police, the Polícia Internacional de Defesa do Estado, PIDE, that had controlled everything ever since António de Salazar's senility had become obvious. In Lisbon, illegally printed flyers circulated placing responsibility for the bloody act on Rui Luís Mendes, a feared officer of the secret police.

'We also had one in the mailbox,' said Adriana. 'Amadeu stared at the photo of Mendes as if he wanted to annihilate him with his look. Then he tore the flyer to shreds and flushed them down the toilet.'

It was early afternoon, and a silent, ominous heat lay over the city. Prado was taking his daily nap which lasted for half an hour almost to the minute. It was the only point in the whole cycle of day and night when he managed to fall asleep easily. During this time, he always had a deep and dreamless sleep, was deaf to all noise, and if anything woke him, he was disturbed and disoriented for a while. Adriana guarded this sleep like a shrine.

Amadeu had just fallen asleep when Adriana heard shrill shouts in the street, shattering the midday silence. She dashed to the window. A man lay on the pavement in front of the house next door. The people who stood around him and blocked Adriana's view were yelling at one another and gesticulating wildly. It seemed to Adriana that one of the women kicked the body with the tips of her shoes. Two big men finally managed to push the people back; they picked up the man and carried him to the door of Prado's office. Only now did Adriana recognize him and her heart stopped: it was Mendes, the man on the flyer, whose photo was captioned: *o carniceiro de Lisboa*, the Butcher of Lisbon.

'At that moment, I knew exactly what would happen. I knew it down to the last detail. It was as if the future had already happened – as if it were already contained in my fear as an existing fact, and now it would simply be a matter of expanding chronologically. It was even horribly clear to me that the next hours would change the course of Amadeu's life and present him with the hardest test he had ever had to endure.'

The men who carried Mendes leaned on the doorbell and it seemed to Adriana that, with the shrill sound now swelling to an unbearable pitch, the violence and brutality of the dictatorship which so far – not without a bad conscience – they had been able to stave off, now made its way into the elegant, guarded silence of her house. For two or three seconds, she considered simply doing nothing and playing dead. But she knew Amadeu would never forgive her for that. So she opened his bedroom door and went to wake him.

'He didn't say a word; he knew I wouldn't have woken him up if it wasn't a matter of life and death. "In the consulting room," I simply said. Barefoot he staggered down the stairs and rushed to the washbasin where he scooped cold water on to his face. Then he went to the examining table, where Mendes lay.

'For two or three seconds he stared in disbelief at the leaden, limp face with the beads of sweat on the forehead. He turned round and looked at me for confirmation. I nodded. For a moment, he raised his hands to his face, petrified. Then a jolt went through my brother. With both hands, he ripped off Mendes's shirt, popping the buttons. He put his ear to the hairy chest, then listened to it with the stethoscope I handed him.

'"Digitalis!"

'He said only this one word but in his choked voice was all the hatred he fought against, a hatred like flashing steel. As I filled the syringe, he massaged Mendes's heart. I heard the dull crack when the ribs broke.

'When I handed him the syringe, our eyes met for a split second. How I loved him at that moment, my brother! With the enormous force of his inflexible iron will, he struggled against the wish to simply let the man on the examining table die, the man who almost certainly had the whole merciless oppression of the state on his conscience. How easy it would have been, how unbelievably easy! A few seconds of inaction would have been enough. Just to do nothing! *Nothing!*

'After Amadeu had rubbed disinfectant on Mendes's chest, he hesitated and shut his eyes. Never, neither before nor after, have I observed a person mastering himself like that. Then Amadeu opened his eyes and thrust the needle directly into Mendes's heart. It looked like the death blow and I froze. He did it with the breathtaking certainty with which he gave every injection; you had the feeling that, in such moments, human bodies were made of glass for him. Without the slightest tremor, with enormous steadiness, he continued to inject the drug into Mendes's heart muscle to start it up again. When he pulled out the syringe, all the violence had been wiped out of him. He put on a dressing and listened to Mendes's heart with the stethoscope. Then he looked at me and nodded. 'The ambulance,' he said.

'They came and carried Mendes out on a stretcher. Just before it reached the door, he came to, opened his eyes, and encountered Amadeu's look. I was amazed to see how calmly, even dispassionately, my brother looked at him. Maybe it was also exhaustion. In any case, he leaned against the door like someone who has weathered a tough crisis and can now count on having some peace.

'But the opposite happened. Amadeu knew nothing of the people who had gathered around the collapsed Mendes out in the street, and I had forgotten about them. So, it took us by surprise when we suddenly heard hysterical voices shouting: *"Traidor! Traidor!"* They must have seen that Mendes was still alive on the orderlies' stretcher, and now they were venting their rage on the person who had saved his life and reprieved him from the punishment he deserved.

'As before, when he had recognized Mendes, Amadeu raised his hands to his face. But now, it happened slowly, having always carried his head high, he lowered it, and nothing could

have expressed better his weariness and grief at what he saw
was in store for him.

'But neither weariness nor grief could dull his mind. With
a confident grip, he took the white coat he hadn't had time
to put on before, off the hook, and slipped it on. Only later
did I grasp the significance of this: he knew, without thinking,
that he had to appear to the people as a doctor and that they
would recognize him best as that if he wore the customary
garment.

'When he appeared at the front door, the shouting ceased.
For a while, he just stood there, head down, his hands in the
pockets of the white coat. Everybody waited for him to say
something in his defence. Amadeu raised his head and looked
around. It was as if his bare feet didn't so much touch the
pavement as press into it.

'"*Sou médico*," he said and once again, imploring, "*Sou
médico*."

'I recognized three or four of our patients from the
neighbourhood, who looked down, embarrassed.

'"*É um assassino!*" someone now yelled.

'"*Carniceiro!*" yelled another.

'I saw Amadeu's shoulders lift and fall in heavy breaths.

'"*É um ser humano, uma pessoa*," He is a human being, a
person, he said loud and clear, and probably only I, who knew
every nuance of his voice, heard the soft tremor when he
repeated, '*Pessoa.*'

'Right after that, a tomato burst on his white coat. As far
as I know, it was the first and only time anyone ever attacked
Amadeu physically. I can't say how much this attack had to
do with what happened next – how much it contributed to
the deep shock triggered in him by this scene at the door. But
I suppose it wasn't much compared with what now occurred:
a woman emerged out of the crowd, stood before him, and
spat in his face.

'If it had only happened once, it might have been seen as an impulsive act, like a furious, uncontrollable twitch. But the woman spat several times and kept on spitting, as if she were spitting her soul out of her body and drowning Amadeu in the slime of her disgust, trickling slowly down his face.

'He withstood this new attack with his eyes closed. But, just like me, he must have recognized the woman: it was Inês Salomão, the wife of a patient who had died of cancer after years of treatment and countless house calls, for which Amadeu hadn't charged a centavo. What ingratitude! I thought at first. But then I saw in her eyes the pain and despair that fuelled the rage, and I understood: she was spitting at him *because* she was grateful for what he had done. He had been a hero, a guardian angel, a divine emissary, who had guided her through the darkness of the disease where she would have lost her way if she had been on her own. And it was he, he of all people, who had stood in the way of justice and allowed Mendes to live. This thought had caused such turmoil in the soul of this misshapen, rather narrow-minded woman that she could relieve herself only with an outburst, and the longer it lasted, the more it took on something mythical, a significance that went far beyond Amadeu.

'As if the crowd felt that a line had been crossed, it broke up; the people went away, eyes down. Amadeu closed the door and returned to the consulting room. I washed the worst off his face with a handkerchief. Over there, at the washbasin, he held his face under the running tap. He turned it on so hard that the water sprayed out of the basin in all directions. The face he rubbed dry was pale. I believe that, at that moment, he would have given anything to be able to weep. He stood there and waited for the tears, but they wouldn't come. Since Fátima's death four years before, he hadn't wept once. He took a few stiff steps towards me as if he had to learn how to walk again. Then he stood before me, in his eyes the tears that wouldn't flow, he grabbed my shoulders with both hands and leaned his forehead against mine. We may have stood like that for three or four minutes, and they are some of the most precious minutes of my life.'

Adriana fell silent. Once again, she lived these minutes. Her face twitched, but her tears wouldn't come either. She went over to the washbasin, let water run into her cupped palms and splashed it over her face. Slowly, she passed the towel over her eyes, cheeks and mouth. As if the story demanded it she went back to the same place before continuing. She also put her hand again on the examining table.

Amadeu, she said, took shower after shower. Then he sat down at the desk, took a fresh sheet of paper and unscrewed his fountain pen.

Nothing happened. Not a single word appeared.

'That was the worst thing of all,' said Adriana, 'to have to watch how the event had so upset him that it had robbed him of words.'

When asked if he wanted something to eat, he nodded absently. Then he went into the bathroom and sponged the traces of tomato off the coat. He came to the dinner table in the white coat – that had never happened before – incessantly wiping the wet patches. Adriana felt that this wiping was an instinctive action, not one he performed deliberately. She was afraid that he would lose his mind before her very eyes and sit there like that for ever, a lost-looking man, always trying mentally to wipe away the filth pelted at him by people to whom he had given all his skill and all his vitality, day and night.

Suddenly, in the middle of the meal, he ran into the bathroom and vomited in a seemingly endless series of retching convulsions. He wanted to lie down, he said flatly afterwards.

'I would like to have taken him in my arms,' said Adriana.

'But it was impossible. It was as if he were burning and everyone who came near him would be scorched.'

The next two days, it was almost as if nothing had happened. Prado was only a little more tense than usual and his kindness to the patients had something ethereal and unreal about it. Now and then he stopped in the middle of doing something and gazed straight ahead with an empty, vague look on his face, like an epileptic during a seizure. And every time he went to the door of the waiting room, there was a hesitation, as if he were afraid to find someone from the crowd who had accused him of treason.

On the third day, he fell ill. Adriana found him trembling at the kitchen table at dawn. He seemed to have aged overnight and didn't want to see anyone. He gratefully handed everything over to her to arrange and sank into a deep, ghostly apathy. He didn't shave or get dressed. The only visitor he allowed was Jorge, the pharmacist. But he hardly said a word to him either, and Jorge knew him too well to press him. Adriana had told him what had happened, and he had nodded silently.

'A week later, a letter arrived from Mendes. Amadeu put it on the hall table, unopened. It lay there for two days. Early on the morning of the third day, he put it, still unopened, in an envelope and addressed it to the sender. He insisted on taking it to the post office himself. They didn't open until nine, I objected. Nevertheless, he left the house with the envelope in his hand. I watched him go and then waited at the window until he came back some hours later. He walked more erectly than when he had left. In the kitchen he checked whether he could bear the taste of coffee again. He could. Then he shaved, got dressed and sat down at the desk.'

Adriana fell silent and her face was closed. She looked forlornly at the examining table where Amadeu had stood when he pushed the life-saving needle into Mendes's heart with a movement like a death blow. As the story came to an end, time also ended for her.

In that moment, it seemed to Gregorius, too, as if time had

been cut off right in front of his nose. He had the impression of having caught a brief glance of the hardship Adriana had lived with for more than thirty years: the hardship of having to live in a time that had long ago come to an end.

Now she took her hand off the examining table and as she did so she also seemed to lose the link with the past, which was her only present. At first, she didn't know what to do with her hand, then she thrust it into the pocket of the white coat. The movement made the coat stand out as something special; now it looked to Gregorius like a magical wrap which Adriana put on to escape from her silent, uneventful present and to be revived in the distant flaming past. Now that this past was extinguished, the coat looked as forlorn on her as a costume in the wardrobe room of an abandoned theatre.

Gregorius could no longer bear the sight of her lifelessness. He would have liked to take himself off into the city, to a pub with a lot of voices, laughter and music. To the kind of place he usually avoided.

'Amadeu sits down at the desk,' he said. 'What does he write?'

The glow of her former life returned to Adriana's face. But her joy of being able to speak of him again was mixed with something else, something Gregorius recognized only slowly. It was anger. Not a short-lived anger kindled by a trifle that flares up and soon goes out, but a profound, creeping anger, like a smouldering fire.

'I wished he hadn't written it. Not even thought it. A creeping poison pulsed in his veins from that day on. It changed him. Destroyed him. He didn't want to show it to me. But he was so different afterwards. I took it out of his drawer and read it while he was asleep. It was the first and last time I did such a thing. For now the poison was also in me. The poison of offended respect, of destroyed trust. And things were never the same between us again.

'If only he hadn't been so mercilessly honest with himself! So possessed by the struggle against self-deception! *Bearing the truth about himself can be demanded of man,* he used to say. It was like a religious confession. A vow that bound him to Jorge. A credo that ultimately undermined even that sacred friendship, that damned sacred friendship. I don't know the details of how it came about, but it had something to do with the fanatical ideal of self-knowledge that, even as students, the two priests of truth carried like the crusaders' banner.'

Adriana went to the wall next to the door and leaned her forehead against it, her hands clasped behind her as if someone had shackled them. Mutely, she quarrelled with Amadeu, with Jorge, and with herself. She braced herself against the irrevocable fact that the drama of Mendes's rescue, which gave her those precious minutes of intimacy with her brother, soon set in motion something that changed everything. She leaned all the weight of her body against the wall so that the pressure on her forehead must have hurt. And then, quite suddenly, she raised her hands high and punched the wall with her fists, over and over, an old woman who wanted to turn back the wheel of time; it was a drumbeat of muted blows, an eruption of helpless fury, a desperate assault against the loss of a happy time.

The blows grew weaker and slower, the excitement subsided. Exhausted, Adriana leaned on the wall for a while. Then she walked backwards into the room and sat down in a chair. Her forehead was covered with white plaster from the wall; now and then a flake came loose and rolled down her face. Her eyes went back to the wall. Gregorius followed her gaze and then he saw it: where she had stood just now, there was a big square lighter than the rest of the wall. The trace of a picture that must have hung there before.

'For a long time I didn't understand why he took away the map,' said Adriana. 'A map of the brain. It had hung there for eleven years, ever since we had set up the practice. Covered with Latin names. I didn't dare ask why, he loses his temper when you ask him the wrong thing. I didn't know anything about the aneurysm, he kept it from me. With a time bomb in your brain, you can't bear the sight of such a map.'

Gregorius was surprised by what he did now. He went to the washbasin, took the towel and approached Adriana to wipe her forehead. At first she sat there stiffly, defensively, but then she let her exhausted head drop gratefully to the towel.

'Would you take what he wrote then?' she asked when she sat up. 'I don't want to have it here in the house any more.'

As she went to get the pages she blamed for so much, Gregorius stood at the window and looked out at the street where Mendes had collapsed. He imagined standing in the doorway, an incensed mob before him. A mob from which a woman broke loose, a woman spat at him, not once, but over and over again. A woman who had accused him of treason, he who had always demanded so much of himself.

Adriana had put the pages in an envelope.

'I often thought of burning them,' she said and gave it to him.

Silently she led him to the door, still in the white coat. And then, quite suddenly, when he was already halfway out, he heard the fearful voice of the little girl she also was: 'Will you bring me back the pages? Please, they are his after all.'

As Gregorius went down the street, he imagined her taking off the white coat some time and hanging it next to Amadeu's. Then she would turn off the light and lock up. Clotilde would be waiting for her upstairs.

21

Breathlessly, Gregorius read what Prado had written. At first, he only skimmed it to know as soon as possible why Adriana had felt his thoughts as a curse on subsequent years. Then he looked up every word. Finally he wrote down the text to understand better what it had been for Prado to think it.

Did I do it for him? *When I wanted him to survive – was it for his sake? Can I honestly say that that was my wish? That's how it is with my patients, even with those I don't like. At least, I hope it is and I wouldn't like the idea that, behind my back, my action is guided by quite different motives than those I think I know. But with* him?

My hand, it seems to have its own memory, and it seems to me that this memory is more trustworthy than every other source of self-examination. And this memory of the hand, which stuck the needle in Mendes's heart, it says: it was the hand of a tyrant's murderer who brought the already dead tyrant back to life in a paradoxical act.

Here what experience always kept teaching me is confirmed, quite against the original temperament of my thought: that the body is less corrupt than the mind. The mind is a charming arena of self-deception, woven of beautiful, soothing words that give us the illusion that we have an unerring familiarity with ourselves, a closeness of discerning that shields us from being surprised by ourselves. How boring it would be to live in such effortless self-knowledge!

So, in reality, did I do it for myself? *To stand before myself as a good doctor and a brave person who has the strength to master his hatred? To celebrate a triumph of self-control and to revel in the frenzy of self-mastering? So, from moral vanity and even worse: from quite normal vanity? The experience in those seconds – it wasn't the experience of appreciative vanity, I'm sure of that; on the contrary, it was the experience of acting against myself and not indulging in the obvious feelings of satisfaction and spite. But maybe that's no proof. Maybe there is a vanity that isn't felt and that hides behind opposing feelings?*

I am a doctor – that is what I argued to the furious mob. I could also have said: I have taken the Hippocratic Oath, it is a sacred oath, and I will never break it, never, no matter how things are. I feel: I like to say it, I love it, they are words that excite me, exhilarate me. Is that because they are like the words of a priestly vow? So was it really a religious act when I gave back to The Butcher the life he had already lost? The act of someone who secretly regrets that he can no longer trust in dogma and liturgy? Who still mourns the unearthly glow of the altar candles? So, not an enlightened act? Is there, in my soul, unnoticed by me, a brief, but violent, bitter struggle between the former pupil of the priest and the tyrant-murderer, who has never taken action? Thrusting the needle with the life-saving poison into his heart, was it an act in which priest and murderer were two of a kind? A movement, in which both got what they longed for?

If I had been in the place of Inês Salomão, who spat at me: What could I have said to me?

'It wasn't a murder that we demanded of you,' I could have said. 'Not a crime, either legally or morally. If you had left him his death: no judge could have prosecuted you and nobody could have judged you by the Sixth Commandment: Thou shalt not murder. No, what we could expect was something plain and simple, obvious: that you wouldn't keep a man alive with all your might, a man who has brought us misery, torture, and death, and whom compassionate

nature finally wanted to get off our back, and that you wouldn't make sure he could go on practising his bloody regime.'

How could I have defended myself?

'Everyone deserves help to remain alive, no matter what he's done. He deserves it as a person, as a human being. We don't have to judge over life and death.'

'And if that means the death of others? Don't we shoot somebody we see shooting somebody? Wouldn't you prevent the obviously murdering Mendes from murdering, with a murder if necessary? And doesn't that go much further than what you could have done: nothing?'

How would it be for me now if I had let him die? If, instead of spitting at me, the others had acclaimed me for my fatal omission? If from the street, an exuberant sigh of relief had come at me instead of an enraged poisonous disappointment? I am sure: it would have haunted my dreams. But why? Because I can't be without something unconditional, absolute? Or simply because it would have meant an alienation from myself to let him die in cold blood? But what I am, I am by accident.

I imagine: I go over to Inês, I ring the bell and say:

'I couldn't have done differently, this is how I am. It might have turned out differently, but in fact, it didn't, and now I am how I am and so I couldn't help doing what I did.'

'It doesn't matter how you are with yourself,' she could say, 'that's completely irrelevant. Just imagine: Mendes is healthy, he puts on his uniform and gives his murderous orders. Imagine. Imagine it precisely. And now judge yourself.'

What could I answer her? What? WHAT?

I want to do something, Prado had said to João Eça, *you understand*: do. *Tell me what I can do.* What exactly was it that he wanted to make up for? *You haven't committed a crime,* Eça had said to him, *you're a doctor.* He himself had so argued to the accusing mob and had also said it to himself, certainly hundreds of times. It hadn't done anything to soothe him. It had seemed too simple to him, too glib. Prado was a man of deep distrust of everything glib and superficial, a man contemptuous and hostile to stock sentences like: *I am a doctor.* He had walked on the beach and wished for icy winds to sweep away everything that sounded like mere linguistic habit, a malicious kind of habit that prevented thinking by producing the illusion that it had already taken place and found its conclusion in the hollow words.

When Mendes lay before him, he had seen him as this particular, individual person whose life was at stake. Only as this individual person. He couldn't have seen this life as something that had to be calculated in terms of others, as a factor in a bigger calculation. And it was precisely this that the woman accused him of in her monologue: that he hadn't thought of the consequences also affecting individual lives, many individual lives. That he hadn't been ready to sacrifice one individual for many individuals.

When he had joined the Resistance, thought Gregorius, it had also been to learn such thinking. He had failed. *One life for many lives. You can't calculate like that. Or could you?* he had asked Father Bartolomeu years later. He had gone to his former mentor to have his feelings confirmed. But he couldn't have done anything different anyway. And then he had taken Estefânia Espinhosa over the border, out of reach of those who thought they had to sacrifice her to prevent something worse happening.

The internal gravity that made him who he was had not permitted any other action. But a doubt had remained because the suspicion of moral indulgence was not to be dispelled, a suspicion that weighed heavily on a man who hated vanity like the plague.

It was this doubt that Adriana cursed. She had wanted her brother all to herself and had realized that you can never have for yourself someone who isn't on good terms with himself.

22

'I don't believe it!' said Natalie Rubin on the phone. 'I simply don't believe it! Where are you?'

He was in Lisbon, said Gregorius and he needed books, German books.

'Books,' she laughed. 'What else!'

He listed: the biggest German–Portuguese dictionary there was; a detailed Portuguese grammar, dry as a Latin textbook, without any junk to make it easy to learn; a history of Portugal.

'And then something that may not exist: a history of the Portuguese Resistance movement under Salazar.'

'Sounds like an adventure,' said Natalie.

'It is,' said Gregorius. 'Somehow.'

'*Faço o que posso*,' said she. I'll do what I can.

At first Gregorius didn't understand, then realization dawned. One of his students knew Portuguese – that mustn't be allowed. It diminished the distance between Bern and Lisbon. It destroyed the magic, the whole crazy magic of his trip. He cursed the phone call.

'Are you still there? My mother is Portuguese, in case you're wondering.'

He also needed a grammar of modern Persian, said Gregorius, and he named the book that had once cost thirteen francs thirty, forty years before. In case the book was still available, or else another. He said it like a defiant boy who doesn't want to give up his dream.

Then he took her address and gave her the name of his

hotel. He'd put the money in the post, he said. If anything was left over – well, maybe he'd need something else later.

'You're opening an account with me, so to speak? I like that.'

Gregorius liked the way she said that. If only she didn't know any Portuguese.

'You caused one hell of a turmoil here,' she said, when he remained silent on the line.

Gregorius didn't want to hear anything about that. He needed a wall of ignorance between Bern and Lisbon.

So what happened? he asked.

'He's not coming back,' Lucien von Graffenried had said into the amazed silence when Gregorius had closed the classroom door behind him.

'You're crazy,' others had said. 'Mundus doesn't just run away, not Mundus, never in his life.'

'You just can't read faces,' von Graffenried had replied.

Gregorius wouldn't have thought von Graffenried was capable of that.

'We went to your house and rang the bell,' said Natalie. 'I could have sworn you were there.'

His letter to Kägi had not arrived until Wednesday. All day Tuesday, Kägi had been calling the police about accident reports. The Latin and Greek classes were cancelled, while the students sat perplexed outside on the steps. Everything was off kilter.

Natalie hesitated. 'The woman . . . I mean . . . we found that thrilling, somehow. Excuse me,' she added when he was silent.

And on Wednesday?

'At break, we found a notice on the blackboard. Until further notice, you would no longer be teaching, it said. Kägi himself would take over the classes. A delegation went to Kägi and asked about it. He was sitting behind his desk with your letter in front of him. He was quite different from his usual self, much more modest, gentler, not like a Rector. "I don't know if I should do that," he said, but then he read the passage from Marcus Aurelius you had quoted. Did he think you were ill? we asked. He was silent a long time and looked out of the window. "I can't know that," he said at last, "but I really don't think so. I think he suddenly felt something, something new. Something subtle and yet revolutionary. It must have been like a silent explosion that changed everything." We told him about . . . about the woman. "Yes," said Kägi. "Yeees." I had the feeling he was somehow envious. "Kägi is cool," Lucien said afterwards, "I wouldn't have expected that of him." Right. But the class is so boring. We . . . we wish you were back.'

Gregorius felt a burning in his eyes and took off the glasses. He swallowed. 'I . . . I can't say anything about that now,' he said.

'But you're . . . you're not ill? I mean . . .'

No, he said, he wasn't ill. 'A little crazy, but not ill.'

She laughed as he had never heard her laugh, altogether without the sound of the courtly maiden. It was a contagious laugh and he laughed too, surprised by his outrageous, unfamiliar, carefree laugh. For a while, they laughed in harmony, he reinforced her and she him; they kept on laughing, for a long time; the reason was no longer important, only the laughing. It was like train rides, like the feeling that the banging sound on the rails, a sound of safety and the future, might never stop.

'Today is Saturday,' said Natalie quickly, when it was over. 'So the bookshops are only open until four. I'm off.'

'Natalie? I'd like to keep this conversation to ourselves. As if it had never taken place.'

She laughed. 'What conversation? *Até logo*.'

Gregorius looked at the sweet wrapper he had put back in his coat pocket that night in the Liceu and had touched this morning when he groped in the pocket. He had picked up the receiver and asked for Inquiries. The operator had given him three numbers for the name Rubin. The second had been the right one. He had felt as if he were jumping off a cliff into emptiness when he dialled. You couldn't say that he had done it rashly or out of blind impulse. Several times he had had the receiver in his hand, had hung up again, and had gone to the window. Monday was March the first, and the light was different this morning. For the first time it was the light he had imagined when the train left Bern railway station in the snowstorm.

Nothing was in favour of calling the girl. A sweet wrapper in a coat pocket was no reason to call a student out of the blue with whom you had never exchanged a personal word. Especially not if you had run away and a call might lead to a drama. Was that what had decided the matter: that nothing was in favour of it and everything was against it?

And now they had laughed together, for some minutes. It had been like a touch. A light, hovering touch without resistance, something that made every physical touch seem like a clumsy, ridiculous manoeuvre. He had once read an article in the paper about a policeman who had let a convicted thief escape. *We laughed together*, the policeman had said as an excuse; *so I could no longer lock him up. It simply didn't work.*

Gregorius then called Mariana Eça and Mélodie. No answer. He set out for the Baixa, for Rua dos Sapateiros, where Jorge O'Kelly, as Father Bartolomeu had told him, still stood behind the counter of his pharmacy. It was the first time since he had arrived that he could wear his coat open. He felt the mild air on his face and noticed how glad he was that he hadn't reached the two women on the phone. He had no idea what he had wanted to say to them.

In the hotel, they had asked him how long he was planning to stay. *'Não faço ideia,'* No idea, he had said, and then he had paid his bill so far. The woman at reception had watched him to the door, he had seen it in the mirror on the pillar. Now he walked slowly to Praça do Rossio. He pictured Natalie Rubin going to the Stauffacher bookshop. Did she know you had to try Haupt on Falkenplatz for the Persian grammar?

At a kiosk a map of Lisbon was spread out, with the city churches marked. Gregorius bought one. Prado – Father Bartolomeu had said – had known all the churches and everything about them. He had been shown round some of them by the priest. *You would have to rip them out!* he had said, when they had gone past the confessional. *Such a humiliation!*

The door and window frames of O'Kelly's pharmacy were dark green and gold. Over the door was a staff of Aesculapius, in the window an old-fashioned pair of scales. When Gregorius entered, several bells rang, and together they produced a soft, clanking melody. He was glad he could hide behind the many customers. And now he saw what he wouldn't have thought possible: a pharmacist behind the counter *smoking*. The whole shop smelt of smoke and medicine and O'Kelly soon lit a new cigarette with the butt of the old one. Then he drank a sip of coffee from a cup on the counter. Nobody seemed surprised. In his rasping voice, he explained something to a customer or made a joke. Gregorius had the impression that he called them all by their first names.

So that was Jorge, the confirmed atheist and disillusioned romantic, whom Amadeu de Prado had needed to be whole. The man whose superiority in chess had been so important for him, the superior one. The man who was the first to burst out laughing when a barking dog had ended the embarrassed silence after Prado's heretical speech. The man who attacked his double bass so violently that the bow broke because he felt he was hopelessly untalented. And finally, the man whom Prado had stood up to when he realized he had condemned Estefânia Espinhosa to death, the woman who – if Father Bartolomeu's assumption was correct – he had approached years later in the cemetery, and didn't meet her eye.

Gregorius left the pharmacy and sat down in the café across the street. He knew there was a note in Prado's book that began with a call from Jorge. Now, out in the street and surrounded by people who were conversing or letting the spring sun shine on them with their eyes shut, when he leafed through the dictionary and began to translate, he sensed that something great and really unprecedented was happening to him: he was occupied with the written word amid voices, street noise, and coffee steam. *But you, too, sometimes read the newspaper in the café*, Florence had objected when he explained to her that books demanded walls that kept the noise of the world away, at best the thick, solid walls of an underground archive. *Come on, newspapers*, he had replied, *I'm talking about books*. And now, all at once, he no longer missed the walls; the Portuguese words before him merged with the Portuguese words next to him and behind him; he could imagine Prado and O'Kelly sitting at the next table and interrupted by the waiter, and that didn't make any difference to the words.

AS SOMBRAS DESCONCERTANTES DA MORTE. THE DISCONCERTING SHADOWS OF DEATH. *'I woke up with a start and was afraid of death,' said Jorge on the phone. 'And even now I'm still in a sheer panic.' It was shortly before three in the morning. His voice sounded different from when he spoke with customers in the pharmacy, offered me something to drink, or said: 'It's your move.' You couldn't say the voice quavered, but it was husky like a voice covering powerful feelings, controlled only with difficulty, that threaten to burst out.*

He had dreamed he was sitting on the stage at his new Steinway grand piano and didn't know how to play. Just recently, he, the passionate rationalist, had done something bewitchingly mad: with the money left him by his brother killed in an accident, he had bought a Steinway even though he hadn't yet played a single bar on the piano. The salesman had been amazed that he simply pointed to the shiny grand piano, without even opening the keyboard cover. Since then, the piano stood in a museum shine in his solitary flat and looked like a monumental tombstone. 'I woke up and suddenly knew: being able to play the grand piano as it deserves – that's no longer within the span of my life.' He sat across from me in his dressing gown and seemed to sink deeper into the chair than usual. Embarrassed, he rubbed his eternally cold hands. 'You must be thinking: that was clear from the start. And somehow, I naturally knew it. But you see; when I woke up, I knew it really for the first time. And now I'm so scared.'

'Scared of what?' I asked and waited until he, a master of the fearless, direct look, would look at me. 'Of what exactly?'

A smile strayed over Jorge's face: Usually he's the one who urges me to be precise and it is his analytically trained mind that counters my tendency to leave final things in hovering uncertainty.

For a pharmacist, it couldn't possibly be fear of pain and the agony of dying, I said, and as for the humiliating experience of physical and mental decay – well, we had often enough talked about ways and means in case the border of the bearable was crossed. So what was the object of his fear?

'The grand piano – since last night, it has reminded me that there are things I can no longer do on time.' He shut his eyes as always when he wanted to forestall a mute objection from me. 'It's not about unimportant little joys and fleeting pleasures as when you toss down a glass of water in dusty heat. It's about things you want to do and experience because only they would make your own, this very special life, whole, and because without them, life remains incomplete, a torso and a mere fragment.'

But from the moment of death on, he would no longer be there to suffer and mourn this lack of completion, I said.

Yes, of course, said Jorge – he sounded irritated as always when he had heard something that seemed irrelevant to him – but it was about the current, living awareness that life would remain incomplete, fragmentary, and without the coherence we hope for. This knowledge, that's what was bad – the fear of death itself.

But the distress was not that his life now, as they spoke, didn't yet possess this internal completion. Or was it?

Jorge shook his head. He wasn't speaking of regret at not yet having experienced everything that had to be part of his life, so that it would be whole. If the awareness of the current lack of completion of his own life were taken as a misfortune, everyone necessarily always had to be unhappy in his life. The awareness of openness, on the other hand, was a condition that it was living and not yet dead life. So, it had to be something different that constituted unhappiness: the knowledge that even in the future it would no longer be possible to have those rounding-off, perfecting experiences.

But if it wasn't true, I said, that the incompleteness in it could turn it into an unhappy moment – why shouldn't that also be true of all those moments filled with the awareness that wholeness was no longer to be achieved? It looked as if the desired wholeness was desirable only in the future, as something you went towards and not something you arrived at. 'I want to put it in yet other words,' I added. 'From which point of view is the unreachable wholeness to be lamented and a possible object of fear? If it is not the point of view of the fleeting moments for which the missing wholeness is not an evil, but rather an incentive and a sign of life?'

Granted, said Jorge, to be able to feel the kind of fear he had woken up with, you had to take another point of view than that of the usual, forward-looking moments: to be able to recognize your missing wholeness as an evil, you had to view your life as a whole, consider it from its end, so to speak – just as you did when you thought of death.

'But why should this view be a reason for panic?' I asked. 'As experienced, the current imperfection of your life is not an evil,

that much we agreed on. It almost seems as if it is an evil only as an imperfection you will no longer experience, as one that can be perceived only from beyond the grave. For as an experiencer, you can't, after all, rush ahead into the future in order, from an end that hasn't yet occurred, to feel despair about a deficiency of your life, which must still creep up to that anticipated end. So your mortal fear seems to have a peculiar object: an imperfection of your life you will never be able to experience.'

'I would have liked to be someone who could make the piano ring,' said Jorge. 'One who – let's say – can play Bach's Goldberg Variations on it. Estefânia – she can, she played them all alone for me, and ever since, I have carried in me the wish to do it too. Until an hour ago, I had, it seems, lived with the vague, never examined feeling that I would still have time to learn it. Only the dream of the stage made me wake up with the certainty: my life will end without playing the Variations.'

All right, I said, but why fear? *Why not simply pain, disappointment, sadness? Or even rage? 'One is afraid of something that's still coming, that's still in store; but your knowledge about the forever mute grand piano is already there, we're talking about it in the present. This evil can last, but it can't grow bigger so that there could be a logical fear of its growth. So, your new certainty may depress and stifle, but it is no reason for panic.'*

That was a misunderstanding, Jorge countered: the fear applied not to the new certainty, but to its object: to what was indeed only a future, but none the less already fixed, imperfection of his life, which, because of its greatness, turned certainty to fear from within.

The wholeness of life, whose anticipated absence drives one to the sweat on the forehead – what can it be? What can it consist of when you recall how rhapsodic, variable, and capricious our life is, outside and inside? We're not monolithic, not at all. Are we simply talking of the need to be sated with experience? Was what tormented Jorge the unattainable feeling of sitting at a shining Steinway and making Bach's music his own, which is only possible if it rises from his hands? Or was it the need to have experienced enough things to narrate *life as a whole?*

Is it ultimately a question of self-image, the determining idea one has made for oneself a long time ago of what one had to have accomplished and experienced so that it would be a life one could approve? Fear of death as fear of the unfulfilled then lay – it seems – completely in my hand, for it is I who draw the image of my own life as it was to be fulfilled. What is more obvious than the thought: Then I'll change the image so my life might now fit it – and the fear of death ought to disappear immediately. If it sticks to me none the less, then it's because of this: the image, even though made by me and nobody else, rises not from temperamental capriciousness and isn't available for random change, but is anchored in me and grows out of the play of forces of my feeling and thought that I am. So, the fear of death might be described as the fear of not being able to become whom one had planned to be.

The bright awareness of finitude that assaulted Jorge in the middle of the night and that I have to inflame in many of my patients with the words announcing the fatal diagnosis to them, disturbs us like nothing else because, often without knowing it, we live towards such wholeness and because every moment we live to the fullest draws its liveliness from the fact that it represents a piece in the puzzle of that unknown wholeness. If the certainty befalls us that it will never be achieved, this wholeness, we suddenly don't know how to live the time that can no longer be part of a whole life. That is the reason for a strange, distressing experience of some of my doomed patients: they no longer know what to do with their time, however short it has become.

When I went into the street after the conversation with Jorge, the sun was just rising and the few people coming towards me looked like silhouettes against the light, faceless mortals. I sat down

*on a window ledge at ground level and waited for the faces of
the passers-by to open to me. The first one to approach was a
woman with a swaying gait. Her face, I now saw, was still veiled
in sleep, but it was easy to imagine it opening in the sunlight and
looking hopefully and expectantly at the events of the day, the eyes
full of future. An old man with a dog was the second one who
passed by me. Now he stood still, lit a cigarette and let the dog
off the leash so it could run over to the park. He loved the dog
and his life with the dog, his features left no doubt of that. The
old woman with the crocheted kerchief, who came a while later,
was also attached to her life, even though it was hard for her to
walk with her swollen legs. She held tight to the hand of the boy
with the schoolbag, a grandson perhaps, whom – it was the first
day of school – she brought to school early so he wouldn't miss this
important beginning of his new future.*

*All of them would die and all were afraid of it, when they
thought of it. Die some time – but not now. I tried to remember
the labyrinth of questions and arguments I strayed through with
Jorge half the night, and the clarity that had been close to being
grasped in order to escape at the last moment. I watched the young
woman stretching, the old man frolicking with the dog leash, and
the hobbling grandmother stroking the child's hair. Wasn't it obvious,
simple and clear what their horror would consist of if, at this
moment, they received tidings of their impending death? I held
the haggard face in the morning sun and thought: they simply
want more of the stuff of their life, no matter how light or heavy,
sparse or lush this life may be. They don't want it to end, even if
they can no longer miss the absent life after the end – and know
that.*

*I went home. How does complicated, analytical thought relate
to intuitive certainty? Which of the two should we trust more?*

*In the consulting room, I opened the window and looked at
the pale blue sky above the roofs, the chimneys, and the laundry
on the line. How would it be between Jorge and me after last*

night? Would we sit across from each other at chess as always, or different? What does the intimacy of death do with us?

It was late afternoon when Jorge came out of the pharmacy and locked it. For an hour, Gregorius had been freezing and drinking one cup of coffee after another. Now he put a banknote under the cup and followed O'Kelly. When he passed by the pharmacy, he realized that a light was still burning inside. He looked through the window but the shop was empty; the antiquated cash register was covered with a dingy wrapper.

The pharmacist turned the corner and Gregorius had to hurry to keep him in view. They walked up the Rua da Conceição, across the Baixa and further into the Alfama quarter, past three churches that rang the hour, one after another. In the Rua da Saudade, Jorge stamped out the third cigarette before he disappeared through the doorway of a house.

Gregorius crossed the street to look up at the building. In none of the flats did a light go on. Hesitantly, he crossed back and entered the dark vestibule. It must have been there, behind the heavy wooden door, that Jorge had disappeared. It didn't look like the door of a flat, more like the door of a bar, but there were no signs of a tavern. Gambling? Was that conceivable for Jorge, after everything he knew about him? Gregorius stood still at the door, his hands in his coat pockets. Now he knocked. Nothing. When he turned the handle, it was like this morning when he had finally dialled Natalie Rubin's number: like a leap into emptiness.

It was a chess club. In a low, smoky room, dimly lit, there were a dozen games going on, all between men. In a corner was a small counter with drinks. There was no heating; the men had on coats and warm jackets, some wore berets. O'Kelly had been expected, for when Gregorius saw him behind a veil of smoke, his partner was holding the pieces in his fist for him to choose. At the next table sat a lone man who kept looking at the clock and then drumming his fingers on the table.

Gregorius flinched. The Portuguese man looked like a man in Jura with whom he had once played chess for ten hours, only to lose in the end. It had been at a tournament in Moutier, on a cold weekend in December, where it never became light and the mountains seemed to arch over the town, as in a mountain fortress. The man, a local who spoke French like a moron, had the same square face as the Portuguese man at the next table, the same stubbly haircut as if by a lawn mower, the same receding forehead, the same jug ears. Only the Portuguese man's nose was different. And the gaze. Black, jet black under bushy brows, a gaze like a cemetery wall.

With this look, he now examined Gregorius. *Not against this man*, thought Gregorius, *by no means against this man*. The man beckoned to him. Gregorius approached. Thus he could see O'Kelly playing at the next table. He could observe him inconspicuously. That was the price. *That damned sacred friendship*, he heard Adriana say. He sat down.

'*Novato?*' asked the man.

Gregorius didn't know: Did that simply mean *new here* or did it mean *beginner*? He decided on the first and nodded.

'Pedro,' said the Portuguese man.

'Raimundo,' said Gregorius.

The man played an even slower game than the man in Jura. And the slowness began at the first move, a leaden, paralysing slowness. Gregorius looked around. Nobody was playing with a clock. Clocks were out of place in this room. Everything except chessboards was out of place here. Even talk.

Pedro laid his forearms flat on the table, leaned his chin on his hands and scanned the board. Gregorius didn't know what bothered him more: this strained, epileptic look with the iris sliding up on a yellowish background or the manic lip-chewing that had made him mad with the man from Jura. It would be a struggle against impatience. He had lost this struggle against the man from Jura. He cursed all the coffee he had drunk.

Now he exchanged the first look with Jorge next to him, the man who had woken up with a fear of death and had outlived Prado for thirty-one years so far.

'*Atenção!*' said O'Kelly and pointed with his chin to Pedro. '*Adversário desagradável.*' Unpleasant opponent.

Pedro grinned without raising his head, and now he looked like a moron. '*Justo, muito justo,*' Quite right, he murmured, and fine bubbles formed in the corners of his mouth.

As long as it was a simple calculation of moves, Pedro wouldn't make any mistakes, Gregorius knew that after an hour's play. You mustn't be deceived by the receding forehead and the epileptic look: he calculated everything thoroughly, ten times if need be, and he anticipated at least the next ten moves. The question was what happened if you made a surprising move. A move that not only seemed not to make sense but in fact didn't. Gregorius had often put strong opponents off with that. Only with Doxiades the strategy didn't work. 'Nonsense,' the Greek simply said and didn't let go of the advantage.

Another hour had passed when Gregorius decided to cause confusion by sacrificing a pawn without attaining the slightest advantage of position.

Pedro pushed his lips in and out several times, then raised his head and looked at Gregorius. Gregorius wished he were wearing the old glasses, which were like a bulwark against such looks. Pedro blinked, rubbed his temples, ran his short, pudgy fingers over his hair stubble. Then he let the pawn alone. '*Novato,*' he murmured, '*diz Novato.*' Now Gregorius knew: it meant beginner.

That Pedro hadn't taken the pawn because he considered the sacrifice a trap had manoeuvred Gregorius into a position from which he could attack. Move after move, he advanced his army and cut off all possibility of defence for Pedro. The Portuguese man started snuffling noisily every few minutes, Gregorius didn't know if it was deliberation or slovenliness. Jorge grinned when he saw how the disgusting noise annoyed Gregorius; the others seemed quite used to Pedro's habit. Whenever Gregorius thwarted one of Pedro's plans, even before it became visible, his look became harder and his eyes were now like glowing slate. Gregorius leaned back and glanced calmly at the game: even if it lasted for hours, nothing more could happen.

Looking ostensibly at the window where a streetlamp swung softly on a loose cable, he began to observe O'Kelly's face. In Father Bartolomeu's tale, the man had only been a figure of light at first, a figure of light without brilliance, an incorruptible, fearless boy, who called things by name and was anything but a show-off. But then, at the end, there had been the tale of Prado's night visit to the priest. *She. She has become the danger. She wouldn't resist. She would talk. The others think so. Jorge too? I don't want to talk about that.*

O'Kelly took a drag at the cigarette before he went across the board with the bishop and captured his opponent's rook. The fingers were yellow with nicotine and black under the nails. His big, fleshy nose with the open pores disgusted Gregorius; it looked to him like an outgrowth of ruthlessness and fitted the man's spiteful grin. But anything that was distasteful about his face was cancelled out by the weary and kind look in the brown eyes.

Estefânia. Gregorius's memory was jolted and he felt hot. The name had appeared in Prado's text this afternoon, but he hadn't made the connection ... *the Goldberg Variations ... Estefânia – she can, she played all alone for me, and ever since, I carried in me the wish to be able to do it too.* Could that have been *this* Estefânia? The woman Prado had to save from O'Kelly? The woman who had broken up the friendship between them – *that damned sacred friendship?*

Gregorius began calculating feverishly. Yes, it could be. Then, however, it was the cruellest thing you could imagine: that someone was willing to sacrifice to the resistance movement the woman who had reinforced with Bach's notes the wonderful, bewitching Steinway illusions Jorge had harboured even at the Liceu.

What had happened all those years ago in the cemetery between the two, after the priest had left. Had Estefânia Espinhosa gone back to Spain? She would have been younger than O'Kelly, so much younger that Prado could have fallen in love with her back then, ten years after Fátima's death. If that were so, then the drama between Prado and O'Kelly had been not only a conflict of morality, but also a drama of love.

What did Adriana know about this drama? Could she have even allowed it into her thoughts? Or did she have to seal her mind against it, as against so many other things? Did the untouched, shiny Steinway still stand in O'Kelly's flat?

Gregorius had made the last moves with the routine, perfunctory concentration he had played in simultaneous tournaments against the students in Kirchenfeld. Now he saw Pedro grinning insidiously and after a careful look at the board, he was jolted. The advantage was gone and the Portuguese man had set in motion a dangerous attack.

Gregorius shut his eyes. Leaden weariness washed over him. Why didn't he just get up and go? How did he happen to be sitting in Lisbon in a smoke-filled room with an unbearably low ceiling and playing chess with a man who didn't matter to him in the least and with whom he couldn't exchange a word?

He sacrificed the last bishop and thus opened the endgame. He couldn't win any more, but it could come to a draw. Pedro went to the WC. Gregorius looked around. The room had emptied and the few people who remained had approached his table. Pedro came back, sat down and snuffled. Jorge's opponent had gone but he himself had sat down at the next table so that he could follow the endgame. Gregorius heard his rattling breath. If he didn't want to lose, he had to forget the man.

Alekhine had once won an endgame, even though he was three pieces down. Incredulous, Gregorius, as a student, had played over the endgame. And for months afterwards he had played every endgame he came across. Ever since, he could see at a glance what had to be done. He saw it now, too.

Pedro deliberated for half an hour and then, nevertheless, walked into the trap. He saw it as soon as he had moved. He could no longer win. He pushed his lips back and forth, back and forth. He stared at Gregorius with his stony look. '*Novato*,' he said, '*Novato*.' Then he stood up quickly and went out.

'*Donde és?*' asked one of those standing around. Where do you come from?

'*De Berna, na Suiça,*' said Gregorius and added: '*Gente lenta.*' Slow people.

They laughed and offered him a beer. They hoped he would come back.

On the street, O'Kelly came up to him.

'Why are you following me?' he asked in English.

When he saw the amazement in Gregorius's face, he laughed harshly.

'There were times when my life depended on noticing when somebody was following me.'

Gregorius hesitated. What would happen if the man was suddenly confronted with Prado's portrait? Thirty years after he had parted from him at the grave? Slowly, he took the book out of his coat pocket, opened it and showed O'Kelly the picture. Jorge blinked, took the book out of Gregorius's hand, went under a street lamp and held the picture close to his eyes. Gregorius was never to forget the scene: O'Kelly observing the picture of his lost friend in the light of the swaying street lamp, unbelieving, frightened, a face that was distraught.

'Come with me,' said Jorge in a hoarse voice that sounded imperious only to hide the tremor in it. 'I live near by.'

His step as he walked ahead was stiffer than before and more uncertain; he was now an old man.

His flat was like a cave, a smoky cave with walls plastered with photographs of pianists. Rubinstein, Richter, Horowitz, Dinu Lipati, Murray Perahia. A gigantic portrait of Maria João Pires, João Eça's favourite pianist.

O'Kelly went through the living room and turned on an endless series of lamps, one spotlight after another highlighting the gallery of photographs. A single corner of the room remained unlit. There was the grand piano, in whose black surface was reflected the gleam of the many lamps. *I wish I could make the piano ring . . . My life will end without playing the Variations.* For decades this grand piano had stood there, a dark *fata morgana* of polished elegance, a monument to the unfulfilled dream of a rounded life. Gregorius thought of the untouchable things in Prado's consulting room, for there didn't seem to be a particle of dust on O'Kelly's grand piano either.

Life is not what we live; it is what we imagine we are living, said a note in Prado's book.

O'Kelly sat in the chair he seemed always to sit in. He looked at Amadeu's picture. His look, interrupted only by an occasional blink, was like someone who had seen a ghost. The black silence of the grand piano filled the room. The howls of the motorcycles outside bounced off the silence. *Human beings can't bear silence,* said one of Prado's brief notes, *it would mean that they would bear themselves.*

Where did he get the book? Jorge asked now, and Gregorius told him. *Cedros vermelhos,* Jorge read aloud.

'Sounds like Adriana, like her kind of melodrama. He didn't

like this side of her, but he did everything to keep Adriana from noticing. "She's my sister, and she helps me live my life," he said.'

Did Gregorius know what the red cedars were supposed to mean? Mélodie, said Gregorius; he had had the impression she knew. How did he know Mélodie and why did all this interest him? asked O'Kelly. Gregorius thought he heard the echo of a sharpness that had once been in the voice, at a time when you had to be continually on your guard.

'I'd like to know what it was like to be him,' Gregorius said.

Jorge looked at him in amazement, then dropped his eyes to the portrait.

'Can you do that? Know what it is like to be another person? Without *being* the other person?'

At least you could find out what it was like when you imagined being the other person, said Gregorius.

Jorge laughed. It must have sounded like that when he had laughed about the barking dog at the graduation ceremony at the Liceu.

'And that's why you ran away? Absolutely crazy. I like it. *A imaginação, o nosso último santuário.* Imagination is our last sanctuary, Amadeu used to say.'

Uttering Prado's name, a change came over O'Kelly. *He hasn't spoken it for decades*, thought Gregorius. Jorge's fingers trembled when he lit a cigarette. He coughed, then opened Prado's book where Gregorius had stuck the receipt from the café between the pages that afternoon. His gaunt ribcage rose and fell, his breath rattled softly. Gregorius would have preferred to leave him alone.

'And I'm still alive,' Jorge said and put the book aside. 'And the fear, the dimly understood fear of back then, is still there. And the grand piano is still standing there, too. Today it's no longer a memorial, it's simply it, the grand piano, without a message, a silent companion. The conversation Amadeu writes about was in late 1970. Even then, yes, I would have sworn that we could never lose each other, he and I. We were like brothers. More than brothers.

'I remember the first time I saw him. It was the beginning of the school year and he arrived a day late. I forget why. He was late for the first lesson, too. His frock coat marked him out as a boy from a wealthy home, for you can't buy such things off the peg. He was the only one without a schoolbag, as if he wanted to say: *I carry everything in my head.* There was no trace of arrogance or haughtiness as he sat down in the empty place. He simply knew there was nothing he couldn't learn easily. As he stood up, said his name, and sat down again, he would have been at home on the stage, not that he wanted or needed one; it was charm, pure grace that flowed from his movements. Father Bartolomeu stopped short when he first saw him and for a moment he was lost for words.'

He had read his graduation address, said Gregorius, when O'Kelly sank into silence. Jorge stood up, went into the kitchen and came back with a bottle of red wine. He poured two glasses and drank his like someone who needs it.

'We worked on it night after night. Meantime he lost his nerve. Then rage helped. "God punishes the Egyptians with plagues because Pharaoh is obstinate," he shouted, "but it was God Himself who made him like that! And He made him like that so He could demonstrate His own power! What a vain, complacent God! What a show-off!" I loved him when he was full of rage like this and offered God his high, beautiful forehead.

'He wanted to call the lecture: "Reverence and Loathing of the *Dying* Word of God." That was bombastic, I said, bombastic metaphysics, and in the end he left it untitled. He tended towards bombast. He didn't want to admit it, but he knew it. Therefore he fought against kitsch, at every opportunity. He could be unfair in his judgements, horribly unfair.

'The only person spared his anathema was Fátima. She could do no wrong. He waited on her hand and foot the whole eight years they were married. He needed someone he could wait on hand and foot, he was like that. It didn't make her happy. She and I, we didn't talk about it. She didn't like me especially, maybe because she was jealous of the intimacy between him and me. But once, I bumped into her in a café. She was reading the Situations Vacant adverts in the newspaper and had circled a few. She folded up the paper when she saw me but I had already seen it. "I wish he thought more of me," she said in that conversation. But the only woman he really thought more of was Maria João. Maria, my God, yes, Maria.'

O'Kelly opened a new bottle of wine. His words began to blur around the edges.

'What was Maria João's last name?' asked Gregorius.

"Ávila. Like Saint Teresa. That's why, in school, they called her a *santa*, the saint. She was furious when she heard it. She married a man with a throughly normal, inconspicious name, but I forget what it is.'

O'Kelly drank and was silent.

'I really thought we could never lose each other,' he suddenly said into the silence. 'I thought it was impossible. Once I read somewhere the sentence *Friendships have their time and end.* Not with us, I thought then, *not with us.*'

O'Kelly was drinking faster now and his mouth no longer obeyed him. He stood up laboriously and went out of the room on uncertain legs. A while later, he came back with a sheet of paper.

'Here. We once wrote this together. In Coimbra when the whole world seemed to belong to us.'

It was a list titled: LEALDADE POR. Prado and O'Kelly had noted all the reasons for loyalty:

Guilt towards the other; common steps of development; shared suffering; shared joy; solidarity of mortals; common intentions;

common struggle against the outside; common strengths, weaknesses; common need for closeness; common taste; common hatred; shared secrets; shared fantasies, dreams; shared enthusiasm; shared humour; shared heroes; common decisions made; common successes, failures, victories, defeats; shared disappointments; common errors.

'You forgot to include love on the list,' said Gregorius. O'Kelly's body tensed and for a while, behind the smoke, he was wide awake again.

'He didn't believe in it. Avoided even the word as too sentimental. There were only three things that were important, he used to say: *desire, pleasure, and security.* All were transitory. The most ephemeral was desire, then came pleasure, and finally, security, the feeling of being safe with someone. The impositions of life, all the things we had to put up with, were just too numerous and powerful for our feelings to weather them intact. That's why loyalty was important. It was not a feeling but an act of will, a commitment, a partisanship of the soul, that turned the accident of encounters and comradeship into a necessity. *A breath of eternity,* he said, *only a breath, but all the same.*

'He was wrong. We were both wrong.

'Later, when we were back in Lisbon, he was often preoccupied with the question of whether there was something like loyalty towards oneself. The duty not to run away from yourself. Neither in thought nor in deed. The willingness to stand up for yourself even if you don't like yourself. He would have liked to reinvent himself and make sure that truth emerged from the process . *I can only bear myself when I'm working,* he said.'

O'Kelly was silent; the tension in his body slackened, his eyes grew dull, his breath slowed as if he was falling asleep. It was impossible to leave just yet.

Gregorius stood up and looked at the bookshelves. A whole row of books about anarchism, Russian, Andalusian, Catalonian.

A lot of books with *justiça* in the title. Dostoevsky and more Dostoevsky. Eça de Queirós, *O Crime Do Padre Amaro*, the book he had bought on his first visit to Júlio Simões's second-hand bookshop. Sigmund Freud. Biographies of pianists. Chess books. And finally, in an alcove, a narrow shelf with his books from the Liceu, some almost seventy years old. Gregorius took out the Latin and Greek grammars and leafed through the inkstained pages. The dictionaries, the workbooks. Cicero, Livy, Xenophon, Sophocles. The Bible, battered and full of notes.

O'Kelly woke up, but when he started talking, it was as if the dream he had just experienced was continuing.

'He bought me the pharmacy. A whole pharmacy in the best location. Just like that. We used to meet in a café and talk about everything under the sun. Not a word about the pharmacy. He was a virtuoso of mystery, a goddamned, lovable virtuoso of mystery, I haven't known anybody who mastered the art of mystery like he did. It was his form of vanity – even if he refused to admit it. On the way home one evening, he suddenly stops. "You see this pharmacy?" he asks. "Naturally I see it," I said, "so what?" "It belongs to you," he says and holds a bunch of keys before my nose. "You always wanted your own pharmacy, now you've got it." And he also paid for all the equipment. And you know what? It didn't even embarrass me. I was overwhelmed, and at first, I rubbed my eyes every morning. Sometimes I called him and said: "Just imagine, I'm standing in my own pharmacy." Then he laughed, a relaxed, happy laugh that became rarer from one year to the next.

'Because he came from a wealthy family, he had a troubled relationship with money. He could throw money out of the window in an expansive gesture, unlike the judge, his father, who didn't allow himself anything. When he saw a beggar in the street, it was always the same. "Why do I give him only a few coins?" he would say. "Why not a bundle of notes? Why not *everything*? And why this beggar and not all the others too? It's quite by chance that we passed him and not another beggar. And anyway, how can you buy an ice cream when someone a few steps away is having to bear this humiliation? That simply doesn't add up! It shouldn't be allowed." Once he was so furious about this illogicality – *this damn, sticky muddle*, as he called it – that he ran back and threw a generous banknote into the beggar's hat.'

O'Kelly's face, which had been relaxed in memory as with someone relieved of pain, darkened again and grew old.

'When we lost each other, at first I wanted to sell the pharmacy and give him back the money. But then I realized it would have been like cancelling everything that had been, the long happy time of our friendship. Like retrospectively poisoning our past closeness and the earlier trust. So I kept the pharmacy. And a few days after this decision, something amazing happened: it was suddenly much more my own pharmacy than before. I didn't understand it. I still don't understand it to this day.'

He had left the light on in the pharmacy, said Gregorius in parting.

O'Kelly laughed. 'That's on purpose. The light is always burning. *Always*. The pure extravagance. My vengeance for the poverty I grew up in. We could only afford to light a single room so you went to bed when it was dark. The few centavos of pocket money I got, I spent on batteries for a torch to read by at night. Books I stole. Books mustn't cost anything, that's what I thought then and still do. They kept turning the electricity off in our house because of unpaid bills. *Cortar a luz*, I will never forget the threat. Those are simple things you never get over. How something smelt; how your skin burned after a smack; how it was when the sudden dark flooded the house; how harsh Father's cursing sounded. At first, the police sometimes checked on the pharmacy because of the light. Now everybody knows it never gets switched off and they leave me alone.'

23

Natalie Rubin had called three times. Gregorius called back. The dictionary and the Portuguese grammar had been no problem at all, she said. 'You'll *love* this grammer book! Like a law book and heaps of lists with exceptions, the man is nuts about exceptions. Like you, sorry.'

The history of Portugal had been harder; there were several and she had decided on the most condensed. All these books were now on the way to him. The Persian grammar he had mentioned was still in print and Haupt could get it by the middle of next week. The history of the Portuguese Resistance, on the other hand – that was a real challenge. The library had been closed when she got there but she would return on Monday. At Haupt, they had advised her to enquire in the department of Romance literature and she knew who to ask for.

Gregorius was frightened by her enthusiasm, even though he had seen it coming. She would prefer to come to Lisbon and help him with his research, he heard her say.

Gregorius woke up in the middle of the night and wasn't sure she had really said this, or whether he had dreamed it. *Cool,* Kägi and Lucien von Graffenried had said all the time he was playing chess against Pedro, the man from Jura, who pushed his pieces over the board with his forehead and banged his head furiously on the table when Gregorius outfoxed him. To play against Natalie had been strange and weird, for she played without pieces and without light. 'I know Portuguese and could assist you!' she said. He tried to answer her in Portuguese and felt as if he were taking an exam when the words didn't come. *Minha Senhora*, he kept repeating, *Minha Senhora*, and then he didn't know how to continue.

He called Doxiades. No, he hadn't woken him up, said the Greek, he was having trouble sleeping again. And not only with sleep.

Gregorius had never heard such an admission from him, and he was scared. What was the problem? he asked.

'Oh, nothing,' said the Greek. 'I'm just tired. I'm making mistakes in my practice. I'd like to stop working.'

Stop? Doxiades *stop?* Then what?

'Go to Lisbon, for example,' he laughed.

Gregorius told him about Pedro, his receding forehead and the epileptic look. Doxiades remembered the man from Jura.

'After that, you played miserably for a while,' he said. 'For you.'

It was already light when Gregorius fell asleep again. When he woke up two hours later, a cloudless sky arched over Lisbon and people were walking around without coats. He decided to take the ferry over to Cacilhas to visit João Eça.

'I thought you'd come today,' João said and from his thin lips, the sparse words sounded enthusiastic.

They drank tea and played chess. Eça's hand trembled when he moved, and there was a clack when he put the piece down. At every one of his moves, Gregorius was horrified by the burn scars on the backs of his hands.

'It's not the pain and the wounds that are the worst,' said Eça. 'The worst is the humiliation. The humiliation when you feel you're going to shit your pants. When I got out, I burned with a need for revenge. White hot. Waited in hiding until the torturers came off duty, in plain coats and with briefcases, like people leaving an office. I followed them home.

To get even. What saved me was the disgust at touching them. Shooting was much too good for them. Mariana thought I had undergone a process of moral maturation. Not a bit. I always rejected becoming mature, as she called it. Didn't like maturity. Considered this so-called maturity opportunism or pure fatigue.'

Gregorius lost. After a few moves, he felt that he didn't *want* to win against this man. The art was not letting him sense that, and he decided on daredevil manoeuvres that a player like Eça would see through.

'Next time, don't let me win,' said Eça when the signal for food came. 'Otherwise I'll get mad.'

They ate the insipid boiled lunch provided by the home. Yes, that's how it always was, said Eça, and when he saw Gregorius's face, he laughed a real laugh for the first time. Gregorius learned something about João's brother, Mariana's father, who had married into a wealthy family, and about the doctor's failed marriage.

This time he hadn't asked at all about Amadeu, said Eça.

'I'm here for your sake, not his,' said Gregorius.

'Even if you haven't come for his sake,' said Eça as evening fell, 'I have something I'd like to show you. He gave it to me after I had asked him one day what he was writing. I've read it so often I know it almost by heart.' And he translated the two sheets for Gregorius.

O BÁLSAMO DA DESILUSÃO. THE BALM OF DISAPPOINTMENT. *Disappointment is considered bad. A thoughtless prejudice. How, if not through disappointment, should we discover what we have expected and hoped for? And where, if not in this discovery, should self-knowledge lie? So, how could one gain clarity about oneself without disappointment?*

We shouldn't suffer disappointment sighing at something our lives would be better without. We should seek it, track it down, collect it. Why am I disappointed that the adored actors of my youth all now show signs of age and decay? What does disappointment teach me about how little success is worth? Many need a whole life to admit the disappointment about their parents to themselves. What did we really expect from them? People who have to live their life under the merciless rule of pain are often disappointed at how others behave, even those who endure with them and feed them the medicine. It's too little, what they do and say, and also too little, what they feel. 'What do you expect?' I ask. They can't say it and are dismayed that, for years, they have carried around an expectation that could be disappointed and they don't know details of it.

One who would really like to know himself would have to be a restless, fanatical collector of disappointments, and seeking disappointing experiences must be like an addiction, the all-determining addiction of his life, for it would stand so clearly before his eyes that disappointment is not a hot, destroying poison, but rather a cool, calming balm that opens our eyes to the real contours of ourselves.

And it should not only be disappointments concerning others or circumstances. When you have discovered disappointment as the guide to yourself, you will be eager to learn how much you are disappointed about yourself: about lack of courage and inadequate honesty, or about the horribly narrow borders drawn by your own feelings, acts, and sayings. What was it we expected and hoped from ourselves? That we were boundless, or quite different than we are?

One could have the hope that he would become more real by reducing expectations, shrink to a hard, reliable core and thus be immune to the pain of disappointment. But how would it be to lead a life that banished every long, bold expectation, a life where there were only banal expectations like 'The bus is coming'?

'I never knew anybody who could get so thoroughly lost in his daydreams as Amadeu,' said Eça. 'And who hated so much to be disappointed. What he writes here – he writes it *against himself.* As he also often *lived* against himself. Jorge would deny that. Have you met Jorge? Jorge O'Kelly, the pharmacist, in whose shop the light burns day and night? He knew Amadeu much longer than I did, much longer. And yet. . .

'Jorge and I . . . well yes. Once we played together. The only time. A draw. But when it came to plans of operation and cunning strategies, we were an unbeatable team, like twins who understood each other instinctively.

'Amadeu was jealous of this understanding; he felt he couldn't keep up with our deviousness and unscrupulousness. *Your phalanx,* he called our alliance, which was sometimes an alliance of silence, even against him. And then you felt: he would like to have broken through it, this phalanx. Then he made assumptions. Sometimes he hit the nail on the head. And sometimes he was completely off-target. Especially when it was about something that . . . yes, that concerned himself.'

Gregorius held his breath. Would he now learn something about Estefânia Espinhosa? He could *ask* neither Eça nor O'Kelly about her; that was out of the question. Had Prado been wrong in the end? Had he taken the woman to safety from a danger that didn't exist? Or did Eça's hesitation concern a completely different memory?

'I've always hated Sundays here,' said Eça in parting. 'Cake without taste, whipped cream without taste, gifts without taste, phrases without taste. The hell of convention. But now . . . the afternoons with you . . . I could get used to that.'

He took his hand out of his jacket pocket and held it out to Gregorius. It was the hand with the missing fingernails. Gregorius felt its solid pressure all the way back on the ferry.

PART III
THE ATTEMPT

24

On Monday morning, Gregorius flew to Zurich. He had woken at dawn and had thought: *I am losing myself.* It wasn't that he had woken up and then had the thought, but the other way round: first the thought had been there and then the waking. So this special, transparent awareness, which was different from the awareness that had filled him on the trip to Paris as something new, had, in a certain sense, been nothing but that thought. He wasn't sure he knew what he thought with it and in it, but, with all its vagueness, the thought had possessed an imperious distinctness. Panic seized him and he had begun to pack with trembling hands, jumbling books and clothes together. When the suitcase was fastened, he forced himself to calm down and stood at the window for a while.

It would be a radiant day. In Adriana's parlour, the sun would illuminate the parquet floor. In the morning light, Prado's writing desk would look even more deserted than usual. On the wall above the desk hung notes with faded, barely legible words, discernible from a distance only by a few points where the pen had pressed harder on paper. He would like to have known what the doctor's words were supposed to have reminded him of.

Tomorrow or the day after, perhaps even today, Clotilde would come to the hotel with a new invitation from Adriana. João Eça was counting on him to come for chess on Sunday afternoon. O'Kelly and Mélodie would be amazed that they never heard anything from him again, from the man who had emerged out of nowhere and had asked about Amadeu as if his salvation depended on understanding who he had been. Father Bartolomeu would find it strange that he returned the copy of Prado's valedictory address in the post. Nor would Mariana Eça understand why he had disappeared off the face of the earth. And Silveira. And Coutinho.

When he settled his bill the woman at the reception desk said that she hoped nothing bad had made him leave so suddenly. He didn't understand a single word of the taxi driver's Portuguese. When he paid him at the airport, he found in his coat pocket the piece of paper on which Júlio Simões, the second-hand book dealer, had written down the address of a language school. He looked at it for a moment and then threw it into the wastepaper basket at the door of the departure lounge. The flight at ten was half empty, they told him at the counter, and gave him a window seat.

At the departure gate, he heard only Portuguese spoken. Once he also heard the word *português*. Now it was a word that scared him but he couldn't have said why. He wanted to sleep in his own bed on Länggasse; he wanted to walk on Bundesterrasse and over the Kirchenfeldbrücke; he wanted to talk about the *ablativus absolutus* and *The Iliad*; he wanted to stand on Bubenbergplatz, where he knew his way around. He wanted to go home.

At the approach to Kloten, he was woken by one of the stewardesses asking a question in Portuguese. It was a long question but he understood it without an effort and answered in Portuguese. He looked down on the lake of Zurich. Large parts of the landscape lay under dirty snow. Rain pelted on the wings of the aircraft.

But it wasn't Zurich where he wanted to be; it was Bern. He was glad he had Prado's book with him. When the plane landed and everyone else put away their books and newspapers, he took it out and began to read.

JUVENTUDE IMORTAL. IMMORTAL YOUTH. *In youth we live as if we were immortal. Knowledge of mortality capers around us like a brittle paper ribbon that barely touches our skin. When in life does that change? When does the ribbon start twining around us tighter, until it ends by strangling us? How do we recognize its soft, but unrelenting pressure that makes us know it will never again subside? How do we recognize it in others? And how in ourselves?*

Gregorius wished the flight were a bus so that you could simply sit there until the final stop, go on reading and then return. He was the last one out of the plane.

At the ticket counter of the main railway station in Zurich he hesitated so long that the woman twisted her bracelet impatiently.

'Second class,' he said at last.

As the train left the station and reached its full speed, it occurred to him that Natalie Rubin would be searching in the libraries today for a book on the Portuguese Resistance and that the other books were on their way to him in Lisbon. In the mid-week, long after he was living on Länggasse again, she would go to the Haupt bookshop only a few houses away from his flat and then take the Persian grammar to the post office. What could he say to her if he should run into her? What could he say to the others? Kägi and his colleagues? The students? Doxiades would be the easiest, and yet: what would be the right words, the words that said it? When Bern cathedral came into view, he had the feeling he would be entering a forbidden city in a few minutes' time.

It was icy cold in the flat. Gregorius pulled up the Venetian blind in the kitchen that he had pulled down two weeks ago in order to hide. The record of the language course was still on the record player, the cover on the table. The telephone receiver was turned around on the cradle and reminded him of the night conversation with Doxiades. *Why do traces of the*

past make me sad even when they're traces of something cheerful?
Prado had asked himself in one of his laconic notes.

Gregorius unpacked the suitcase and put the books on the
table. O GRANDE TERRAMOTO. A MORTE NEGRA. He turned on
the heat in all the rooms, put on the washing machine, and
then started reading about the Portuguese plague in the
fourteenth and fifteenth centuries. It wasn't difficult Portuguese
and he progressed well with it. After a while, he lit the last
cigarette from the packet he had bought in the café near
Mélodie's house. In the fifteen years that he had lived here,
this was the first time that cigarette smoke hung in the air.
Now and then, when a passage in the book came to an end,
he thought of his first visit to João Eça and it was as if he
could feel in his throat the burning tea he had poured into
himself to make it easier for Eça's trembling hands.

As he went to the cupboard to get a thicker sweater, he recalled
the sweater in which he had wrapped the Hebrew Bible at the
abandoned Liceu. It had been good to sit at Senhor Cortês's desk
and read the Book of Job, while the cone of sunlight wandered
through the room. Gregorius thought of Eliphaz of Teman, Bildad
of Shuah, and Zophar of Na'ama. He pictured the railway station
sign at Salamanca and remembered how, in preparation for Isfahan,
he had written the first Persian letters on the blackboard in his
room not far from here. He took a sheet of paper and tried to
recall them now. A few lines and loops came, a dot for the
vocalization. Then he ripped it up.

He was startled when the doorbell rang. It was Frau Loosli,
his neighbour. She had seen from the change in the doormat
that he was back, she said, and gave him the post and the
mailbox key. Had he had a good trip? And was there always
a school holiday this early in the year?

The only thing in the mail that interested Gregorius was a
letter from Kägi. Contrary to habit, he didn't use the letter
opener, but ripped the letter open quickly.

Dear Gregorius,

I didn't want to leave the letter you wrote me unanswered: It touched me too much. And I assume that, wherever your travels take you, you will have the mail forwarded.

The first thing I'd like to tell you is this: our Gymnasium feels remarkably empty without you. How empty may be shown by the fact that today in the staffroom Virginie Ledoyen said quite suddenly: 'I sometimes hated him for his blunt, uncouth manner; and it really wouldn't have hurt if he had sometimes dressed a little better. Always this worn-out, baggy stuff. But I must say, I must say: somehow I miss him. Étonnant.' And what our esteemed French colleague says is nothing compared to what we hear from the students. And, I might add, from quite a few female students. When I take your classes now, I feel your absence as a big, dark shadow. And what will happen now with the chess tournament?

Marcus Aurelius, indeed! If I may confide this to you, more and more my wife and I have had the feeling of losing our two children recently. It's not a loss through sickness or accident, it's worse: they reject our whole way of life and aren't at all afraid of saying so. There are moments when my wife looks as if she's going to pieces. So your reminder of the wise emperor was right on target. And let me add something you hopefully won't regard as importunate: whenever I see the envelope with your letter, I feel a twinge of envy. Simply to get up and go: what courage! 'He just got up and went,' the students keep saying. 'Just got up and went.'

Your job is still open, you should know that. I've taken over some of the teaching; for the rest, we've found students as substitutes, even for Hebrew. As for the financial aspect, you'll be sent the necessary papers by the school administration.

What should I say in conclusion, dear Gregorius? Perhaps simply this: we all wish that your trip really takes you where you want to go, outside and inside.

   Yours,

     Werner Kägi

P.S. Your books are in my cabinet for safekeeping. In practical matters, I have one more request: at some time – no hurry – would you let me have your keys?

Kägi had added by hand: *Or would you like to keep them? Just in case?*

Gregorius sat there a long time. Outside it grew dark. He wouldn't have thought that Kägi would write him such a letter. A long time ago, he had seen him in the city with the two children and everything seemed to be fine. He liked what Virginie Ledoyen had said about his clothes and he had misgivings when he looked down at the trousers of the new suit he was wearing. *Blunt*, yes. But *uncouth?* And aside from Natalie Rubin and maybe Ruth Gautschi, which girl students missed him?

He had returned because he wanted to be back in the place where he knew his way around. Where he didn't have to speak Portuguese or French or English. Why did Kägi's letter make this plan, the simplest of all plans, suddenly seem so difficult? Why was it now more important to him than a while ago in the train that it was night-time when he went down to Bubenbergplatz?

An hour later, when he stood in the square, he had the feeling he couldn't touch it any more. Yes, even though it sounded strange, that was the right word: he couldn't *touch* Bubenbergplatz any more. He had already walked around the square three times, had waited at the traffic lights and looked in all directions: towards the cinema, the post office, the war memorial, the Spanish bookshop where he had come upon

Prado's book, straight ahead at the tram stop, at Heiliggeistkirche and the Loeb department store. He had stood still, closed his eyes and concentrated on the pressure his heavy body exerted on the pavement. The soles of his feet had become warm, the street seemed to come towards him, but the feeling persisted: he no longer succeeded in touching the square. The streets and buildings, the lights and sounds, of the square with its decades of familiarity no longer managed to reach him, to bridge this final gap and present themselves to his memory as something he not only *knew*, knew by heart, but as something he *was*, had always been. Only now did it dawn on him that he was no longer the same person.

The persistent, inexplicable gap was in no way like a protective shield. Instead, it made Gregorius panic; it was the fear that in losing the familiar things he had evoked to recapture himself he was also losing himself. He was experiencing much the same thing here as he had at dawn in Lisbon, only more perniciously and much, much more dangerously, for while there had been Bern as well as Lisbon, there was nowhere to replace the lost Bern. With his eyes on the solid yet receding ground, he bumped into a passer-by and for a moment everything was spinning. He grasped his head with both hands as if to hold on to it, and when he was calm and collected again, he saw a woman glance back at him, in her look a question of whether he might be in need of help.

The clock on Heiliggeistkirche now showed eight o'clock and the traffic had subsided. The cloud cover had thinned and you could see the stars. It was cold. Gregorius went through the Kleine Schanze and on to the Bundesterrasse. Excited, he saw the moment approaching when he could turn on to the Kirchenfeldbrücke, as he had done every morning for decades at a quarter to eight.

The bridge was closed until early the following morning while tramlines were being repaired. 'There's been a bad accident,' a passer-by explained when he saw Gregorius staring bewildered at the sign.

Feeling that he was making a habit of it he entered Hotel Bellevue and went into the restaurant. The subdued music, the waiter's light beige jacket, the silver tableware. He ordered something to eat. *The Balm of Disappointment.* 'He had often joked,' João Eça had said of Prado, 'that we humans regard the world as a stage for the acting out of our wishes. He considered this illusion the origin of all religion. "None of it is true," he used to say. "The universe is simply there, and it's completely indifferent, really completely indifferent to what happens to us."'

Gregorius took out Prado's book and looked for a heading with the word *cena.* By the time his meal arrived, he had found what he was looking for:

CENA CARICATA. COMICAL STAGE. *The world as a stage, waiting for us to present the important and sad, funny and meaningless dramas of our imaginations. How touching and charming it is, this idea! And how unavoidable!*

After Gregorius left the hotel he walked slowly to Monbijou and from there over the bridge to the Gymnasium. It had been many years since he had seen the building from this direction and it seemed strange to him. He had always entered it through the back door but now the main entrance was in front of him. Everything was dark. The church bell rang nine thirty.

He saw a man park his bicycle, unlock the main door and disappear inside the building. It must be Burri, the major, he decided. Gregorius knew that he sometimes came in the evening to prepare a physics or chemistry experiment for the next day. The light went on in the lab at the back of the building.

Without a sound, Gregorius slipped inside. He had no idea

what he wanted here. On tiptoe he sneaked up to the first floor. The classroom doors were locked and the high door to the auditorium couldn't be opened either. He felt locked out, even if, obviously, that made no sense at all. His rubber soles squeaked softly on the linoleum. The moon shone through a window. In its pale light he looked at everything as he had never looked at it before, not as a teacher and not as a student either. The door handles, the banister, the students' lockers. Despite their familiarity he looked at them now as if seeing them for the first time. He put his hand on the door handles, felt their cool resistance and crept along the corridor like a big, sluggish shadow. On the ground floor, at the other end of the building, Burri dropped something and the sound of smashing glass reverberated through the hall.

One of the classroom doors yielded. Gregorius entered the room where, as a student, he had seen the first Greek words on the blackboard. That was forty-three years ago. He had always sat at the back on the left and he sat in that seat now, too. Back then, Eva, Unbelievable, sat two rows in front of him, her red hair in a ponytail, which she would swish from side to side. Beat Zurbriggen, who had been his benchmate, had often fallen asleep in class, and was teased about it. Later, they found out that this was due to a metabolic disorder that killed him in his youth.

When Gregorius left the classroom, he knew why it was so strange to be here: he was viewing the school through the eyes of a former student, forgetting that for decades he had walked through the corridors as a teacher. How could one, as a teacher, forget what it was like to be a student?

Downstairs, Burri ran through the hall cursing. The door he slammed had to be the door to the staffroom. Now Gregorius heard the main door slam shut. The key was turned. He was locked in.

It was as if he woke up. But it was no awakening into the

teacher, no return to Mundus, who had spent his life in this building. The alertness was that of the secret visitor who hadn't managed to touch Bubenbergplatz earlier that evening. Gregorius went down to the staffroom, which Burri in his anger had forgotten to lock. He looked at the chair where Virginie Ledoyen always sat. *I must say, I must say: somehow I miss him.*

For a while, he stood at the window and looked out at the night. He pictured O'Kelly's pharmacy with the words IRISH GATE inscribed on the glass of the green-gold door. He went to the phone, called Inquiries and asked to be connected to the pharmacy. He felt like letting it ring all night in the empty, brightly lit pharmacy, until Jorge had slept off his drunkenness, entered the shop, and lit his first cigarette behind the counter. But after a while the engaged signal came and Gregorius hung up. When he called Inquiries again, he asked for the Swiss Embassy in Isfahan. A foreign, hoarse male voice answered. Gregorius hung up. *Hans Gmür,* he thought, *Hans Gmür.*

Next to the back door, he climbed out of a window and dropped to the ground. Momentarily he blacked out and held on to the bicycle stand to steady himself. Then he went to the annexe and approached the window from which he had once climbed during a Greek lesson. He saw Unbelievable turn to her benchmate to point out the unbelievable event. Her breath stirred the other girl's hair. The eyes with the squint seemed to expand and the freckles seemed to increase her look of amazement. Gregorius turned away and walked towards Kirchenfeldbrücke.

He had forgotten that the bridge was closed. Annoyed, he went through Monbijou. As he came to the Bärenplatz, midnight was striking. Tomorrow morning was market day, and that meant market women and cashboxes with money. *Books I stole. Books mustn't cost anything, that's what I thought then and still do*, he heard O'Kelly say. He went on towards Gerechtigkeitsgasse.

In Florence's flat, there was no light showing. She never went to bed before one o'clock. Had never gone to bed any earlier. Gregorius crossed to the other side of the street and waited behind a pillar. The last time he had done that was more than ten years ago. She had come home alone and her step had been tired, listless. When he saw her coming now, she was with a man. *You really might buy something new for a change. After all, you don't live alone. And Greek isn't enough for that.* Gregorius looked down at his new suit: he was better dressed than the other man. When Florence stopped under the street lamp he was shocked: she had grown grey in the intervening years. And although in her mid-forties, she was dressed as if she were at least fifty. Gregorius felt anger rise in him: hadn't she ever been back to Paris? Had her sloppily dressed companion who looked like a neglected tax clerk, deadened her sense of elegance? Afterwards, when Florence opened the window upstairs and leaned out, he was tempted to emerge from behind the pillar and wave to her.

Later, he went over to the doorbell. Florence de l'Arronge was her maiden name. If he interpreted the order of the bells correctly, her name was now Meier. He wasn't even worth a *y*. How elegant the doctoral student had looked back then, sitting in La Coupole! And how dowdy and worn the woman looked now! On the way up to the railway station and on to Länggasse, he felt a mounting anger that he understood less with each step. It subsided only when he stood before the shabby house where he had grown up.

The door was locked, but a piece of cloudy glass was missing from it. Gregorius put his nose to the opening: even today it smelt of cabbage. He looked for the window of the room where he had written Persian letters on the board. It had been enlarged and had acquired a new frame. It had made his blood boil when his mother imperiously called him to eat while he was excitedly reading the Persian grammar. He saw the sentimental novel by Ludwig Ganghofer on her bedside table. *Kitsch is the most misleading of all prisons*, Prado had noted. *The bars are covered with the gold of simplistic, unreal feelings so that you mistake them for the pillars of a palace.*

That night, Gregorius didn't sleep much and the first time he woke up, he didn't know where he was. He had rattled many doors of the Gymnasium and climbed through many windows in his dreams. When the city woke up in the morning and he stood at the window of his flat, he was no longer sure if he really had been in Kirchenfeld.

In the editorial offices of the big Bern newspaper, they weren't very helpful and Gregorius missed Agostinha of the *Diario de Noticias* in Lisbon. An advertisement from April 1966? Reluctantly, they left him alone in the archive and by noon he had found the name of the industrialist who had once sought a tutor for his children in Isfahan. There were three Hannes Schnyders in the phone book, but only one a licensed engineer. An address in the Elfenau.

Gregorius went to the house and rang the bell with the feeling of doing something completely absurd. The Schnyders in their impeccable villa apparently considered it a welcome change to drink tea with the man who had almost become their children's tutor thirty years ago. The two of them were approaching eighty and spoke of the wonderful times under the Shah when they had become rich. Why had he withdrawn his application all that time ago? A boy studying ancient languages – that would have been exactly what they were looking for. Gregorius spoke of his mother's illness and changed the subject.

How was the climate in Isfahan? he asked. Hot? Sand storms? Nothing you needed to be afraid of, they said, laughing, at least not when you had a house like they had. And then they

brought out photos. Gregorius stayed until evening and the
Schnyders were amazed and pleased at his interest in their
memories. They gave him a book about Isfahan.

Before he went to bed, Gregorius looked at the photographs
of mosques of Isfahan and listened to the Portuguese language
course. He fell asleep feeling that both Lisbon and Bern had
failed him. And that he no longer knew how it was when a
place *didn't* fail you.

When he woke up at about four, he felt like calling Doxiades.
But what could he have said to him? That he was here but
not here? That he had used the the telephone in the staffroom
of the Gymnasium to act out his crazy wishes? And that he
wasn't even sure it had all really taken place?

To whom, if not the Greek, could he have told that?
Gregorius thought of the strange evening when they had tried
calling each other by their Christian names.

'My name's Constantine,' the Greek had said suddenly during
the chess game.

'Raimund,' he had replied.

There had been no ritual confirmation, no raised glasses,
no handshake; they hadn't even looked at each other.

'But that's mean of you, Raimund,' said the Greek as he
fell into Gregorius's trap.

It didn't sound right, and Gregorius had the impression
that they both felt it.

'You shouldn't underestimate my meanness, Constantine,'
he said.

For the rest of the evening, they avoided that form of address.

'Good night, Gregorius,' said the Greek in parting, 'sleep
well.'

'You too, Doctor,' said Gregorius.

That was as far as it went.

Was that a reason not to tell Doxiades about his floating
confusion as he stumbled through Bern? Or was the distancing

closeness between them precisely what was needed for such a tale? Gregorius dialled and hung up on the second ring. Sometimes the Greek had this rough way typical of taxi drivers in Thessaloniki.

He took out Prado's book. As he sat reading at the kitchen table with the Venetian blind pulled down, as he had two weeks before, he had the feeling that the sentences the Portuguese aristocrat had written in the attic room of the blue house helped him to be in the right place: neither in Bern nor in Lisbon.

AMPLIDÃO INTERIOR. INTERNAL EXPANSE. *We live here and now, everything before and in other places is past, mostly forgotten and accessible as a small remnant in disordered slivers of memory that light up in rhapsodic contingency and die out again. This is how we are used to thinking about ourselves. And this is the natural way of thinking, when it is others we look at: they really do stand before us here and now, no other place and no other time, and how should their relationship to the past be thought of if not in the form of internal episodes of memory, whose exclusive reality is in the present of their happening?*

But from the perspective of our own inside, it's quite different. We're not limited to our own present, but, expanded far into the past. That comes through our feelings, especially the deep ones, those that determine who we are and how it is to be us. For these feelings know no time, they don't know it and they don't acknowledge it. It would naturally be false if I said: I am still the boy on the steps in front of the school, the boy with the cap in his hand, whose eyes strayed to the girls' school hoping to see Maria João. Naturally it is false; more than thirty years have passed since then. And yet it is also true. The heart pounding at difficult tasks is the heart pounding when Senhor Lanções, the maths teacher, entered the classroom; in the anxiety about all authorities, my bent father's words of authority resonate; and if the twinkling look of a woman strikes me, it takes my breath away as every time, from school window to school window, my look seemed to meet Maria João's. I am still there, at that distant place in time, I never left it, but live expanded in the past, or out of it. It is present, this past, and not simply in the form of brief episodes of flashing memory. The thousand changes that have driven time – measured by this timeless present of feeling, they are fleeting and unreal as a dream, and deceptive as dream images: they delude me into believing that I, a doctor that people come to with their pains and cares, possess fabulous self-confidence and fearlessness. And this anxious trust in the look of those who seek help forces me to believe in it as long as they stand before me. But as soon as they're gone, I'd like to shout: I'm still that scared boy on the school steps, it's absolutely irrelevant, really a lie, that I sit in the white coat behind the mighty desk and give advice, don't be deceived by what, in ridiculous superficiality, we call the present.

And not only in time are we expanded. In space, too, we stretch out far over what is visible. We leave something of ourselves behind when we leave a place; we stay there, even though we go away. And there are things in us that we can find again only by going back there. We go to ourselves, travel to ourselves, when the monotonous beat of the wheels brings us to a place where we have covered a stretch of our life, no matter how brief it may have been. When we set foot for the second time on the platform of the foreign railway station, hear the voices over the loudspeaker, smell the unique odours, we have come not only to the distant place, but also to the distance of our own inside; to a perhaps thoroughly remote corner of our self which, when we are somewhere else, is completely in the dark and invisible. Otherwise, why should we be so excited, so outside ourselves when the conductor calls the names of the places, when we hear the screech of the brakes and are swallowed up in the suddenly appearing shadow of the railway station? Otherwise, why should it be a magical moment, a moment of silent drama when the train comes to a complete halt with a final jolt? It is because, from the first steps we take on the strange and not strange platform, we resume a life we had interrupted and left, when we felt the first jolts of the moving train. What could be more exciting than resuming an interrupted life with all its promises?

It is an error, a nonsensical act of violence, when we concentrate on the here and now with the conviction of thus grasping the essential. What matters is to move surely and calmly, with the appropriate humour and the appropriate melancholy, into the temporally and spatially expanded internal landscape that we are. Why do we feel sorry for people who can't travel? Because, unable to expand externally, they are not able to expand internally either, they can't multiply and so they are deprived of the possibility of undertaking expansive excursions in themselves and discovering who and what else they could have become.

When it grew light, Gregorius went down to the railway station and took the first train to Moutier in the Jura. There were actually people travelling to Moutier. Real people. Moutier wasn't only the city where he had lost playing chess against the man with the square face, receding forehead and crew cut, because he couldn't bear how long he took over every move. Moutier was a real city with a city hall, supermarkets and teashops. For two hours, Gregorius searched in vain for the place where the tournament was played. You couldn't search for something you knew so little about. The waiter in the café was surprised at his confused, incoherent questions and afterwards Gregorius saw him whispering about him to his colleague.

In the early afternoon, he was back in Bern and took the tram to the university. It was the vacation. He sat down in an empty lecture hall and thought of the young Prado in the lecture halls at Coimbra. According to Father Bartolomeu, he could be merciless in the face of vanity. *Merciless. The knife opened in his pocket.* And he carried a few pieces of chalk about with him in case he was summoned to the board to be made a fool of. It was many years ago that Gregorius had sat here listening to a lecture on Euripides. He had been stunned at the high-flown gibberish being tossed about. 'Why don't you read the text again?' he had wanted to shout to the young lecturer. 'Read! Just *read!*' As the man kept introducing more and more French notions that seemed invented to suit the colour of his politics he had left the lecture hall amid the surprised looks of the other students. Too bad, he thought now, that he hadn't challenged the lecturer back then.

Outside the university, he paused after a few steps and held his breath. At that moment Natalie Rubin was coming out of the Haupt bookshop. In the bag she was carrying, he thought, was the Persian grammar and as she was now walking towards the post office she must be going to send it to him in Lisbon.

Perhaps that in itself would not have been enough, Gregorius thought later. Perhaps he would have remained in Bern nevertheless and stood in Bubenbergplatz until he could feel in touch with it again. But then, in the early dusk of the dull day, the light went on it all pharmacies. *Cortar a luz*, he heard O'Kelly say and, as the words wouldn't go away, Gregorius went to his bank and transferred a large sum to his current account. 'Well, at last you are using some more of your money!' said the woman who managed his savings.

He told Frau Loosli, his neighbour, that he had some more travelling to do. Could she take in his mail again and forward it to him if he called and told her where? The woman would like to have known more, but didn't trust herself to ask. 'Everything's fine,' said Gregorius, and held out his hand.

He called the hotel in Lisbon and asked them to reserve the same room for him as before for an indefinite time. It was as well that he had called, the receptionist said, since a package had come for him and the old woman had delivered another note. There had also been phone calls asking for him; they had written down the numbers. And they had found a chess set in the cupboard. Was it his?

In the evening, Gregorius went to have dinner at the Bellevue, the safest place not to run into anybody. The waiter was gracious as with an old acquaintance. Afterwards, Gregorius walked on to the Kirchenfeldbrücke, which was open again. He went to the place where the Portuguese woman had read the letter. When he looked down, he became dizzy. Back at home, he read the book about the Portuguese plague until late into the night. He turned the pages feeling like someone who knew Portuguese.

The next morning, he took the train to Zurich. The plane to Lisbon left shortly before eleven. When it landed in the early afternoon, the sun appeared out of a cloudless sky. The taxi drove with the windows open. The hotel porter, who carried his suitcase and the package containing Natalie Rubin's books to his room, recognized him and wouldn't stop talking. Gregorius didn't understand a word.

25

'*Quer tomar alguma coisa?* Will you come and have a drink with me? said the note Clotilde had brought on Tuesday. And this time the signature was simpler and more familiar: *Adriana*.

Gregorius looked at the three phone messages. Natalie Rubin had called on Monday evening and had been confused when they told her he had left. Then maybe she hadn't posted off the Persian grammar he had seen her with yesterday?

He called her. A misunderstanding, he said, he had only made a small trip and was now back in the hotel. She told him about her unsuccessful search for literature on the Resistência.

'If I were in Lisbon – I bet I'd find something,' she said.

Gregorius said nothing.

He had sent her much too much money, she said into the silence. And she was mailing his copy of the Persian grammar today.

Gregorius was silent.

'You don't object if I study it, too?' she asked and suddenly there was a note of trepidation in her voice that really didn't suit the courtly maiden, much less than the laughter she had drawn him into again.

No, no, he said and strove for a cheerful tone; why should I?

'*Até logo,*' she said.

'*Até logo,*' he said too.

Tuesday night Doxiades and now the girl: why was he suddenly such an illiterate about closeness and distance? Or had he always been, without noticing it? And why had he never had a friend like Jorge O'Kelly had been to Prado? A friend with whom he could have talked about things like loyalty and love, and about death?

Mariana Eça had called without leaving a message. José António de Silveira, on the other hand, had left him a message inviting him for dinner if he should ever come back to Lisbon.

Gregorius opened the package of books. The Portuguese grammar was so similar to a Latin book that he had to laugh, and he read it until it grew dark. Then he opened the history of Portugal and discovered that Prado's lifespan had coincided almost exactly with the length of the Estado Novo. He read about Portuguese fascism and the secret police, PIDE, which Rui Luís Mendes, the Butcher of Lisbon, had belonged to. Tarrafal, he learned, had been the worst camp for political prisoners. It had been on the Cape Verde islands of Santiago and its name had become a symbol for ruthless political persecution. But what interested Gregorius the most was what he read about the Mocidade Portuguesa, a paramilitary organization modelled on the Italian and German pattern. All young people, from grammar school to university, had to join it. That started in 1936, at the time of the Spanish Civil War, when Amadeu de Prado was sixteen. Had he too worn the compulsory green shirt? Raised his arm, as they did in Germany? Gregorius looked at the portrait: inconceivable. But how had he avoided joining it? Had his father used his influence? The judge, who, despite the atrocities of Tarrafal, had his chauffeur pick him up at ten to six in the morning in order to be the first one in the courthouse?

Late that night, Gregorius stood in the Praça do Rossio. Would he ever be able to touch the square as he had once touched Bubenbergplatz?

Before he went back to the hotel, he went to the Rua dos Sapateiros. In O'Kelly's pharmacy, a light was burning, and on the counter he saw the antiquated phone he had rung on Monday night from Kägi's office.

26

On Friday morning, Gregorius called Júlio Simões, the second-hand bookseller, and again asked for the address of the language school, which he had thrown away before the flight to Zurich. The school secretary was amazed when he said he couldn't wait until Monday and wanted to start lessons right away, if possible.

The woman who was delegated to give him individual instruction was dressed all in green, and even her eyeshadow matched. She sat down behind a desk in the well-heated room and shivered as she pulled the scarf around her shoulders. Her name was Cecília, she said in a light, melodious voice that didn't fit the sullen, sleepy face. Please would he tell her who he was and why he wanted to learn the language. In Portuguese, naturally, she added with an expression that seemed to express profound boredom.

It wasn't until three hours later, when Gregorius left the school, dizzy with exhaustion, that he realized, what had happened to him during that time: he had treated the sullen woman's impudent challenge like a surprise opening on the chess board. *Why do you never fight in life when you do it so well in chess!* Florence had said more than once. *Because I find fighting in life absurd*, he had answered; *you've got enough to fight with yourself.* And now he had himself actually provoked a fight with the green lady. Had she felt with unbelievable clairvoyance that she had to accept him as he was at this point in his life? Sometimes it had seemed to him to be so, especially when, behind the sullen façade, a triumphant smile had appeared, which told him she enjoyed his progress. *'Não, não,'* she had protested when he took out the grammar book, *'tem que aprender falando'*. You have to learn by speaking.

In the hotel, Gregorius lay down on the bed. Cecília had forbidden him the grammar book. Him, Mundus. She had even taken it away from him. Her lips moved incessantly and so did his lips and he had no idea where the words came from; *mais doce, mais suave,* she said constantly, and when she pulled the filmy green scarf over her lips, so that it blew when she spoke, he waited for the moment when he could see her lips again.

When he woke up, it was beginning to get dark, and by the time he rang Adriana's doorbell, it was night. Clotilde led him into the parlour.

'Where were you?' Adriana asked as soon as he entered the room.

'I've come to return your brother's note,' said Gregorius and handed her the envelope with the sheets.

Her features hardened, her hands remained in her lap.

'What did you expect?' asked Gregorius and it seemed like a bold move on the board whose consequences he couldn't foresee. 'That a man like him wouldn't think about what was right? After an emotional shock like that? After an accusation that put everything he stood for in question? That he would simply go on with business as usual? You can't be serious!'

He was alarmed by the ferocity of his last words. He was prepared for her to throw him out.

Adriana's features smoothed out and an almost happy amazement spread over her face. She held out her hands to him and Gregorius gave her the envelope. For a while, she stroked it with the back of her hand, as she had done with the furniture on his first visit to Amadeu's room.

'Ever since then, he's been going to see the man he met a long time ago in England, on the trip with Fátima. He told me about him when he . . . came back early, because of me. João is his name, João something. He often visits him. Doesn't come home at night so I have to send the patients away. Lies upstairs on the floor and studies train routes. He's always been crazy about trains, but not like that. It's not good for him, you can see that. His cheeks are hollow, he has lost weight, he's unshaven. It will be the death of him, I feel it.'

In the end, her voice had become fretful again, an audible refusal to acknowledge the past as something that was irrevocably past. But before, when he had snapped at her, there was something in her face that could be interpreted as the willingness and even the yearning wish to shake off the tyranny of memory and be freed from the dungeon of the past. And so he risked it.

'He hasn't studied train routes for a long time, Adriana. He hasn't visited João for a long time. He hasn't been practising for a long time. Amadeu is dead, Adriana. And you know that. He died of an aneurysm. Thirty-one years ago, half a human lifetime. In the morning. On Rua Augusta. They called you.' Gregorius pointed to the grandfather clock. 'At six twenty-three. That's how it was, wasn't it?'

Dizziness gripped Gregorius, and he held tight to the back of the chair. He wouldn't have the strength to resist another outburst from the old woman, such as he had experienced in the consulting room a week before. As soon as the dizziness had passed, he would leave the house and never come back. Why, for God's sake, had he thought it was his duty to free this woman, with whom he really had nothing to do, from the frozen past and bring her back to real life? Why had he seen himself as destined to break open the seals of her mind? What had given him this ludicrous idea?

They fell silent. The dizziness subsided and Gregorius opened his eyes. Adriana sat slumped on the sofa, had raised her hands to her face and was weeping; the gaunt body twitched, the hands with the dark veins shook. Gregorius sat down next to her and put his arm around her shoulders. Once more, the tears burst out of her, and now she clung to him. Then slowly, the sobs grew weaker and the calm of exhaustion set in.

When she sat up and reached for her handkerchief, Gregorius stood up and went to the clock. As if in slow motion, he opened the glass in front of the clock face and set the hands to the present time. He didn't dare turn round; one wrong move, one wrong look could make everything collapse. With a soft snap, the glass closed in front of the face. Gregorius opened the pendulum case and set it in motion. The ticking was louder than he had expected. In the first seconds, there seemed to be nothing in the parlour but this ticking. A new time had begun.

Adriana looked at the clock and it was the look of a disbelieving child. The hand with the handkerchief had stopped short as if frozen in time. And then something happened that seemed to Gregorius like a seismic shift: Adriana's eyes flickered, smouldered, went blank, refocused and all of a sudden took on the certainty and brightness of a look thoroughly attuned to the present. Their eyes met and Gregorius put into his all the confidence he possessed so that he could hold hers when they began to flicker again.

Clotilde appeared with the tea and stood motionless in the doorway, her eyes directed at the ticking clock. *Graças a Deus!* she said softly. She looked at Adriana and when she put the tea on the table, her eyes glittered.

What kind of music did Amadeu listen to? Gregorius asked after a while. At first Adriana didn't seem to understand the question. Her attention apparently had to travel a long way before she could return to the present. The clock ticked and, with every beat, seemed to announce the message that everything had changed. Then, all of a sudden, Adriana stood up without a word and put on a record of Hector Berlioz. *Les Nuits d'Été, La Belle Voyageuse, La Captive, La Mort d'Ophélie.*

'He could listen to it for hours,' she said. 'What am I saying? – for days.' She sat down on the sofa again.

Gregorius was sure she wanted to add something. She pressed the cover of the record so hard that her knuckles grew white. She swallowed. Fine drops formed in the corner of her mouth. She ran her tongue over her lips. Now she leaned back against the sofa, like someone yielding to fatigue. The black velvet ribbon slipped out of place and showed a small part of a scar.

'It was Fátima's favourite music,' she said.

When the music had died away and the ticking of the clock again broke the silence, Adriana sat erect and straightened the velvet ribbon. Her voice possessed the amazed calm and relieved confidence of someone who has just overcome an insurmountable internal hurdle.

'Cardiac arrest. At thirty-five. He couldn't believe it. My brother, who adapted to everything new with tremendous, almost inhuman speed and whose presence of mind grew by leaps and bounds when challenged, so that he seemed to be really alive only when the avalanche of an unexpected event threatened to submerge him – this man who could never get enough of reality, he couldn't believe, didn't want to admit that the stillness in her face was not the calm of repose. He refused a postmortem, the idea of the knife was unbearable to him, he kept postponing the funeral, shouted at people who reminded him of realities. He lost track of things, ordered a requiem mass, cancelled it, forgot that he had done so and blasted the priest when nothing happened. *I should have known it, Adriana,* he said, *she had heart arrhythmia, I didn't take it seriously. I'm a doctor and didn't take it seriously. In every other patient I would have taken it seriously but in her I attributed it to nerves. There was an argument with the other women in the nursing home; she wasn't a trained kindergarten teacher, they said, but only a spoiled daughter from a good family and the wife of a rich doctor, who didn't know how else to kill time. Her pride was wounded, for she had a natural way with children, they ate out of her hand. The others were just jealous. She thought she had succeeded in diverting attention from her childlessness so well and that's why her pride was hurt. Unable to fight back, she suffered in silence and then her heart started to beat unevenly. Sometimes it also looked like tachycardia. I should have taken it seriously, Adriana, why didn't I send her to a specialist? I knew one I studied with in Coimbra, he was a leading authority; all I had to do was call him. Why didn't I, my God, why didn't I? I didn't ausculate her even once, just imagine, not even once.*

'So, one year after Mamã's death, we were again at a requiem mass. *Fátima would have wanted it*, he said, *and besides you have to give death a form, at any rate, religion says that, I don't know.* Suddenly his thoughts were unsettled; *não sei, não sei,* he said constantly. At the mass for Mamã, he had sat in a dark corner so that it wouldn't be noticed that he wasn't taking part in the liturgy. Rita didn't understand it. *They're only gestures, a framework,* she said, *you were an altar boy, and it was all right in Papá's case.* Now, with Fátima, he was so off balance that one moment he participated and the next he sat still, as if frozen, instead of praying, and the worst thing was: he made mistakes in the Latin text. *Him! Mistakes!*

'He never wept in public, and not at the grave either. It was February the third, an unusually mild day, but he kept rubbing his hands, his hands were easily cold, and then, when the coffin was lowered into the ground, he buried his hands in his pockets and watched it, with a look I had never seen in him before, the look of someone who is burying everything he has, absolutely everything. Quite different from at the grave of Papá and Mamã, where he stood like someone who had prepared himself for this parting a long time and knew that it also meant a step forward in his own life.

'Everyone felt that he wanted to be alone at the grave and so we left. When I looked back, he was standing next to Fátima's

father, who had also remained, an old friend of Papá's. Amadeu
had met Fátima at his house and had come home in a trance.
Amadeu embraced the big man, who wiped his eyes with his
sleeve and then went away with ostentatiously bold steps. My
brother stood head down, eyes shut, and hands folded alone
at the open grave, for at least a quarter of an hour. I could
swear he was praying, I really hope so.'

*I love people who pray. I need the sight of them. I need it to
withstand the superficial and the thoughtless.* Gregorius pictured
the student Prado as he had spoken about his love of cathedrals
in the auditorium of the Liceu. *O sacerdote ateu,* he heard João
Eça say.

Gregorius had expected Adriana to give him her hand at
parting, for the first time. But instead, the old woman, whose
strands of grey hair now fell on her face, slowly came towards
him until she stood right in front of him and he could smell
the peculiar blend of perfume and medicine on her. He felt
like withdrawing, but the way she now shut her eyes and ran
her hands over his face had something imperious about it. Like
a blind person, she ran along his features with cold, trembling
fingers that sought only the slightest touch. Touching the glasses,
she faltered. Prado had worn glasses with round lenses in gold
frames. He, Gregorius, was the foreigner, who had set time in
motion again and had sealed the death of her brother. And he
was also this very brother, who had come back to life in the
telling. The brother – at that moment, Gregorius was sure of
it – who had something to do with the scar under the velvet
ribbon and with the red cedars.

Adriana stood embarrassed before him, her arms at her
sides, looking down. Gregorius grasped her shoulders with
both hands. 'I'll come back,' he said.

27

He hadn't been in bed half an hour when the hotel porter informed him that he had a visitor. He couldn't believe his eyes: it was Adriana, leaning on a cane, who stood in the middle of the hotel lobby, wrapped in a long black coat, the crocheted kerchief around her head. She had the touching yet bombastic look of a woman who had left her house for the first time in years and found herself in a world she no longer knew so that she didn't even trust herself to sit down in it.

Now she unbuttoned the coat and took out two envelopes.

'I . . . I'd like you to read that,' she said stiffly and uncertainly, as if speaking in the world outside was more difficult, or very different, from inside. 'One letter I found when we cleared out the house after Mamã's death. Amadeu came within a hair's-breadth of seeing it, but I decided to keep it to myself when I found it in the secret compartment of Papá's desk. The other I found in Amadeu's desk after his death, buried under a pile of other papers.' She looked at Gregorius shyly, dropped her eyes, looked at him again. 'I . . . I wouldn't like to remain the only one who knows about the letters. Rita, yes, Rita wouldn't understand them. And I don't have anybody else.'

Gregorius shifted the envelopes from one hand to the other. He searched for words and didn't find them. 'How did you get here?' he asked at last.

Outside in the taxi, Clotilde was waiting. When Adriana sank into the cushions of the back seat, it was as if this excursion into the real world had consumed all her strength.

'*Adeus*,' she had said to him before she got in. When she had given him her hand, he had felt the bones and the veins on the back of it yield under the pressure. He was amazed to feel how strong and decisive her handshake was, almost like that of someone who lived in the outside world from morning to night and shook dozens of hands every day.

This surprisingly strong, almost routine handshake reverberated in Gregorius as he watched the taxi drive off. In his mind, he turned Adriana back into the forty-year-old woman described by old Coutinho when he had mentioned the arrogant way she treated the patients. If there hadn't been the shock of the abortion and if she had lived her own life afterwards, instead of her brother's life, what a different person she would be today!

Back in his room, he first opened the thicker envelope. It was a letter from Amadeu to his father, the judge. A letter that had never been sent. That it had been constantly revised over the years could be inferred from the many corrections showing how the handwriting had changed and the inks of different vintages.

Dear Father, was the original form of address, which later became *Honoured feared Father*. Even later Amadeu had added *Beloved Papá*, and the last version had opened with *Secretly beloved Papá.*

When your chauffeur took me to the railway station today and I sat on the seat where you sit every morning, I knew I would have to capture in words all the contradictory feelings that threaten to tear me to pieces so as not to be their victim. I believe that by expressing a thing its power is retained and its terror diminished, writes Pessoa. At the end of this letter I will know if he is right. However, I will have to wait a long time for this knowledge; for I already feel that it will be a long and rocky road to achieve the clarity I seek in writing this. And when I think of something that

Pessoa failed to mention, I'm afraid: the possibility that a thing can be lost through expressing it. What happens then to all the power and the terror?

I wish you a successful term, *you say every time I go back to Coimbra. Never – at this parting or any other – have you used words that would have expressed the wish that the new term might give me* satisfaction *or* pleasure. *In the car, when I ran my hand over the upholstery, I thought: Does he even know the word* prazer? *Was he ever young? At some point he must have met Mamã. Some time.*

But even though it was the same as always, this time it was also different, Papá. In a year, hopefully you'll come home, *you said when I was already outside. The sentence choked me and I felt I was stumbling. It was a sentence that came from the tormented man with the crooked back and not from the mouth of the judge. Sitting in the car, I tried to hear it as an expression of a pure and simple affection but the tone didn't convince me, for I knew that most of all he wanted his son, the doctor, to be near him and to help him in the fight against pain. 'Does he ever mention me?' I asked Enrique at the wheel and he seemed to be preoccupied with the traffic. His answer was slow in coming. 'I believe he's very proud of you,' he said finally.*

Gregorius knew that Portuguese children, even in the fifties, still addressed their parents formally, but used the indirect form with *o pai, a mãe.* He had learned that from Cecília, who had first called him *você,* but interrupted him after a while and suggested that they should say *tu,* the other was so stiff; after all, it was the abbreviated form of *Vossa Mercê,* or *Your Grace.* In the letter the young Prado had decided to alternate between the two extremes, regarding the familiar *tu* and the formal *você.* Or had it not been a decision, but rather the natural, unthinking expression of his wavering feelings?

One sheet of the letter ended with the question to the chauffeur. Prado hadn't numbered the pages. The continuation was abrupt and written in different ink. Was that Prado's own order, or had Adriana determined the sequence?

You are a judge, Father – a person who judges, condemns, and punishes. 'I no longer know how it happened,' Uncle Ernesto once said to me; 'it seems to me that it was fixed at his birth.' Yes, I thought at the time; exactly.

I realize that you didn't behave like a judge at home; you didn't make judgements more often than other fathers, on the contrary, very seldom. And yet, Father, I often found your silent presence judgemental.

You are – I imagine – a fair judge, filled with and determined by benevolence, not a judge whose harsh, unsparing judgements come from resentment at the deprivations and failures of his own life, or from the denied guilt of his secret failures. You were as lenient as the law allowed you to be. Nevertheless, I have always suffered from the fact that you are one who sits in judgement over others. 'Are judges people who send others to prison?' I asked you after my first day at school, where I had to reveal my father's profession. That's what the others were talking about at break. What they said didn't sound scornful or accusing; rather it was curiosity and the desire for sensation, much the same as their curiosity about another student's father who worked in the slaughterhouse. From then on, I would make every possible detour to avoid having to pass the prison.

I was twelve when I slipped past the guard into the courtroom to see you sitting in your robes on the judge's bench. At that time, you were a regular judge and not yet on the Supreme Court. What I felt was pride but at the same time I was terrified. You were sentencing a habitual thief to prison, without probation because of recidivism. The woman was middle-aged, careworn and ugly, not a face that could charm. Nevertheless, everything in me recoiled when she was led away and disappeared into the bowels of the court, which I imagined as dark, cold and damp.

I thought the defence didn't make a good case. He delivered his sentences listlessly, you learned nothing about the woman's reasons for committing the crime. She couldn't explain herself, I wouldn't be surprised if she was illiterate. Later, I lay awake in the dark and defended her and it was not so much a defence against the state attorney as a defence against you. I talked myself hoarse until the stream of words ran dry. In the end, I stood before you paralysed by a lack of words. When I woke up, I realized that ultimately I had defended myself against a charge you had never made. You never accused me, your idolised son, of anything serious, not once, and sometimes I think what I did, I did for this reason: to pre-empt a possible accusation that I seemed to recognize, without knowing anything about it. Isn't that ultimately the reason why I became a doctor? To do what is humanly possible to cure the devilish affliction of vertebral arthritis? To be protected from the reproach of not sympathizing enough with your silent suffering? A reproach meant to drive away Adriana and Rita.

But back to the court. Never will I forget the incredulousness and horror that gripped me when I saw the prosecution and the defence turn to each other after the verdict and laugh together. I would have thought such a thing was impossible and, to this day, I can't grasp it. I'll say this for you: when you left the chamber, with the books under your arm, your face was serious, regret could be read in it. How much I wished it was really genuine, this regret that a heavy cell door would now close behind the thief and that enormous, unbearably loud keys would turn in the lock!

I could never forget her, that thief. Many years later, I observed another thief in a department store, a young woman of bewitching beauty, a wizard at making glittering things disappear into her coat pockets. Confused by the joy I felt as I watched her on her reckless raid of the store, I followed her. Only very gradually did it occur to me that, in my imagination, the woman was avenging that other thief you had sent to prison. When I saw a man approaching her with a purposeful step, I went up to her and whispered: 'Cuidado!' Her presence of mind left me speechless.

'Vem, armor,' *she said and hung on to me, her head on my shoulder. In the street, she looked at me and now anxiety could be read in her eyes, in amazing contrast to her nonchalant, cold-blooded actions.*

'Why?' The wind blew her hair into her face and hid her expression for a moment. I stroked it off her forehead.

'It's a long story,' I said. 'But to cut it short: I love thieves. Assuming I know their names.'

She pursed her lips and considered for a moment. 'Diamantina Esmeralda Ermelinda.'

She smiled, pressed a kiss on my lips and disappeared round the corner. Afterwards I sat at the table opposite you with a feeling of triumph. At this moment, all the thieves in the world mocked all the law books in the world.

Your law books: for as long as I can remember, the uniform black leather volumes have filled me with awe. Those weren't like other books, they possessed a special status and a unique dignity. They were so grand that it surprised me to find Portuguese words in them — even though they were heavy, baroque, and squiggly words, invented, it seemed to me, by denizens of a different planet. Their foreignness and remoteness were underlined even more by the sharp smell of dust that penetrated from the shelf and made me think vaguely that it had to be part of the nature of these books that no one ever took them down and they kept their sublime content entirely to themselves.

Much later, when I began to grasp what the arbitrariness of a dictatorship meant, I sometimes pictured those unused law books from my childhood, and then I blamed you, rather childishly, for not taking them out to fling them in the face of Salazar's thugs.

You never ordered me not to take the books off the shelf. No, it wasn't you who stopped me, it was the heavy, majestic volumes themselves that forbade me with draconian rigour to do so, or even to shift them very slightly. How often when I was a little boy did I creep into your study and, with heart pounding, struggle

*against the wish to pick up a volume and glance at the sacred
contents! I was ten when I finally did so, with trembling fingers
and after looking over my shoulder to avoid being caught. I
wanted to track down the mystery of your profession and understand
who you were in the outside world. It was a powerful disappointment
to see that the brittle, formal language contained between the
covers held absolutely nothing revelatory, nothing that could make
one feel the hoped-for frisson of fear.*

*Back then, when the court rose after the trial of the thief, our
eyes met. In any case, that's how it seemed to me. I had hoped —
and it lasted for weeks, this hope — that you would bring up the
matter yourself. Finally, the hope turned to disappointment, which
gradually metamorphosed into something closer to protest and rage:
did you think I was too young for it, too limited? But that didn't
agree with the fact that otherwise you demanded everything from
me and and took it for granted. Was it painful for you that your
son had seen you in your judge's robes? But I never had the feeling
that you were embarrassed by your profession. In the end, were
you scared of my doubts? You knew that I would have them, even
if I was still half-child; you knew me well enough for that; at
least I hope so. So, was it cowardice — a kind of weakness I never
otherwise connected with you?*

*And I? Why didn't I bring it up myself? The answer is simple
and clear: to take you to task — that was something one simply*
could not do. *It would have brought down the whole edifice of
the family. And it wasn't only something one couldn't* do; *it was
something one couldn't even* think. *Instead of thinking and doing
it, I combined the two images in my imagination: the familiar,
private father, master of silence, and the man in the robes, who
measures his words in the courtroom and speaks in a sonorous
voice, overflowing with eloquence. And whenever I imagined this,
I flinched, for no consoling contradiction emerged. It was hard,
Father, that everything fitted together in this way and when I
could no longer bear your presence in me like a monolithic figure,*

I indulged a thought that I generally avoided because it seemed to defile the sacredness of intimacy: that now and then you must have embraced Mamã.

Why did you become a judge, Papá, and not a defence attorney? Why did you come down on the side of the prosecution? There must be judges, you would probably say, and naturally I know that it would be difficult to argue with this. But why did my father, of all people, have to be one of them?

So far, it was a letter to a father who was still alive, a letter the student Prado had written in Coimbra; you could imagine he had started it immediately after the return he mentioned. On the next sheet, the ink and the handwriting changed. The pen-stroke was now more self-confident, more relaxed, and as if it were refined by the professional routine of medical notes. And the verb forms indicated when sentences had been added after the judge's death.

Gregorius calculated: there were ten years between the time Prado finished college and the time of his father's death. Had the silent conversation between father and son come to a halt for so long? When feelings ran deep ten years could pass in a second; nobody knew that better than Prado.

Did the son have to wait until the father's death before he could continue writing the letter? When he had finished at medical school, Prado had returned to Lisbon where he worked in the neurological clinic. Gregorius had learned that from Mélodie.

'I was nine then and glad he was back; today I would say it was a mistake,' she had said. 'But he was homesick for Lisbon, he was always homesick. As soon as he went away, he wanted to come back. As well as this homesickness he had a crazy love of trains. He was full of contradicitons, my big, beaming brother. There was the traveller in him, the man with wanderlust, who was fascinated by the Trans-Siberian Railway

– *Vladivostok* was a holy name to him – and there was the other side of him, the homesick one. *It's like thirst,* he'd say, *when it attacks me, homesickness; it's like an unbearable thirst. Maybe I have to know all the train routes so I can come home at any time. I couldn't bear to go to Siberia – just imagine: the pounding of the wheels over many days and nights; it would take me farther away from Lisbon, ever farther.'*

It was already getting light when Gregorius laid the dictionary aside and rubbed his burning eyes. He closed the curtain and lay down under the covers in his clothes. *I am losing myself:* that had been the thought that had made him go to Bubenbergplatz, which he found he could no longer touch. When had that been?

And if I want *to lose myself?*

Gregorius slipped into a light sleep, swept by a whirlwind of thoughts. The green-clad Cecília constantly addressed the judge as *Your Grace,* she stole expensive glittering things, diamonds and other gems, but most of all she stole names, names and kisses carried by pounding wheels through Siberia to Vladivostok, much too far from Lisbon, the place of court-houses and pain.

A warm wind greeted him when he pulled back the curtain and opened the window at noon. He stood still for a few minutes and felt his face dry and become hot under the onslaught of the desert air. For the second time in his life, he ordered a meal in his room and when he saw the tray of food was reminded of the other time, in Paris, on that crazy trip Florence had suggested after the first breakfast in his kitchen. *Desire, pleasure, and security.* Desire was the most fleeting, Prado had said, then came pleasure, and finally security. Therefore, it was loyalty that counted, a partisanship of the soul that went beyond feeling. *A breath of eternity. You never really meant me,* he had said to Florence at the end, and she hadn't said no.

Gregorius called Silveira, who invited him for supper. Then he wrapped up the picture book about Isfahan which the Schnyders in Elfenau had given him, and asked at reception where he could buy scissors, pins, and tape. As he was about to leave, Natalie Rubin called. She was disappointed that the Persian grammar hadn't yet arrived, despite having sent it by express mail.

'I should have just brought it to you!' she said, and then, scared and a little embarrassed at her own words, she asked what he was doing over the weekend.

Gregorius couldn't resist replying, 'I'm sitting without electricity in a school with rats and reading about the difficult love of a son for his father, who took his own life because of pain or guilt, nobody knows.'

'You're pulling . . .' said Natalie.

'No, no,' said Gregorius, 'I'm not pulling your leg. It's exactly as I say. Only it's impossible to explain, simply impossible, and then there is also this wind from the desert . . .'

'You're hardly . . . hardly recognizable any more. If I . . .'

'You said it, Natalie, I can't believe it myself sometimes.'

Yes, he would call her as soon as the grammar had come.

'Will you also learn Persian in the fabulous rat school?' She laughed at her own linguistic creation.

'Naturally. That's where Persia *is*.'

'I give up.'

They laughed.

28

Why, Papá, did you never talk to me about your doubts, your inner struggles? Why didn't you show me your letters to the Minister of Justice, your requests to resign? Why did you destroy everything so that now it's as if you had never written them? Why did I have to hear about your attempts to fight for freedom from Mamã, and why was she ashamed to tell me about something which should have been a cause for pride?

If it was the pain that finally drove you to death: well, I couldn't have done anything to prevent that. With pain, the force of words is soon exhausted. But if it wasn't the pain that cast the decisive vote, but rather the feeling of guilt and failure because in the end you didn't muster the strength to break away from Salazar and no longer close your eyes to blood and torture: why didn't you talk it over with me? With your son who once wanted to be a priest?

Gregorius looked up. The tropical air streamed out of Africa through the open window of Senhor Cortês's office. The wandering cone of light on the rotting floorboards was a stronger yellow today than recently. On the walls hung the pictures of Isfahan he had cut out. Dark blue and gold, gold and dark blue, and more and more of it, domes, minarets, markets, bazaars, women's faces veiled in black, eyes with a zest for life. Eliphaz of Teman, Bildad of Shuah, and Zophar of Na'ama.

The first thing he looked for was the Bible on his sweater, which already smelt of mould and mildew. *God punishes the Egyptians with plagues because Pharaoh is obstinate*, Prado had said to O'Kelly. *But it was God Himself who made him like that! And He made him like that so He could demonstrate His own power! What a vain, complacent God! What a show-off!* Gregorius re-read the story: it was right.

For half a day, O'Kelly had said, they had argued about whether Prado should really talk about God as a show-off, a *gabarola* or *fanfarrão*, in his speech. Whether it wasn't going too far to place the Lord – even if only for the tiny length of a single impudent word – on a level with a loud-mouthed punk. Jorge had won out over Amadeu and he had left it out. For a moment, Gregorius had been disappointed in O'Kelly.

Gregorius went through the building, avoiding the rats, and sat down on the seat where he had recently imagined Prado making eye contact with Maria João. In the basement he finally found the former library where, according to Father Bartolomeu, the young Amadeu had sometimes spent the whole night reading. *When Amadeu finishes reading a book, it has no more letters.* The dusty shelves were now empty. The only book still there lay propping up a shelf to keep it from tipping over. Gregorius broke off the corner of a rotten floorboard and wedged it in instead of the book. Then he brushed the dust off the book and leafed through it. It was a biography of Juana la Loca. He took it with him to Senhor Cortês's office, then he returned to Prado's letter.

It was much easier to be taken in by António de Oliveira Salazar, the aristocratic professor, than by Hitler, Stalin or Franco. You would never have associated with such scum, you would have been immune to them through your intelligence and your unerring sense of style, and you never raised your arm in the fascist salute, I'd stake my life on that. But the man in black with the intelligent, strained face under the bowler hat: sometimes I thought you may have had a fellow feeling with him. Not his merciless ambition or his ideological blindness, but with the iron discipline you both imposed upon yourselves. But, Father, he made a pact with the others! And allowed those crimes for which there will never be an appropriate word, as long as humans live! And we had Tarrafal! Why did you turn a blind eye to Tarrafal, Father! TARRAFAL! You would only have had to look once on such hands as I saw on João Eça: burned, scarred, maimed hands that had once played Schubert. Why didn't you ever look at such hands, Father?

Was it because you were afraid, out of physical weakness, to pick a fight with the power of the State? And therefore looked the other way? Was it your bent back that forbade you to show any backbone? But no, I refuse to accept such an explanation; it would be unfair because it would negate the dignity you always showed: the strength never to surrender to your suffering in thoughts and deeds.

Once, Father, one single time, I was glad you could pull strings in the circle of well-dressed, top-hatted criminals, I have to admit that: when you managed to release me from the Mocidade. *You saw my horror when I imagined having to put on the green shirt and raise my arm.* It won't happen, *you said simply, and I was happy at the affectionate implacability in your look. I wouldn't have wanted to be your enemy. Of course, you yourself didn't want to imagine your son as a trendy camp-fire proletarian either. Nevertheless I felt your action – for whatever reason – as an expression of deep affection, and on the night after my release, my feelings of gratitude were overwhelming.*

It was more complicated when you saved me from being arrested for causing bodily harm to Adriana. The judge's son: I don't know what strings you pulled, what talks you engaged in. I tell you today: I would rather have faced the judge and fought for the moral right to be able to put life above the law. Nevertheless, what you did moved me deeply, whatever it was. I can't explain it, but I was sure that neither of the two things I couldn't have accepted decided you: fear of scandal or the joy of being able to use your influence. You did it simply to protect me. I am proud of you, *you said when I explained the medical facts to you and showed you the passage in the textbook. Then you hugged me, the only time since childhood. I smelled the tobacco on your clothes and the soap on your face. I still smell them and I can still feel the pressure of your arms holding on longer than I had expected. I dreamed of these arms and they were imploring arms, stretched out with a fervent plea to the son to free the father from pain like a kindly magician.*

One element in this dream was the enormous expectation and hope that always appeared on your face when I explained the mechanism of your illness, the irreversible curvature of the spine named after Vladimir Bechterev, and when we spoke about the mystery of pain. Those were moments of great intimacy when you, hung on every word of the future doctor. Then I was the knowing father and you the needy son. How did your father behave towards you, I asked Mamã after one of these conversations. 'He was unbearable,' she said. 'A proud, solitary, tyrant who ate out of my hand. A fanatical colonialist. He would turn in his grave if he knew what you think of that.'

That evening Gregorius arrived for dinner with Silveiras wearing his new clothes. The man lived in a villa in Belém. A maid opened the door and Silveira came to meet him in a vast hall, lit by a chandelier, that looked like the entrance to an embassy. He noticed Gregorious looking around admiringly.

'When the children moved out after the divorce, everything was suddenly much too big. But I didn't want to move out either,' said Silveira, on whose face Gregorius detected the same weariness as in their first meeting on the night train.

Later, when they were sitting over dessert, Gregorius no longer knew how it had come about but he was telling Silveira about Florence, about Isfahan, and his crazy visits to the Liceu. It was a little like the time in the sleeping car when he had told this man how he had stood up in front of the students and left the classroom. 'Your coat was damp when you took it from the hook, I remember precisely, it was raining,' Silveira had said during the soup course, 'and I also still know what light is in Hebrew.' Then Gregorius had told him about the nameless Portuguese woman whom he had omitted to mention on the train.

'Come with me,' said Silveira after coffee and led him to the cellar. 'Look, this was the children's camping equipment. Everything of the finest quality, nothing missing. One day they simply left the stuff, no more interest, no thanks, nothing. A heater, a lamp, a coffee machine, everything battery-operated. Why don't you just take them? For the Liceu? I'll tell the driver; he'll check the batteries and take them over there.'

It wasn't only the generosity. It was the Liceu. A while ago, Silveira had made him describe the abandoned school and had kept wanting to know more; but that could have been mere curiosity, a curiosity like that about the bewitched fairy-tale castle. The offer of the camping equipment however, showed an understanding of his bizarre act – or, if not understanding, then respect – Gregorius hadn't expected that from anybody, least of all from a businessman whose life was calculated on money.

Silveira saw his surprise. 'I simply like the idea of the Liceu and the rats,' he said, smiling. 'Something so completely different, something that doesn't involve money. It seems to me it has something to do with Marcus Aurelius.'

When he was alone in the living room, Gregorius looked at the books. Lots of literature about porcelain. Commercial law. Travel books. Dictionaries of English and French business language. A lexicon of child psychology. A shelf with an odd assortment of novels.

On a table in the corner was a photograph of the two children, a boy and a girl. Gregorius thought of Kägi's letter.

In their conversation that morning, Natalie Rubin had mentioned that the Rector had cancelled classes as his wife was in as hospital, in the Waldau. *There are moments when my wife looks as if she's going to pieces,* the letter had said.

'I called a business friend of mine who is often in Iran,' said Silveira when he came back. 'You need a visa, but otherwise it's no problem to travel to Isfahan.'

He paused when he saw the expression that appeared on Gregorius's face.

'I see,' he said slowly. 'I see. *Naturally.* It's not *this* Isfahan. And not Iran, but *Persia.*'

Gregorius nodded. Mariana Eça had been interested in his eyes which she said revealed a lack of sleep in him. But otherwise, Silveira was the only person here who had shown any interest in him. In *him* for himself. The only one for whom he wasn't just a sympathetic ear, as he had been to those who inhabited Prado's world.

As they stood in the hall saying goodbye and the maid brought Gregorius's coat, Silveira's eyes wandered to the gallery and on to other rooms. He looked at the floor, then back up.

'The children's wing. Former wing. Do you want to see it?'

Two generous-sized, light rooms with their own bath. Long rows of Georges Simenon novels on the bookshelves.

They stood in the gallery. Silveira suddenly seemed not to know what to do with his hands.

'If you like, you could live here. For free, of course. As long as you like.' He laughed. 'If you're not in Persia. Better than a hotel. You won't be disturbed, I'm away a lot. Like tomorrow morning again. Julieta, the maid, will take care of you. And some day I'll win a game against you.'

'*Chamo-me José,*' he said as they sealed the agreement with a handshake. '*E tu?*'

29

Gregorius packed. He was as excited as if he were setting out on a trip around the world. He imagined clearing a few Simenons off the shelf in the boy's room and putting out his own books: the two about the plague and the earthquake, the New Testament Coutinho had given him an eternity ago, Pessoa, Eça de Queirós, the picture biography of Salazar, Natalie Rubin's books. In Bern, he had packed Marcus Aurelius and his old Horace, the Greek tragedies and Sappho. At the last moment, also Augustine's *Confessions. Books for the next stretch of the way.*

The bag was heavy, and when he picked it up from the bed and carried it to the door, he felt dizzy again. He lay down. After a few minutes, it passed and he continued reading Prado's letter.

I start trembling at the very thought of the unplanned and unknown, but inevitable and unstoppable force with which parents leave traces in their children that, like traces of branding, can never be erased. The outlines of parental will and fear are written with a white-hot stylus in the souls of the children who are helpless and ignorant of what is happening to them. We need a whole life to find and decipher the branded text and we can never be sure we have understood it.

And you see, Papá, that's also what happened to me with you. Not long ago it finally dawned on me that there is a powerful text in me that has dominated everything I have felt and done so far, a hidden white-hot text, whose insidious power lies in the fact that, despite all my education, it never occurred to me that it might not possess the validity I had unwittingly granted it. The text is brief and of Old Testament finality: OTHERS ARE YOUR COURT OF JUSTICE.

I can't prove it in court, but I know that, from an early age, I read this text in your eyes, Father, in the look that penetrated full of deprivation, pain and severity from behind your eyeglasses and seemed to follow me wherever I went. The only place it couldn't follow me was the big chair in the library of the Liceu, where I hid at night to be able to go on reading. The solid concreteness of the chair along with the darkness resulted in an impenetrable wall that protected me from all intrusions. There, your look didn't penetrate, and so neither was there a court of justice I had to account to when I read of the women with white limbs and all the things you may do only in secret.

Can you imagine my rage when I read in the Prophet Jeremiah: Can any man hide himself in secret places that I shall not see him? saith the Lord. Do not I fill heaven and earth? saith the Lord.

'What do you want?' said Father Bartolomeu. 'He is God.'

'Yes, and that's precisely what speaks against God: that he is God,' I replied.

The priest laughed. He didn't hold it against me. He loved me.

How much, Papá, would I have liked to have a father to talk to about these things! About God and His complacent cruelty, about cross, guillotine and garrotte. About the madness of turning the other cheek. About justice and revenge.

Your back, it couldn't bear the church pews, so that I saw you kneeling only one single time, at the requiem mass for Uncle Ernesto. The silhouette of your tortured body remains unforgettable to me; it had something to do with Dante and Purgatory, which I always imagined as a flaming sea of humiliation. For what is worse than humiliation? The fiercest pain is nothing compared to it. And we never got to talk about these things. I think I heard the word Deus *from you only in hackneyed idioms, never properly, never as if it were spoken from belief. And yet you didn't do anything against the mute impression that you bore not only the secular law books in you, but also the ecclesiastical ones from which the Inquisition emerged. Tarrafal, Father,* TARRAFAL!

30

Silveira's chauffeur came for Gregorius in the late morning. He had charged the batteries of the camping equipment and packed two blankets, with coffee, sugar and biscuits lying on top of them. At the hotel, they weren't happy that he was moving out. '*Foi um grande prazer*,' they said.

It had rained during the night and fine sand from the desert wind lay on the car. Filipe, the driver, opened the door to the back seat of the big, shining car for Gregorius. *In the car, when I stroked the upholstery* – that's where Prado's plan to write a letter to his father had been born.

Gregorius had ridden in a taxi with his parents only once, on the way back from a holiday on Thunersee, where his father had sprained his foot and they had to take a cab because of the luggage. He had seen from the back of his father's head how uneasy he was. For his mother, it had been like a fairy tale; her eyes lit up and she didn't want to get out.

After delivering Gregorius's things to the villa, they went on to the Liceu. They arrived to find that the road which was once used to deliver supplies to the school kitchen was completely overgrown. 'Here?' Filipe asked, flabbergasted. The heavy-set man with shoulders like a horse anxiously avoided the rats when they entered the building. He walked gingerly around the Rector's office, cap in hand, looking at the pictures of Isfahan.

'And what are you doing here?' he asked. 'I mean, it's not my place . . .'

'Hard to say,' said Gregorius. 'Really hard. You know what daydreaming is. It's a little like that. But also quite different. More serious. And crazier. When life is short, rules no longer apply. And then it looks as if you have cracked and are fit for the loony bin. But basically it's the other way around: the ones who belong there are those who don't want to admit that time is short. You understand?'

'Two years ago, I had a heart attack,' said Filipe. 'I found it strange to go back to work afterwards. Now it comes back to me, I had completely forgotten it.'

'Yes,' said Gregorius.

When Filipe had gone, the sky clouded over; it became cool and dark. Gregorius put on the heater, turned on the light and made coffee. The cigarettes. He took them out of his pocket. What brand of cigarettes had he smoked the first time in his life? Silveira had asked him. Then he had left the room and returned with a packet of this very brand. *Here. It was my wife's brand. Been lying for years in the drawer of the night table. On her side of the bed. Couldn't throw them away. The tobacco must be dry as dust.* Gregorius tore open the packet and lit one. By now he could inhale without coughing. The smoke was sharp and tasted like burned wood. A wave of dizziness washed over him and his heart seemed to skip a beat.

He read the passage in Jeremiah that Prado had written about and leafed back in Isaiah. *For my thoughts are not your thoughts, neither are your ways my ways, saith the Lord. For as the heavens are higher than the earth, so are my ways higher than your ways, and my thoughts than your thoughts.*

Prado had taken seriously the idea that God was a person who could think, feel, and had a will. Then he had heard himself saying: I won't have anything to do with such an arrogant character. Did God have a *character*? Gregorius thought of Ruth Gautschi and David Lehmann and of his own words about poetic seriousness, the greatest seriousness of all. Bern was far away.

Your remoteness, Father. Mamā as the interpreter, who had to translate your reticence to us. Why didn't you learn to talk about yourself and your feelings? I want to tell you why: it was too comfortable for you, it was so wonderfully comfortable for you to hide behind the Mediterranean role of the aristocratic head of the family. And there was also the role of the sufferer in whom taciturnity is a virtue, that is, the virtue of not complaining about the pain. And so, your illness was an excuse for not wanting to learn to express yourself. You were arrogant: others were left to guess how much you were suffering.

Didn't you see what you forfeited in terms of autonomy, which we only have if we know how to express ourselves?

Did you never think, Papá, how much of a burden it was for us that you didn't *talk about your pain and humiliation? That your mute, heroic endurance, which was not without vanity, could be more oppressive for us than if you had sometimes cursed and shed tears of self-pity? For that meant that we children, and mainly I, the son, imprisoned by your imposed bravery, we had no right to complain. Every such right, even before one of us claimed it – was negated, destroyed by your courage and your bravely endured suffering.*

You refused to take painkillers, you didn't want to lose your lucidity, you were dogmatic about that. Once, when you believed you were unobserved, I watched you through a crack in the door. You took one tablet and after a brief struggle, you also put another one in your mouth. After a while, when I looked in again, you were leaning back in the chair, your head on the cushion, your glasses in your lap, your mouth slack. Naturally it was unthinkable, but how I would have liked to go in and give you a hug!

Not once did I see you weep. You stood there with a rigid face when we buried Carlos, the beloved dog – even beloved by you.

You weren't a soulless person, far from it. But why did you act all your life as if the soul was something to be ashamed of, something unseemly, a place of weakness that must be kept hidden, at almost any cost?

Through you, we all learned from childhood on are that there is nothing in our minds that wasn't first in the body. And then – what a paradox! – you withheld from us every sign of affection so that we really couldn't believe that you had ever come close enough to Mamã to conceive us. It wasn't him, *Mélodie once said,* it was the Amazon. *Only once did I feel that you recognized what a woman is: when Fátima came into the room. Nothing changed in you and everything changed. For the first time I grasped what a magnetic field was.*

Here the letter ended. Gregorius put the sheets back in the envelope. As he did so, he noticed a pencilled note on the back of the last page. *What did I know of your fantasies? Why do we know so little about the fantasies of our parents? What do we know of somebody if we know nothing of the images passed to him by his imagination?* Gregorius put the envelope away and looked at his watch. He was due to play chess with João Eça that afternoon, and it was time to set out for the ferry.

31

Eça chose white, but didn't start. Gregorius had made tea and poured both of them half a cup. He smoked one of the cigarettes Silveira's wife had left behind in the bedroom. João Eça also smoked. He smoked and drank and said nothing. Twilight descended over the city. They would soon be called for supper.

'No,' said Eça when Gregorius went to the light switch. 'But lock the door.'

It grew dark fast. The glow of Eça's cigarette expanded and contracted. When he started speaking, it was as if he had put a mute on his voice, as on an instrument, a mute that made the words not only softer and darker, but also rougher.

'The girl. Estefânia Espinhosa. I don't know what you know about her. But I'm sure you have heard of her. You've wanted to ask me about her for a long time. I feel that. You haven't dared. I've been thinking about it since last Sunday. It's better if I tell you my story. It is, I think, only a part of the truth. If there is a truth here. But this part you should know. Whatever the others will say.'

Gregorius refilled the teacup. Eça's hands shook as he drank.

'She worked in the post office. The post office was important for the Resistance. Post office and railway. She was young when O'Kelly met her. Twenty-three or twenty-four. That was in the spring of 1970. She had this unbelievable memory. Forgot nothing, neither what she had seen nor what she had heard. Addresses, phone numbers, faces. We used to joke that she knew the phone directory by heart. "How come you can't, too?" she said in retaliation. "I don't understand how one can be so forgetful." Her mother had run away or had died young, I don't remember, and her father was arrested and dragged off one morning, a railway worker they suspected of sabotage.

'She became Jorge's lover. He was smitten with her; we were worried about it because such things are always dangerous. She liked him, but he wasn't her passion. That gnawed at him, made him edgy and sick with jealousy. "Don't worry," he said when I looked at him pensively. "You're not the only one who's not a beginner."'

'The school for illiterate people was her idea. Brilliant. Salazar had started a campaign against illiteracy, learning to read as a patriotic duty. We hired a room, stocked it with old benches and a desk. Enormous blackboard. The girl got hold of whatever educational materials there were, pictures illustrating letters, things like that. Such a class was open to anybody, people of all ages. That was the deception: nobody needed to justify his presence to the outside world, and moreover, with stool pigeons, you could rely on discretion; it's a stigma not to know how to read. Estefânia sent out the invitations, made sure they weren't opened, even though all they said was: *Shall we see each other on Friday? Kisses, Noëlia*, the imaginary name as a password.

'We met. Discussed plans.

If somebody from, the PIDE showed up, or anyone else who hadn't been invited, she would simply pick up a piece of chalk. That was also part of the deception: we could meet openly, we didn't need to hide. We could do whatever we wanted with the pigs. Resistance isn't anything to laugh at. But sometimes we laughed.

'Estefânia's memory became increasingly important. We didn't have to write anything down, didn't have to leave a paper trail. The whole network was in her head. Sometimes I thought:

what if she had an accident? But she was so young and so beautiful, full of life, you pushed such thoughts aside. We landed one blow after another.

'One evening, in the autumn of 1971, Amadeu entered the room. He saw her and was spellbound. When the meeting broke up, he went across to speak to her. Jorge waited in the doorway. She hardly looked at Amadeu, lowered her eyes immediately. I saw it coming.

'Nothing happened. Jorge and Estefânia stayed together. Amadeu stopped coming to meetings. Later, I found out that she used to go to his office. She was crazy about him. Amadeu turned her away. He was loyal to O'Kelly. Loyal to the point of self-denial. Through the winter, a semblance of calm prevailed. Sometimes Jorge was seen with Amadeu. Something had changed between them, something intangible. When they walked beside each other, it was as if they were no longer walking in step as before. As if the solidarity had become an effort. And something had also changed between O'Kelly and the girl. He managed to control himself, but now and then irritability flared, he blamed her for mistakes but was proved wrong by her memory and left the group. Even so, things might have come to a head, but it would have been harmless, compared to what actually happened.

'In late February, one of Mendes's minions burst into the meeting. An intelligent, dangerous man – we all knew him – he had opened the door silently and slipped into the room. Estefânia was unbelievable. As soon as she saw him, she broke off a sentence about a dangerous operation, picked up the chalk and the pointer and pretended to be giving us a lesson. Badajoz – that was the man's name, like the Spanish city – sat down, I can still hear the bench squeak in the breathless silence. Estefânia took off her jacket although it was cool in the room. To be safe, she always dressed seductively at our meetings. With bare arms and the see-through blouse, she was

. . . you could lose your mind on the spot. O'Kelly hated it. Badajoz crossed his legs.

'With a provocative spin of her body, Estefânia ended the would-be lesson. "Until next time," she said. Everyone stood up, you could feel the collective self-control. Estefânia's music professor, sitting next to me, also got up to leave. Badajoz went over to him.

'I knew it. I knew that disaster had struck.

'"An illiterate professor," said Badajoz and his face twisted into a nasty grin. "Something new. Congratulations on the educational experience."

'The professor turned pale and ran his tongue over his dry lips. But he held up well under the circumstances.

'"I've recently met someone who has never learned to read. I knew about Senhora Espinhosa's course, she is one of my students, and I wanted to sample it myself before recomending it to the person in question," he said.

'"Ah," said Badajoz. "What's his name?"

'I was glad the others had disappeared. I didn't have my knife on me. I cursed myself.

'"João Pinto," said the professor.

'"How original," grinned Badajoz. "And the address?"

'The address the professor gave didn't exist. They arrested him and kept him in custody. It wasn't safe for Estefânia to go home any more. I forbade her to stay at O'Kelly's place too. "Be reasonable," I said to him. "That's much too dangerous. If she's busted, you'll be busted with her." I arranged for her to stay with an old aunt of mine.

'Amadeu asked me to come to the office. He had spoken with Jorge. He was out of his mind with anxiety. Thoroughly beside himself. In this quiet, subdued way that was peculiar to him.

'"He wants to kill her," he said flatly. "He didn't say it in as many words, but it's clear: he wants to kill Estefânia. To wipe out her memory before they catch her. Just imagine: Jorge, my old friend Jorge, my best friend, my only real friend. He's gone crazy, he wants to sacrifice his lover. *It's about many lives*, he kept saying. One life against many, that's his calculation. Help me, you must help me, it mustn't be allowed to happen."

'If I hadn't always known it – I realized during this conversation that Amadeu loved her. Naturally, I couldn't know how it had been with Fátima. I had seen them together only that one time in Brighton, and yet I was sure: this was something completely different, something much wilder, like a volcano about to erupt. Amadeu was a walking paradox: self-confident and fearless, but also someone who constantly felt under scrutiny. That was why he had come to us; he wanted to defend himself against the accusation about Mendes. Estefânia, I think, was his chance to finally leave the courthouse, go out into the wider world and live his life according to his own wishes, according to his passions, and to hell with the rest.

'He was aware of this, I'm sure, he knew himself relatively well, better than most, but there was this barrier, the iron barrier of loyalty to Jorge. Amadeu, was the most loyal person alive, loyalty was his religion. But sometimes loyalty had to be sacrificed for freedom and maybe happiness. He had steeled himself to suppress the desire he felt for the girl. He wanted to keep on being able to look Jorge in the eye; he didn't want a forty-year-old friendship to break up because of a daydream, however painful.

'And now, Jorge wanted to take away from him the girl who had never belonged to him. Wanted to test his sense of loyalty beyond acceptable limits.

'I talked with O'Kelly. He denied saying anything of the sort or even implying it. Some red spots had appeared on his unshaved face and it was hard to say if they were connected more with Estefânia or with Amadeu.

'He was lying. I knew it and he knew that I knew. He had

started drinking. He felt that Estefânia was slipping away from him, with or without Amadeu, and he couldn't bear it.

"'We could take her out of the country," I said.

"'They'll catch her," he said. "The professor is strong, but not strong enough. They'll crack him, then they'll find out that she carries everything in her memory, and they'll hunt her down. They'll use all the means at their disposal to find her. Imagine, *the whole Lisbon network* could be at risk. They won't rest until they have her, and they're an army.'"

The nurse had knocked on the door to call them for dinner. Eça had ignored her and gone on talking. It was dark in the room by now and Eça's voice sounded to Gregorius as if it came from another world.

'What I say now may shock you: I understood O'Kelly. I understood both him and his arguments, for those were two different things. If they gave her an injection and cracked her memory, all of us would be implicated, some two hundred people, and it would be many times that if they dragged every individual over the coals. It was inconceivable. You only needed to imagine some of the consequences and you thought: *She has to go.*

'In this sense, I understood O'Kelly. I still believe it would have been a justifiable murder. Whoever disagreed simply didn't get it. A lack of imagination, I'd say. The wish for clean hands as the highest principle I find repulsive.

'I think that, in this matter, Amadeu couldn't think clearly. He pictured her shining eyes, the unusual, almost Asian features the contagious, thrilling laugh, the swaying walk, and he simply didn't want all that to be snuffed out. *He could not want it* and I am glad he couldn't, for anything else would have made him a monster, a monster of self-denial.

'O'Kelly, on the other hand – I suspect that he also saw her death as a redemption, redemption from the torment of knowing that passion drew her to Amadeu. And in that, too,

I understood him, but in a completely different sense, that is, without approval. I understood him because I recognized myself in his feelings. A long time ago I had also lost a woman to somebody else and she had also brought music into my life, not Bach as with O'Kelly, but Schubert. I knew what it meant to dream of such a redemption and I knew how easily you can find a pretext for such a plan.

'And precisely because of that, I threw a monkey wrench into O'Kelly's plan. I got the girl out of hiding and took her to the blue house. Adriana hated me for it, but then she already hated me. To her, I was the man who had hijacked her brother into the Resistance.

'I spoke with people who knew their way around the mountains on the border and gave Amadeu the necessary instructions. He stayed away for a week. When he came back, he was ill. I never saw Estefânia again.

'They caught me shortly after, but that had nothing to do with her. They said she was at Amadeu's funeral. Much later, I heard that she was working in Salamanca, as a lecturer in history.

'I haven't spoken a word to O'Kelly for ten years. Today it's all right again, but we don't seek each other out. He knows what I thought back then, which doesn't make it any easier.'

As Eça took a fierce drag on his cigarette, the burning ash ate along the paper that shimmered bright in the dark room. He coughed.

'Every time Amadeu visited me in the slammer, I was tempted to ask him about O'Kelly, about their friendship. I didn't dare. Amadeu never threatened anybody, that was part of his credo. But, without knowing it, he could *be* a threat. There was always the danger that he might go to pieces in front of the others. Naturally, I couldn't ask Jorge either. Maybe today, after more than thirty years, I don't know. Can a friendship survive such a thing?

'When I came out, I searched for the professor. Nobody had heard from him since the day of the arrest. Those pigs. Tarrafal. Have you ever heard of Tarrafal? I had counted on being sent there. Salazar was senile and the PIDE did just what it wanted. I think it was only by chance that I wasn't. In that case, I had planned to ram my head against the wall of the cell until my skull broke.'

They fell silent. Gregorius was lost for words.

Finally, Eça stood up and turned on the light. He rubbed his eyes and made the opening move he always made. They played until the fourth move, then Eça pushed the board aside. The two men stood up. Eça took his hands out of the sweater pockets. They approached each other and embraced. Eça's body shook. A raw sound of animal strength and helplessness came out of his throat. Then he grew limp and held on tight to Gregorius. Gregorius stroked his head. When he quietly unlocked the door, Eça was standing at the window and looking out into the night.

32

Gregorius stood in the living room of Silveira's house and looked at a row of photographs, snapshots of a big party. Most of the men wore frock coats, the ladies long evening gowns whose trains brushed the shining parquet floor. José António da Silveira was also to be seen, many years younger, with a woman, a voluptuous blonde who reminded Gregorius of Anita Ekberg in the Trévi Fountain. The children, maybe seven or eight, chased each other under the endless buffet table. Behind one table was the family coat of arms, a silver bear with a red sash. In another picture, they all sat and listened to a young woman playing the grand piano, an alabaster beauty with a distant resemblance to the nameless Portuguese woman on the Kirchenfeldbrücke.

After arriving in the villa, Gregorius had sat on the bed for a long time and waited for the shock of parting from João Eça to subside. The raw sound from his throat, a dry sob, a cry for help, a memory of torture, all of those things – he would never erase from his memory, He wished he could pour so much hot tea into himself that it would wash away Eça's pain.

Then, slowly, the details of the story about Estefânia Espinhosa came back into his mind. Salamanca. She had become a lecturer in Salamanca. The railway station sign with the dark medieval name emerged before him. Then the sign disappeared and he thought of the scene Father Bartolomeu had described: how O'Kelly and the woman, without looking at each other, had walked towards each other and had then stood at Prado's

grave. *That they avoided each other's eyes created a greater closeness
between them than any exchange of looks could have done.*

Finally, Gregorius had unpacked his suitcase and put his
books on a shelf. It was very quiet in the house. Julieta, the
maid, had gone home, leaving a note for him on the kitchen
table about where to find the food. Gregorius had never
been in a house as grand as this and everything seemed
forbidden, even the sound of his footsteps. Switch by switch,
he had turned on the lights. The dining room, where they
had eaten together. The bathroom. He had even cast a brief
glance into Silveira's study, only to close the door again
straight away.

And now he stood in the living room where he and Silveira
had drunk coffee and said the word *nobreza*; he liked it, and
he kept repeating it. And *aristocracy*, he now became aware
that he had always liked it, too; it was a word things flowed
into, or vice versa. De l'Arronge – Florence's maiden name –
had never made him think of aristocracy, and she didn't set
much store by it either. Lucien von Graffenried: that was
something else, old Bern aristocracy; it made him think of a
noble sandstone structure, at the corner of Gerechtigkeitsgasse,
and that there had been a von Graffenried who had played
some vague role in Beirut.

And naturally, of Eva von Muralt, Unbelievable. It had only
been an end-of-term party, not comparable to the one in
Silveira's photos and yet he had sweated with excitement in
the high rooms. 'Unbelievable!' Eva had said when a boy asked
her if an aristocratic title could be bought. 'Unbelievable!' she
had also shouted when Gregorius wanted to wash the dishes
at the end.

Silveira's record collection made little impression. As if the
period in his life when music had played a role was long gone.
Gregorius found Berlioz, *Les Nuits d'Été, La Belle Voyageuse*
and *La Mort d'Ophélie*, the music Prado had loved because it

reminded him of Fátima. *Estefânia was his chance to finally leave the courthouse, go out into the wider world.*

Maria João. He had to find Maria João. If anybody knew what had happened to Prado on the way back from Spain and why he became ill on his return, it would be her.

He spent an uneasy night, listening to every unfamiliar sound. The scattered dream images teemed with aristocratic women, limousines and chauffeurs. And they hunted Estefânia. They hunted her, and he didn't see even a single image of the hunt. He woke up with his heart racing, had to fight dizziness, and sat down at the kitchen table at about five o'clock with the other letter Adriana had brought him.

My esteemed, dear son,

Over the years, I have started so many letters to you and thrown them away, so that I don't know what number this one is. Why is it so difficult?

Can you imagine what it is like to have a son blessed with so many talents? A son powerful with words who gives his father the feeling that all he has left is silence if he is not to sound like a bungler? As a law student, I enjoyed the reputation of being deft with words. And I was introduced to the Reis family, mother's family, as an eloquent attorney. My speeches against Sidónio Pais, the gallant fraud in uniform, and for Teófilo Braga, the man with the umbrella in the tram, made an impression. So why did I fall silent?

You were four when you came to me with your first book to read me two sentences: Lisbon is our capital. It is a beautiful city. *It was Sunday afternoon, after a downpour, muggy, heavy air streamed in through the window, steeped with the smell of wet flowers. You had knocked on the door, stuck your head in and asked: 'Do you have a minute?' Just like the grown-up son of an aristocratic household who approaches the head of the family respectfully and requests an audience. I liked your precocious manners, but at the same time I was alarmed. What had we done wrong that you didn't come crashing in like other children? Your mother hadn't told me anything about the book and I was flabbergasted when you read me the sentences without the slightest hesitation and with the clear voice of a lecturer. And your voice was not only clear but also full of love for words, so that the two simple sentences sounded like poetry. (I know it is childish, but sometimes I thought that this was the origin of your homesickness, the legendary homesickness you savoured, without it being any the less real for that; indeed you had never even been out of Lisbon, and couldn't possibly know what homesickness is; you have to experience it before you can feel it, but who knows, you are capable of everything, even the inconceivable.)*

A radiant intelligence filled the room and I still recall that I thought: How little the naïveté of the sentences suits him! Later, when I was alone again, pride gave way to another thought: from now on, his mind will be like a dazzling spotlight that mercilessly illuminates all my weaknesses. I believe that was the beginning of my fear of you. For yes, I was afraid of you.

How hard it is for a father to confront his children, and how hard to endure the thought that one is registered in their souls with all one's weaknesses, blindness, errors and cowardice! I had these thoughts when I worried that the Morbus Bechterev might be hereditary, but you were spared, thank God. Later, I thought more of the soul, our inside, that is as receptive to impressions as a wax tablet and records everything with seismographic precision. I stood before the mirror and thought: How will this stern face be judged by you?

But what can you do to alter your face? Only a little, for I don't mean the simple physiognomy. But not much. We aren't the sculptors of our facial features or the stage managers of our seriousness, our laughing and weeping.

After you read me the first two sentences came hundreds, thousands, millions of words. Sometimes, it seemed as if the books you held were as much a part of you as the hands that held them. Once when you were reading outside on the steps, a ball from a children's game landed near you. Your hands left the book and threw the ball back. How strange the movement of the hand was!

I loved you as a reader, I loved you very much. Even if your compulsion for words seemed strange to me.

Even stranger was your fervour as you carried the candles to the altar. Unlike your mother, I didn't believe for a moment that you could become a priest. You have the soul of a rebel and rebels don't become priests. So where would your ardour finally lead you, what outlet would it seek? That it possessed an explosive force, this ardour, that was palpable. I was afraid of the explosions it could produce.

I felt this fear when I saw you in court. I had to condemn the thief and send her to prison, the law demanded it. Why did you look at me as if I were a torturer? Your look paralysed me, I couldn't talk about it. Do you have a better idea of what we should do with thieves? Do you?

As I watched you grow up, I was amazed at the breadth of your mind, I heard you cursing God. I didn't like your friend Jorge, anarchists frighten me, but I was glad you had a friend, a boy like you. It could have been so different: your mother dreamed of you pale and quiet behind the walls of an institution. She was deeply horrified by the text of your graduation address. 'A blasphemous son, what did I do to deserve it?' she said.

And I read the text. And was proud! And jealous! Jealous of the independent thought and of the morality that spoke through every one of your lines. They were like a shining horizon I would also have liked to have reached, but never could; the leaden gravity of my upbringing was too great for that. How could I have explained my proud jealousy to you? Without making myself feel small, even smaller and more dejected than I already was?

It was crazy, thought Gregorius: the two men, father and

son, had lived on opposite hills of the city like opposing actors in an ancient drama, linked by an archaic fear of each other and an affection they couldn't find words for, and had written letters to each other that they didn't trust themselves to send. Confined in a mutual silence neither understood, and blind to the fact that one led to the other.

'Madam sometimes sat here, too,' said Julieta, when she came in the late morning and found him at the kitchen table. 'But she didn't read any books, only magazines.'

She observed him. Hadn't he slept well? Or was there something wrong with the bed?

He was fine, said Gregorius, he hadn't felt so good in a long time.

She was glad there was someone else in the house now, she said, Senhor da Silveira had become so quiet and closed in. 'I hate hotels,' he had said recently when she had helped him pack. 'Why do I go on? Can you tell me that, Julieta?'

33

He was the strangest student she had ever had, Cecília said.

'You know more literary words than most people in the tram, but when you curse, go shopping, or try to book a trip, you have no idea what to say. Not to mention flirting. Or do you know what you'd like to say to me?'

Shivering, she pulled the green shawl around her shoulders.

'And the man has the slowest quick-wittedness I've ever encountered. Slow and yet quick-witted – wouldn't have thought that possible. But with you . . .'

Under her withering look, Gregorius took out the grammar book and pointed to a mistake.

'Yes,' she said and the green scarf billowed in front of her lips, 'but sometimes the informal way is the right way. That was certainly so even with the Greeks.'

On the way to Silveira's house, Gregorius drank coffee in a bar across the street from O'Kelly's pharmacy. Now and then he saw the smoking pharmacist through the display window. *He was smitten with her*, he heard João Eça say. *She liked him, but he wasn't her passion. It made him edgy and sick with jealousy . . . Amadeu entered the room. He saw her and was spellbound.* Gregorius took out Prado's book and leafed through it until he found the following passage:

But when we set out to understand someone on the inside? Is that a trip that ever comes to an end? Is the soul a place of facts? Or are the alleged facts only the deceptive shadows of our stories?

On the tram to Belém, he felt suddenly that his sense of

the city had changed. So far, it had been exclusively the place
of his investigations, and the time that had flowed through it
had taken its shape from the plan to keep finding out more
about Prado. Now, when he looked out of the tram window,
the time when the car crept along creaking and groaning was
all his own; it was simply the time when Raimund Gregorius
was living his new life. He saw himself standing again in the
Bern tram depot and asking about the old cars. Three weeks
ago, he had had the feeling of travelling here through the Bern
of his childhood. Now he was travelling through Lisbon and
only Lisbon. He felt as if something had been rearranged deep
inside himself.

In Silveira's house, he called Frau Loosli and dictated his
new address to her. Then he called the hotel and found out
that the Persian grammar had arrived. The balcony on which
he was sitting was bathed in warm spring sunshine. He listened
to the people passing in the street and was amazed at how
much he understood. From somewhere came the smell of
food. He was reminded of the tiny balcony of his childhood,
where the repulsive cooking smells had hovered. Later, when
he lay under the blanket in Silveira's son's room, he had fallen
asleep after a few moments and found himself in a contest of
quick-wittedness in which the slowest won. He stood with
Eva von Muralt, Unbelievable, at the sink and washed the
dishes after the school party. Finally, he sat in Kägi's office
and spent hours calling distant countries where nobody picked
up the phone.

In Silveira's house, too, time began to be his own. For the
first time since he had arrived in Lisbon, he turned on the
television and saw the evening news. He moved very close to
the set so that there was as little distance as possible between
him and the words. He was surprised by how much had
happened and how different Portuguese priorities were. On
the other hand, it was also amazing that the familiar here was

the same as at home. He thought: *I'm living here. Vivo aqui.* He couldn't follow the film that came next, so he put on the record of Berlioz's music that Prado had listened to for days after Fátima's death. It echoed through the whole house. After a while, he sat down at the kitchen table and finished reading the letter the judge had written to the son he feared.

Sometimes, my son, increasingly often, you seem to me like a self-righteous judge who reproaches me for still wearing the robes. For seeming to shut my eyes to the cruelty of the regime. Then I feel your look on me as a scorching light. And would like to pray to God to fill you with more understanding and take the executioner's gleam out of your eyes. Why didn't You grant him more imagination about me? – *I'd like to shout at Him and it would be a shout full of resentment.*

For you see: great, even excessive, as your imagination can be, you have no idea what pain and a twisted back make of a person. Well, nobody *seems to have an idea of that except the victims.* Nobody. *You gave me a splendid explanation of what Vladimir Bechterev discovered. And I wouldn't want to miss a single one of these conversations, they are precious hours when I feel secure with you. But then it's past, and I return to the hell of being stooped and enduring. And the one thing that you never seem to consider is that you can't expect as much from those who are slaves to humiliating curvature and incessant pain as from those who can forget their bodies.* You can't expect the same thing from them! *And that they depend on* not having to tell people about their suffering, *for that would be a new humiliation!*

The truth – yes, the truth – is quite simple: I don't know how I should have endured my life if Enrique didn't pick me up every morning at ten to six. Sundays – you have no idea what a torture they are. Sometimes I don't sleep on Saturday night because I anticipate how it will be. That even on Saturdays at a quarter past six, I enter the empty building: they joke about it. Sometimes

I think that more cruelty is produced by thoughtlessness than by any other human weakness. I keep asking for a key for Sundays. They refuse. Sometimes I wish they had my pain for one day, one single day, so they'd understand.

When I enter the office, the pain subsides a little; it's as if the room becomes like a prop inside my body. Until shortly before eight, it's quiet in the building. I usually study the files for the day. I have to be sure there are no surprises, a man like me is scared of that. Sometimes I also read poetry and my breathing calms down; it's as if I were looking at the sea and sometimes that helps to relieve the pain. Now do you understand?

But Tarrafal, you will say. Yes, Tarrafal, I know. Should I give up the key because of that? I've tried it out, more than once. I took it off the key ring and put it on the desk. Then I left the building and walked through the streets as if I had really done it. I breathed into my back as the doctor recommended, the breathing grew louder and louder. I walked through the city gasping, sweating with fear that some day the imagined scenario might become real. In a shirt damp with sweat, I later sat at the judge's bench. Now do you understand?

It isn't only to you that I have written countless letters that I later destroyed. I've also kept writing to the minister. And one of the letters I put in the house mail. I caught the postman on the street before he delivered it to the minister. He was annoyed to have to rummage through his bag and he looked at me with the contemptuous curiosity many people show for an error. I threw the letter where the others went: into the river. So that the treacherous ink would be washed away. Now do you understand?

Maria João Flores, your loyal classmate, understood. One day, when I could no longer bear how you looked at me, I arranged to meet her.

'He would like to respect you,' she said and put her hand on mine; 'revere and love you as one loves a paragon. "I don't want to see him as a sick man who is forgiven everything," he said. "It

would then be as if I no longer had a father.' He assigns a very definite role to others and is merciless when they don't fit it. A refined kind of egoism.'

She looked at me and gave me a smile that came from the experience of a well-lived life.

'Why don't you try showing your anger?'

Gregorius picked up the last sheet. The few sentences were written with a different-coloured ink and the judge had dated it June 8, 1954, a day before his death.

The struggle is at an end. What, my son, can I say to you in farewell?

You became a doctor for my sake. What would have happened if you had not grown up in the shadow of my suffering? I am in your debt. You are not responsible that the pain remained and my resistance has now broken.

I left the key in the office. They'll blame it all on the pain. That a failure can also die – the idea is foreign to you.

Will my death satisfy you?

Gregorius was freezing and turned on the heating. *Amadeu came within a hair's-breadth of seeing it, but I decided to keep it to myself,* he heard Adriana say. The heating didn't help. He turned on the television and sat watching a soap opera he didn't understand a word of; it could have been in Chinese. In the bathroom, he found a sleeping pill. By the time it started to take effect, it was growing light outside.

34

There were two Maria João Flores who lived in Campo de Ourique. The next day, after language school, Gregorius went there. The first doorbell he rang was answered by a young woman with two children hanging on her skirt. In the other house, he was told that Senhora Flores had gone away two days earlier.

He picked up the Persian grammar book from the hotel and went out to the Liceu. Migratory birds swooshed over the abandoned building. He had hoped the hot African wind would come back, but the mild March air remained, with a whiff of wintry sharpness.

In the grammar book was a note from Natalie Rubin: *I made it up to here!* The letters were difficult, she had said when he called her to say that the book had arrived. For days, she had done nothing else; her parents were amazed at her diligence. When was he planning his trip to Iran? Wouldn't that be a little dangerous these days?

The year before, Gregorius had read in the newspaper an ironic commentary about a man who had started learning Chinese at the age of ninety. The author had made fun of the man. *You have no idea* – with this sentence, Gregorius had begun his draft of a letter to the editor. 'Why do you waste time on such things?' Doxiades had said when he saw his anger devouring him. He hadn't sent the letter. But the Greek's casual manner had bothered him.

A few days ago, in Bern, when he had tested himself on

how many Persian letters he still remembered, only a few had
come back to him. But now, with the book before him, it
went more quickly. *I am still there, in that distant place in time,
I never left it, but live expanded in the past, or out of it,* Prado
had noted. *The thousand changes that time has accelerated – they
are, measured by this timeless present of feeling, fleeting and unreal
as a dream.*

The cone of light in Senhor Cortês's office moved.
Gregorius thought of the irrevocably silent face of his dead
father. He would like to have turned to him back then with
his fear of the Persian sandstorm. But he hadn't been that
kind of a father.

He made the long journey to Belém on foot and arranged
it so that he passed by the house where the judge had lived
with his silence, his pain, and the fear of his son's judgement.
The cedars stood out in the black night sky. Gregorius thought
of the scar under the velvet ribbon on Adriana's neck. Behind
the lighted windows, Mélodie went from room to room. She
knew whether these were the red cedars. And what they had
to do with the fact that a court could have accused Amadeu
of bodily injury.

It was now the third evening he had spent in Silveira's
house. *Vivo aqui.* Gregorius went out of the house, through
the dark garden, and on to the street. He strolled through the
neighbourhood and looked through windows at people,
cooking, eating, watching television. When he returned, he
looked at the pale yellow façade and the illuminated porch
with its columns. An elegant house in a wealthy neighbourhood.
I live here now. In the parlour, he sat down in a chair. What
could that mean? He could no longer touch the Bubenbergplatz.
Would he eventually be able to touch the ground of Lisbon?
What kind of touch would it be? And how would he place
his feet on this ground?

To live for the moment: it sounds so right and so beautiful,

Prado had remarked in one of his brief notes, *but the more I want to, the less I understand what it means.*

In all his life, Gregorius had never been bored. There were few things he found as incomprehensible as somebody who didn't know what to do with their time. Even now he wasn't bored. What he felt in the silent, much-too-big house was something else: time stood still, or no, it didn't stand still, but it didn't pull him along with it, didn't approach any future, flowed past him indifferently, without touching him.

He went into the boy's room and looked at the titles of the Simenon novels. *L'homme qui regardait passer les trains.* It was the novel whose stills had hung in the window of the Bubenberg Cinema, black-and-white pictures featuring Jeanne Moreau. It had been three weeks ago yesterday, Monday, when he had passed by there. The film must have been made in the sixties. Forty years ago. How long was that?

Gregorius hesitated to open Prado's book. Reading the letters had changed something. The father's letter even more than the son's. Finally, he started leafing through it. There weren't many pages left that he hadn't yet read. How would it be after the last sentence? He had always feared the last sentence and from the middle of a book, had always been tormented by the thought that there would inevitably be one. But this time his fear was much greater than usual. When he finished the last sentence it would be as if the invisible thread that had bound him to the Spanish bookshop on Hirschengraben would be broken. He would delay turning the last page and read as slowly as he could, but it wasn't entirely in your hands. The last look into the dictionary, more exhaustive than necessary. The last word. The last full stop. Only then would he would arrive in Lisbon. In Lisbon, Portugal.

TEMPO ENIGMÁTICO. ENIGMATIC TIME. *It took me a year to find out how long a month is. It was in October last year, on the last day of the month. What happens every year happened and what nevertheless throws me off every year, as if I had never before experienced it: the new faded morning light announced winter. No more burning light, no painful dazzle, no sweltering air you want to flee from to the shadows. A mild, conciliatory light that visibly contained the impending shortness of the days. Not that I would meet the new light as an enemy, as one who rejects and fights it in comical helplessness. It saves strength when the world loses the sharp corners of summer and shows us more blurred outlines that demand less resolve.*

No, it wasn't the pale, milky veil of the new light that made me flinch. It was the fact that the broken, weakened light once again indicated the irrevocable end of a period in nature and a temporal segment in my life. What had I done since the end of March, since the day when the cup on the table had become hot in the sun again so that I winced when I picked it up? Had it been a lot of time that had flowed since then, or a little? Seven months – how long was that?

I usually avoid the kitchen, that's Ana's domain and there is something about her vigorous juggling of the pans that I don't like. But that day, I needed somebody to whom I could express my silent fear, even if I couldn't put a name to it.

'How long is a month?' I asked out of the blue.

Ana, who was about to light the gas, blew out the match.

'You mean?'

Her forehead was wrinkled like someone confronting an insoluble puzzle.

'What I say: how long is a month?'

Looking down, she rubbed her hands in embarrassment.

'Well, sometimes they're thirty days, sometimes . . .'

'I know that,' I said gruffly. 'But the question is: how long is that?'

Ana reached for the spoon to give her hands something to do.

'Once, I took care of my daughter for almost a month,' she

said hesitantly and with the caution of a psychiatrist afraid his words could cause a collapse in his patient that could never be restored. 'Up and down the steps many times a day with the soup that mustn't be spilled – that was long.'

'And how was it afterwards, looking back?'

Now Ana risked a smile of relief that her answer apparently hadn't been wrong. 'Still long. But somehow it kept getting shorter, I don't know.'

'The time with all the soup – do you miss it now?'

Ana moved the spoon back and forth, then she took a handkerchief out of her apron and blew her nose. 'Naturally I wanted to take care of the child, she really wasn't so sulky at the time. Nevertheless, I wouldn't like to have to do it again, I was constantly scared because we didn't know what it was or whether it was dangerous.'

'I mean something else: whether you regret that that moment is past; that time has run out; that you can't do anything more with it.'

'Well, yes, it's past,' said Ana, and now she no longer looked like a pensive doctor, but like an intimidated schoolgirl.

'It's all right,' I said and turned to the door. As I went out, I heard her strike a new match. Why was I always so short, so curt, so ungrateful for the words of others when it was something really important to me? Why the need to defend what's important rabidly against the others, when they really didn't want to take it away from me?

The next morning, the first day of November, I went at dawn to the arch at the end of Rua Augusta, the most beautiful street in the world. The sea in the wan morning light was like a smooth surface of flat silver. To experience with special alertness how long a month is – that was the idea that had driven me out of bed. In the café, I was the first one. When there were only a few sips left in the cup, I slowed down the usual pace of drinking. I was uncertain what I should do when the cup was empty. It would

*be very long, this first day, if I simply sat still. And what I wanted
to know wasn't how long a month is for those who are completely
inactive. But what was it I did want to know?*

*Sometimes I am so slow. Only today, when the light of early
November breaks again do I notice that the question I asked Ana
– about the irrevocability, the transience, the regret, the sadness
– wasn't really the question that had preoccupied me. The question
I had wanted to ask was completely different: What does it depend
on when we have experienced a month as a fulfilled time, our
time, instead of a time that has passed as by, which we only
suffered, that ran through our fingers, so that it seems to us like
a lost, past time, and we're not sad because it's past, but because
we couldn't do anything with it? So, the question was not how
long is a month, but rather: What can you do for yourself with
the time of a month? When is it that I have the impression that
this month was all mine?*

*So it is wrong when I say it took me a year to find out how
long a month is. It was different: it took me a year to find out
what I wanted to know when I posed the misleading question
about the length of a month.*

Early the next afternoon, when he left the language school,
Gregorius ran into Mariana Eça. When he turned the corner
and saw her coming towards him, he knew all at once why
he had been afraid to call her: he wanted to tell her about
the attacks of dizziness but he didn't want to hear what she
thought might be causing them.

While they were having coffee she told him about João.
'I waited all Sunday morning for him,' he had said of
Gregorius. 'I don't know why, but I can talk to him about
things that are weighing on me. Not that they would go
away, but for a few hours, it gets easier.' Gregorius told her
about Adriana and the clock, about Jorge and the chess club,
and about Silveira's house. He was about to mention the trip

to Bern, but then he decided that he wanted to keep it to himself.

When he had finished, she asked him about the new glasses and then she narrowed her eyes observantly. 'You're sleeping too little,' she said. He thought of the morning when she had examined him and he hadn't ever wanted to get up from the chair in front of her desk. Of the thorough eye examination. Of the boat trip together to Cacilhas and the red-gold Assam tea he had later drunk in her house.

'Recently I've been feeling dizzy sometimes,' he said. And after a pause: 'I'm scared.'

An hour later, he left her office. She had tested his eyes again and taken his blood pressure; he had to do knee bends and balancing exercises and she asked him to describe the dizziness very precisely. Then she had written down the address of a neurologist for him.

'It doesn't seem serious to me,' she had said, 'and it's not surprising when you think of how much has changed in your life in a short time. But the usual things have to be examined.'

He pictured the empty square on the wall of Prado's office where the map of the brain had hung. She saw the panic in him.

'A tumour would present completely different symptoms,' she said and stroked his arm.

It wasn't far to Mélodie's house.

'I knew you'd come again,' she said when she opened the door to him. 'After your visit, Amadeu was very real to me for a few days.'

Gregorius gave her the letters of father and son to read.

'That's unfair,' she said when she had read the last words of her father's letter. 'Very unfair. As if Amadeu had driven him to take his life. His doctor was a shrewd man. He only prescribed small quantities of sleeping pills at a time. But Papá could wait. He had infinite patience. He had the patience of a stone. Mamã saw it coming. She always saw everything coming. She didn't do anything to prevent it. "Now his back doesn't hurt him any more," she said when we stood at the open coffin. I loved her for these words. "And he doesn't have to torment himself any more," I said. "Yes," she said, "that, too."'

Gregorius told her about his visits to Adriana. She hadn't been to the blue house after Amadeu's death, said Mélodie, but she wasn't surprised that Adriana had turned it into a museum and a shrine where time stood still.

'She admired him even as a little girl. He was the big brother who could do everything. Who dared to stand up to Papá! A year after he had gone to college in Coimbra, she moved to the girls' school across from the Liceu. The same school that Maria João had attended. There, Amadeu was a legend and she enjoyed being his sister. Nevertheless, things would have taken a different, more normal turn if not for the drama when he saved her life.'

It had happened when Adriana was nineteen. Amadeu, who was soon to take the official exams, was at home and sat at his books day and night. He left his room only for meals. It was at one such family meal that Adriana choked.

'We all had food on our plates and didn't notice anything at first. Suddenly, a strange noise, a horrible gasp came from Adriana, she clasped her neck and stamped her feet. Amadeu was sitting next to me, deep in thought about the coming exam. We were used to him sitting there like a ghost and blindly shovelling in the food. I nudged him with my elbow and pointed to Adriana. He looked up, confused. Adriana's face had turned purple, she wasn't able to breathe and she was looking helplessly at Amadeu. His face wore the look of furious concentration he always had on the rare occasions when he didn't understand something immediately.

'Now he jumped up, the chair toppled back, and with a few steps he was next to Adriana, had grabbed her under the arms and stood her up, turned her with her back to him; then he clutched her shoulders, took a deep breath and jerked her torso back violently. A choked gasp came from Adriana. Nothing else. Amadeu jerked twice more in the same way, but the piece of meat stuck in her windpipe still wasn't dislodged.

'What happened next was etched on the minds of all of us for ever, second by second, movement by movement. Amadeu sat Adriana back on her chair and ordered me to come and help. He bent her head back.

'"Hold on," he said in a strained voice. "Tight."

'Then he took the sharp meat knife from his place and wiped it on the napkin. We held our breath.

'"No!" shouted Mamã. "No!"

'I don't think he even heard her. He straddled Adriana's lap and looked her in the eye.

'"I have to do this," he said, and even now I'm amazed at how calm his voice was. "Otherwise, you'll die. Take your hands away. Trust me."

'Adriana took her hands from her neck. He groped with his index finger for the gap between thyroid cartilage and annular cartilage. Then he put the tip of the knife in the middle of the gap. A deep breath, a brief shutting of the eyes, then he stabbed.

'I was concentrating on holding Adriana's head tight as in a vice. I didn't see the blood spray out, saw it only afterwards on his shirt. Adriana's body convulsed. That Amadeu had found clear the windpipe was from Adriana's whistling as she sucked in air through the new opening. I opened my eyes and saw with horror that Amadeu was turning the blade of the knife in the wound; it looked like an act of special brutality. I realized only later that he had to keep the air passage open. Now, Amadeu took a ballpoint pen out of his shirt pocket, stuck it between his teeth, unscrewed the top with his free hand, ripped out the cartridge and put the bottom part in the wound as a cannula. Slowly, he pulled out the blade and held the pen tight. Adriana's breathing was jerky and rasping, but she was alive and the colour of the choking slowly subsided from her face.

'"Ambulance!" Amadeu ordered.

'Papá shook off his paralysis and went to the phone. We carried Adriana with the pen sticking out of her neck to the sofa. Amadeu stroked her hair.

'"It wouldn't have worked otherwise," he said.

'The doctor, who appeared a few minutes later, put his hand on Amadeu's shoulder. "That was close," he said. "What presence of mind. What courage. At your age."

'When the ambulance had left with Adriana, Amadeu sat down at his place at the table in his bloodstained shirt. Nobody said a word. I think that was the worst thing for him: that nobody said anything. With his few words, the doctor had confirmed that Amadeu had done the right thing and had saved Adriana's life. Nevertheless, the silence that filled the dining room was one of horrified amazement at his cold-bloodedness. "The silence made me look like a butcher," he said years later, the only time we talked about it.

'He never got over the fact that we left him so completely alone at this moment and it changed his relationship with the family for ever. After that he came home less often and then only as a polite guest.

Amadeu started shaking and suddenly the silence was shattered. He put his hands to his face and even now I can still hear the dry sobs that racked his body. And again, we left him alone. I stroked his arm, but that was much too little. I was only the eight-year-old sister, he needed something quite different.

'That it didn't come was the last straw. All of a sudden, he leapt up, raced to his room, ran back down with a medical textbook and banged the book on the table with all his might; the cutlery rattled on the plates, the glasses clinked. "Here," he shouted, "it says so here. The intervention is called a tracheotomy. Why are you all gawking at me like that? You sat there like dummies! If not for me, we would have had to carry her out in a coffin!"

'They operated on Adriana and she stayed in hospital for two weeks. Amadeu went to see her every day, always alone, he didn't want to go with us. Adriana was filled with an overwhelming gratitude which was almost religious. She lay white on the pillows with her neck bandaged and kept going over the dramatic scene. When I was alone with her, she talked of nothing else.

"'Shortly before he cut into me, the cedars in the window were red, blood red," she said. "Then I blacked out."'

She left hospital, said Mélodie, with the conviction that she had to devote her life to the brother who had saved hers. That gave Amadeu the creeps and he tried everything to talk her out of the idea. For a while, it seemed to work; she met a Frenchman who fell in love with her and the dramatic episode seemed to recede in importance. But this love collapsed the moment Adriana got pregnant. And again Amadeu intervened. He cut short his trip to England with Fátima because of it. Adriana had trained to be a nurse and three years later, when Amadeu opened the blue office, it was clear that she would work as his assistant. Fátima refused to let her live in the house. There were dramatic scenes when she was told to go. After Fátima's death, it took less than a week for Adriana to move back in. Amadeu was completely thrown by the loss of his wife and incapable of resistance. Adriana had won.

35

'Sometimes I've thought Amadeu's spirit consisted mainly of words,' Mélodie had said at the end of the conversation. 'That his soul was made up of them, in a way I had never experienced with anybody else.'

Gregorius had shown her the note on aneurysms. She hadn't known anything about that either, but she now remembered something significant.

'He flinched when anybody used words that had to do with going, flowing, passing, I remember mainly *correr* and *passar*. He was generally somebody who reacted to words as fiercely as if they were much more important than things. If you wanted to understand my brother, that was the most important thing you had to know. He talked of the dictatorship of the wrong words and the freedom of the right ones, of the invisible dungeon of kitsch language and the light of poetry. He was a person possessed by language, bewitched by it; a wrong word hurt him more than a knife wound. And he always reacted fiercely to words dealing with ephemerality and transience. After one of his visits when he revealed this new jumpiness, my husband and I puzzled about it half the night. "Not these words, please not these words," he had said. We didn't dare ask why. My brother, he could be like a volcano.'

Gregorius sat down in a chair in Silveira's living room and began reading the text by Prado that Mélodie had given him just before he left.

'He was in a panic that it could fall into the wrong hands,' she had said. "Maybe I should have destroyed it," he said. But then he gave it to me for safekeeping. He asked me not to open the envelope until after his death. The scales fell from my eyes.'

Prado had written the text in the winter following his mother's death and given it to Mélodie shortly before Fátima's death in the spring. There were three notes on separate sheets of paper and written in different inks. Even though they added up to a farewell letter to his mother, there was no address. Instead, the text had a tittle like many of the notes in the book.

DESPEDIDA FALHADA À MAMÃ. FAILED FAREWELL FROM MAMA. *My farewell from you has to fail, Mamã. You aren't here any more, and a real farewell would have to be an encounter. I have waited too long and naturally, that's no accident. What distinguishes an honest farewell from a cowardly one? An honest farewell from you – that would have been the attempt to come to some understanding with you about how it was with us, you and me. For that is the meaning of a farewell in the full, important sense of the word: that the two people, before they part, come to an understanding of how they have seen and experienced each other. What succeeded between them and what failed. That takes fearlessness: you have to be able to endure the pain of dissonance. It is also about acknowledging what was impossible. Parting is also something you do with yourself: to stand by yourself under the look of the other. The cowardice of a farewell re-sides in the transfiguration: in the attempt to bathe what was in a golden light and deny the dark. What you forfeit in that is nothing less than the acknowledgment of your self in those features produced by darkness.*

You played a trick on me, Mamã, and I now write down what I should have told you a long time ago: it was a perfidious trick that burdened my life like nothing else. That is, you let me know

– in no uncertain terms – that you expected from me, your son – your *son* – nothing less than that he be the best. Never mind what, just that whatever I did had to surpass the achievements of all others and not only surpass somehow, but tower high above them. The perfidy: you never *said* that to me. Your expectation was never explicit, which would have allowed me to take a position on it, to think about it and argue with my feelings about it. And yet I knew it, for that exists: a knowledge you drip into a defenceless child, drop by drop, day by day, without him noticing in the slightest this silently growing knowledge. The inconspicuous knowledge spreads in him like a pernicious poison, seeps into the tissue of body and soul and determines the colours and shades of his life. From this knowledge working unknown, whose power lay in its secrecy, an invisible, undiscoverable web emerged in me of inflexible, merciless expectations of myself, woven by the horrible spiders of an ambition born of fear. How often, how desperately and comically did I later lash out to free myself – only to be caught even more! It was impossible to defend myself against your presence in me: your trick was too perfect, too faultless, a masterpiece of overwhelming, breathtaking perfection.

Part of its perfection was that you not only left your suffocating expectations unspoken, but hid them under words and gestures that expressed the opposite. I'm not saying it was a conscious, cunning, insidious plan. No. You believed your own *deceptive* words and were a victim of the mask whose intelligence went far beyond yours. Since then, I've known how people can be entwined deeply with one another and present to one another without having the slightest idea of it.

And there's something else about the intricate way you created me according to your will – like a wanton sculptress of an alien soul: the names you gave me. Amadeu Inácio. Most people don't think anything of it, now and then somebody says something about the melody. But I know better, for I have the sound of your voice in my ear, a sound full of conceited devotion. I was to be a genius.

I was to possess godlike grace. And at the same time – the same time! – I was to embody the murderous rigidity of the holy Ignacio and his abilities to perform as a priestly general.

It's a nasty term, but it fits the case to a T: my life was determined by a maternal poisoning.

Was there in him, too, a secret, life-determining, parental presence, perhaps disguised as its opposite? Gregorius asked himself as he walked through the quiet streets of Belém. He pictured the slim book in which his mother had written down what she earned from cleaning. The shabby glasses with the cheap frames and the eternally dirty lenses over which she looked at him wearily. *If I could see the sea just once, but we simply can't afford that.* There had been something in her, something beautiful, even radiant, that he hadn't thought about for a long time: her dignity when she met on the street the people whose homes she cleaned. Her look was on the same level as those who paid her for crawling around on her knees, without a trace of obsequiousness. As a small boy he had wondered about this, only to feel proud later on when he had observed it again. If only there hadn't been the sentimental novels of Ludwig Ganghofer she had picked up in the rare hours of reading. *Now you're also cursed with books.* She hadn't been a reader. It hurt, but she hadn't been a reader.

What bank will give me a loan, Gregorius heard his father saying, *and for such a thing?* He could still see his big hand with the short fingernails, counting out the thirteen francs thirty for the Persian grammar, coin after coin, into his son's hand. *Are you sure you want to go there?* he had said. *It's so far away, so far away from what we're used to. Even the letters, they're so different, not like letters at all. We won't know anything about you.* When Gregorius had given him back the money, his father had stroked his hair with the big hand, a hand much too seldom capable of affection.

The father of Eva, Unbelievable, old man von Muralt, had also been a judge. He had looked in briefly at the school party, a giant of a man. How would it have been, thought Gregorius, if he had grown up as the son of a strict, pain-ridden judge and an ambitious mother who lived her life through the life of the idolized son? Would he still have been known as Mundus, The Papyrus?

When Gregorius came into the heated house from the cold night air, he had another of his dizzy spells. He sat down in a chair and waited for it to pass. *Not surprising when you think of how much has changed in your life in a short time*, Mariana Eça had said. *A tumour would present quite different symptoms.* He banished the doctor's voice from his head and went on reading.

My first big disappointment with you was that you didn't want to hear about my doubts concerning Papá's profession. I asked myself: Did you – as a neglected wife in backward Portugal – believe yourself incapable of thinking about it? Because law and justice were things that concerned only men? Or was it worse: that you simply didn't question or have doubts about Papá's work? That the fate of the people in Tarrafal just didn't interest you?

Why didn't you force Papá to talk to us about it? Were you glad about the power you gained from that? You were a virtuoso of the passive when it came to your children. And you were also a virtuoso as a diplomatic intermediary between Papá and us. You took a certain pride in the role. Was that your revenge for the limitations of your marriage? Compensation for the lack of social recognition and the burden of Father's pain?

Why did you give in whenever I protested? Why didn't you hold out against me and so teach me to face up to conflict? So that I could learn by observation rather than from a textbook, with a grim thoroughness that often led me to lose my sense of proportion?

Why did you burden me with my perferential treatment? Why did you and Papá expect so little from Adriana and Mélodie? Why didn't you sense the humiliation in your lack of confidence in them?

But it would be unjust, Mamã, if that were all I said to you in farewell. In the six years since Papá's death, I have discovered new feelings for you and I am glad of that. Your desolation by his grave moved me deeply and I was glad there were religious customs to shore up your spirit. I was really happy when the first signs of liberation became visible in you, much faster than expected. It was as if you had awoken to your own life for the first time. In the first year, you often came to the blue house and Fátima was afraid you would cling to me, to us. But no: now, when the scaffolding of your old life had collapsed, you seemed to discover what had been denied you by marrying much too early: your own life beyond your role in the family. You started asking about books, and leafed through them like a curious schoolgirl. Once when you didn't notice me, I saw you standing in bookshop, an open book in your hand. At this moment, I loved you, Mamã, and was tempted to go to you. But that would have been exactly the wrong thing: it would have pulled you back into the old life.

36

Gregorius paced back and forth in Senhor Cortês's room, calling everything by its familiar German name. Then he walked through the cold dark corridors of the Liceu and did the same with everything he saw there. He spoke aloud and furiously, the guttural words resounding through the building. An amazed observer would have judged that someone thoroughly demented had run amok in the abandoned building.

It had begun that morning in the language school. Suddenly, he could no longer remember the simplest things in Portuguese, things he knew from the first lesson on the first record of the language course, things he had learned before he left Bern. Cecilia, who appeared late because of a migraine, started on an ironic comment, stopped, frowned and made a calming gesture.

'*Sossega*,' she said, 'calm down. That happens to everybody who studies a foreign language. Suddenly it deserts you. This will pass. Tomorrow you'll be back up to standard.

Then his memory went on strike with Persian, a language he had always been able to count on remembering. In sheer panic, he had recited verses from Horace and Sappho to himself, had called up rare Homeric words and leafed frantically through Solomon's Song of Songs. To his relief everything came to mind as usual: there was no abyss of sudden memory loss. And yet he felt as if he had survived an earthquake. Dizziness. Dizziness and loss of memory. It would pass.

He had stood quietly at the window in the Rector's office.

Today there was no cone of light wandering through the room. It was raining. All of a sudden, he had become furious. It was a violent, hot fury, mixed with despair that the anger had no recognizable cause. Only very slowly did he realize that he was experiencing a revolt, a resistance against all the linguistic foreignness he had inflicted on himself. At first it seemed to apply only to Portuguese, and maybe the French and English he occasionally had to speak here. Then, gradually and reluctantly, he admitted to himself that the surge of rage also extended to the ancient languages he had lived with for more than forty years.

He was alarmed at the depth of his rebellion. The ground swayed. He had to do something, hold on to something; he closed his eyes, imagined he was standing on Bubenbergplatz and called the things he saw by their familiar German names. He talked to the things and to himself in slow, clear sentences of dialect. The earthquake subsided, he felt solid ground beneath his feet again. But the fear had an echo; he faced it with the fury of someone who has been exposed to a great danger, and so it happened that he strode through the corridors of the empty building like a lunatic, as if the essential thing was to defeat the spirits lurking in the dark corridors with familiar German words.

Two hours later, when he sat in the living room of Silveira's house, the whole thing seemed to him like a nightmare, like something he may only have dreamed. Reading Latin and Greek was the same as always, and when he opened the Portuguese grammar, everything came back to him and he made good progress with the conjunctive. Only the dream images still reminded him that something had temporarily stopped.

When he nodded off in the chair for a moment, he dreamed he was the only student in an enormous classroom and defended himself with sentences in dialect against questions aimed at him from the front row by somebody in a foreign language.

He woke up with his shirt damp, had a shower, and then made his way to Adriana's house.

Clotilde had reported that Adriana had changed since time and the present had returned to the blue house with the ticking clock in the living room. Gregorius had run into her on the tram on his way back from the Liceu.

'Sometimes,' the maid had said and repeated the words patiently when he didn't understand, 'she stands looking at the clock as if she wants it to stop again, but then she turns away. Her walk has become faster and firmer. She gets up earlier. It is as if she would no longer . . . yes, as if she would no longer only endure the day.'

She ate more and once she had asked Clotilde to take a walk with her.

When the door of the blue house opened, Gregorius experienced a surprise. Adriana wasn't wearing black. Only the black ribbon over the scar on her neck had remained. Skirt and jacket were a light grey with thin blue stripes and she had put on a shiny white blouse. The trace of a smile showed that she enjoyed the amazement on Gregorius's face.

He gave her back the letters to father and son.

'Isn't it insane?' she said. 'This silent communication. *Éducation sentimentale*, Amadeu used to say, would have to initiate us in the art of revealing our feelings and the experience that feelings become richer through words. How little that helped him with Papá!' She looked at the floor. 'And how little with me!'

He would like to read the notes on the scraps of paper on Amadeu's desk, said Gregorius. When they entered the attic room, another surprise awaited Gregorius: the office chair was no longer diagonal to the desk. After thirty years, Adriana had managed to rescue it from the past and straighten it so that it was no longer as if her brother was about to stand up from it. When he looked at her, she stood looking down, her hands in her jacket pockets, a devoted old woman who was at the same time like a schoolgirl who has solved a difficult task and waits bashfully for praise. Gregorius put his hand on her shoulder for a moment.

He noticed that the blue china cup on the copper tray had been washed, the ashtray was empty. Only the sweets were still in the sugar bowl. Adriana had screwed the top on the ancient fountain pen and now she turned on the desk lamp with the emerald green shade. She pushed the desk chair back and, with a final hesitation, beckoned to Gregorius to sit down.

The gigantic book still lay on the reading desk, open in the middle, and the stack of papers was still there, too. After a questioning glance at Adriana, he picked up the book to be able to see the author and title. João De Lousada De Ledesma, *O Mar Tenebroso*, the dark, dreadful sea. It contained big, calligraphic fonts, engravings of coasts, Indian ink drawings of seafarers. Gregorius looked questioningly at Adriana.

'I don't know,' she said, 'I don't know why that suddenly interested him, but he was fascinated by books that dealt with the fear that people in the Middle Ages experienced when they found themselves at the westernmost point of Europe and questioned what might be on the other side of the apparently endless sea.'

Gregorius pulled the book towards him and read a Spanish quotation: *Más allá no hay nada más que las aguas del mar, cuyo término nadie más que Dios conoce. Beyond that there is nothing except the water of the sea, whose borders no one knows but God.*

'Cabo Finisterre,' said Adriana, 'up in Galicia. The westernmost point of Spain. He was obsessed by that. The end of the world at the time. "But here in Portugal there is a point that is even further west, so why Spain?" I said and pointed to it on the map. But he didn't want to hear anything about it and kept talking about Finisterre; it was like an *idée fixe*.

He had a haunted, feverish expression on his face when he spoke of it.'

SOLIDÃO, LONELINESS, was at the top of the last page Prado had written on. Adriana had followed Gregorius's look.

'He often complained in his last year that he didn't understand what it really meant, the loneliness we all feared so much. *What is it that we call loneliness?* he said. *It can't simply be the absence of others. You can be alone and not lonely, and you can be among people and yet be lonely. So what is it?* It always concerned him that we could be lonely in the middle of the hustle and bustle. *All right,* he said, *it isn't only when others are there, when they occupy the space next to us. Even when they praise us or give us advice in a friendly way, clever, sensitive advice: even then we can be lonely. So loneliness is not something simply connected with the presence of others or with what they do. Then what? What on earth is it?*

'He didn't talk to me about Fátima and his feelings for her, *Intimacy is our last sanctuary,* he used to say. Only once that I can remember did he get carried away with a remark. *I lie next to her, I hear her breathe, I feel her warmth – and am horribly lonely,* he said. *What is it? WHAT?*'

Solidão por proscrição. *Loneliness through ostracism,* Prado had written. *When others withdraw affection, respect and recognition from us, why can't we simply say to them: 'I don't need all that, I am self-sufficient?' Isn't it a horrible form of bondage that we can't acknowledge that? Doesn't it make us the slaves of others? What feeling can we summon to protect ourselves?*

Gregorius bent over the desk and read the faded words on the notes on the wall.

Extortion through trust. 'Patients confided the most intimate things to him, and also the most dangerous,' said Adriana. 'Politically dangerous, I mean. And then they expected him to reciprocate. So they wouldn't have to feel vulnerable. He hated that. He hated it from the bottom of his heart. *I don't want anybody to expect anything of me,* he said and stamped his foot. *And why the devil is it so hard to keep my distance?* "Mamã," I was tempted to say, "Mamã." But I didn't. He knew it himself.'

The dangerous virtue of patience. 'Paciência: in the last years of his life he developed a real allergy to this word. His face darkened abruptly whenever anybody mentioned patience to him. *Nothing more than a blessed way of missing out on yourself,* he said, annoyed. *Fear of the fountains that can shoot up inside us.* I understood that properly only when I learned of the aneurysm.'

The last note was longer than the others: *If the force of the soul is more powerful than we are: why then attach praise and blame? Why not simply say: "was lucky," "had bad luck"? And it* is *more powerful than we are, this surge; it* always *is.*

'Before, the whole wall was filled with notes,' said Adriana. 'He was constantly writing down something and pinning it to the wall. Until that wretched trip to Spain a year and a half before his death. After that, he seldom picked up his pen; he often sat here at the desk and simply stared into space.'

Gregorius waited. Now and then he glanced at her. She sat in the reading chair next to the mountain of books on the floor, which she hadn't touched; the big book with the reproduction of the brain was still there. She clasped her dark-veined hands, released them, clasped them again. Her face contorted with the strain. The resistance to remembering seemed to have gained the upper hand.

He would like to learn something about this time, too, said Gregorius. 'To understand him even better.'

'I don't know,' she said and then relapsed into silence. When she started talking again, the words seemed to come from far away.

'I thought I knew him. Yes, I would have said: I know him, I know him inside and out; after all, I had seen him every day for years and heard him talk about his thoughts and feelings, even his dreams. But then he came home from this meeting, that was two years before his death, in December; he would have been fifty-one. It was one of those meetings where João was also present, João something. The man who wasn't good for him. Jorge was also there, I think, Jorge O'Kelly, sacred friend. I wished he hadn't gone to these meetings. They weren't good for him.'

'There, the people of the Resistance met,' said Gregorius. 'Amadeu was working for the Resistance, you must have known that. He wanted to do something, he wanted to strike a blow against people like Mendes.'

'*Resistência*,' said Adriana, and then again, '*Resistência*.' She said the word as if she had never heard anything about it, and refused to believe such a thing could have been.

Gregorius cursed his need to force her to acknowledge reality because for a moment it looked as if she would fall silent again. But then the annoyance died out of her face and she was back with the brother who came home after one of those mysterious meetings.

'He hadn't slept and was still wearing the clothes from the night before when I met him in the kitchen the next morning. I always knew when he hadn't slept. But this time it was different. He didn't look tormented as usual, despite the dark circles under his eyes. And he did something he never did: he tipped the chair back and rocked back and forth. Later, when I thought about it, I said to myself: it's as if he had set off on a trip. In the office, he was incredibly fast and light in the way he did everything; things seemed to require little effort, and he hit the waste paper basket whenever he threw things into it.

'In love, you might think. Weren't those clear signs that he was in love? Naturally, I also thought of that. But at one of those meetings, meetings of men? And it was so different from his manner with Fátima. Wilder, more boisterous, lustier. Thoroughly unbridled, so to speak. He scared me. He was a stranger to me. Especially after I had seen her. As soon as she entered the waiting room, I felt that she wasn't simply a patient. Early to middle twenties. A remarkable blend of innocent maiden and vamp. Glittering eyes, Asian features, swaying walk. The men in the waiting room glanced at her furtively, the women narrowed their eyes.

'I led her into the consulting room. Amadeu was just washing his hands. He turned around and it was as if he was struck by lightning. The blood shot into his face. Then he got himself under control.

'"Adriana, this is Estefânia," he said. "Would you please leave us alone for a moment? We have something to discuss."

'That had never happened before. Nothing was said in this room that I wasn't allowed to hear. *Nothing.*

'She came back, four or five times. He always sent me out of the room, spoke with her and then escorted her to the door. Every time, his face was flushed and for the rest of the day, he was jumpy and his hand shook when he gave injections, he who was renowned for his sure touch. The last time, she didn't come to the office, but rang the bell up here; it was after midnight. He took his coat and went downstairs. I saw the two of them turn the corner; he was talking intensely to her. An hour later, he came back with ruffled hair and smelling of scent.

'After that, she stayed away. Amadeu started to have blackouts. As if a hidden force was sucking him down. He was edgy and sometimes rough, even with patients. For the first time I thought: he doesn't like the medical profession any more; it doesn't suit him. He would like to escape from it.

'Once I came across Jorge and the same girl. He had his arm around her waist and she didn't seem to like it. I was confused. Jorge acted as if he didn't know me and pulled the girl into a side street. The temptation to tell Amadeu was great but I didn't. He was suffering enough already. Once, on an especially bad evening, he asked me to play Bach's Goldberg Variations. He sat there with his eyes shut and I was absolutely sure he was thinking of her.

'The chess games with Jorge, which had become part of the rhythm of Amadeu's life, were dropped. All winter long, Jorge didn't come to us once, not even at Christmas. Amadeu didn't mention him.

'One evening in early March, O'Kelly stood at the door. I could hear Amadeu opening it.

'"You," he said.

'"Yes, me," said Jorge.

'They went downstairs to the office so I wouldn't hear the conversation. I opened the door of the flat and tried to listen but could hear nothing, not a single word. Later, I heard the front door slam. O'Kelly, his coat collar pulled up, a cigarette between his lips, vanished round the corner. Silence. Amadeu didn't come up. Finally, I went downstairs. He was sitting in the dark and didn't move.

'"Leave me alone," he said. "I don't want to talk."

'Late at night when he came upstairs, he was pale, silent and thoroughly distraught. I didn't dare ask what was going on.

'The next day, the practice was closed. João came. I didn't learn anything from their conversation. Ever since the girl had appeared, Amadeu had overlooked me. All the pleasure had gone out of our working together. I hated this person, the long black hair, the swaying walk, the short skirt. I didn't play the piano any more. I didn't matter to him any more. It was . . . it was humiliating.

'Two or three days later, in the middle of the night, João and the girl stood at the door.

"I would like Estefânia to stay here," said João.

'The way he said it, refusal was impossible. I hated him and his domineering way. Amadeu didn't say a word when he saw her, but he fumbled with the keys and dropped the key ring when he took her upstairs to the office. He made up a bed for her on the examining table, I saw it later.

'Towards morning, he came up, had a shower and made breakfast. The girl looked bleary-eyed and scared; she was wearing jeans or something, and now there was nothing provocative about her. I controlled myself, made a second pot of coffee and another one for the road. Amadeu didn't explain anything to me.

'"I don't know when I'll be back," was all he said. "Don't worry."

'He stuffed a few things in a bag, put in a few medications, and then they went into the street. To my surprise, Amadeu took a car key out of his pocket and unlocked a car that hadn't been there the day before. But he can't drive, I thought, and then the girl got in behind the wheel. That was the last time I saw her.'

Adriana sat still, her hands in her lap, her head resting on the back of the chair, her eyes closed. Her breathing was rapid, she was reliving those events. The black velvet ribbon had slid up her neck and Gregorius could see the scar, an ugly, jagged scar with a small greyish bulge. Amadeu had sat astride her lap. *I have to do this,* he had said, *otherwise you'll die. Take your hands away. Trust me.* Then he had cut into her. And half a lifetime later, Adriana had seen him get into a car with a young woman and be driven away for an undetermined time without any explanation.

Gregorius waited until Adriana's breathing had calmed down. How had it been when Amadeu came back? he asked.

'I happened to be standing at the window when I saw him getting out of a taxi. Alone. He must have come back by train. He had been gone for a week. He didn't say a word about that time, not then and not later either. He was unshaven and hollow-cheeked, I think he had hardly eaten anything while he had been away. Famished, he devoured everything I put before him. Then he went upstairs to bed and slept for a day and a night. He must have taken a pill. I found the packet later.

'When he reappeared he had washed his hair, shaved, and dressed carefully. I had cleaned the office in the meantime.

'"Everything's gleaming," he said and attempted a smile. "Thanks, Adriana. What would I do without you?"

'We let the patients know that the practice was open again and an hour later, the waiting room was full. Amadeu was slower than usual, or maybe it was the after-effects of the sleeping pill or maybe it was the onset of the illness. The patients felt he wasn't the same person and looked at him uncertainly. In the middle of the morning, he asked for coffee. He had never done that before.

'Two days later, he developed a fever and raging headaches. No medicine helped.

'"No reason for panic," he said to calm me, his hands on his temples. "After all, the body is also the mind."

'But I observed him secretly. I saw his fear, he must have been thinking of the aneurysm. He asked me to put on Berlioz, Fátima's music.

'"Turn it off!" he yelled after a few bars. "Turn it off right now!"

'Maybe it was the headaches, maybe he also felt that he couldn't bear memories of Fátima after what happened with the girl.

'Then they caught João. We found out through a patient. Amadeu's headaches became so violent that he paced back and forth up here like a lunatic, with his head in his hands. A blood vessel burst in one eye, turning the eye dark red. He looked horrible, desperate and a bit brutalized. Shouldn't I fetch Jorge? I asked helplessly.

'"Don't you dare!" he yelled.

'He and Jorge didn't meet again until a year later, a few months before Amadeu's death. In that year, Amadeu had changed. After two or three weeks, the fever and the headaches disappeared. They left my brother like a man sunk in deep melancholy. *Melancolia* – he had loved the word even as a little boy and later had read books about it. One of them said it was a typically modern phenomenon. "Rubbish" he said. He considered it to be a timeless affliction and thought it was one of the most precious conditions known to humans.

'"Because it shows all the fragility of man," he said.

'It wasn't harmless. Naturally he knew that melancholy and clinical depression aren't the same thing. But when he had to treat a depressed patient, he sometimes hesitated much too long before sending him to a psychiatrist. He told the patient he was suffering from melancholy. He tended to idealize the condition of such people and to offend them with his particular interest in their suffering. After the trip with the girl, this tendency became stronger and sometimes bordered on gross negligence.

'His physical diagnoses remained sound to the end. But he was a marked man and when he had to deal with a difficult patient, sometimes he was no longer up to it. With women, on the other hand, he became over-zealous and sent them to specialists sooner than before.

'Whatever happened on that trip, it distressed him as nothing else had, even more than Fátima's death. It was as if a tectonic plate had shifted the deepest layers of his soul. Everything that rested on these layers of rock had become shaky and fragile. The whole atmosphere in this house changed. I had to shelter and protect him as if we were living in a sanitorium. It was horrible.'

Adriana wiped a tear from her eye.

'But wonderful. He belonged . . . He belonged to me again.

Or he would have belonged to me if Jorge hadn't stood at the door one evening.'

O'Kelly had brought Amadeu a chessboard and carved pieces from Bali.

'It's been a long time since we played,' he said. 'Too long. Much too long.'

The first time they played, there was little conversation. Adriana brought them tea.

'There was a tense silence,' she said. 'Not hostile, but tense. They searched for each other. Searched in themselves for a possibility to be friends again.'

Now and then they tried a joke or reliving a memory from their schooldays, but the laughter died before it reached their lips. A month before Prado's death, they went down to the office after playing chess and stayed there talking late into the night. Adriana stood in the doorway of the flat the whole time.

'The door of the office opened and they came out. Amadeu didn't turn on a light and the light from the office door barely illuminated the hall. They walked slowly, almost in slow motion, to the front door. They seemed to be standing unnaturally far apart.

'"So," said Amadeu.

'"Yes," said Jorge.

'And then they fell . . . yes, they fell into each other, I don't know how I can express it better. They must have wanted to embrace each other one last time. The action once begun seemed impossible, but was not to be stopped any more. They stumbled against each other, groped for each other, clumsy as blind men. Their heads butted into each other's shoulders, then they straightened up, recoiled, and didn't know what to do with their arms and hands. One, two seconds of horrible embarrassment, then Jorge tore open the door and stormed out. The door slammed shut. Amadeu turned to the wall, leaned his forehead against it and started sobbing. They were deep, raw, almost animal sounds, accompanied by violent twitches of his whole body. I know that I thought: How much a part of him Jorge has been, for almost a lifetime! And will remain so, even after this parting. It was the last time the two men met.'

Prado's sleeplessness became even worse than before. He complained of dizziness and had to take breaks between seeing patients. He sometimes asked Adriana to play the Goldberg Variations. Twice he went to the Liceu and came back with traces of tears on his face. At the funeral, Adriana learned from Mélodie that she had seen him coming out of a church.

There were a few days when he took up his pen. On those days he ate nothing. On the evening before his death, he had another bad headache. Adriana stayed with him until the sleeping pill took effect. When she left him, he looked as if he was about to fall asleep. But when she looked in on him at five in the morning, the bed was empty. He was on his way to the beloved Rua Augusta, where he collapsed an hour later. At six twenty-three, Adriana was notified. Later, when she came home, she put the clock back and stopped the pendulum.

37

Solidão por proscrição, loneliness through ostracism, that was what had preoccupied Prado at the end. That we need the respect and affection of others and that that makes us dependent on them. How far he had come! Gregorius sat in Silveira's living room and re-read the previous note about loneliness that Adriana had put into the book.

SOLIDÃO FURIOSA. FURIOUS LONELINESS. Is it so that everything we do is done out of fear of loneliness? Is that why we renounce all the things we will regret at the end of life? Is that why we so seldom say what we think? Why else do we hold on to all these broken marriages, false friendships, boring birthday parties? What would happen if we refused all that, put an end to the skulking blackmail and stood on our own? If we let our enslaved wishes and the fury at our enslavement rise high as a fountain? For the feared loneliness – what does it really consist of? Of the silence of absent reproaches? Of not needing to creep through the minefield of marital lies and friendly half-truths while holding our breath? Of the freedom not to have anybody across from us at meals? Of the fullness of time that yawns when the barrage of appointments falls silent? Aren't those wonderful things? A heavenly situation? So why the fear of it? Is it ultimately a fear that exists only because we haven't thought through its object? A fear we have been talked into by thoughtless parents, teachers and priests? And why are we so sure the others wouldn't envy us if they saw how great our freedom has become? And that they didn't seek our company as a result?

He hadn't then known the icy wind of the ostracism he was to experience twice later: when he saved Mendes and when he took Estefânia Espinhosa out of the country. This earlier note showed him as the open-minded iconoclast who didn't shrink from delivering a blasphemous speech to a faculty of teachers, including priests. He had written as a result of the security given him by his friendship with Jorge. This security, thought Gregorius, must have helped him endure being spat upon before the enraged mob. And then it had been withdrawn. The demands of life were simply too many and too massive for our feelings to survive them intact, he had said when he was at college in Coimbra. To Jorge, of all people.

Now his shrewd prediction had come true and he had remained in the chill of unbearable isolation, which even his sister's care could do nothing to alleviate it. The loyalty he had considered an anchor against the tides of feelings – it too had turned out to be fragile. Never again did he go to meetings of the Resistance, Adriana had said. He only visited João Eça in prison. Permission for that was the one token of gratitude he he would accept from Mendes. *His hands, Adriana,* he had said when he came back, *his hands. They once played Schubert.*

After Jorge's last visit Amadeu had forbidden Adriana to open the office windows to dispel the lingering smell of smoke. The patients complained about it but the windows remained closed for days. He inhaled the stale air like a memory drug. When ventilation could no longer be avoided, he sat slumped in a chair and his life force seemed to leave the room along with the smoke.

'Come,' Adriana had said to Gregorius. 'I want to show you something.'

They went down to the office. In a corner of the floor was a small rug. Adriana shoved it aside with her foot. The mortar had been loosened and one of the floor tiles had been removed. Adriana went down on her knees and lifted out the tile. Underneath, a hollow had been chiselled into the floor in which there was a folded chessboard and a box. Adriana opened the box and showed Gregorius the carved chess pieces.

Gregorius couldn't catch his breath, and opened a window to inhale the cool night air. He was overcome by dizziness and had to hold on to the windowsill.

'I surprised him at that,' said Adriana. She had replaced the tile and had come to stand next to Gregorius.

'His face flushed flaming red. "I only wanted . . ." he began. "No reason to be embarrassed," I said. That evening he was as vulnerable and fragile as a small child. Naturally, it *looked like* a grave for the chess set, for Jorge, for their friendship. But he hadn't *felt* it like that at all, I discovered. It was more complicated. And somehow, also more hopeful. He hadn't wanted to *bury* the set. He only wanted *to push it over the borders of his world,* without destroying it, and he wanted the certainty that he could take it out at any time. His world was now a world without Jorge. But Jorge was still there. He *was still there.* "Now, where he no longer is, it is as if I am no longer, either," he had once said.

'After that, for days he lacked self-confidence and his manner was almost servile to me. "So sentimental, the business with the chess set," he finally burst out, as if I had made him speak.'

Gregorius thought of O'Kelly's words: *He tended to bombast, he didn't want to admit it, but he knew it, and therefore he fought against kitsch at every opportunity, and he could be unjust in that, horribly unjust.*

Now, in Silveira's living room, he re-read the note about kitsch in Prado's book:

Kitsch is the most misleading of all prisons. The bars are covered with the gold of simplistic, unreal feelings so that you mistake them for the pillars of a palace.

Adriana had given him a pile of papers, one of the piles from Prado's desk, pressed between cardboard and tied with a red ribbon. 'Those are things that aren't in the book. The world mustn't know of their existence,' she had said.

Gregorius untied the ribbon, pushed back the cover, and started to read:

Jorge's chess set. The way he handed it to me. Only he can do that. I don't know anyone who can be so compelling. A compulsion I wouldn't miss for anything in the world. Like his compelling moves on the board. What did he want to make up for? Is it even right to say: he wanted to make up for something? He didn't say: "You misunderstood me back then about Estefânia." He said: "I thought back then that we could talk about everything, everything that came into our heads. That's what we had always done, don't you remember?" When he said that, I thought for a few seconds, only a few seconds, that we could find each other again. It was a wonderful feeling. But it died out again. His gigantic nose, his tear ducts, his brown teeth. Earlier, that face had been inside me, a part of me. Now it remained outside me, stranger than the face of a stranger. There was such an ache in my chest, such an ache.

Why should it be sentimental, what I did with the chess set? Really, a simple, genuine gesture. And I did it only for myself, not for an audience. If someone does something just for himself and others happen to see him doing it, and think it sentimental, why should we care?

An hour later, when Gregorius entered the chess club, O'Kelly was involved in a complicated endgame. Pedro was also there, the man with the epileptic eyes and the snuffle, who reminded

Gregorius of the lost tournament in Moutier. There was no board free.

'Sit down here,' said O'Kelly and pulled an empty chair up to his table.

All the way to the club, Gregorius had asked himself what he expected of it. What he wanted from O'Kelly. Clearly he couldn't *ask* him what had happened back then with Estefânia Espinhosa and whether he would have been willing in all seriousness to sacrifice her. He hadn't found the answer, but he couldn't go back either.

Now, with the smoke of O'Kelly's cigarette in his face, he suddenly knew that he wanted once more to experience sitting next to the man Prado had carried inside him for a lifetime, the man, as Father Bartolomeu had said, he had needed in order to be *whole*. The man he enjoyed losing to and to whom he had given a whole pharmacy without expecting gratitude. The man who was the first to laugh when the barking dog had broken through the painful silence after his scandalous speech at the Liceu.

'Shall we?' asked O'Kelly after he had won the endgame and parted from his partner.

Gregorius had never played like that against anybody. It wasn't the game but the presence of the other person. Only his presence. And the question of what it must have felt like to be somebody whose life was filled with this man whose nicotine-stained fingers with the dirty nails moved the chess pieces with such merciless precision.

'What I recently told you, about Amadeu and me, I mean: forget it.'

O'Kelly looked at Gregorius with a look blending bashfulness and a furious willingness to throw everything away.

'It was the wine. Everything was quite different.'

Gregorius nodded and hoped O'Kelly could see on his face his respect for that deep and complex friendship. Prado had asked himself if the soul was a place of facts or whether the alleged facts were only the deceptive shadows of stories we tell ourselves, about others and about ourselves.

Yes, said O'Kelly, that had been what had preoccupied Amadeu all his life. Inside a person, he said, it was much more complicated than our schematic, ridiculous explanations wanted to have us believe. *Everything is much more complicated. The further one goes, the more complicated it becomes. 'They got married because they fell in love and wanted to share their life'; 'she stole because she needed money'; 'he lied because he didn't want to hurt someone': what ridiculous stories! We are stratified creatures, full of abysses, with souls of quicksilver, with minds whose colour and shape change as in a kaleidoscope that is constantly shaken.*

That sounded as if there *were*, after all, psychological facts, even very complicated ones, Jorge had objected.

No, no, Amadeu protested, we could improve our explanations to infinity and they'd still be false. *And what is false is the assumption that there are truths to be discovered. The soul, Jorge, is a pure invention, our most brilliant invention, and its brilliance resides in the suggestion, the overwhelmingly plausible suggestion, that there is something in the soul to be discovered as in a real part of the world. The truth, Jorge, is quite different: we invented the soul to have a topic of conversation, something we can talk about when we meet one another. Just imagine if we couldn't talk about the soul: what should we talk about with one another? It would be hell!*

'He could work himself up into a state of intoxication about that, then he really glowed, and when he saw that I was enjoying his intoxication, he said: *You know, thinking is the second most beautiful thing. The most beautiful is poetry. If there were poetic thinking and thinking poetry – that would be paradise.* Later when he began on his notes he wrote: *I think they were an attempt to pave the way to this paradise.*'

O'Kelly looked close to tears. He didn't see that his queen was in danger. Gregorius made an insignificant move. They were the only two people in the room.

'Once the intellectual argument became bitter and deadly serious. But it's none of your business, it's *nobody's* business.'

He bit his lip.

'Neither is João's business up in Cacilhas.'

He took a drag at the cigarette and coughed.

'"You're fooling yourself," he said to me. "You want it for another reason than the one you've fabricated for yourself."

'Those were his words, his damned, insulting words: *the one you've fabricated for yourself.* Can you imagine how it feels when somebody says that you're only fabricating your reasons? Can you imagine how it feels when a *friend, the* friend, says that?

'"How do you know that?" I yelled at him. "I think there is no true or false, or don't you admit that any more?"'

On O'Kelly's unshaven face some red spots appeared.

'You know, I had simply believed we could talk about everything that came into our minds. *Everything.* Romantic. Damned romantic, I know. But that's how it was between us for more than forty years. Ever since the day he appeared in class in his expensive frock coat and without a satchel.

'*He* was the one who had no fear of any thought. *He* was the one who had wanted to talk of the dying word of God in front of priests. And when I wanted to try out a bold and, I admit, horrible thought – I saw that I had overestimated him and our friendship. He looked at me as if I was a monster. Usually he could distinguish between a mere tried-out thought and one that actually set us in motion. *He* was the one who taught me this liberating difference. And suddenly he didn't know anything about it any more. All the blood had drained from his face. In this one single second, I realized that the most horrible thing had happened: our lifelong affection had turned into hate. That was the moment, the dreadful moment, when we lost each other.'

Gregorius wanted O'Kelly to win the game. He wanted him to mate him with compelling moves. But Jorge had lost interest in the game and so Gregorius arranged a draw.

'It's simply not possible, unlimited openness,' said Jorge, when they shook hands in the street. 'It's beyond us. Loneliness through the need to conceal, there's that too.'

He exhaled smoke.

'It's been a long time, over thirty years. As if it were yesterday. I'm glad I have the pharmacy. I can live there in our friendship. And occasionally I succeed in thinking that we never lost each other. That he just died.'

38

For a good hour, Gregorius had been sneaking around Maria João's house and asking himself why his heart was pounding. *The great, untouched love of his life*, Mélodie had called her. *It wouldn't surprise me if he never even kissed her. But nobody, no woman, measured up to her. If there was anybody who knew all his secrets, it was Maria João. In a certain sense, she, only she, knew who he was.* And Jorge had said that she had been the only woman Amadeu really had thought something of. *Maria, my God yes, Maria*, he had said.

When she opened the door, everything became clear to Gregorius. She held a steaming cup of coffee in one hand and warmed the other hand on it. The look in the clear brown eyes was scrutinizing but not threatening. She wasn't a beautiful woman. She wasn't a woman you'd turn round to look at in the street. Nor had she been such a woman in her youth. But Gregorius had never met a woman who radiated such inconspicuous and yet such perfect confidence and independence. She must have been over eighty, but it wouldn't have been surprising if she were still confidently practising her profession.

'Depends on what you want,' she said when Gregorius asked if he might come in. He didn't want to stand in a doorway again and produce the portrait of Prado like a calling card. The calm, open look gave him the courage for a direct opening.

'I'm interested in the life and notes of Amadeu de Prado,'

he said in French. 'I have learned that you knew him. Knew him better than anybody else.'

You might think from looking at her that nothing could disturb her equilibrium. But it happened now. Not on the surface. In her dark blue wool dress, she leaned on the door frame as sure and calm as before, and the free hand kept rubbing the warm cup, only a little more slowly. Her eyelids twitched and lines of concentration appeared on her forehead as if she had suddenly been confronted with something unexpected that could have consequences. She said nothing. For a few seconds, she closed her eyes. Then she had herself under control again.

'I don't know if I want to go back there,' she said. 'But it doesn't make sense for you to stand out here in the rain.'

The French words came without hesitation, and her accent had the sleepy elegance of a Portuguese woman who also speaks fluent French.

Who was he? she wanted to know after she had given him a cup of coffee, not with the affected movements of an attentive hostess, but with the sober, plain movements of someone carrying out the practical essentials.

Gregorius told her about the Spanish bookshop in Bern and the sentences the bookseller had translated for him. *Of the thousand experiences we have, we find language for one at most and even this one merely by chance and without the care it deserves. Among all these unexpressed experiences are those that are hidden and that have given our life its shape, its colour and its melody.*

Maria João closed her eyes and her lips began to shake imperceptibly. She sank a little deeper into the chair. Her hands clasped a knee and let go of it as if she didn't know what to do with them. Slowly her breath grew calmer. She opened her eyes.

'You heard that and ran away from school,' she said.

'I ran away from school and heard that,' said Gregorius.

She smiled. *She looked at me and gave me a smile that came from the experience of a well-lived life,* Judge Prado had written.

'Good. But it fits. It fits so well that you wanted to meet him. How did you get to me?'

When Gregorius had finished his story, she looked at him.

'I don't know anything about the book. I'd like to see it.'

She opened it, saw the picture and it was as if a double force of gravity pressed her into the chair. Behind her veined, almost transparent eyelids, the pupils raced. She made another attempt, opened her eyes and fixed them on the picture. Slowly, she ran her shrivelled hand over it and then she repeated the action. Now she leaned her hands on her knees, stood up and went out of the room without a word.

Gregorius picked up the book and studied the picture. He thought of the moment when he had sat in the café in Bubenbergplatz and had seen it for the first time. He thought of Prado's voice from Adriana's old tape recorder.

'So now I've gone back there,' said Maria João, sitting down in the chair again. 'If it's about the soul, there is little we can do. He used to say.'

Her face was more composed and he noticed that she had combed the stray strands of hair out of her face. She took the book and looked at the picture again.

'Amadeu.'

In her mouth, the name sounded completely different than when spoken by the others. As if it couldn't possibly belong to the same man.

'He was so white and quiet, so terribly white and quiet. Perhaps it was because he consisted so much of language. I could hardly believe that words would never come from him again. Never again. The blood from the burst vein had washed them away, the words. All words. A bloody break in the dam of destructive force. As a nurse, I've seen a lot of dead people.

But never did death seem so horrible to me. As something that simply shouldn't have happened. As something absolutely unberable. Unbearable.'

Despite the noise of traffic outside the window, silence filled the room.

'I can see him now coming towards me, the hospital report in his hand; it was in a yellowish envelope. He had gone there because of piercing headaches and dizziness. He was afraid it could he a tumour. Angiography, radiography revealed nothing. Only an aneurysm. "You could live to be a hundred with that," the neurologist had told him. But Amadeu was pale as a ghost. "It can burst any minute, any minute. How can I live with this time bomb in my brain?" he said.'

'He took the map of the brain off the wall,' said Gregorius.

'I know, that was the first thing he did. What it meant, you can guess only if you know what unbounded admiration he had for the human brain and its enigmatic achievements. A proof of God's existence, he said, it's a proof of God's existence. Only there is no God. And from now on he steered clear of every thought of the brain. Every clinical syndrome with the remotest connection to the brain, he immediately referred to the specialists.'

Gregorius pictured the big book that lay in Prado's room on top of the heap of books. *O cérebro sempre o cérebro,* he heard Adriana say. *Porquê não disseste nada?*

'Nobody but me knew about it. Not Adriana. Not Jorge.'

The pride was barely audible, but it was there.

'Later we seldom talked about it, and never for long. There wasn't much to say. But the threat lay like a shadow over the last seven years of his life. There were moments when he wished it would finally happen. To get rid of the fear.'

She looked at Gregorius. 'Come.' She led the way into the kitchen. From the top shelf of a cupboard she took a big flat box of lacquered wood, its cover embellished with marquetry, and sat down at the kitchen table.

'A few of his notes were written in my kitchen. It was another kitchen, but it was at this table. The things I write here are the most dangerous, he said. He didn't want to talk about them. Writing doesn't require speech, he said. He'd sit here all night and then go to the office without having had any sleep. He ruined his health. Adriana hated it. She hated everything connected with me. "Thanks," he said when he left. "With you it's like being in a quiet, protected port." I always kept the notes in the kitchen. They belonged here.'

She opened the engraved clasp of the box and took out the top three sheets. After she had read a few lines to herself, she pushed the papers towards Gregorius.

He read. Whenever he didn't understand something, he looked at her and she translated it.

MEMENTO MORI. Dark monastery walls, downcast look, snow-covered cemetery. Must it be that?

Reflecting on what you may really want. The awareness of limited, ephemeral time as a source of strength to withstand your own habits and expectations, but mostly the expectations and threats of others. So something that opens up and doesn't lock the future. Understood like this, the memento is a danger for the powerful, the oppressors who try to keep the oppressed from finding an ear for their wishes, not even in themselves.

'Why should I think about it, the end is the end, it comes when it comes, why do you tell me that, that doesn't change in the least.'

What is the reply?

'Don't waste your time, do something worthwhile with it.'

But what can that mean: worthwhile? Finally to start realizing long-cherished wishes. To attack the error that there will always be time for it later. The memento as an instrument in the struggle against indolence, self-deception and fear, linked with the necessary change. Take the long-dreamed-of trip, learn this language, read those books, buy yourself this jewellery, spend a night in that famous hotel. Don't miss out on yourself.

Bigger things are also part of that: to give up the loathed profession, break out of a hated milieu. Do what contributes to making you more genuine, moves you closer to yourself.

Lying on the beach or sitting in the café from morning to night: that can also be the answer to the memento, the answer of one who has only worked up to now.

'*Think that you have to die someday, maybe this morning.*'

'*I think of it all the time, and so I play hooky from the office and let myself bask in the sun.*'

The apparently gloomy warning doesn't lock us up in the snow-covered monastery garden. It opens the way out and wakes us to the present.

With death in mind straightening out the relationship with others. Ending a hostility, excusing yourself for an injustice done, expressing an acknowledgement that pettiness kept us from doing. Stop taking trivialities seriously, the jibes of others, their pompousness, their entire bad judgement of us. The memento as a demand to feel different.

The danger: relations are no longer genuine and alive because they lack the momentary seriousness assumed by a certain lack of distance. And: for much of what we experience, it is crucial not to be linked with thoughts of finitude, but rather with the feeling that the future will still be very long. It means nipping this experience in the bud if the awareness of impending death would seep in.

Gregorius told her about the Irishman who had dared to appear at the evening lecture in All Souls College at Oxford with a bright red football.

'Amadeu noted: *What wouldn't I have given to be the Irishman!*'

'Yes, that fits,' said Maria João, 'that fits precisely. Above all, it fits the beginning, our first meeting, when, as I would say today, everything was already predestined. It was in my first year at the girls' school of the Liceu. We were all in awe of the boys on the other side of the fence. Latin and Greek! One day, it was a warm morning in May, I simply went over there, I'd had enough of the stupid awe in which we held them. They played, they laughed, they played. Amadeu was the only one who didn't. He sat on the steps his arms wrapped around his knees, and was looking at me. As if he had been waiting years for me. If he hadn't looked like that – I wouldn't have simply sat down next to him. But it seemed to be the most natural thing in the world.

"'You're not playing?" I said. He shook his head, short and sweet, almost a little gruffly.

"'I read this book," he said in the soft, irresistible tone of a dictator who doesn't yet know anything of his despotism and in a certain sense would never know it. "A book about saints, Thérèse of Lisieux, Teresa of Ávila and so on. After that, everything I do seems so banal. Simply not *important* enough. You understand?"

'I laughed. "My name's Ávila, Maria João Ávila," I said.

'He laughed too, but it was a tormented laugh; he felt he wasn't being taken seriously.

"'Not *everything* can be important, and not *always*," I said. "That would be awful."

'He looked at me and now his smile wasn't tormented. The Liceu bell rang for the end of break.

"'Will you come back tomorrow?" he asked. No more than five minutes had passed, and it felt as if we had known each other for years.

'Naturally I went back the next day and by then he knew everything about my last name. He gave me a lecture about Vasco Ximeno and Count Raimundo de Borgonha, who had been dispatched to the town by King Alfonso VI of Castile, about Antão and João Gonçalves de Ávila, who brought the name to Portugal in the fifteenth century, and so on.

'"We could go to Ávila together," he said.

'The next day, I looked out of the classroom towards the Liceu and I saw two dazzling points of light in the window. It was the sunlight on the lenses of his opera glasses. Everything moved so fast, everything always moved so fast with him.

'At break, he showed me the opera glasses. "They belong to Mamã," he said. "She likes going to the opera, but Papá . . ."

'He wanted to make me a good student so I could become a doctor. I really didn't want that, I said. I wanted to be a nurse.

'"But you . . ." he began.

'"A nurse," I said. "A simple nurse."

'It took him a year to accept it. That I stuck to my guns and couldn't be compelled by him – that shaped our friendship. For that's what it was: a lifelong friendship.

'"You have such tanned knees, and your dress smells so good, of soap," he said two or three weeks after our first encounter.

'I had given him an orange. The others in the class were really jealous: the aristocrat and the peasant girl. *Why Maria of all people?* one of them asked, not knowing I was near by. They imagined things. Father Bartolomeu, Amadeu's favourite teacher, didn't like me. When he saw me, he turned round and went the other way.

'On my birthday, I was given a new dress. I asked Mamã to shorten it a little. Amadeu didn't comment on it.

'Sometimes he came over to the girls' side and we went for a walk at break. He told me about his home, his father's back, his mother's silent expectations. I learned about everything that mattered to him. I was his confidante. Yes, that's what I was: his lifelong confidante.

'He didn't invite me to the wedding. "You'd only be bored," he said. I stood behind a tree when they came out of the church. It was an expensive society wedding. Big, shiny cars, a gown with a long white train. Men in tailcoats and top hats.

'It was the first time I set eyes on Fátima. A well-proportioned, beautiful face, white as alabaster. Long black hair, a boyish figure. Not a fashion plate, I'd say, but somehow ... withdrawn. I can't prove it, but I think he patronized her. Without noticing it. He was that sort of man. Not a domineering nature, not at all, but controlling, glorious, superior. Basically, there was no place in his life for a woman. When she died, it was a deep shock for him.'

Maria João fell silent and looked out of the window. When she continued, it was hesitantly, as if with a bad conscience.

'As I said: a deep shock. No doubt. And yet ... how should I put it: not a shock that would penetrate to the deepest part of him. In the first days after her death, he often sat with me. Not to be comforted. He knew that he ... that he couldn't expect *that* from me. Yes, he knew that. He *must* have known. He simply wanted me to be there. That's how it often was: I had to be *there*.'

Maria João got up, went to the window and stood there looking out, her hands clasped behind her back. When she went on talking, it was in the soft voice of secrecy.

'The third or fourth time, he finally found the courage; the inner need had become too great, he had to tell somebody. He couldn't produce any children. He had had an operation not to become a father under any circumstances. That was long before he met Fátima.

'"I don't want little, defenceless children, who have to bear the burden of my soul," he said. "I know how it was with me – and still is."'

Gregorius told Maria João what Amadeus had written to his father. *Parental will and fear are branded on the souls of the children, who are helpless and ignorant of what is happening to them. It would take a lifetime to decipher the marks of the branding iron and we can never be sure we have understood it.*

'Yes,' she said, 'yes. What weighed on him wasn't the operation, he never regretted it. It was that he hadn't told Fátima about it. She suffered from childlessness and he almost choked on his bad conscience. He was a brave man, a man of really extraordinary courage. But in this he was cowardly and he never got over this cowardice.'

He's a coward when it comes to Mamã, Adriana had said. The only cowardice in him. He who usually faces up to unpleasant things.

'I understood it,' said Maria João. 'Yes, I believe I can say that I understood it. After all, I experienced how deeply he was influenced by his father and mother. And yet I was upset. Also because of Fátima. But what upset me even more was the finality, even brutality of his decision. In his mid-twenties he committed himself in this matter. For ever. It took me about a year before I could say: He wouldn't be Amadeu if he couldn't do such a thing.'

Maria João picked up Prado's book, put on a pair of glasses and started leafing through it. But her thoughts were still in the past and she took the glasses off again.

'We never talked about Fátima, about what she meant to him. She and I once met in café; she came in and felt obliged to sit with me. Even before the waiter came, we both knew it was a mistake. Fortunately, it was only an espresso.

'I don't know if I understood the whole thing or if I didn't. I'm not even sure if *he* understood it. And here is *my* cowardice: I didn't read what he wrote about Fátima. "You may read it only after my death," he said when he gave me the sealed envelope. "But I don't want it to fall into Adriana's hands." More than once, I've picked up the envelope. At some point, I decided I didn't want to open it. And so it is still here in the box.'

Maria João put the text about the warning of death back in the box and pushed it aside.

'One thing I do know: when the thing happened with Estefânia, I wasn't a bit surprised. It happens: one doesn't know what a person is missing until he gets it and then all of a sudden it's quite obvious.

'He changed. For the first time in forty years he seemed embarrassed with me and to want to hide something about himself from me. I learned only that there was somebody, somebody from the Resistance who was also connected with Jorge. And that Amadeu wouldn't allow it, couldn't allow it. But I knew him: he thought constantly of her. From his silence, it was clear that I was not to meet her. As if I could learn something about him from seeing her that he didn't want me to know. That no one was to know. Not even himself, so to speak. I went there and waited in front of the house where the Resistance met. Only one woman came out and I realized at once: That's her.'

Maria João's glance fixed on a distant point in the room.

'I won't describe her to you. I'll only say this: I could immediately imagine what had happened to him. That the world suddenly looked quite different for him. That the previous order had been turned upside down. That all of a sudden, quite different things mattered. That's the kind of woman she was. And she was only in her mid-twenties. She wasn't only the ball, the red Irish ball in the Oxford college. She was much more than all red Irish balls together. He must have felt that she was the chance for him to be *whole*. As a man, I mean.

'That's the only way to explain why he staked everything on it: the respect of others, the friendship with Jorge, which had been sacred to him, even his life. And that he came back from Spain as if he . . . was destroyed. Destroyed, yes, that's the right word. He slowed down, had trouble concentrating.

There was no more of the earlier quicksilver in his veins, no more of his boldness. His life glow was extinguished. He spoke of having to learn life all over again.

"'I was out at the Liceu," he said one day. "Back then, everything was still ahead of me. So much was still possible. Everything was open."'

Maria João had a lump in her throat. She cleared her throat and when she went on, her voice sounded hoarse.

'He said something else. "Why didn't we ever go to Ávila together?" he said.

'I thought he had forgotten it. He hadn't. We wept. It was the only time we wept together.'

Maria João went out of the room. When she came back, she had a scarf around her neck and a thick coat over her arm.

'I'd like to go to the Liceu with you,' she said. 'What's left of it.'

Gregorius imagined her looking at the pictures of Isfahan and asking questions. He was amazed that he wasn't embarrassed. Not with Maria João.

39

She, the eighty-year-old woman, drove the car with the calm and precision of a cab-driver. Gregorius looked at her hands on the steering wheel and the gearshift. They weren't elegant hands, nor did she take the time to look after them. They were hands that had cared for sick people, emptied bedpans, applied bandages. Hands that knew what they were doing. Why hadn't Prado made her his assistant?

They stopped and walked through the park. She wanted first to go to the girls' school.

'I haven't been here in thirty years. Not since his death. Back then I was here almost every day. I thought, the shared place, the place of our first meeting, could teach me to part from him. I didn't know how I was to do it: part from him. How do you part from somebody who shaped your own life like nobody else?

'He gave me something I didn't know before and have never experienced since: his unbelievable ability to empathize. He was often preoccupied and he could be dreadfully self-referential. But at the same time, as far as others were concerned, he possessed an imagination so fast and precise it could make you dizzy. He seemed to tell me how I felt even before I had begun to look for the words. Wanting to understand others was a passion with him. But he wouldn't have been Amadeu if he hadn't also questioned the possibility of such an understanding and been so radical in his doubts that it could make one's head spin to see him swing in the opposite direction.

'It created an unbelievable, breathtaking closeness when he was like that with me. In our family we were very serious with each other, practical so to speak. And then came someone who could see inside me. It was like a revelation. And it let a hope emerge.'

They stood in Maria João's old classroom. The benches had been removed but the blackboard was still there. The windows were missing a pane of glass here and there. Maria João opened one and its squeaking spoke of decades. She pointed to the Liceu.

'There. Over there, on the third floor, were the points of light of the opera glasses.' She swallowed. 'That someone, a boy from an aristocratic family, was looking for me with opera glasses: that . . . was really something. And as I said, it let a hope emerge. It still had a childish form, this hope, and naturally it wasn't clear what it was about. Nevertheless, it was, in a vague form, the hope for a shared life.'

They went down the stairs which were coated with a film of damp dust and rotting moss, as in the Liceu. Maria João was silent until they had crossed the park.

'Somehow that's what it was then, too. A shared life, I mean. Shared in a close distance; in a distant closeness.'

She looked up at the façade of the Liceu.

'There, at this window, he sat and because he already knew everything and was bored, he wrote me little notes on scraps of paper that he slipped to me at break. They weren't . . . weren't *billets-doux*. There wasn't what I kept hoping for, in every note. They were his thoughts about something. About Teresa of Ávila and many other things. He made me into an inhabitant of his world of thought. "Only you live there, apart from me," he said.

'Nevertheless, what I grasped only very slowly and much later was true: He didn't want me to be involved in his life. In a sense that's very hard to explain; he wanted me to stay outside it. I waited for him to ask me to work in the blue office. In my dreams, I worked there, many times, and it was wonderful; we understood each other without words. But he didn't ask, didn't even hint at it.

'He loved trains, they were a symbol of life for him. I would like to have travelled in his compartment. But he didn't want me there. He wanted me on the platform. He wanted always to be able to open the window and ask me for advice. And he wanted the platform to move when the train started moving. Like an angel, I was to stand on the moving platform, on the angels' platform moving at exactly the same speed.'

They entered the Liceu. Maria João looked around.

'Girls weren't allowed in here, but he smuggled me in after classes and showed me everything. Father Bartolomeu caught us. He was furious. But because it was Amadeu he said nothing.'

They were standing in Senhor Cortês's office. Now Gregorius was apprehensive. Maria João burst out laughing. The laughter of a merry schoolgirl.

'You?'

'Yes.'

She went to the wall with the pictures of Isfahan and looked at him questioningly.

'Isfahan, Persia. As a student, I wanted to go there. To the *Morgenland*.'

'And now, since you have run away, you make up for it. Here.'

He nodded. He hadn't known that there were people who cottoned on so fast. You could open the train window and ask the angel.

Then Maria João did something surprising. She came over to him and put her arm around his shoulders.

'Amadeu would have understood that. And not only understood. He would have loved you for it. *A imaginação, o nosso último santuário*, he used to say. Imagination and intimacy, those were the only two sanctuaries he allowed, aside from language. *And they have a lot to do with each other, a lot*, he said.'

Gregorius hesitated. Then he opened the desk drawer and showed Maria João the Hebrew Bible.

'I bet that's your sweater!'

She sat down in a chair and put one of Silveira's blankets over her legs.

'Read to me from it, please. He did. Naturally I didn't understand a thing, but it was wonderful.'

Gregorius read the story of the Creation. He, Mundus, read the story of the Creation in a dilapidated Portuguese Gymnasium to an eighty-year-old woman he hadn't known yesterday and who didn't speak a word of Hebrew. It was the craziest thing he had ever done and he enjoyed it as he had never enjoyed anything before. It was as if he had cast off all his internal shackles to fight unimpeded just this one time, like someone who knows his end is near.

'And now let's go into the auditorium,' said Maria João. 'It was locked in those days.'

They sat in the first row in front of the raised lectern.

'So that's where he gave his speech. His notorious speech. I loved it. It was so much from him. He *was* it. But there was something about it that scared me. Not in the version he presented – he took it out. You remember the conclusion, where he says that he needs both, the holiness of words and the hostility against everything cruel. Then comes: *And no one may force me to choose*. That was the last sentence he delivered. But originally, there was another sentence: *Seria uma corrida atrás do vento*. It would be reaching for the wind.

'"What a wonderful image!" I shouted.

'Then he picked up the Bible and read to me from Ecclesiastes: *I have seen all the works that are done under the sun; and behold, all is vanity and reaching for the wind.* I was afraid.

'"You can't do that!" I said. "The priests all know that quotation and will consider you a megalomaniac!"

'What I didn't say was that, at that moment, I was worried about his emotional health.

'"But why?" he said in amazement. "It's just poetry."

'"But you can't speak biblical poetry! *Biblical* poetry! In your name!"

'"Poetry trumps everything," he said. "It annuls all rules."

'But he had become uncertain and deleted the sentence. He felt that I was worried, he always felt everything. We never talked about it again.'

Gregorius told her of Prado's discussion with O'Kelly about the dying word of God.

'I didn't know that,' she said and was silent for a while. She folded her hands, released them, folded them again.

'Jorge. Jorge O'Kelly. I don't know. I don't know if he was good fortune or bad for Amadeu. A great misfortune disguised as great good fortune, there is that. Amadeu, he longed for Jorge's strength, a coarse strength. He really longed for his coarseness, which could be seen in his rough, chapped hands, his unruly, tangled hair and the unfiltered cigarettes he smoked nonstop. I don't want to do him an injustice, but I didn't like Amadeu's uncritical enthusiasm for him. I was a peasant girl, I know how peasant boys are. No reason for romanticism. When it came to the crunch, Jorge would put himself first.

'What fascinated him about O'Kelly, and even intoxicated him, was that Jorge had no trouble keeping his distance from others. He just said no and grinned over his big nose. Amadeu, on the other hand, struggled for his boundaries as for his salvation.'

Gregorius told her of the sentence in Amadeu's letter to his father: *Others are your court of justice.*

'Yes, exactly. It made him a profoundly insecure person, the thinnest-skinned person you can imagine. He had this overwhelming need to trust people and to be accepted by them. He felt he had to hide this uncertainty and much that looked like courage and boldness was simply a subterfuge. He demanded infinitely too much from himself, much too much, and he became self-righteous and judgemental about it.

'Everyone who knew him closely talked of never feeling able to satisfy him and his expectations, of always falling short. That he didn't think much of himself made everything even worse. You couldn't even defend yourself with the accusation of complacency.

'How intolerant he was of kitsch! Above all, in words and gestures. And what fear he had being kitsch himself! "You have to be able to accept the kitsch in yourself in order to be free," I said. Then he breathed more calmly, more freely for a while. He had a phenomenal memory. These were things he quickly forgot, only for them to re-emerge and draw him back into its merciless grip.

'He had fought against justice. My God, he fought! And he lost. Yes, I think you have to say that he lost.

'In quiet times, when he simply practised medicine and people were grateful to him, he sometimes looked as if he had done it. But then the story with Mendes. The spit on his face haunted him; to the last he kept dreaming of it. An execution.

'I was against him going into the Resistance. He wasn't the man for it, didn't have strong enough nerves, although he did have the mind. And I didn't see that he had to make up for anything. But there was nothing I could do. *When it has to do with the soul, there's little we can do*, he said. I've already told you these words.

'And Jorge was also in the Resistance. Jorge, whom he finally lost because of it. Listless, he brooded over it in my kitchen and didn't say a word.'

They went upstairs and Gregorius showed her the school bench where he had seated Prado in his thoughts. It was the wrong floor, but otherwise almost right. Maria João stood at the window and looked over to her seat in the girls' school.

'*Others are your court of justice.* He had also experienced it when he cut open Adriana's neck. The others sat at the table and looked at him as if he was a monster. And he did the only possible thing. When I lived in Paris, I attended a course in emergency medicine and they showed us that. Tracheotomy. You have to split the *ligamentum conicum* and keep the windpipe open with a trachea cannula. Otherwise the patient dies of bolus. I don't know if I could have done it or if I would have thought of a pen as a substitute for the cannula. "If you want a job here . . ." the doctors who operated on Adriana said to him afterwards.

'For Adriana, it had devastating consequences. When you've saved somebody's life, especially then, you must have a quick and easy parting. Saving a life is a burden nobody can bear, neither the life-saver nor the one who is saved. Therefore, it should have been treated as a stroke of luck, something like a spontaneous cure. Something impersonal.

'Adriana's gratitude was difficult for Amadeu. There was something religious, almost fanatical about it. Sometimes he was disgusted by it, she could be as servile as a slave. But there was her unfortunate love affair, the abortion, the fear of loneliness. Sometimes I tried to persuade myself that he didn't take me into his practice because of Adriana. But it's not the truth.

'With Mélodie, his sister Rita, it was completely different, light and easy. He had a photo of him wearing one of the Mao caps of her girls' orchestra. He envied her flightiness. He didn't hold it against her that, as the unplanned latecomer, she bore much less of the emotional burden of her parents than the older siblings. But he could also be furious when he thought of how much easier his life as a son might have been.

'I was in the family home only once. When we were still at school. The invitation was a mistake. They were nice to me, but we all felt that I didn't belong there, not in a rich, aristocratic house. Amadeu was unhappy about the afternoon.

"'I hope . . ." he said, "I can't . . ."

"'It's not important," I said.

'Much later, I had a meeting with the judge; he had requested it. He felt that Amadeu was offended that he worked for a government that had Tarrafal on its conscience. *He loathes me, my own son loathes me*, he blurted out. And then he talked of his pains and how his profession helped him to go on living. He accused Amadeu of a lack of empathy. I told him what Amadeu had said to me: *I don't want to see him as a sick man who is forgiven everything. It would be as if I didn't have a father any more.*

'What I didn't tell him was how unhappy Amadeu was in Coimbra. Because he had doubts about his future as a doctor. Because he wasn't sure if he was only following his father's wish rather than the dictates of his own will.

'He shoplifted in the oldest department store in the city, was almost caught, and then suffered a nervous breakdown. I visited him in hospital.

"'Do you know the reason?" I asked. He nodded.

'He never explained it to me. But I think it was connected with his father, a court case he once witnessed. A kind of helpless, suppressed revolt. I ran into O'Kelly in the hospital corridor.

"'If he had at least pinched something really valuable!" was all his father said. "Not this junk!"

'I don't know if I liked him at that moment, or the opposite. To this day I don't know.

'The accusation of a lack of empathy was anything but justified. How often in my presence had Amadeu assumed the position of a Bechterev sufferer and held it until he got back backache! And then remained bent over, his head stretched forward like a bird, his teeth gnashing.

"'I don't know how my father stands it," he said. "Not only the pain. The humiliation!"

'If his imagination failed anywhere, it was with his mother. His relationship with her remained a mystery to me. She was pretty, well-groomed, but a nondescript woman. "Yes," he said. "That's it. No one can understand it." He blamed her for so much that it couldn't possibly be true. His problem with boundaries; his passion for work; the excessive demands he made on himself; his inability to play and dance. Everything was supposed to be connected with her and her gentle dictatorship. But you couldn't talk to him about it. "I don't want to talk, I want to be furious! Just furious! *Furioso! Raivoso!*"'

Twilight fell. Maria João was driving with her headlights on.

'Do you know Coimbra?' she asked.

Gregorius shook his head.

'He loved the Biblioteca Joanina at the university. Not a week went by that he wasn't there. And the Sala Grande dos Actos, where he received his certificate. He kept going back later to see the rooms.'

When Gregorius got out, he became dizzy and had to hold on to the roof of the car.

'Does that happen often?' Maria João asked.

He hesitated. Then he lied.

'You shouldn't take it lightly,' she said. 'Do you know a neurologist here?'

He nodded.

She drove off slowly as if she were considering coming back. Only at the intersection did she accelerate. The world was spinning and Gregorius had to hold on to the handle on the front door before he could unlock it. He drank a glass of milk from Silveira's refrigerator and then went upstairs slowly, step by step.

40

I hate hotels. Why do I keep doing it? Can you tell me that, Julieta? At midday on Saturday, when Gregorius heard Silveira unlock the door, he thought of these words of his, which the maid had told him. Silveira's actions fitted his words: he simply dropped his suitcase and coat, sat down in a chair in the hall and shut his eyes in exhaustion. When he saw Gregorius coming down the stairs, his face lit up.

'Raimundo. You're not in Isfahan?' he asked laughing.

He had a cold and was sniffling. The business deal in Biarritz hadn't gone as expected; he had twice lost at chess to the sleeping-car waiter and Filipe, the chauffeur, hadn't arrived at the railway station on time. Moreover, Julieta was also off today. Exhaustion was written on his face, an exhaustion greater and deeper than when they had met on the train. *The problem is,* Silveira had said when the train stopped at Valladolid station, *that we have no overview of our life. Neither forward nor backward. If something goes well, we simply have good luck.*

They ate what Julieta had prepared yesterday and then drank coffee in the living room. Silveira saw Gregorius looking at the photos of the grand party.

'Dammit,' he said. 'I completely forgot that. The party, the damn family party tonight.'

He wasn't going, *he simply wasn't going*, he said, and banged the fork on the table. Something in Gregorius's face made him stop.

'Unless you're coming along,' he said. 'A formal family party
The very last one! But if you like . . .'

It was close to eight when Filipe picked them up and he
was amazed to find them standing in the hall and shaking
with laughter. He had nothing suitable to wear, Gregorius had
said an hour earlier. Then he had tried on Silveira's things,
which were all tight. And now he looked at himself in the big
mirror: a pair of trousers that were too long, lying in folds on
the unsuitable, thick shoes, a smoking jacket that didn't close,
a shirt whose collar choked him. He was shocked when he
saw himself, but then was carried away by Silveira's fit of
laughter and now he began to enjoy the clowning. He couldn't
have explained it, but he had the feeling that he was taking
revenge on Florence with this masquerade.

Yet the obscure revenge didn't really get going until they
entered Silveira's aunt's villa. Silveira enjoyed introducing his
snooty relatives to his friend from Switzerland, Raimundo
Gregorio, a real scholar, who had mastered countless languages.
When Gregorius heard the word *erudito*, he flinched like an
impostor about to be exposed. But at the table, he suddenly
felt an attack of mischief and, to prove his multilingualism,
he spoke a wildly jumbled blend of Hebrew, Greek and Bernese
German and got drunk on the abstruse combinations of words
that became crazier by the minute. He hadn't known he was
capable of so much wordplay; he seemed to be carried away
by his imagination into a bold, broad loop in space, ever
farther and higher. Dizziness gripped him, a pleasant dizziness
of crazy words, red wine, smoke and background music; he
wanted this dizziness and did everything to make it last. Silveira's
relatives seemed to welcome his presence and Gregorius was
the star of the evening while Silveira chain-smoked and enjoyed
the show. The women watched Gregorius in a way he wasn't
used to; he wasn't sure whether their looks meant what they
seemed to mean, but it didn't matter.

What did matter was that he, Mundus who, because of his love of ancient texts, was nicknamed 'The Papyrus', was attracting such ambiguous looks.

Some time during the night he found himself in the kitchen. It was the kitchen of Silveira's relatives, but it was also the von Muralts' kitchen, and Eva watched what he was doing in horror. He had waited until the two maids had gone before slipping into the kitchen and now he was standing there, dizzy and swaying, leaning on the sink and washing the plates. He wanted the dizziness now, he wanted to enjoy the lunacy of the evening, the luxury of making up for what he had been unable to do at the school party forty years ago. Can you buy a title in Portugal, he had asked at dessert, but the question failed to provoke the expected embarrassment. To them, it was the mere stammering of someone who didn't know the language. Silveira was the only one who smiled.

The glasses were steamy with hot water. Gregorius groped in the washing-up bowl and a plate slipped out of his hand and shattered on the stone floor.

'*Espera, eu ajudo,*' said Silveira's niece Aurora, who suddenly appeared in the kitchen. Together, they crouched down and gathered up the slivers of china. Gregorius accidentally bumped into Aurora, whose perfume, he thought later, was a perfect antidote to his dizziness.

'*Não faz mal.*' Never mind, she said when he apologized and he was amazed to feel her press a kiss on his forehead. What was he doing here? she asked when they were back on their feet and pointed, giggling, at the apron he was wearing. Washing dishes? He? The guest? The polyglot scholar? '*Incrível!*' Unbelievable!

Then Aurora had taken off his apron, turned on the kitchen radio, taken hold of his hand and shoulder, and waltzed him around the kitchen. Gregorius, who had fled from dancing school back in his youth after one and a half lessons, now spun like a bear, stumbling over the trousers that were too long, gripped by vertigo. *I'm going to fall*, he thought. He tried to hold on to Aurora who didn't seem to notice his giddiness and whistled to the music. His knees buckled, and it was only Silveira's strong grip that prevented the fall.

Gregorius couldn't understand what Silveira said to Aurora, but from his tone he was clearly telling her off. He helped Gregorius sit down and brought him a glass of water.

Half an hour later, they left. He had never seen anything like that, said Silveira in the back of the car. Gregorius had stood this whole stiff company on its head. Well, Aurora always had this reputation . . . But the others . . . They had made him promise to bring Gregorius along to the next family party!

They let the chauffeur drive himself home, then Silveira sat down behind the wheel of the car and they went to the Liceu. 'It seems right to go there now, somehow, doesn't it?' Silveira had suddenly said on the way back.

In the light of the camping lamp, Silveira looked at the pictures of Isfahan. He nodded. He glanced at Gregorius and nodded again. On a chair lay the blanket as Maria João had folded it. Silveira sat down. He asked Gregorius questions no one here had asked, not even Maria João. How had he come to study ancient languages? Why wasn't he teaching at the university? He still remembered everything Gregorius had told him about Florence, but hadn't there been any other women afterwards?

And then Gregorius told him about Prado. It was the first time he had talked about him with someone who hadn't known him. Silveira was amazed at everything Gregorius had discovered about him and listened without once interrupting, while he warmed his hands on the camp stove. Could he see the book of the red cedars? he asked at the end.

He looked at the portrait for a long time. He read the introduction about the thousand unexpressed experiences. And then he re-read it. Then he began leafing through the book. He laughed and read aloud: *Petty book-keeping about generosity: there is that, too.* He turned some more pages, stopped, leafed back and read aloud:

AREIAS MOVEDIÇAS. QUICKSAND. *When we have understood that no matter how hard we try it's a matter of pure luck whether we succeed or not; when we have understood that in all our actions and experiences we are as quicksand before ourselves and for ourselves: what then happens to all the intimate respected feelings like pride, remorse and shame?*

Now Silveira stood up and paced back and forth, Prado's text before his eyes. Feverishly. He read aloud: *To understand yourself: is that a discovery or a creation?* He turned a few more pages and read aloud again: *Is anyone really interested in* me, *and not only in his interest in me?* He had come upon a longer piece of text, sat down on the edge of Senhor Cortês's desk and lit a cigarette.

PALAVRAS TRAIÇOEIRAS. TREACHEROUS WORDS. *When we talk about ourselves, about others, or simply about things, we want – it could be said – to reveal ourselves through our words: we want to show what we think and feel. We let others have a glimpse into our soul.* (We give them a piece of our mind, *as they say in English. An Englishman said that to me when we stood at a ship's railing. That's the only good thing I brought from that absurd country. Maybe also the memory of the Irishman with the red football in All Souls.) In this understanding of the case, we're the sovereign director, the self-appointed dramaturge as far as exposing our self is concerned. But maybe this is utterly false? A self-deception? For not only do* we reveal *ourselves with our words, we also* betray *ourselves. We give away a lot more than we had intended to reveal, and sometimes it's the exact opposite. And others can interpret our words as symptoms of something we ourselves may not even be aware of. As symptoms of the sickness of being us. It can be amusing when we regard others like this; it can make us more tolerant, but also put ammunition in our hands. And if we think that others are doing the same thing with us, the moment we start speaking words can stick in our throat and fear can silence us for ever.*

On the way back from the Liceu, they stopped at a building with a lot of steel and glass.

'That's my office,' said Silveira. 'I'd like to make a photocopy of Prado's book.'

He turned off the engine and opened the door. A look at Gregorius's face made him stop.

'I *see*. Yes. This book and a photocopying machine – they don't go together.' He ran his hand round the steering wheel. 'And besides, you want to keep the text all to yourself. Not only the *book*. The *text*.'

Later, when Gregorius lay awake, he kept thinking of these sentences. Why hadn't there been anybody before in his life who had understood him so quickly and easily? Before they went to bed, Silveira had embraced him for a moment. He was someone he could tell about his dizziness. The dizziness and the fear of the neurologist.

41

When João Eça stood in the doorway of his room in the home on Sunday, Gregorius saw from his face that something had happened. Eça hesitated before asking him in. It was a cold March day, yet the window was wide open. Eça straightened his trousers before he sat down. He struggled with himself as he set up the chess pieces with shaking hands. The struggle, Gregorius later thought, was about both his feelings and the question of whether he should talk about them.

Eça moved the pawns. 'I wet the bed last night,' he said in a rough voice. 'And I didn't notice it.' He kept his eyes lowered to the board.

Gregorius knew that he mustn't remain silent for too long. He told João that he had reeled dizzily around a strange kitchen last night and had almost landed up in the arms of a hysterical woman; unintentionally, he added.

That was entirely different. Eça was irritated.

Because it didn't concern the lower body? asked Gregorius. In both cases, it was about losing normal control of the body.

Eça looked at him. The incident had obviously upset him.

Gregorius made tea and poured him a half-cup. Eça saw the look that fell on his shaking hands.

'*A dignidade,*' he said.

'Dignity,' said Gregorius. 'I have no idea what that really is. But I don't think it's something that gets lost just because the body fails.'

Eça botched the opening move.

'When they led me away to be tortured, I went in my underpants and they laughed at it. It was a horrible *humiliation*, but I didn't feel I was losing my *dignity*. But what is it *then*?'

Did he believe he would lose his dignity if he had talked? asked Gregorius.

'I didn't say a word, not a single word. I locked away all the possible words inside me. Yes, that's it: I *locked* them away and bolted the door irrevocably. So it was *impossible* for me to talk, it was no longer *negotiable*. That had a remarkable effect: I stopped regarding the torture as an activity that others had to endure, and saw it instead as a form of behaviour. I sat there like a mere body, a heap of flesh in a hailstorm of pain. The torturers didn't know it, but I *degraded* them, degraded what was happening to a meaningless piece of theatre. That helped to reduce the torture to an agony.'

And if they had loosened his tongue with a drug?

He had often asked himself that, said Eça, and he had dreamed about it. He had come to the conclusion that they could have *destroyed* him with that, but they could never take away his *dignity*. To lose your dignity, you had to *forfeit* yourself.

'And then you get worked up about a wet bed?' said Gregorius and shut the window. 'It's cold and the room doesn't smell, not at all.'

Eça ran a hand over his eyes. 'I don't want all those tubes and pumps. I just want to live a few weeks longer.'

That there are things a person wouldn't do or allow at *any* price: maybe that's what dignity was about, said Gregorius. It didn't need to be moral boundaries, he added. You could forfeit your dignity in other ways. A teacher who played the crowing cock in the variety show against his will. Ass-kissing for the sake of a career. Unbounded opportunism. Duplicity and avoiding conflict to save a marriage. Such things.

'A beggar?' asked Eça. 'Can a person be a beggar with dignity?'

'Maybe, if there's an inevitability in his story, something unavoidable, something he can't do anything about. And if he stands by it. Stands by himself,' said Gregorius.

To stand by yourself – that was also part of dignity. That way, a person could get through a public flogging with dignity. Galileo. Luther. Even somebody who resisted the temptation to deny his guilt. Something politicians couldn't do. Honesty, the courage for honesty. With others and yourself.

Gregorius stopped. You knew what you thought only when you expressed it.

'There's a disgust,' said Eça, 'a very special disgust you feel when someone constantly deceives himself. Maybe it's the lack of dignity that disgusts me even today. At school I sat next to someone who kept wiping his sticky hands on his trousers, and I can still picture him doing it: as if it wasn't *true* that he wiped them. He wanted to be my friend but it just wasn't possible. And not because of the trousers. That's how he was *in general.*'

There was a question of dignity in forgiveness, too, he added. Amadeu had spoken of that sometimes. He had been particularly concerned with the difference between a forgiveness that leaves the other person his dignity and one that takes it away from him. *It must not be a forgiveness that demands subordination,* he said. *Thus, not as in the Bible, where you must regard yourself as a servant of God and Jesus. A servant! That's what it says!*

'He could get white-hot with rage,' said Eça. 'And often afterwards he also spoke of the lack of dignity in the New Testament relationship with death. *To die in dignity means recognizing the fact of dying. And all immortality kitsch must be resisted.* On Ascension Day, his office was always open and he worked even harder than usual.'

On the ferry back to Lisbon Gregorius reflected on Prado's words. *When we have understood that in all our actions and experiences we are as quicksand . . .* What did that imply for dignity?

42

On Monday morning, Gregorius sat in the train to Coimbra, the city where Prado had lived with the tormenting question of whether studying medicine had perhaps been a great mistake because he was mainly following his father's wish and going against his own will. One day, he had gone into the oldest department store in the city and stolen goods he didn't need. He who could afford to give his friend Jorge a complete pharmacy. Gregorius thought of his letter to his father and the beautiful thief, Diamantina Esmeralda Ermelinda, to whom Prado's imagination had assigned the role of avenging the thief sentenced by his father.

Before he left, he had called Maria João and asked her about the street in Coimbra where Prado had lived. He had given an evasive answer to her worried question about his dizziness. This morning, he hadn't felt dizzy. But something was different. It was as if he had to overcome a paper-thin air cushion of the softest resistance in order to touch things. He could have experienced the layer of air to be pierced as a protective cover if not for the flickering fear that the world was incessantly slipping past him. On the railway platform in Lisbon, he had walked briskly back and forth to reassure himself. It had helped and when he took a seat in the empty train compartment, he felt calmer.

Prado must have made this trip countless times. On the telephone, Maria João had spoken of his passion for railways. João Eça had also mentioned it when explaining how Amadeu's knowledge of such things, *his crazy patriotism for the railway*, had saved the lives of people in the Resistance. The working of the points had particularly fascinated him João had reported. Maria João had emphasized something else: train travel as a riverbed of imagination, a movement where fantasy liquefied and passed you images from closed chambers of the soul. The conversation with her this morning had lasted longer than planned; the particular, precious trust that had emerged when he had read to her from the Bible yesterday was still there. Gregorius again heard O'Kelly's sighing words: *Maria, my God, yes, Maria.* Exactly twenty-four hours had passed since she had opened the door to him, and it was already perfectly clear to him why Prado had written the thoughts he considered most dangerous in her kitchen and nowhere else. What was it? Her fearlessness? The impression that this was a woman who, in the course of her life, had found an internal demarcation and independence that Prado could only dream of?

They had talked on the phone as if they were still sitting in the Liceu, he at Senhor Cortês's desk, she in the chair with the blanket over her legs.

'Concerning travel, he was remarkably split,' she had said. 'He wanted to travel, ever farther, he wanted to lose himself in the space opened up to him by fantasy. But, as soon as he was away from Lisbon, he became homesick, a horrible homesickness that it was painful to witness. "Look, Lisbon is indeed beautiful, but . . ." people said to him.

'They didn't understand that it wasn't really about Lisbon, but about him, Amadeu. That is, his homesickness wasn't the yearning for the familiar and beloved. It was something much deeper, something that concerned his core: the wish to take refuge behind the solid, reliable defences that protected him from the malicious undercurrents of his soul. He knew from experience that these defensive walls were strongest when he was in Lisbon, in his parents' house, in the Liceu, but above all in the blue office. *Blue is the colour of my security*, he said.

'That it was about self-protection explains why his homesickness always smacked of panic and catastrophe. When it came over him, he broke off a trip from one moment to the next and fled home – often to Fátima's great disappointment.'

Maria João had hesitated before adding, 'It's good that she didn't understand what his homesickness was about. Otherwise, she would have had to acknowledge that she hadn't managed to rid him of his fear of himself.'

Gregorius opened Prado's book and read for the nth time a note that seemed to be the key to all the others.

ESTOU A VIVER EM MIM PRÓPRIO COMO NUM COMBOIO A ANDAR. I LIVE IN MYSELF AS IN A MOVING TRAIN. *I didn't board voluntarily, didn't have the choice and don't know the name of the destination. One day in the distant past I woke up in my compartment and felt rolling. It was exciting, I listened to the pounding of the wheels, held my head in the wind and savoured the speed of the things passing by me. I wished the train would never interrupt its journey. By no means did I want it to stop somewhere for ever.*

It was in Coimbra, on a hard bench in the lecture hall, that I became aware: I can't get off. I can't change the tracks or the direction. I don't determine the pace. I don't see the locomotive and can't see who's driving it and whether the engineer makes a reliable impression. I don't know if he reads the signals correctly and notices if a switch is worked wrong. I can't change the compartment. In the corridor, I see people passing by and think: Maybe it looks completely different in their compartment than in mine. But I can't go there and see, a conductor I never saw and never will see has bolted and sealed the compartment door. I open the window, lean far out and see that everybody else is doing the same thing. The train makes a soft curve. The last cars are still in the tunnel and the first are going on. Maybe the train is travelling in a circle, over and over, without anybody noticing it, not even the engineer? I have no idea how long the train is. I see all the others craning their neck to see and understand something. I call a greeting, but the wind blows away my words.

The lighting in the compartment changes and I can't determine it. Sun and clouds, twilight and again twilight, rain, snow, storm. The light on the ceiling is dim, grows lighter, a glistening glow, it begins flickering, goes out, comes back, it's a miserable light, a chandelier, a dazzling coloured neon light, all in one. The heating doesn't work right. It might heat when it's hot and break down when it's cold. If I move the switch, it clicks and clacks, but doesn't change anything. Strangely, my coat doesn't always warm me evenly either. Outside, things seem to take their usual, reasonable course. Maybe in the other compartments, too? In mine, it's different from what I expected, completely different. Was the designer drunk? A madman? A diabolical charlatan?

Train schedules are available in the compartment. I want to see where we'll stop. The pages are empty. At the railway stations where we stop, place signs are missing. The people outside glance curiously at the train. The windowpanes are murky from frequent fierce storms. I think: they distort the image of what is inside. Suddenly I'm overcome by the need to put things right. The window's stuck. I shout myself hoarse. The others bang indignantly on the wall. Beyond the station comes a tunnel. It takes my breath away. Leaving the tunnel, I ask myself if we really did stop.

What can you do on the trip? Tidy up the compartment. Fasten things so they don't rattle. But then I dream that the wind billows up and smashes the window-panes. Everything I have carefully straightened up flies away. I dream a lot on the endless journey, dreams of missed trains and wrong information in the schedules, of stations that vanish when you arrive, of level-crossing attendants and stationmasters in red caps suddenly standing in the emptiness. Sometimes I fall asleep out of sheer weariness. Falling asleep is dangerous, only seldom do I awake refreshed and am glad about the changes. What usually happens is that I'm bothered by what I find on awakening, both inside and out.

Sometimes I'm startled and think the train can go off the rails any time. Indeed I usually frighten myself with the thought. But in rare, incandescent moments, it flashes through me like a blessed lightning bolt.

I wake up and the landscape of the others draws past. Sometimes at breakneck speed so that I hardly keep up with their moods and their exuberant nonsense; then again with tormenting slowness when they keep saying and doing the same thing. I'm glad about the window-pane between them and me. So I see their wishes and plans but they can't open fire on me unhindered. I'm glad when the train picks up speed and they disappear. The wishes of others: What do we do with them when they strike us?

I press my forehead to the compartment window and concentrate with all my might. I would like once, one single time, to grasp what is going on outside. Really grasp *it. So that it doesn't slip away from me again immediately. It fails. Everything goes much too fast, even when the train stops between stations. The next impression wipes away the last one. Memory is overheated, I'm breathlessly busy retrospectively assembling the fleeting images of the event into an illusion of something intelligible. I always come too late, how fast the light of attention to things scurries off. Everything is always already past. I'm always left behind empty-handed. Never am I* there. *Not even when the inside of the compartment is reflected at night in the windowpane.*

I love tunnels. They're the symbol of hope: some time it will be bright again. If by chance it is not night.

Sometimes I get a visit in the compartment. I don't know how that's possible despite the bolted and sealed door, but it does happen. Usually the visit comes at the wrong time. They're people from the present, often also from the past. They come and go as they like, they're inconsiderate and bother me. I have to talk with them. It's all temporary, not binding, doomed to oblivion;

conversations on a train. A few visitors disappear without a trace. Others leave sticky and stinking traces, ventilating doesn't help. Then I'd like to rip out all the furnishings of the compartment and replace them with new ones.

The trip is long. Some days I wish it were endless. Those are rare, precious days. Other days I'm glad to know that there will be a last tunnel, where the train will come to a halt for ever.

When Gregorius got off the train, it was late afternoon. He took a room in a hotel on the other side of the Mondego, where he had a view of the old city on the Alcáçova Hill. The last sunbeams bathed the majestic buildings of the university, towering over everything, in a warm, golden light. Up there, in one of the steep narrow streets, Prado and O'Kelly had lived in a República, one of the student hostels dating from the Middle Ages.

'He didn't want to live differently from the others,' Maria João had said. 'Even though the noise from the room next door sometimes drove him to despair; he wasn't used to that. But the family wealth from the big estates of previous generations sometimes weighed heavily on him. There were two words that wound him up like no others: *colónia* and *latifundiário*. Then he looked like a person who's ready to shoot.

'When I visited him, his clothes were deliberately casual. Why didn't he wear the yellow ribbon of the college like the other medical students? I asked him.

'"You know I don't like uniforms; even the cap in the Liceu was repellent to me," he said.

'When I was about to leave and we were standing in the railway station, a student came on the platform wearing the dark blue ribbon of the literature faculty.

'I looked at Amadeu. "It's not the *ribbon*," I said. "It's the fact that it's *yellow*. You'd be happy to wear the *blue* ribbon."

'"You do know," he said, "that I don't like people to see through me. Come again soon. Please."

'He had a way of saying *por favor* – I would have gone to the ends of the earth to hear it.'

The street where Prado had lived was easy to find. Gregorius glanced into the hostel entrance and went up a few steps. *In Coimbra, when the whole world seemed to belong to us.* That's how Jorge had described that time. In this house he and Prado had written down what it was that endowed *lealdade*, loyalty between people. A list that didn't include love. *Desire, pleasure, security*. All feelings that disintegrate sooner or later. Loyalty was the only one that lasted. *An act of a will, a commitment, a partisanship of the soul.* Something that changed to necessity by chance encounters and the contingency of feelings. *A breath of eternity, only a breath, but all the same*, Prado had said. Gregorius pictured O'Kelly's face. *He deluded himself. We both deluded ourselves*, he had said with the slowness of a drunk.

In the university, Gregorius wanted to go immediately to the Biblioteca Joanina and the Sala Grande dos Actos, the places that had kept drawing Prado back here. But that was only possible at certain times, and he had missed the opening hours today.

The Capela de São Miguel *was* open and Gregorius was the only visitor. He looked at the overwhelmingly beautiful baroque organ. *I want to hear the swelling of the organ, this deluge of ethereal tones. I need it to counter the shrill absurdity of marches*, Prado had said in his speech. Gregorius recalled the times he had been to church. Confirmation classes, the funerals of his parents. *Our Father . . .* How dull, joyless and naïve it had sounded! And all that, he thought now, had nothing to do with the sweeping poetry of the Greek and Hebrew texts. Nothing, absolutely nothing!

Gregorius gave a start. Without meaning to, he had banged his fist on a bench and now looked round ashamed, but he was still alone. He dropped to his knees and did what Prado had done with his father's twisted back: he tried to imagine how the posture felt from within. *You would have to rip them out,* Prado had said when he had passed the confessionals with Father Bartolomeu. *Such humiliation!*

When Gregorius straightened up, the chapel was spinning rapidly. He clung to the bench and waited until the dizziness had passed. Then, as students rushed past him, he walked slowly along the corridors and entered a lecture hall where a lecture on jurisprudence was in progress. Sitting in the front row, he thought first of the lecture on Euripides when he had once failed to express his opinion. Then his thoughts slid back to other lectures he had attended as a student. And finally, he imagined the student Prado standing up in this very room and posing critical questions. Staid, prizewinning professors, leading authorities in their field, felt tested by him, Father Bartolomeu had said. But Prado had sat here not as an arrogant, know-it-all student. He had lived in the purgatory of doubt, tormented by the fear that he could miss himself. *It was in Coimbra, sitting on a hard bench in the lecture hall, that I became aware: I can't get off.*

Gregorius stayed until darkness fell on the grounds of the university and kept trying to be aware of the confusing feelings that accompanied him. Why did he suddenly think that here, in the most famous university of Portugal, he might have liked to stand in a lecture hall and share his comprehensive philosophical knowledge with students? Had he perhaps missed a possible life, one he could easily have led with his abilities and knowledge? Never before, not for a single hour, had he considered it a mistake that, as a student, he had stayed away from lectures after a few terms and devoted all his time to the ceaseless reading of texts. Why now, all of a sudden, this particular nostalgia? And was it really nostalgia?

He had ordered a meal in a small pub. But when it arrived, it revolted him and he wanted to be out in the cool night air. The paper-thin cushion of air that had enclosed him this

that was a trace stronger. As on the railway platform in Lisbon
he walked with exaggerated firmness and that helped now, too.

Joao de Lousada de Ledesma, *O Mar Tenebroso*. The title
caught his eye he walked along the shelves of books in a
second-hand bookshop. The book on Prado's desk. The last
thing he read. Gregorius took it off the shelf. The big calligraphic
font, the engravings of coastlines, the Indian ink drawings of
seafarers. *Cabo Finisterre*, he heard Adriana say, *up in Galicia.
It was like an* idée fixe. *He had a haunted, feverish expression
on his face when he spoke of it.*

Gregorius sat down in a corner and leafed through the book
until he came on the words of the twelfth-century Muslim
geographer El Edrisi: *From Santiago we went to Finisterre, as
the peasants call it, a word that means the end of the world. You
see nothing more than sky and water, and they say that the sea
is so stormy that no one could travel on it, and so you can't know
what is on the other side. They told us that some, eager to fathom
it, disappeared with their ships and none ever came back.*

It took a while for the thought to take shape in Gregorius's
mind. *Much later I heard that she was working in Salamanca
as a lecturer in history*, João Eça had said about Estefânia
Espinhosa. When she was working for the Resistance, she had
a job in the post office. After the flight with Prado, she had
stayed in Spain and had studied history. Adriana had seen no
connection between Prado's trip to Spain and his sudden
fanatical interest in Finisterre. Was there a link? If he and
Estefânia Espinhosa had travelled to Finisterre because she had
always been interested in the medieval fear of the endless stormy
sea, an interest that had led to her studies? Had something
happened on this trip to the end of the world that had upset
Prado and moved him to return?

But no, it was too absurd, too preposterous. And it was
just as ridiculous to assume that the woman had also written
a book about the fearsome sea. He really couldn't waste the

a book about the fearsome sea. He really couldn't waste the
bookseller's time with that.

'Let's see,' said the bookseller. 'The same title – that's almost
out of the question. Violates good academic practice. We'll
check it with the name.'

Estefânia Espinhosa, said the computer, had written two
books. Both dealt with the beginnings of the Renaissance.

'Not so far away, eh?' said the bookseller. 'But we can get
much more precise information. Watch,' and he called up the
history department of the University of Salamanca.

Estefânia Espinhosa had her own website, and right at the
top they came upon the list of her publications: two entries
about Finisterre, one in Portuguese, the other in Spanish. The
second-hand bookseller grinned.

'Don't like the machine, but sometimes . . .'

He called a specialized bookshop and they had one of the
two books in stock.

The shops would soon be closing. Gregorius, with the book
about the dark sea under his arm, took off. Would there be a
picture of the woman on the cover? He almost ripped the book
out of the saleswoman's hand and turned it over.

Estefânia Espinhosa, born 1948 in Lisbon, currently a professor
of early modern Spanish and Italian history at the University of
Salamanca. And a portrait that explained everything.

Gregorius bought the book and on the way to the hotel
he stopped every few feet to look at the picture. *She wasn't
only the ball, the red Irish ball in the Oxford college. She was
much more than all red Irish balls together. He must have felt
that she was the chance for him to be whole. As a man, I mean,*
he heard Maria João say. And the words of João Eça could
not have been more apt: *Estefânia, I think, was his chance to
leave the courthouse at last, to be free to live his life according
to his own wishes, according to his own passions, and to hell
with the rest.*

So she had been twenty-four when she sat behind the steering wheel in front of the blue house and drove across the border with Prado, twenty-eight years older, away from O'Kelly, away from danger, into a new life.

On the way back to the hotel, Gregorius passed the psychiatric clinic. He thought of Prado's nervous breakdown after the shoplifting incident. Maria João had told him that he was mainly interested in those patients who, in a world of their own, paced back and forth and talked to themselves. Afterwards he was always on the lookout for such people and was amazed by how many of them there were on the street, in the bus, on the ferry, who shouted out their rage at imaginary enemies.

'He wouldn't have been Amadeu if he hadn't spoken to them and listened to their stories. That had never happened to them and when he made the mistake of giving them his address, they arrived at his door the next day and Adriana had to throw them out.'

In the hotel, Gregorius read one of the few notes in Prado's book he didn't yet know.

O VENENO ARDENTE DO DESGOSTO. THE WHITE-HOT POISON OF ANGER. *When others make us angry at them – at their shamelessness, injustice, inconsideration – then they exercise power over us, they proliferate and gnaw at our soul, then anger is like a white-hot poison that corrodes all mild, noble and balanced feelings and robs us of sleep. Sleepless, we turn on the light and are angry at the anger that has lodged like a succubus who sucks us dry and debilitates us. We are not only furious at the damage, but also that it develops in us all by itself, for while we sit on the edge of the bed with aching temples, the distant catalyst remains untouched by the corrosive force of the anger that eats at us. On the empty internal stage bathed in the harsh light of mute rage, we perform all by ourselves a drama with shadow figures and shadow words we hurl against enemies in helpless rage we feel as icy blazing fire in our bowels. And the greater our despair that it is only a shadow play and not a real discussion with the possibility of hurting the other and producing a balance of suffering, the wilder the poisonous shadows dance and haunt us even in the darkest catacombs of our dreams. (We will turn the tables, we think grimly, and all night long forge words that will produce in the other the effect of a fire bomb so that now he will be the one with the flames of indignation raging inside while we, soothed by* schadenfreude, *will drink our coffee in cheerful calm.)*

What could it mean to deal appropriately *with anger? We really don't want to be soulless creatures who remain thoroughly indifferent to what they come across, creatures whose appraisals consist only of cool, anemic judgements and nothing can shake them up because nothing really bothers them. Therefore, we can't seriously wish not to know the experience of anger and instead persist in an equanimity that wouldn't be distinguished from tedious insensibility. Anger also teaches us something about who we are. Therefore this is what I'd like to know: what can it mean to train ourselves in anger and imagine that we take advantage of its knowledge without being addicted to its poison?*

We can be sure that we will hold on to the deathbed as part of the last balance sheet — and this part will taste bitter as cyanide — that we have wasted too much, much too much strength and time on getting angry and getting even with others in a helpless shadow theatre which only we, who suffered impotently, knew anything about. What can we do to improve this balance sheet? Why did our parents, teachers and other instructors never talk to us about it? Why didn't they tell something of this enormous significance? Not give us in this case any compass that could have helped us avoid wasting our soul on useless, self-destructive anger?

Gregorius lay awake for a long time. Now and then he stood up and went to look out of the window. The upper part of the city with the university and the bell tower now, after midnight, looked barren, sacred, and a little menacing. He could imagine a surveyor waiting in vain to be allowed into the mysterious district.

His head leaning on a mountain of pillows, Gregorius re-read the sentences in which Prado had revealed more about himself than in all the others: *Sometimes I have the startling thought: the train could go off the rails at any moment. Indeed I usually frighten myself with this thought. But in rare moments, it flashes through me like a lightning bolt.*

He didn't know where the image came from, but all at once, Gregorius saw this Portuguese doctor who had dreamed of poetic thinking as paradise sitting among the pillars of a cloister, that had become a silent shelter for the derailed passenger. His derailment had been created when the incandescent lava of his tortured soul had scorched and washed away every trace of enslavement and strain in him. He had disappointed all expectations and broken all taboos, and that was his happiness. In the end, he was at peace with his disabled, judgemental father, the gentle dictatorship of the ambitious mother, and the lifelong stifling gratitude of the sister.

And with himself, too, he had finally found peace. The homesickness had passed, he no longer needed Lisbon and the blue colour of safety. Now that he had let go of the internal storm tide and had become one with it, there was no longer any need for a defensive wall. Unhampered by himself, he could travel to the other end of the world. At last, he could travel the snowy steppes of Siberia to Vladivostok without having to think at every pounding of the wheels that the train was taking him farther and farther away from his blue Lisbon.

Now the sunlight flooded the cloister garden, the pillars

grew lighter and lighter and finally turned completely pale, so that only a shining depth remained where Gregorius lost his hold.

He woke with a start, reeled to the bathroom and washed his face. Then he called Doxiades. The Greek asked him to describe all the symptoms of his dizziness. Then he was silent for a few moments. Gregorius felt a creeping fear.

'It can mean anything,' said the Greek finally in his calm doctor's voice. 'It's probably harmless, nothing that can't be brought under control quickly. But you would be wise to have some tests. The Portuguese can do them just as well as we can here. But my gut feeling is that you should come home. Talk to the doctors in your mother tongue. Fear and foreign languages don't go well together.'

When Gregorius finally fell asleep again, the first glimmer of dawn was visible behind the university.

43

There were three hundred thousand volumes, said the tourist guide, and her high heels clacked on the marble floor of the Biblioteca Joanina. Gregorius hung back and looked around. Never had he seen anything like it. Rooms panelled in gold and in tropical woods, linked by arches reminiscent of triumphal arches, topped by the coat of arms of King João V who had founded the library in the early eighteenth century. Baroque shelves with galleries of delicate pillars. A portrait of João V. A red carpet that enhanced the impression of splendour. It was like a fairy tale.

Homer, *The Iliad* and *The Odyssey*, several editions in magnificent bindings that gave them the appearance of sacred texts. Gregorius let his eyes glide on.

After a while, he felt his gaze travelling along the shelves carelessly. His thoughts had remained with Homer. It must have been these thoughts that made his heart pound, but he couldn't figure out what they were about. He went into a corner, took off his glasses and closed his eyes. In the next room, he could hear the guide's shrill voice. He pressed the palms of his hands to his ears and concentrated on the muffled silence. The seconds passed by and he could feel his blood throbbing.

Yes. What he had been looking for, without being aware of it, was a word that appeared in Homer only one single time. It was as if something hidden in the wings of memory wanted to test whether his ability to remember was still as good as ever. His breath speeded up. The word didn't come. *It didn't come.*

The guide moved through the room with a group of chattering people. Gregorius pushed past them as far back as he could. He heard the door to the library close and the key turn in the lock.

His heart still pounding, he ran to the shelf and took out *The Odyssey*. The old, stiff leather cut his palms with its sharp edges. He leafed through the volume frantically and blew the dust into the room. The word wasn't where he had expected to find it. *It wasn't there.*

He tried to breathe calmly. As if a layer of cloud went through him, he felt a dizziness that came and went. Methodically, he went through the whole epic in his mind. No other passage was possible. But the result of the exercise was that now the supposed certainty at the start of his search began to crumble. The floor began to sway and this time it wasn't dizziness. Had he deceived himself in the worst way, and it was *The Iliad*? He took the book off the shelf and leafed through it mindlessly. The movements of his hand were empty and mechanical, the goal forgotten; from one moment to the next, Gregorius felt the cushion of air surrounding him, he tried to stamp his feet, flailed his arms, the book fell from his hand, his knees gave way, and he slid to the floor in a feeble motion.

When he came to, he struggled to find his glasses that lay an arm's length away. He looked at his watch. No more than a quarter of an hour could have passed. Sitting up, he leaned his back against the wall. Minutes went by when he only breathed, glad that he hadn't hurt himself and that his glasses had remained intact.

And then, quite suddenly, panic flared up in him. Was this forgetting the beginning of something? A first, tiny island of forgetting? Would it grow and would others join it? *We are gravel-covered slopes of forgetting*, Prado had written somewhere. What if an avalanche of gravel now overcame him and ripped away all the precious words? He grabbed his head with his hands and pressed it as if he could thus prevent more words from disappearing. He examined object after object in his field of vision and gave every item its name, first in dialect, then in High German, French and English and finally in Portuguese. None was lacking and slowly he calmed down.

When the door was unlocked for the next group of visitors, he waited in the corner, mingled with the people for a moment and then disappeared. A dark blue sky arched over Coimbra. At a café, he drank a camomile tea in small sips. His stomach relaxed and he felt he could eat something.

The students lay on the grass in the warm March sunshine. A man and a woman, entangled in each other, suddenly burst into loud laughter, threw away their cigarettes, got up with fluid, supple movements and started dancing, as lightly and loosely as if there were no gravity. Gregorius felt the undertow of memory and let himself go. And suddenly it was there, the scene he hadn't thought about in decades.

No errors, but a bit clumsy, the Latin professor had said when Gregorius translated Ovid's *Metamorphoses* in the lecture hall. A December afternoon, snowflakes, electric light. Girls grinning. *A little more dancing!* the man in the bow tie and the red scarf had called. Gregorius had felt the whole weight of his body on the bench. The bench had creaked when he moved. The remaining time, when the others' turn came, he had sat there numb. The numbness had lasted until the end of the class when he went through the arbour decorated for Christmas.

After the holidays, he hadn't gone to this class any more. He had avoided the man with the red scarf and evaded the other professors as well. From then on, he had studied only at home.

Now he paid and went through the Mondego, called *O Rio dos Poetas,* back to the hotel. *Do you find me boring? How? But*

Mundus, you can't ask me such questions! Why did all these things hurt so much, even now? Why hadn't he managed in twenty, thirty years to *shake them off?*

When Gregorius woke up in the hotel two hours later, the sun was just going down. Natalie Rubin had walked with clacking high heels over the marble of the corridors in the University of Bern. Standing at the front of an empty lecture hall, he had given a lecture about words that appeared in Greek literature only once. He wanted to write down the words, but the board was so slippery that the chalk slid off and when he tried to say the words, he had forgotten them. Estefânia Espinhosa had also flitted through his fitful sleep, a figure with shining eyes and an olive complexion, silent at first, then giving a lecture under a gigantic, gold-covered dome about subjects that didn't exist. Doxiades had interrupted her. *Come home*, he had said, *we'll examine you on Bubenbergplatz.*

Gregorius sat on the edge of the bed. The Homeric word didn't come now either. And the uncertainty about the passage in which it appeared began to torment him again. There was no point picking up *The Iliad.* It was in *The Odyssey*. It was *there*. He *knew* it. But where?

The next train to Lisbon, they had found out downstairs at the reception desk, wasn't until the next morning. He reached for the big book about the dark sea and read more of what El Edrisi, the Muslim geographer, had written: *Nobody knows – we are told – what is in this sea, nor can it be explored, for there are many obstacles that confront the sailor: the profound darkness, the high waves, the frequent storms, the countless monsters that inhabit it, and the strong winds.* He would have liked to make photocopies of Estefânia Espinhosa's two articles about Finisterre, but had been unable to ask the library staff because he lacked the vocabulary.

He sat still for a while. *You would be wise to have some tests,*

Doxiades had said. And he also heard the voice of Maria João: *You shouldn't take it lightly.*

He took a shower, packed and asked the baffled woman at the reception desk to call a taxi. The car rental agency at the railway station was still open. They would also have to charge for today, said the man. Gregorius nodded, signed for two more days and went to the parking lot.

He had learned to drive as a student, with the money he earned from teaching. That had been thirty-four years ago. Since then, he hadn't driven; the yellowed licence with the youthful photo and the stipulation, in bold print, about wearing glasses and not driving at night, had lain unused in the folder of his travel documents. The man at the car rental agency had frowned as he looked back and forth between the photo and the real face, but he hadn't said anything.

Behind the wheel of the big car, Gregorius waited until his breathing had calmed down. Slowly, he tried all the knobs and switches. With cold hands he started the engine, put it in reverse, released the clutch and stalled the engine. Frightened by the violent jolt, he shut his eyes and waited again until his breath was calm. At the second attempt, the car lollopped along, and Gregorius backed out of the parking space. He took the curves to the exit ramp at snail's pace. At a traffic signal on the edge of the city, the car stalled, then it settled down.

He did the highway to Viana do Castelo in two hours. He sat calmly behind the wheel and stayed in the right lane. He began to enjoy the trip. He managed to push the issue of the Homeric word so far into the background that it could almost be called forgetting. Becoming cocky, he pressed the accelerator and held the steering wheel with outstretched arms.

A car with blinding headlights came towards him in the opposite lane. Everything began to spin, Gregorius eased up on the throttle, slid on to the hard shoulder at the right, pulled up on the grass and came to a stop centimetres from the guardrail. Dashing cones of light flowed away above him. At the next rest stop, he got out and carefully inhaled the cool night air. *You should come home. Talk to the doctors in your mother tongue.*

An hour later, beyond Valença do Minho, he reached the border. Two members of the Guardia Civil with machine guns waved him through. From Tui, he took the highway through Vigo, Pontevedra and further north to Santiago. Shortly before midnight, he stopped and studied the map as he ate in a diner. There was no other solution: if he didn't want to make an enormous detour through the Cape of Santa Eugenia, he had to go through Padrón on the mountain road to Noia; the rest was straightforward: keep along the coast to Finisterre. He had never driven on mountain roads and his mind pictured the Swiss passes where the driver of the post van constantly had to swing the steering wheel back and forth.

The people around him spoke Galician. He didn't understand a word. He was tired. He had forgotten the word. He, Mundus, had forgotten a word in Homer. Under the table, he pressed his feet on the floor to dissipate the cushion of air. He was afraid. *Fear and foreign language don't go well together.*

It was easier than he had thought. In sharp, blind curves, he slowed down to a crawl, but at night, because of the headlights, you had more warning of oncoming cars than in the day. The traffic thinned out; it was after two o'clock in the morning. When he realized that he couldn't simply stop on the narrow mountain road if the dizziness came on, he panicked. But then, when a sign indicated that Noia was close, he grew bold and cut corners. *A little hard. But Mundus, you can't ask me such things!* Why hadn't Florence simply lied! *You boring? Why,* absolutely *not!*

Was it really that you simply shook off offences? *We are expanded far into the past,* Prado had noted. *That comes from our feelings, especially the deep ones, those that determine who we are and what it is like to be us. For these feelings are not related to time; they don't know it and they don't acknowledge it.*

From Noia to Finisterre, it was a hundred and fifty kilometres on good roads. You didn't see the sea, but you imagined it. It was coming up to four o'clock. Now and then Gregorius stopped. It wasn't dizziness, he decided every time, it was simply that his brain seemed to be swimming in his skull with fatigue. After four dark petrol stations, he finally found one that was open. How far was Finisterre? he asked the sleepy garage attendant. '*Pues, el fin del mundo!*' he laughed.

When Gregorius entered Finisterre, dawn was beginning to break through a cloud-covered sky. The first customer, he drank a cup of coffee in a bar. Wide awake and very solid, he stood on the stone floor. The word would come to him when he least expected it, that's how memory was, he knew that. He was enjoying this crazy trip and being here now, and took the cigarette the innkeeper offered him. After the second drag, he felt slightly dizzy. '*Vértigo*,' he said to the innkeeper. 'I'm an expert in dizziness. There are a whole lot of kinds and I know them all.' The innkeeper didn't understand and wiped the counter vigorously.

Gregorius drove the few kilometres to the Cape with the window open. The salty sea air was wonderful and he drove very slowly like someone savouring anticipation. The road ended in a harbour with fishing boats. The fishermen had recently returned and were standing smoking together. All of a sudden – he no longer knew how it had happened – he was standing with the fishermen and smoking their cigarettes.

Were they content with their life? Mundus, a Bernese philologist of ancient languages, had asked the Galician fishermen at the end of the world about their outlook on life. Gregorius enjoyed it; he enjoyed it enormously. Joy at the absurdity of his questions blended with fatigue, euphoria and an unfamiliar feeling of liberation.

The fishermen didn't understand his questions and Gregorius had to repeat them twice in his broken Spanish. '*Contento?*' one of them finally shouted. 'We don't know anything else!' They laughed and kept on laughing until the laughter became more like a roar, Gregorius joining in so passionately that his eyes began to water.

He put his hand on the shoulder of one of the men and turned him to face the sea.

'*Siempre derecho, más y más – nada!*' he shouted into a gust of wind.

'*America!*' shouted the man. '*America!*'

From the inside pocket of his jacket, he took out the photo of a girl in blue jeans, boots, and a cowboy hat.

'*Mi hija!*' My daughter! He gestured towards the sea.

The others ripped the picture out of his hand.

'*Qué guapa es!*' How pretty she is, they all shouted together.

Gregorius laughed and gesticulated and laughed. The others tapped him on the shoulders, right and left and right. They were rough blows and Gregorius staggered. The fishermen were spinning around, the sea was spinning around, the roar of the wind became a roar in the ear, it swelled on and on, to disappear quite suddenly in a silence that swallowed everything.

When he came to, he was lying on the seat of a boat with frightened faces looking down on him. He sat up. His head hurt. He refused the bottle of liquor they offered him. The dizziness had passed, he said, and added: '*El fin del mundo!*' They laughed with relief. He shook off calloused, gigantic hands, clambered out of the boat, and sat down behind the steering wheel of the car. He was glad the engine started immediately. The fishermen, their hands in the pockets of their oilskins, watched him go.

In the town, he took a room in a boarding house and slept until early afternoon. It had cleared up in the meantime and become warmer. Nevertheless, he was freezing when he drove to the Cape at dusk. He sat down on a rock and watched the light in the west grow weaker until it finally died out completely. *O mar tenebroso.* The black waves crashed, the light foam washed over the beach with a menacing rustle. The word from Homer didn't come. *It didn't come.*

Was this word *there* at all? Was it ultimately not his memory but his mind that had failed him? How could a person almost lose his mind because a word, a single word, that occurred one single time, had escaped him? He might torment himself in the lecture hall taking an examination. But facing the raging sea? Shouldn't the black water merging seamlessly into the night sky simply wash away such cares as completely meaningless, absurd, of concern only to someone who had lost all sense of proportion?

He was homesick. He shut his eyes. He imagined walking from Bundesterrasse to the Kirchenfeldbrücke. Through the arcades of Spitalgasse, Marktgasse and Kramgasse, he went down to the Bärengraben. In the cathedral, he heard the Christmas Oratorio. He got off the train in Bern and entered his flat. He took the Portuguese language course off the record player and put it in the broom cupboard. Then he lay down on the bed, glad to know that nothing had changed in his absence.

It was quite unlikely that Prado and Estefânia Espinhosa had come here, he thought, returning to the present. More than unlikely. Nothing suggested it, nothing in the least.

Freezing cold and with his jacket damp, Gregorius went to the car. In the dark, the car looked enormous. Like a monster that nobody could drive back to Coimbra intact, least of all him.

Later, he tried to get something to eat from a café opposite the boarding house, but it was just about to close. At the reception desk, he asked for a few sheets of paper, then he sat down at the tiny table in his room and translated what El

Edrisi, the Muslim geographer, had written into Latin, Greek and Hebrew. He had hoped that writing Greek letters would bring back the lost word. But nothing happened; the space of memory remained silent and empty.

No, it wasn't that the rippling expanse of the sea made retaining and forgetting of words and phrases meaningless. It wasn't so at all. A single word among words, a single phrase among phrases: they were untouchable, absolutely untouchable by the mass of blind, wordless water, and that would remain so even if the whole universe became a world of countless deluges, dripping nonstop from the skies. If there was only one word in the universe, one single word, then it wouldn't be a *word*, but if it were one, it would be mightier and more illuminating than all floods beyond all horizons.

Slowly Gregorius calmed down. Before he went to sleep, he looked out of the window at the parked car. Tomorrow morning, it would take him back to Coimbra.

Exhausted and fearful after an uneasy sleep, he took the journey in short shifts. During the breaks, he was regularly haunted by dream images of the night. He had been in Isfahan and it had been by the sea. The city with its minarets and domes of shining dark blue and glittering gold, had risen against a bright horizon and therefore he was frightened when he looked at the sea and saw it raging black and roaring before the desert city. A hot, dry wind drove damp, heavy air into his face. For the first time, he had dreamed of Prado. The goldsmith of words was only present in the broad arena of the dream, wordless and elegant, and with his ear to Adriana's enormous tape recorder. Gregorius searched for the sound of his voice.

In Viana do Castelo, shortly before reaching the highway to Porto and Coimbra, Gregorius felt that the lost word from *The Odyssey* was on the tip of his tongue. Behind the wheel, he shut his eyes instinctively and tried with all his might to keep himself from sinking back into forgetting. A cacophony of horns startled him. At the last second, he was able to turn the wheel sharply, pull the car back from the oncoming lane where it had drifted, and prevent a head-on collision. At the next rest stop, he sat quietly in the car until the painful throbbing of the blood in his brain subsided. Then he drove behind a slow truck to Porto. The woman at the car rental agency was not exactly pleased that he wanted to return the car here and not in Coimbra. But seeing the tension in his face, she finally agreed.

When the train to Coimbra and Lisbon pulled out of the station, Gregorius leaned his head back, exhausted. He thought of the farewells in store for him in Lisbon. *That's the meaning of a farewell in the full, important sense of the word: that two people, before they part from each other, reach an understanding of how they have seen and experienced each other,* Prado had written in his letter to the mother. *Saying goodbye is something that only you can do, but it means subjecting yourself to the scrutiny of the other.* The train got under way. The fear of the accident he had missed by a hair's-breadth began to fade. Until he reached Lisbon, he didn't want to think of anything at all.

Just as he had managed to empty his mind, helped by the monotonous beat of the wheels, the lost word was suddenly there: λίοτσον, an iron shovel for cleaning the floor of the hall. And now he also knew where to find it: in *The Odyssey,* at the end of the twenty-second book.

Then the compartment door opened and a young man entered. He sat down opposite Gregorius and unfolded a tabloid newspaper with bold headlines. Gregorius stood up, took his bag and went to the end of the train where there was an empty compartment. λίοτσον, he said to himself, λίοτσον.

When the train reached Coimbra, he thought of the university on the hill and of the surveyor who went over the bridge in his imagination with an old-fashioned doctor's bag, a thin, bent man in a grey smock, who wondered how he could make the people in the castle let him in.

When Silveira came home from the office that night, Gregorius met him in the hall. Silveira hesitated and narrowed his eyes.

'You're going home.'

Gregorius nodded.

'Explain!'

44

'If you'd given me time – I'd have made a Portuguese out of you,' said Cecília. 'When you're back in your raw, guttural country, think of that: *doce, suave*, and we leap over the vowels.'

She pulled the green scarf over her lips and it blew when she spoke. She laughed when she saw his look.

'The thing with the scarf, you like it. Don't you?' And she blew into it again.

She gave him her hand. 'Your unbelievable memory. Because of that I won't forget you.'

Gregorius held her hand too long. He hesitated. Finally he ventured, 'Is there any reason why . . .'

'You mean, why I always wear green? Yes, there is. You'll hear it when you come back.'

Quando voltares. When you come back. *Quando*, she had said, not *se*. On the way to Vítor Coutinho, he imagined how it would be if he turned up at the language school on Monday morning. How her face would look; how her lips would move when she told him the reason for the eternal green.

'*Que quer?*' Coutinho's voice roared an hour later.

The door buzzed; the old man came down the steps with his pipe between his teeth. For a moment, he had to search in his memory.

'Ah, *c'est vous*,' he said then.

Today, too, the house smelled of stale food, dust and pipe tobacco, and today, too, Coutinho wore a washed-out shirt of indefinable colour.

Prado. *O consultório azul.* Had Gregorius found the man?

No idea why I give this to you, but that's how it is, the old man had said to him when he had given him the New Testament on his previous visit. Gregorius had it with him but it remained in his pocket. He didn't even mention it; the right words wouldn't come. *Intimacy, it is fleeting and deceptive as a mirage,* Prado had written.

He was in a hurry, said Gregorius, and gave the old man his hand.

'One more thing,' the old man shouted at him across the courtyard. 'Will you call the number now that you're here again? The number on your forehead?'

Gregorius made the sign of uncertainty and waved.

He went to the Baixa, the lower part of the city, and paced the chessboard of the streets. In the café across from O'Kelly's pharmacy, he had something to eat and kept waiting for the figure of the smoking pharmacist to appear behind the glass door. Did he want to have another talk with him? Did *he want to*?

All morning he felt that something wasn't right with his farewells. That something was lacking. Now he knew what it was. He went to the photo shop and bought a camera with a telephoto lens. Back in the café, he aimed it at the part of the glass door through which O'Kelly could sometimes be seen and shot a whole roll of film.

Later he went back to Coutinho's house in the Cemitério dos Prazeres and photographed the dilapidated building overgrown with ivy. This time he aimed at the window, but the old man didn't appear. Finally, he gave up and went to the cemetery where he took pictures of the Prado family plot. Near the cemetery, he bought more film and then took the old tram through the city to visit Mariana Eça.

Red-gold Assam with biscuits. Big dark eyes. Reddish hair. Yes, she said, it would be better if he could explain his symptoms in his mother tongue. Gregorius said nothing about fainting in the library at Coimbra. They talked about João Eça.

'His room is a little small,' said Gregorius.

For a moment, anger flitted over her face, then she had herself under control again.

'I suggested other homes to him, more comfortable ones. But that's what he wanted. *It should be basic*, he said. *After everything that was, it has to be basic.*'

Gregorius left before the teapot was empty. He wished he hadn't said anything about Eça's room. It was ridiculous to have done so, as if, after spending four afternoons with João, he was closer to him than she, who had known him as a little girl. As if he understood João better. It was ridiculous. Even if it was right.

When he returned to Silveira's house that afternoon, he put on the old, heavy glasses but they no longer felt comfortable.

It was too dark to take a photograph when he arrived at Mélodie's house. The flash worked when he took a few pictures anyway. Today she wasn't to be seen behind the illuminated windows. *A girl who didn't seem to touch the floor.* The judge had got out of the car, stopped the traffic with his cane, made his way through the audience, and without looking at his daughter in the Mao cap, had tossed a handful of coins into the open violin case. Gregorius gazed up at the cedars that had looked blood red to Adriana just before her brother had stuck the knife in her throat.

Now Gregorius saw a man at one of the windows. That decided the issue of whether or not he should ring the bell. In a bar where he had once been, he drank a coffee and smoked a cigarette, as before. Then he went over to the citadel and imprinted Lisbon at night on his memory.

At closing time O'Kelly was there to lock up the shop. A few minutes later, when he entered the street, Gregorius followed him again, but at a safe distance this time. When he saw him turn into the side street where the chess club was, Gregorius went back to take a picture of the lighted pharmacy.

45

On Saturday morning, Filipe drove Gregorius to the Liceu. They packed up the camping gear and Gregorius took the pictures of Isfahan off the walls. Then he sent the chauffeur away.

It was a warm sunny day and April was only a week away. Gregorius sat down on the moss on the front steps. *I sat on the mossy steps and thought of my father's imperious wish that I might become a doctor – one who might release people like him from pain. I loved him for his trust and cursed him for the crushing burden he imposed on me with his touching wish.*

Suddenly Gregorius began to weep. He took off the glasses, buried his head between his knees and let the tears drip freely on to the moss. *Em vão,* In vain, had been one of Prado's favorite phrases, Maria João had said. Gregorius said the words and repeated them, slowly, then faster, until they merged into one another and with the tears.

Later he went up to Prado's classroom and photographed the view of the girls' school. From the girls' school, he got the opposite view: the window where Maria João had seen the points of light in Prado's opera glasses.

He told Maria João about the pictures when he sat in her kitchen at noon. And then, all at once, it broke out of him; he talked of fainting in Coimbra, of forgetting the Homeric word, and of the panicky fear of a neurological examination.

Later they sat together at the kitchen table and read what Maria João's encyclopaedia said about dizziness. It could have completely harmless causes, Maria João said, and showed him the sentences, moving her index finger along as she translated the important words.

Tumour. Gregorius pointed silently to the word. Yes, of course, said Maria João, but he had to read what it said, mainly, that in this case dizziness doesn't appear without other, more serious signs of breakdown, which didn't appear in him.

She was glad, she said at parting, that he had taken her along on the trip into the past. In this way, she could feel the peculiar blend of closeness and distance that was the essence of her relationship with Amadeu. Then she went to the cupboard and took out the big box with the marquetry lid. She handed him the sealed envelope with Prado's notes about Fátima.

'I won't read it, as I said,' she said. 'And I think it's better off with you. Maybe, in the end, you're the one who knows him best of all of us. I'm grateful for the way you've talked about him.'

Later, when Gregorius sat on the ferry across the Tagus, he pictured Maria João waving goodbye until he had disappeared from view. She was the one he had met last, and she was the one he would miss most. Would he write and tell her how the examination had turned out? she had asked him.

46

When Gregorius stood at the door, João Eça squinted and his features hardened as if he was anticipating great pain.

'It's Saturday,' he said.

They sat down in the usual places. The chessboard wasn't there; the table looked naked.

Gregorius told him about the dizziness, the fear, the fishermen at the end of the world.

'So you won't be coming any more,' said Eça.

Instead of Gregorius and his worries, he spoke about himself, which, in anyone else, would have seemed strange to Gregorius. But not in this tortured, taciturn, lonely man. Eça's words were some of the most precious he had heard.

If the dizziness turned out to be nothing and the doctors managed to treat it, he would come back, he said. To learn Portuguese properly and write the history of the Portuguese Resistance. He said it in a firm voice, but the confidence he forced into it sounded hollow, and he was sure that it sounded hollow to Eça too.

With shaking hands, Eça took the chessboard off the shelf and lined up the pieces. For a while, he sat there with his eyes closed. Then he stood up and took a book of chess games from the shelf.

'Here. Alekhine against Capablanca. I'd like us to play it together.'

'Art against science,' said Gregorius.

Eça smiled. Gregorius wished he could have captured this smile on film.

Sometimes he tried to imagine how the last minutes were after you took a lethal dose, Eça said in the middle of the game. First perhaps relief that it was now finally over and you had escaped from your undignified disability. A soupçon of pride at your own bravery. A regret that you hadn't been so brave more often. A final summing-up, a final assurance that it was right and it would be wrong to call the ambulance. Hope and composure to the last. Waiting for the cloudiness and numbness in fingertips and lips.

'And then suddenly a tremendous panic, a convulsion, the crazy wish that it might not be the end. An internal flooding, a hot current of will to live that sweeps everything aside and makes all thoughts and decisions appear artificial, stilted, absurd. And then? What *then*?'

He didn't know, said Gregorius, and then he took out Prado's book and read aloud:

Wasn't it obvious, simple and clear what her horror consisted of when she received news of her impending death at this moment? I held the bleary-eyed face in the morning sun and thought: They simply wanted more of the stuff of their life, however light or heavy, barren or lush this life may be. They don't want it to end, even if they can no longer miss the lacking life after the end — and know that.

Eça took the book and read, first, this passage, then the whole conversation with Jorge about death.

'O'Kelly,' he said finally. 'Smoking himself to death. "So what?" he said when anyone mentioned it. I picture his face: *Kiss my ass*, he used to say And then fear got to him after all. *Merda.*'

By the time the game was over and Alekhine had won, it

was beginning to grow dark. Gregorius took Eça's cup and drank the last sip of tea. At the door, they stood facing each other. Gregorius felt himself shaking. Eça's hands grabbed his shoulders and now he felt his head against his cheek. Eça sobbed aloud, Gregorius could feel the movement of his Adam's apple. With a violent shove that made Gregorius totter, Eça pushed away from him and opened the door, looking down. Before Gregorius turned the corner in the hall, he looked back. Eça stood in the middle of the hall and watched him. He had never done that before.

On the street, Gregorius went behind some bushes and waited. Eça came out on to the balcony and lit a cigarette. Gregorius shot a whole roll of film.

On the return journey he saw nothing of the Tagus, but saw and felt João Eça. From the Praça do Comércio, he walked slowly towards Bairro Alto and sat down in a café near the blue house.

47

He let one quarter-hour after another pass. Adriana. That would be the hardest goodbye.

She opened the door and immediately read his face correctly. 'Something's happened,' she said.

A routine medical examination with his doctor in Bern, said Gregorius. Yes, he might well come back. He was amazed at how calmly she took it; it almost offended him a little.

She started breathing more heavily than before. Then she pulled herself together, stood up and took out a notebook. She'd like to have his phone number in Bern, she said.

Gregorius raised his eyebrows in surprise. Then she pointed to the little table in the corner where there was a telephone.

'Since yesterday,' she said. And she wanted to show him something else. She led the way to the attic.

The mountains of books on the bare floorboards in Amadeu's room had disappeared. The books were now on a shelf in the corner. She watched him expectantly. He nodded, went to her and touched her arm.

Now she pulled out the drawer of Amadeu's desk, untied the ribbon holding the cardboard cover together and took out three sheets of paper.

'He wrote it afterwards, after the girl,' she said. Her gaunt breasts rose and fell. 'The writing is suddenly so small. When I saw it, I thought: he wanted to hide it from himself.'

She slid her eyes over the text. 'It destroys everything. *Everything.*'

She put the sheets in an envelope and handed it to Gregorius.

'He was no longer himself. I'd like . . . please take it. Far away. Very far away.'

Later Gregorius cursed himself. He asked to have a last look at the examining room where Prado had saved Mendes's life, where the map of the brain had hung and where he had buried Jorge's chess set.

'He really likes to work down here,' said Adriana, when they stood in the office. 'With me. Together with me.' She stroked the examination table. 'They all love him. Love and admire him.'

She smiled a ghostly light, distant smile.

'Many come, even when they don't need to. They make up something. Just to see him.'

Gregorius's thoughts raced. He went to the table with the antiquated syringes, and picked one up. Yes, this was the way syringes used to look, he said. How different they were today!

The words didn't reach Adriana; she was tugging at the paper cloth on the examination table. A remnant of the smile he had seen before still lay on her features.

Did she know what had become of the map of the brain? he asked. Today, it had to be a rarity.

'"Why do you need it?" I sometimes ask him. "Bodies are transparent to you." "It's just a map," he says then. He loves maps. Land maps. Railway maps. In Coimbra, when he was at college, he once criticized a standard work of anatomy. The professors didn't like him. He is impudent. Simply superior.'

Gregorius knew only one solution to her lapse into the present tense. He looked at the clock.

'I'm late,' he said. 'Can I use your phone?'

He opened the door and went out, into the vestibule of the house.

Her face was distraught as she locked the office. A vertical line divided her forehead and made her look like somebody ruled by darkness and confusion.

Gregorius went to the stairs.

'*Adeus*,' said Adriana and unlocked the front door.

It was the bitter, hostile voice he remembered from the first visit. She stood straight as a candle and faced the whole world brazenly.

Gregorius went to her slowly and stood still before her. He looked her in the eye. Her look was sealed and cold. He didn't hold out his hand. He knew she wouldn't take it.

'*Adieu*,' he said. 'All the best.' Then he was outside.

48

Gregorius gave Silveira the photocopy of Prado's book. He had wandered through the city for more than an hour until he found a shop that was still open where you could make copies.

'That's . . .' said Silveira in a hoarse voice. 'I . . .'

Then they talked about the dizziness. His sister, whose eyesight was failing, said Silveira, had suffered from dizziness for decades; they couldn't find the cause, she simply got used to it.

'I went to the neurologist with her once. And left his office with the feeling of being in the Stone Age. Our knowledge of the brain is still so primitive. A few areals, a few examples of neural activity, a few bits of brain tissue. We don't know more. I had the feeling they don't even know where they should *search*.'

They spoke of the fear that comes with uncertainty. Suddenly Gregorius felt that something was bothering him. It lasted until he realized what it was: the day before yesterday, on his return, the conversation with Silveira about the trip; today the conversation with João Eça; now Silveira again. Could two intimacies coexist? He was glad he hadn't told Eça anything about the fainting in the library at Coimbra so that he had something he shared only with Silveira.

So what was the Homeric word he had forgotten? Silveira asked now. λίοτςον, said Gregorius, an iron shovel to clean the floor of the hall.

Silveira laughed and Gregorius joined in. They laughed and laughed, they roared with laughter, two men, who, for a moment, were able to rise above all fear, all sadness, all disappointment and over all their weariness of life. Who were linked in laughter in a precious way, even if the fear, the sadness and the disappointment were all their own and created their own loneliness for them.

When his laughter subsided and he felt the weight of the world again, Gregorius thought of how he had laughed with João Eça about the overcooked lunch at the home.

Silveira went into his study and came back with the napkin from the dining car on which Gregorius had written the Hebrew words: *And God said, Let there be light: and there was light.* He asked Gregorius to read it to him once more, then he asked him to write something from the Bible in Greek.

Gregorius couldn't resist writing: *In the beginning was the Word, and the Word was with God, and the Word was God. The same was in the beginning with God. All things were made by him; and without him was not any thing made that was made. In him was life; and the life was the light of men.*

Silveira picked up his Bible and read these opening sentences of the Gospel of St John:

'So the word is the light of men,' he said. 'And so things exist properly only when they are grasped in words.'

'And the words have to have a rhythm,' said Gregorius. 'A rhythm such as the words have in St John, for example. Only then, only when they are poetry, do they really shed light on things. In the changing light of the words the same things can look quite different.'

Silveira looked at him.

'And therefore, when, faced with three hundred thousand books and one word is missing, it has to make you dizzy.'

They laughed and laughed some more. They looked at each other and knew that they were also laughing at the earlier laughter and because you laughed best about the most important things there were.

Would he leave him the photographs of Isfahan? Silveira

asked later. They hung them in his study. Silveira sat down behind his desk, lit a cigarette and looked at the pictures.

'I wish my ex-wife and my children could see that,' he said.

Before they went to bed, they stood silently in the hall for a while.

'That's also past now,' said Silveira. 'Your stay here, I mean. Here in my house.'

Gregorius couldn't fall asleep. He imagined how his train would start up the next morning, he felt the first, soft jolts. He cursed the dizziness and the fact that Doxiades was right.

He turned on a light and read what Prado had noted about intimacy:

INTIMIDADE IMPERIOSA. IMPERIOUS INTIMACY. *In intimacy, we are clasped into one another, and the invisible bonds are liberating shackles. This clasping is imperious: it demands exclusivity. To share is to betray. But we want to love and touch not only one single person. What to do? Control the various intimacies? Strict bookkeeping of subjects, words, gestures? Mutual knowledge and secrets? It would be a silent trickling poison.*

It was already growing light when he slipped into a restless sleep and dreamed of the end of the world. It was a melodious dream without musical instruments or notes, a dream of sun, wind and words. The fishermen with their rough hands shouted coarse things to one another; the salty wind blew away the words, and the word that had escaped him, too. Now he was in the water and he swam deeper with all his might and felt the desire and warmth in his muscles when they braced against the cold. He had to leave the banana boat because he was in a hurry; he assured the fishermen it had nothing to do with them, but they defended themselves and regarded him as a stranger when he went ashore with his sailor's kitbag, accompanied by sun, wind, and words.

PART IV
THE RETURN

49

Silveira had long ago disappeared from sight, but Gregorius still kept waving. 'Is there a company that produces porcelain in Bern?' he had asked on the platform. Gregorius had taken a picture from the compartment window: Silveira, shielding his cigarette against the wind so he could light it.

The last houses of Lisbon. Yesterday in the Bairro Alto, he had gone once more to the religious bookshop where he had leaned his forehead on the foggy damp windowpane before ringing the doorbell of the blue house for the first time. Back then, he had had to struggle against the temptation to go to the airport and take the next plane to Zurich. Now he had to resist the temptation to get out at the next station.

If a memory was extinguished with every metre travelled, and if, in addition, the world reverted to what it had been, so that, when he arrived in Bern, everything would be as before: would the time of his stay also be destroyed?

Gregorius took out the envelope Adriana had given him. *It destroys everything. Everything.* What he was about to read, Prado had written after the trip to Spain. *After the girl.* He thought of what she had said about his return from Spain: he had got out of the taxi unshaven and hollow-cheeked, had gulped down everything as if he hadn't eaten for a week, taken a sleeping pill and slept for a day and a night.

As the train arrived in Vilar, where it would cross the border, Gregorius translated the text Prado had written in tiny letters.

ZINZAS DA FUTILIDADE. ASHES OF FUTILITY. *It has been an eternity since Jorge called me in the middle of the night because he was assailed by the fear of death. No, not an eternity. It was in a* different time, *a* completely *different time. And it was hardly three years, three perfectly normal, boring calendar years. Estefânia. He spoke then of Estefânia. The Goldberg Variations. She had played them for him, and he wanted to play them himself on his Steinway.* Estefânia Espinhosa. *What an enchanting, bewitching name! I thought that night. I wanted never to see the woman; no woman could live up to this name, it had to be a disappointment. How could I know that it was the other way around: the name couldn't live up to* her.

The fear that life remained incomplete, a torso; the awareness of no longer being able to become the one we aimed to be. That's how we had finally interpreted the fear of death. But how, I asked, can the missing wholeness and coherence of life be feared when it's not experienced at all as soon as it has become an irrevocable fact? Jorge seemed to understand it. What did he say?

Why don't I leaf through, why don't I watch? Why don't I want to know what I thought and wrote back then? Whence this indifference? Is it indifference? Or is the loss greater, deeper?

To want to know how one thought before and how it became what one thinks now: that too, if it existed, was also part of the wholeness of a life. So had I lost what makes death fearsome? The belief in a coherence of life worth struggling for and which we try to wrest from death?

Loyalty, I tell Jorge, loyalty. That's how we invent our coherence. Estefânia. Why couldn't the surf of accident wash her up someplace else? Why to us of all places? Why did she have to put us to a test we weren't up to? Which neither *of us passed, each in his own way?*

'You're too hungry for me. It's wonderful with you. But you're too hungry for me. I can't want this trip. You see, it would be

your *trip, yours alone. It couldn't be* ours.' And she was right: you mustn't make others into the building blocks of your own life, into water bearers in the race for your own bliss.

Finis terrae. *Never have I been so awake as there. And so sober. Since then, I know: my race is at an end. A race I didn't know I was running, always. A race without rivals, without purpose, without reward. Wholeness? Espejismo, say the Spaniards, I read the word in the newspapers on those days, it's the only one I still know. Mirage. Fata morgana.*

Our life, those are fleeting formations of quicksand, formed by one gust of wind, destroyed by the next. Images of futility that blow away even before they have properly formed.

He was no longer himself, Adriana had said. And she wanted nothing to do with her strange, estranged brother. *Far away. Very far away.*

When was anybody himself? When he was unchanged? As he saw himself? Or as he was when the passion of thoughts and feelings buried all lies, masks, and self-deceptions? Usually it was others who complained that somebody was no longer himself. Perhaps this is what it really meant: he's no longer as we would like him to be? So was the whole thing ultimately no more than a kind of rallying cry against a menacing disruption of the usual, masquerading as concern and worry about the alleged welfare of the other?

On the way to Salamanca, Gregorius fell asleep. And then something happened that he hadn't ever experienced: he woke feeling dizzy. Nervous irritation flooded through him, threatening to draw him into the depths, so that he clutched the armrest of the seat. Shutting his eyes made it worse. Then he buried his face in his hands and it was over.

λίοτςον. Everything's fine.

Why hadn't he flown? Tomorrow morning, in eighteen hours, he would in Geneva, and three hours later at home. At noon he would be with Doxiades, who would arrange all the rest.

The train slowed down. SALAMANCA. Then a second sign: SALAMANCA. Estefânia Espinhosa.

Gregorius stood up, heaved the suitcase down from the rack, and held on to it until the dizziness had passed. On the platform, he walked firmly as if to crush the cushion of air surrounding him.

50

Later, when he thought back on his first evening in Salamanca, he seemed to have struggled for hours against the dizziness, reeling through cathedrals, chapels and cloisters, blind to their beauty, but overwhelmed by their dark force. He looked at altars, domes, and choir stalls that immediately overlapped in his memory, wound up twice at mass and finally came to rest in an organ concert. *I would not like to live in a world without cathedrals. I need their beauty and grandeur. I need them against the vulgarity of the world. I want to let myself be wrapped in the austere coolness of the church. I need their imperious silence. I need it against the witless bellowing of the barracks yard and the witty chatter of the yes-men. I want to hear the rustling of the organ, this deluge of ethereal notes. I need it against the shrill farce of marches.*

That had been written by the seventeen-year-old Prado. A boy who glowed. A boy who went soon after with Jorge to Coimbra, where the whole world seemed to belong to them and where he reprimanded the professors in the lecture hall. A boy who had not yet experienced the tide of accident, of blowing quicksand and the ashes of futility.

Years later, he had written these lines to Father Bartolomeu: *There are things that are too big for us humans: pain, loneliness and death, but also beauty, sublimity and happiness. For them we created religion. What happens when we lose it? Those things are still too big for us. What is left for us is the poetry of the individual life. Is it strong enough to bear us?*

From his hotel room, Gregorius could see the old and the new cathedrals. When the hour struck, he went to the window and looked out at the floodlit facades. San Juan de la Cruz had lived here. Florence had travelled here several times when she was writing about him. He had never felt like making the trip so she had gone with other students. He hadn't liked the way she and the others had gushed over the mystical verse of the great poet.

Over poetry, you didn't *gush*. You *read* it. You read it with the tongue. You lived it. You felt how it moved you, changed you. How it contributed to shaping your own life, giving it colour and melody. You didn't talk about it and you certainly didn't make it the cannon fodder of an academic career.

In Coimbra, he had asked himself if he hadn't missed a possible life in the university. The answer was no. He felt once again how he had when he had sat in La Coupole in Paris and had put down Florence's chattering colleagues with his Bernese tongue and knowledge. *No.*

Later he dreamed that Aurora was whirling him around to organ music in Silveira's kitchen. The kitchen expanded and he swam down only to be caught in a vortex where he lost consciousness. Then he woke up.

He was the first at breakfast. Afterwards he went to the university and asked for the history department. Estefânia Espinhosa's lecture was in an hour's time: Isabel la Católica.

In the inner courtyard of the university, students huddled under the cloisters. Gregorius didn't understand a word of their rapid Spanish and went to the lecture hall early. It was a panelled room of bare, monastic elegance, with a raised lectern at the front. The room filled up. It was a big room, but soon every seat was taken and students sat on the floor of the aisles.

I hated this person, the long black hair, the swaying walk, the short skirt. Adriana had seen her as a girl in her mid-twenties. The woman who came in now was in her late fifties. *He*

pictured her shining eyes, the unusual, almost Asian features the
contagious, thrilling laugh, the swaying walk, and he simply didn't
want all that to be snuffed out. He could not want it, João Eça.
had said of Prado.

Nobody could want that, thought Gregorius. Not even
today. And especially not when he heard her speak. She had
a dark, smoky alto voice and spoke the harsh Spanish words
with a remnant of Portuguese softness. Right at the beginning,
she had turned off the microphone. It was a voice that would
fill a cathedral. And her manner made you hope the lecture
might never end.

Gregorius understood hardly anything of what she said. He
listened to her as to a musical instrument, sometimes with his
eyes shut, sometimes concentrating on her gestures: her hand
stroking the grey-streaked hair off her forehead, the other hand
holding the silver pen and drawing a line in the air to emphasize
things, the elbows leaning on the lectern, her two arms
outstretched as if to embrace the lectern when she introduced
something new. A girl who had once worked in the post office;
a girl with a phenomenal memory retaining all the secrets of
the Resistance; the woman who objected when O'Kelly held
her around the waist in the street; the woman behind the
steering wheel of the car outside the blue house who had
travelled for her life to the end of the world; the woman who
hadn't let Prado take her on his trip, a disappointment and a
setback that had provoked in him the most painful awareness
of his life, the consciousness that the race for his bliss had
finally been lost, the feeling that his life, begun so glowingly,
had been extinguished and fallen into ashes.

The shoving of the students as they stood up to leave
startled Gregorius. Estefânia Espinhosa packed her papers in
her briefcase and came down the steps from the podium. A
number of students approached her. Gregorius went outside
and waited.

He had placed himself where he could see her from afar. Should he address her? She approached accompanied by a woman, possibly an assistant. Gregorius's heart pounded as she passed him. He followed the two upstairs and along a corridor. The assistant went off and Estefânia Espinhosa disappeared through a door. As Gregorius passed the door he saw her name. *The name couldn't live up to* her.

Slowly he returned, gripping the banister. At the foot of the stairs he paused for a moment. Then he ran back upstairs. He waited to catch his breath, then he knocked on the door.

She had her coat on and was about to leave. She looked at him questioningly.

'I . . . can I speak French with you?' asked Gregorius.

She nodded.

He introduced himself falteringly and then, as so often of late, he took out Prado's book.

Her light brown eyes narrowed. She stared at the book without reaching for it. The seconds passed.

'I . . . why . . . Come in.'

She went to the phone and told someone in Portuguese that she couldn't come now. Then she took off her coat. She asked Gregorius to sit down and lit a cigarette.

'Is there anything about me in there?' she asked, exhaling smoke.

Gregorius shook his head.

'How do you know about me?'

Gregorius explained. He told her about Adriana and João Eça; of the book about the dark sea that Prado had read at the end. About the second-hand bookseller's investigations. About the blurb on her books. O'Kelly he didn't mention. Nor did he say anything about the handwritten note with the small letters.

Now she wanted to see the book. She read, lighting another cigarette. Then she looked at the portrait.

'That's how he looked earlier. I've never seen a picture from this period.'

He hadn't planned to break his journey here, Gregorius said. But then he couldn't resist it. The picture of Prado, it was so . . . so incomplete without meeting her. But naturally he knew that it was unreasonable to simply burst in here.

She went to the window. The phone rang. She let it ring.

'I don't know if I want to,' she said. 'To talk about those days, I mean. At any rate not here. Can I take the book home with me? I'd like to read it and think about it. Come to my house this evening. Then I'll tell you how I feel about it.'

She gave him her card.

Gregorius bought a guidebook and spent the afternoon visiting monasteries, one after another. He wasn't one for sightseeing. If people gathered around something, he tended to keep his distance; that equated with his habit of reading bestsellers only years later. So, it wasn't the tourist instinct that drove him now. It wasn't until late afternoon that he began to understand: the preoccupation with Prado had changed his feelings about churches and monasteries. *Can there be anything more serious than poetic seriousness?* he had objected to Ruth Gautschi and David Lehmann. That linked him with Prado. Maybe was this the strongest link. But the man who had changed from a glowing altar boy to a godless priest had gone a step further, a step that Gregorius tried to understand as he walked through the cloisters. Had he managed to extend the poetic depth of the biblical words to the buildings that these words had created? Was *that* it?

A few days before his death, Mélodie had seen him coming out of a church. *I want to read the mighty words of the Bible. I need the unreal force of their poetry. I love praying people. I need the sight of them. I need them against the malicious poison of the superficial and the thoughtless.* Those had been the feelings of his youth. With what feelings had the man entered the church, the man who was waiting for the time bomb in his brain to explode? The man for whom, having journeyed to the end of the world, everything had become ashes?

While the taxi that took Gregorius to Estefânia Espinhosa's address waited at the traffic lights he saw a poster with domes and minarets in the window of a travel agent's. How would it have been if, in the blue Orient with its golden domes, he had heard the Muezzin every morning? If Persian poetry had been the soundtrack of his life?

Estefânia Espinhosa wore blue jeans and a dark blue sailor's sweater. Despite the strands of grey, she looked as if she were in her mid-forties. She had made sandwiches and poured Gregorius a cup of tea. She needed time, she said.

Seeing Gregorius's eyes slide over the bookshelves, she said he could take a closer look. He picked up the thick history books. How little he knew of the Iberian Peninsula and its history, he said. Then he told her of the books about the earthquake of Lisbon and the Black Death.

She made him tell her about the philology of ancient languages and kept asking questions. She wanted to know, he thought, what kind of person she would be telling about the trip with Prado. Or was she just playing for time?

Latin, she said at last. In a certain sense, Latin had been the beginning. 'There was this boy, this student, who helped out in the post office. A timid boy who was in love with me and thought I didn't notice it. He was studying Latin. *Finis terrae*, he said one day, when he picked up a letter to Finisterre. And then he recited a long Latin poem that also talked about the end of the world. I liked the way he recited Latin poetry while still sorting letters. He sensed that I liked it and kept on doing it all morning.

'I started learning Latin secretly. I didn't want him to know or he would have misunderstood. It was so improbable that somebody like me, a girl from the post office with a rotten education, would learn Latin. *So improbable!* I don't know what appealed to me more: the language or this improbability.

'I made rapid progress, I have a good memory. I began getting interested in Roman history. Read everything I could lay my hands on, and later, books about Portuguese, Spanish, Italian history. My mother had died when I was a child. I lived with my father who was on the railways. He had never read books. At first he was upset that I did. Later he was proud, a touching pride. I was twenty-three when the PIDE arrested him and sent him to Tarrafal for sabotage. But I can't talk about that, not even today.

'I met Jorge O'Kelly a few months later at a Resistance meeting. Papá's arrest had been spoken about in the post office, and to my amazement, it turned out that a lot of my colleagues belonged to the Resistance. As for political things, I woke up to them with a jolt because of Papá's arrest. Jorge was an important man in the group. He and João Eça. He fell head over heels in love with me. It flattered me. He tried to make me a star. I had this idea of starting a school for illiterates where everybody could meet unsuspected.

'And there it happened. One evening Amadeu entered the room. After that everything was different. A new light fell on everything. It was the same for him, I felt that from the start.

'I wanted it so much. I couldn't sleep any more. I went to his office, kept going, despite his sister's hateful looks. He wanted to take me in his arms. Inside him was an avalanche that could let go at any moment. But he rejected me. Jorge, he kept saying. What about Jorge? I began to hate Jorge.

'Once I rang Amadeu's doorbell at midnight. We walked a few streets, then he pulled me under an archway. The avalanche broke. 'That mustn't happen again,' he said afterwards and forbade me to come back.

'It was a long, tormenting winter. Amadeu didn't come to meetings any more. Jorge was sick with jealousy.

'It would be an exaggeration to say that I saw it coming. Yes, that would be an exaggeration. I was, however, aware that they were relying more and more on my memory. "What if something happens to me?" I said.'

Estefânia went out of the room. When she came back, she looked different. As if to pull herself together, she had washed her face and her hair was now tied in a ponytail. She stood at the window and smoked a whole cigarette with hasty drags. Then she went on.

'It all went wrong at the end of February. The door opened much too slowly. Silently. He was wearing boots. No uniform, but boots. His boots, that was the first thing I saw when the door opened. Then the intelligent, cunning face. We knew it was Badajoz, one of Mendes's people. As so often before, we started talking about the ç. Later, for a long time, I couldn't see a *ç* without being forced to think of Badajoz. The bench creaked when he sat down. João Eça slipped me a warning look. *Now everything depends on you*, the look seemed to say.

'As always, I was wearing my see-through blouse, my working clothes, so to speak. Jorge hated it. Now I took off the jacket. I hoped Badajoz would save us. But Badajoz just crossed his legs. It was disgusting. I brought the lesson to an end.

'When Badajoz approached Adrião, my piano teacher, I knew it was over. I didn't hear what they said, but Adrião turned pale and Badajoz grinned deviously.

'Adrião didn't come back from the interrogation. I don't know what they did to him, I never saw him again.

'João insisted that I live with his aunt from then on. Safety, he said, it was about keeping me safe. By the first night, I realized that was so, but it wasn't only me, it was mainly my memory. What it might reveal if they caught me. I met Jorge only once in those days. We didn't touch, not even our hands. It was eerie. I didn't understand why. I didn't understand until Amadeu told me why I had to leave the country.'

Estefânia came back from the window and sat down. She looked at Gregorius.

'What Amadeu said about Jorge – it was so monstrous, so inconceivably cruel that at first I simply laughed. Amadeu made up a bed for me in the consulting room before we left the next day.

'"I simply don't believe it," I said. "Kill me." I looked at him. "We're talking about Jorge, your friend."

'"Exactly," he said flatly.

'What *precisely* did he say? I wanted to know, but he didn't want to repeat the words.

'Afterwards, as I lay alone in the office, I went over everything I had experienced with Jorge. Was he *capable* of thinking such a thing? *Seriously* thinking it? I was tired and confused. I thought of his jealousy. I thought of the times when he had seemed brutal and inconsiderate, even if not to me. I didn't know what to make of him any more.

'At Amadeu's funeral, we stood together at the grave, he and I. The others had left.

'"You didn't really *believe* it, did you?" he asked after a while. "He *misunderstood* me. It was a misunderstanding, just a misunderstanding."

'"It's not important now," I said.

'We parted without touching. I've not heard anything more of him. Is he still alive?'

After Gregorius's answer, there was silence for a while. Then she stood up and took from the shelf her copy of *O Mar Tenebroso*, the big book that had lain on Prado's desk.

'And at the end he was reading that?' she asked.

She sat down, with the book on her lap.

'It was simply too much, much too much for a twenty-five-year-old girl like me. Badajoz, being spirited off to João's aunt, the night spent in Amadeu's office, the dreadful thoughts of Jorge, the journey with the man who had robbed me of my sleep. I was a complete mess.

'The first hours, we drove without saying anything. I was glad I could still handle the steering wheel and gears. We were to go north, to Galicia, over the border, João had said.

'"And then we'll drive to Finisterre," I said and told him the story of the Latin student in the post office.

'He asked me to stop and he embraced me. After that, he kept questioning me. Was he searching for me, or was he searching for *life?* He wanted more of it, and he always wanted it faster and greedier. Not that he was coarse or violent. On the contrary, I hadn't known such tenderness. But he almost swamped me with it; he had such a ravenous hunger for life, its warmth, its lust. And he was just as hungry for my mind as for my body. He wanted, in a few hours, to know my whole life, my memories, thoughts, fantasies, dreams. *Everything.* After the first joyous amazement, he began to scare me. His quick mind tore down all my defences.

'In the years after that, I fled as soon as anyone began to understand me. But not now. One thing, however, has remained: I don't want anybody to understand me *completely.* I want to go through life incognito. The blindness of others is my safety and my freedom.

'Even though now it sounds as if Amadeu was passionately interested in *me,* it wasn't so. It was just an *encounter.* He drew in everything that he experienced, he couldn't get enough of life. To put it another way, I wasn't really *somebody* for him, but rather some *aspect* of life he craved as if he had previously been cheated of it. It was as if he wanted to live a full life before death claimed him.'

Gregorius told her of the aneurysm and the map of the brain.

'My God,' she said softly.

They had sat on the beach in Finisterre. Beyond, a ship had passed.

"'Let's sail away," he said, "perhaps to Brazil. Belém, Manaús. The Amazon. Where it's hot and damp. I'd like to write about it, about colours, smells, sticky plants, the rain forest, animals. I've only ever written about the soul.'"

This man who could never get enough of reality, Adriana had said of him.

'It wasn't adolescent romanticism, or the dreams of an ageing man. It was *genuine*, it was *real*. But on the other hand, it had nothing to do with *me*. He wanted to take me on a trip that would have been *his* alone, his voyage to the inner depths of his soul.

"'You're too demanding for me," I said. "I can't do it, I *can't*."

'Back then, when he had pulled me into the doorway, I would have followed him to the end of the world. But then I didn't know of his instatiable hunger. This hunger for life was also horrible. A devouring, destructive force. Terrifying. Dreadful.

'My words must have wounded him dreadfully. Quite dreadfully. He no longer wanted to take a double room, paid for two singles. Later, when we met, he had changed his clothes. He looked composed and stood there stiffly, very correct. My words had lost him his dignity. The stiffness, the correctness were a hapless attempt to show that he had won it back. I didn't see it like that at all. There was nothing undignified in his passion, or in his lust. Lust in and of itself isn't undignified.

'I didn't close my eyes, even though I was tired out.

'He would stay a few days, he said abruptly the next morning. Nothing could have expressed his complete withdrawal better than this abruptness.

'In parting, we simply shook hands. He went back to the

hotel, without even turning round. Before driving off, I waited in vain for a sign from the window.

'After an unbearable half-hour behind the wheel, I drove back to the hotel. I knocked. He stood calmly in the doorway, without hostility, almost without emotion. He had shut me out of his soul for ever. I have no idea when he returned to Lisbon.'

'A week later,' said Gregorius.

Estefânia gave him back the book.

'I read it all afternoon. First I was horrified. Not about him. About me. That I had no idea who he was. How aware he was of himself. And how sincere. Mercilessly sincere. Hence his verbal force. I was upset to have said to such a man: "You're too demanding for me." But then I slowly realized: it was right to say that. It would have been right even if I had seen his writings.'

It was close to midnight. Gregorius didn't want to leave Bern, the railway, the dizziness – everything was far away. He asked how a girl from the post office who learned Latin had become a professor. Her reply was curt, almost cold. That could happen: that someone receptive to the distant past would be reticent about what came later and about the present. There was a time for intimacy.

They stood in the doorway. Then he made up his mind. He proffered the envelope with Prado's last note.

'I think these most likely belong to you,' he said.

51

Gregorius stood by the window of an estate agent. In three hours' time, his train would leave for Irún and Paris. His bag was at the station in a locker. He stood motionless on the pavement, studying the prices and thinking of his savings. To learn Spanish, the language he had previously left to Florence. To live in the city of her holy hero. Attend Estefânia Espinhosa's lectures. Study the history of the many monasteries. Translate Prado's notes. Discuss his writings with Estefânia, one by one.

The agent set up three inspections within the next two hours. Gregorius stood in empty, echoing apartments taking in the view, the traffic noise, imagining the daily walk downstairs. He made offers on two apartments. Then he rode back and forth through the city in a taxi. *'Continue!'* he kept saying to the driver. *'Siempre derecho, más y más!'*

Back at the railway station, he made a mistake about his locker number and had to run to catch the train.

In the compartment, he nodded off and woke up only when the train stopped in Valladolid. A young woman came into the compartment. Gregorius heaved her suitcase on to the luggage rack. *'Muito obrigada,'* she said, sat down next to the door and began reading a French book. There was a light, rustling sound when she crossed her legs.

Gregorius looked at the sealed envelope Maria João hadn't wanted to open. *To be read only after my death*, Prado had said.

And I don't want it to fall into Adriana's hands. Gregorius broke the seal, took out the sheets, and began to read.

PORQUÊ TU, ENTRE TODAS? WHY YOU, OF ALL WOMEN? *A question that forms sometimes in everyone. Why does it seem dangerous to allow it, even if it happens only in silence? What is so frightening about the idea of contingency that is expressed in it and is not the same idea as those of randomness and interchangeability? Why can one not acknowledge this contingency and joke about it? Why do we think it would trivialize, really cancel affection, if we acknowledge it as something obvious?*

I saw you pass through the living room, past heads and champagne glasses. 'That is Fátima, my daughter,' said your father. 'I could imagine you passing through my rooms,' I said to you in the garden. 'Can you still imagine me in passing through your rooms?' you asked in England. And on the ship: 'Do you also think in passing we were destined for each other?'

No one is destined for another. Not only because there is no Providence and no one else who could arrange it. No: because there is simply no inevitability between people beyond accidental needs and the powerful force of habit. I had spent five years in a clinic, five years, when no one had passed through my rooms. I stood here absolutely by chance, you stood there absolutely by chance, between us the champagne glasses. That's how it was. No different.

It is good that you won't read that. Why did you think you had to ally with Mamã against my Godlessness? An advocate of contingency loves no less. Nor is he less loyal. Rather more.

The reading woman had taken off her glasses and was cleaning them. Her face didn't look like the face of the Portuguese woman on the Kirchenfeldbrücke. But they did have one thing in common: the unequal distance between the eyebrows and the bridge of the nose, with one eyebrow stopping before the other.

Gregorius said he would like to ask her something. Whether the Portuguese word *glória*, apart from fame, could also mean *bliss* in the religious sense.

She thought, then she nodded.

And whether a non-believer could make use of it when he wanted to refer to a bliss that was other than religious.

She laughed. '*Que c'est drôle! Mais . . . oui. Oui.*'

The train left Burgos. Gregorius read on.

UM MOZART DO FUTURO ABERTO. A MOZART OF THE OPEN FUTURE. *You came down the steps. Like thousands of times before, I watched as more and more of you became visible, while the head remained hidden to the last behind the banister opposite. I had always completed what was still concealed in thoughts. And always the same.* It was certain, *who was coming down.*

On this morning, it was different all of a sudden. Children playing had thrown the ball against the colored window the day before and smashed the pane. The light on the stairs was different than usual – instead of the gold, veiled light, reminiscent of the illumination in a church, unbroken daylight flowed in. It was as if this new light made a breach in my usual expectations, as if something ripped open that demanded new thoughts from me. I was suddenly curious *about how your face would look. The sudden curiosity made me happy and yet also made me flinch. It was years since the time of wooing curiosity had come to an end and the door had shut on our shared life. Why, Fátima, did a window have to shatter for me to be able to meet you again with an open look.*

I also tried it with you, Adriana. But our familiarity had become leaden.

Just why is the open look so hard? We are sluggish creatures who need familiarity. Curiosity as a rare luxury on home ground. To be certain and be able to play with the openness, in every moment, it would be an art. You had to be a Mozart. A Mozart of the open future.

San Sebastián. Gregorius looked at the timetable. Soon he would have to change trains in Irún for Paris. The woman crossed her legs and went on reading. He picked up the last note from the sealed envelope.

MINHA QUERIDA ARTISTA NA AUTO-ILUSÃO. MY BELOVED VIRTUOSO OF SELF-DELUSION. *We are in the dark about so many of our wishes and thoughts, and others sometimes know more about them than we do. Who ever believed anything* different?

No one. No one who lives and breathes with another. We know each other down to the smallest twitches of body and words. We know and often don't want to know what we know. Especially when the gap between what we see and what the other believes becomes unbearably wide. It takes divine courage and divine strength to live with oneself in perfect truth. So much we know, even of ourselves. No reason for self-justification.

And if she is a true virtuoso of self-deception, always a step ahead of me? Would I have had to confront you and say: No, you're fooling yourself, you're not like that? I owed you that. If I owed you.

How does one know what he owes the other in this sense?

Irún. *Isto ainda não é Irún.* This is not yet Irún. These were the first Portuguese words he had said to anyone. Five weeks before, and also on a train. Gregorius lifted down the woman's suitcase.

Shortly after he had taken a seat in the Paris train, the woman passed by his compartment. She had almost disappeared, then she paused, saw him, hesitated a moment and came in. He put her suitcase up on the rack.

She had taken the slow train, she explained, because she wanted to read this book. *Le Silence du Monde avant les mots.* Nowhere else did she read as well as she did on a train. Nowhere else was her mind so receptive. This made her quite an expert on slow trains. She was also travelling to Switzerland, to Lausanne. Yes, they would arrive in Geneva tomorrow morning. Obviously they had both chosen the slow train for the same reason.

Gregorius pulled his coat over his face. His reason had been different. He didn't want to reach Bern. He didn't want Doxiades to pick up the phone and reserve a bed in the clinic. There were twenty-four stops before Geneva. Twenty-four opportunities to get off the train.

He sank ever deeper. The fishermen laughed as he danced with Estefânia Espinhosa through Silveira's kitchen. All these monasteries that led to all these empty apartments. Their echoing emptiness had extinguished the Homeric word.

He woke with a start. λίστσον. He went to the toilet and washed his face.

While he slept, the woman had turned off the ceiling light and turned on her reading lamp. She read and read. When Gregorius came back from the toilet, she glanced up and smiled remotely.

Gregorius pulled his coat over his face again and imagined the reading woman. *I stand here completely by chance, you stand there completely by chance, between us the champagne glasses. That's how it was. No different.*

They could share a taxi to the Gare de Lyon, said the woman, as they pulled into Paris shortly after midnight. La Coupole. Gregorius breathed the perfume of the woman beside him. He didn't want to go to the clinic. He didn't want to smell clinical air. The air he had fought his way through when he had visited his dying parents in the overheated ward where the air always smelt of urine.

At close to four in the morning, when he woke up beneath his coat, the woman had fallen asleep with the open book in her lap. He turned off the reading lamp over her head. She turned to the side and pulled her coat over her face.

Dawn broke. Gregorius didn't want it to grow light.

The dining-car waiter passed by with the drinks trolley. The woman woke up. Gregorius handed her a cup of coffee. Silently they watched the sun rise behind a fine veil of clouds. It was strange, said the woman suddenly, that *glória* could stand for two completely different things: external, noisy glory and internal, silent bliss. And after a pause: 'Bliss – what are we really talking about?'

Gregorius carried her heavy suitcase through Geneva station. People in the Swiss train were talking loudly and laughing. Seeing his anger, the woman pointed to the title of her book and laughed. Then he laughed too. In the middle of his laughter, the loudspeaker announced Lausanne. The woman stood up, he took down her suitcase. She looked at him. '*C'était bien, ça,*' she said. Then she left the train.

Fribourg. Gregorius slept. He dreamt he was climbing up the mountain and looking down on Lisbon at night. He was on the ferry crossing the Tagus. He was sitting with Maria João in the kitchen. He was visiting the monasteries of Salamanca and listening to Estefânia Espinhosa's lecture.

Bern. Gregorius got out. He put down the suitcase and waited. When he picked it up and went on, it was as if he were wading through lead.

52

After leaving his luggage in the cold flat, Gregorius went out to the photo shop. Then he sat in the living room. In two hours, he could pick up the developed pictures. What should he do until then?

The telephone receiver was still turned around on the cradle and reminded him of the night-time conversation with Doxiades five weeks ago. Back then it had snowed; now people were walking around without coats. But the light was still pale, so unlike the light on the Tagus.

The language-course record was still on the turntable. Gregorius switched it on. He compared the voices with the voices on the old trams of Lisbon. He imagined travelling from Belém to the Alfama quarter and taking the Metro on to the Liceu.

The doorbell rang. The doormat, Frau Loosli, always knew from the position of the doormat when he was at home, she said. She gave him a letter from the school office that had come the day before. The other mail had been forwarded to Silveira's address. He looked pale, she said. Was everything all right?

Gregorius read the communication from the school and forgot the details even as he read them. He arrived early at the photo shop and had to wait. He almost ran the short distance home.

A whole roll of film for the lighted glass door of O'Kelly's pharmacy. He had almost always been too late. The smoking pharmacist was visible in only three of them. The tangled hair.

The big, fleshy nose. The eternally slipped tie. *I began to hate Jorge.* Ever since he had known the story of Estefânia Espinhosa, thought Gregorius, O'Kelly's look seemed devious to him. Mean. As in the chess club when he sat at the next table and Gregorius saw how annoyed he was by the repulsive sound of Pedro's constant sniffing.

Gregorius looked closely at the photos. Where was the kind, weary look he had also seen on the peasant face? The look of grief for his lost friend? *We were like brothers. More than brothers. I really thought we could never lose each other.* Gregorius no longer found that earlier look. *It's simply not possible, unlimited openness. It's beyond us. Loneliness through having to suppress, there's that too.* Now they were back, the other looks.

Is the soul a place of facts? Or are the alleged facts only the deceptive shadows of our stories? Prado had asked himself. That's also true of looks, thought Gregorius. Looks are only meaningful when they are interpreted. Only then do they *exist*.

João Eça in the twilight on the balcony of the home in Cacilhas. *I don't want all these tubes and pumps. I just want to live a few weeks longer.* Gregorius felt the scalding tea he had drunk from Eça's cup.

The pictures of Mélodie's house had not come out because it was too dark when they were taken.

Silveira, on the platform, trying to light his cigarette in the wind. Today he would be returning to Biarritz and would ask himself as he did so often, 'Why do I go on?'

Gregorius went through the pictures once more. And then again. The past began to freeze beneath his look. Memory would select, arrange, retouch, lie. The pernicious thing was that the omissions, distortions and lies were later no longer recognized. There was no point of view beyond memory.

A normal Wednesday afternoon in the city where he had spent his life. What should he do with it?

The words of the Muslim geographer, El Edrisi, about the

end of the world. Gregorius took out the pages on which he had translated his words into Latin, Greek and Hebrew in Finisterre.

Suddenly he knew what he wanted to do. He wanted to photograph Bern. To record where he had lived all these years. The buildings, streets, squares that had been much more than just the stage set of his life.

In the photo shop, he bought more film and in the time that remained until twilight he walked through the streets of the Länggasse, where he had spent his childhood. Considering them from various angles and with a photographer's eye, they were quite different, these streets. He photographed until sleep overtook him. Sometimes he woke up and didn't know where he was. Then, when he sat on the edge of the bed, he was no longer sure whether the detached, calculating eye of the photographer was the right one to capture the world of a life.

He continued on Thursday. He went down to the Old City where he took the lift from Universitätstrasse and cut through the railway station. That way, he could avoid Bubenbergplatz. He shot one roll of film after another. He saw the cathedral as he had never seen it. An organist was practising. For the first time since his arrival, the dizziness returned, and Gregorius held on to a pew.

He took the most recent film to be developed. Going on to Bubenbergplatz, it was as if he was attempting something beyond his strength. At the memorial he rested for a while. The sun had disappeared, a leaden grey sky arched over the city. He had expected to find out whether he could touch the square again. He didn't think so. It wasn't the same as before. Nor was it as it had been on his short visit three weeks ago. Why was that? He was tired and turned to go.

'How did you like the goldsmith's book?'

It was the bookseller from the Spanish bookshop. He held out his hand to Gregorius.

'Did it live up to expectations?'

Yes, said Gregorius, absolutely.

He said it stiffly. The bookseller noted that he wasn't in the mood to talk and quickly took his leave.

At the Bubenberg Cinema, the programme had changed. The Simenon film starring Jeanne Moreau was no longer showing.

As Gregorius waited impatiently for his film standing in the doorway of a shop, Kägi, the Rector, turned the corner. *There are moments when my wife looks as if she's going to pieces*, he had written. Now he had heard she was in the psychiatric clinic. Kägi looked tired and seemed hardly to notice what was going on around him. For a moment, Gregorius felt the impulse to talk but the feeling soon passed.

When he had collected the latest batch of photos, he sat down in the restaurant of the Hotel Bellevue and opened the folders. The pictures were strange and meant nothing to him. He ate his meal wondering what he had hoped to find out from them.

On the stairs up to his flat, a violent dizziness grabbed him and he had to hold on to the banister with both hands. After that, he sat by the phone all evening and imagined what would inevitably happen when he called Doxiades.

Shortly before falling asleep, he was always afraid of sinking into dizziness and unconsciousness and waking up without a memory. As it slowly became light over the city, he summoned his courage. When Doxiades's receptionist appeared, he was already at his office.

A few minutes later, the Greek arrived. Gregorius waited for him to complain about the new glasses. But Doxiades only frowned when he saw them, led the way into the examination room and then listened to everything about them and the dizziness.

He saw no reason for panic, he said at last. But a series of tests was necessary, and Gregorius would have to remain in the clinic under observation. He picked up the phone, let his hand rest on it, and looked at Gregorius.

Gregorius inhaled and exhaled a few times, then he nodded.

They could admit him on Sunday evening, said the Greek after he had hung up. There was nobody better than this doctor for miles around, he added.

Gregorius walked slowly through the city, past the many buildings and squares that had been important to him. That seemed the right way to do it. He ate where he had usually eaten, and in the early afternoon he went to the cinema where, as a student, he had seen his first film. The film bored him, but the cinema still smelt the same and he stayed to the end.

On the way home, he ran into Natalie Rubin.

'New glasses!' she greeted him.

Both of them felt a little awkward. Their phone conversations were now something of the past, like the echo of a dream.

Yes, he said, he might well go back to Lisbon. The medical examination? No, no, only a minor problem with his eyes.

Her Persian had ground to a halt, said Natalie. He nodded.

Had they got used to the new teacher? he asked finally.

She laughed. 'A boring man by the grace of God!'

Both of them turned after a few steps and waved.

On Saturday, Gregorius spent several hours gathering up his Latin, Greek and Hebrew books. He looked at the many marginal notes and the changes his handwriting had undergone over the decades. In the end, a small pile of books lay on the table, which he packed in the holdall he was taking to the clinic. Then he called Florence and asked if he might visit her.

When they met, she told him that she had had a stillborn child, and had been operated on for cancer a few years earlier. The disease hadn't returned. She was working as a translator. She was far less tired and dowdy than he had recently thought when he had watched her come home.

He told her about the monasteries in Salamanca.

'Back then, you didn't want to,' she said.

He nodded. They laughed. He didn't tell her anything about the clinic, which he regretted when he went to the Kirchenfeldbrücke afterwards.

He walked all the way around the dark Gymnasium. As he did so, he thought of the Hebrew Bible in Senhor Cortês's desk in the Liceu, still wrapped in his sweater.

On Sunday morning, he called João Eça. What should he do this afternoon? Eça asked him. Could Gregorius please tell him? .

He was going in to the clinic tonight, Gregorius said.

'It may be nothing,' said Eça after a pause. 'And if – nobody can keep you there.'

In the afternoon, Doxiades called and asked if he felt like a game of chess. He would take him to the clinic afterwards.

Did he still think of retiring? Gregorius asked the Greek after the first game. Yes, said Doxiades, he thought about it often. But maybe it would pass. In the next month, he was going to Thessaloniki; it was more than ten years since he had been there.

The second game was over and it was time to leave for the clinic.

'What if they find something bad?' asked Gregorius. 'Something that would make me lose myself?'

The Greek looked at him. It was a calm and solid look.

'I have a prescription pad,' he said.

Silently, they drove in the twilight to the clinic. *Life is not what we live; it is what we imagine living*, Prado had written.

Doxiades gave him his hand. 'It's probably nothing,' he said. 'And the man, as I said, is the best.'

At the entrance to the clinic, Gregorius turned around and waved. Then he went in. As the door closed behind him, it started raining.